SINISTER BY DESIGN

Madison Shaw and Jack Wyatt Medical Mysteries

Book 4

GARY BIRKEN, M.D.

Erupen Titles

Copyright © 2026 by Erupen titles

All rights reserved.

This is a work of fiction. Names, characters, places, and incidents are products of the author's imagination or used fictitiously. Any resemblance to actual persons, living or dead, is purely coincidental. All products and brand names are registered trademarks of their respective holders/companies.

No part of this book may be reproduced in any form or by any electronic or mechanical means, including information storage and retrieval systems, without written permission from the author, except for the use of brief quotations in a book review.

Cover provided by Get Covers

Editing services provided by Mighty Oak Publishing Services

Prologue

PALM BEACH COUNTY, FLORIDA

NOVEMBER 2025

Although he was an educated man, Marcus Parry oftentimes found himself stifled by the simplest of choices.

When recent circumstances called for a change in his name, the selection of an alias became a daunting task. It wasn't that he disliked his given name, but the course he'd charted for himself demanded an alternative to the one his mother had given him. After a time, he settled on Marcus Parry, regarding his choice as functional but uninspired. With natural black hair and a small port-wine stain birthmark at the corner of his mouth, he was a man who was spoiled by his own cunning, having long ago convinced himself that he was far too crafty to ever suffer any consequences arising from his questionable life choices.

With the dwindling warmth of the sun on his shoulders, he stood at the southwest corner of his thirty-two-acre farm, delighting in the beginning of what promised to be another serene South Florida sunset. Even though he'd never had an interest in planting a fruit or vegetable crop, nor raising livestock, he had no regrets about his decision to make the sprawling farm his permanent home.

When the sunset was nearing its end, he strolled over to his ATV and made the fifteen-minute ride back to his luxury barn-house that had taken one of the county's most prestigious general contractors a year to build. Before constructing the timber-framed house that attached directly to the barn via a closed breezeway, the contractor completely restored the oak-frame barn, to include a gable roof and a raftered loft. The final part of the project was to remove the pens and stalls and build a modest office and two tack rooms in the loft.

Entering the barn through the red paneled front doors, Marcus made his way up the stairs toward his office. Turning his eyes toward the rafters, he watched as several dozen bats silently roosting upside down. He'd always been fascinated by the many aspects of animal behavior, but few phenomena intrigued him more than the nocturnal awakening of the bats and how quickly they flew from the barn to spend the evening devouring thousands of insects.

His mind shifted back to the task at hand, which was an ambitious and complex project, even by his standards. If Marcus was anything, he was meticulous and compulsive about the projects he took on. Not being prone to impulsive thinking, his pragmatic approach to problem-solving had always served him well. Over the past fourteen months, he'd dedicated himself heart and soul to assuring a smooth implementation of the plan.

Opening the top drawer of his desk, he removed a large stack of handwritten notes that he'd created specifically to identify issues that needed to be further refined or updated. After spending almost an hour poring over the pages, he returned the notes to the drawer and left his office. Before making his way to his home, he stopped at the larger of the two store rooms. The only item of furniture present was a plain folding card table. Atop the table sat a Styrofoam container filled with dry ice that contained a small black insulated canister.

With the Styrofoam container in hand, Marcus left the tack room, traversed the flat-roofed breezeway to the barn-house, and went directly to the master suite. Being well practiced in the art of disguise, he took his time to significantly change his appearance by using facial make-up, a hairpiece, and an artificial mustache. When he was done, he gazed at his reflection in the mirror. Pleased with the result, he estimated he'd successfully made himself look at least twenty years older.

After he tidied up, he went into his den and removed from the closet a brown leather satchel that he'd purchased ten years earlier while touring Southern Asia. Earlier that day, he'd packed it with everything he'd need for his short trip to Sarasota. Assuming a normal amount of traffic on US-27, he estimated his arrival time would be a few minutes after ten. The date he'd been anticipating for weeks was upon him, although he wasn't a bit unnerved about it. His mind took him back to his high school days and his gymnastics coach who had drummed the same lesson into his head time after time: *The best hedge against performance anxiety is flawless preparation.*

Having considered every possible adverse contingency and how to deal with it, he was confident tomorrow's undertaking would be an unqualified success. His certainty was bolstered by his knowledge that one week earlier he'd artfully gained access to a different hospital for the same purpose.

Chapter 1

THREE WEEKS LATER

LAKE WORTH, FLORIDA

OUTBREAK—DAY 1

For as long as anybody could remember, Emma Collymore had been on a first-name basis with the world. Erudite, with a commanding personality, she seldom flinched when faced with the type of situation that would cause the eyes of most of her friends and colleagues to cross. A lawyer of some repute, she had the neck and back of a prima ballerina from a Degas painting, shoulder-length auburn hair, and high, angulated cheekbones.

A month earlier had been a time of extreme joy in her life when she'd delivered her first baby, Alyssa Marie. A week after the uneventful pregnancy and delivery, she was back at her desk at Eversole, Myers, and Jones, picking up right where she'd left off on several high-profile cases.

It was almost eleven a.m., and Emma had been hard at work since sunrise preparing for a critically important meeting with a potential new client that was scheduled for two o'clock. She was just about to have another look at one of their financial spreadsheets when she was suddenly struck by an overpowering sense of nausea. For the first few minutes, she did her best to ignore the sickening feeling, but the waves of nausea persisted and soon made it impossible for her to continue working.

Having recently celebrated her thirty-third birthday, Emma had always enjoyed excellent health. Looking for a reason to explain her sudden illness, she thought about how she'd spent the last twenty-four hours. Yesterday, her workday was long but fairly routine. She hadn't eaten anything out of the ordinary, and with the help of an excellent baby nurse, she'd had an undisturbed night's sleep. Leaning back in her chair and inhaling one deep breath after another, she thought about her upcoming afternoon meeting and prayed the intense nausea would pass as quickly as it had begun. But her prayer remained unanswered when all at once she felt lightheaded. Reaching up, Emma swept a few droplets of perspiration from her clammy brow.

With her anxiety soaring and fearing she was minutes away from vomiting, she came to her feet, steadied herself on the corner of her desk, and began wondering if her unexpected symptoms could in any way be related to giving birth. Forcing out a breath from the bottom of her lungs, she took a few moments to reassess the situation. To her dismay, the intense nausea continued to twist the pit of her stomach. Wishful waiting for improvement was no longer a viable option. She had to figure out a way to get to the restroom as quickly as possible.

Still holding on to the corner of her desk, Emma gathered the strength to take her first cautious step toward the door. Instantly, she was consumed by the sensation of the floor spinning and undulating, reminding her of riding a calliope-type merry-go-round when she was a child.

With her equilibrium rapidly faltering, she began a sideways topple. More from instinct than anything else, she grabbed for the armrest of the upholstered chair that sat in front of her desk. Fortunately, it was sufficiently well placed to allow her to redirect her fall into the chair, and she was able to maintain the presence of mind to slow her breathing and stop gulping for air. Because she suspected closing her eyes would only make her vertigo worse, she chose a spot on the wall and set a firm gaze on it.

It didn't take her but a moment to realize there was no way she could get back to her desk where her phone was located. The thought of calling out for help crossed her mind, but she hesitated, still praying the nausea and dizziness would pass on their own. Emma continued to hold her head perfectly still and train her eyes on the wall. By what she assumed was the grace of divine intervention, she began feeling slightly better. Another minute or so passed, and she noted her head was beginning to clear.

She was clinging to the hope that her faintness and abdominal discomfort were coming to an end when one of the senior law partners, Al Pritchard, came through the door. A look of grave concern came to rest on his face the moment he laid eyes on her.

Approaching slowly, he said in a guarded voice. "I just thought I'd see if you had any last-minute thoughts on this afternoon's..." Al's words were still suspended in mid-air when he got a closer look at her white face. "My God, Emma. You look like a ghost. Are you okay?"

"I think I must be coming down with something. I was fine until a few minutes ago, but then suddenly something hit me like a freight train, and I began feeling awful."

"Maybe you should head home and give your doctor a call."

"I can't... Not with the meeting with Kazimierz's people at two. This is potentially a huge case for the firm, and it's our first face-to-face with them. I need to be there to answer their questions."

"Look, Emma. If you feel the way you look, there's no way you'll be anywhere near your best for the meeting." He held up a hand, as he so often did to indicate that when he wanted her opinion he'd give it to her. "The other problem is that, if you're contagious and get everybody in the room sick...well, you won't have to worry about us landing Kazimierz Innovations as a new client. We'll be lucky if they don't sue us." Taking a couple of steps back, he continued, "I may not be a CPA, but I've been around the block enough times to know how to get through an exploratory first tax meeting without tripping over a bunch of rugs I've never seen before." He gazed at her through his quintessential Dutch uncle eyes. "Just go ahead on home and do whatever it is you need to do to get better...and for goodness' sake, don't come back to work until you feel up to it. I'll give you a call tomorrow to brief you on the meeting."

"Thanks, Al."

"I knew this would happen if you came back to work so soon after having the baby. Trying to take care of her and maintain a full schedule here at work is just too much. I should have insisted you take more time off."

"I don't know. You may be right, but on the other hand, maybe whatever I'm getting has nothing to do with giving birth."

"Spoken like a true lawyer," he said, leaning forward and focusing his gaze directly on her face. "Your eyes look a little yellow to me. I'm going to have Chuck call our car service to take you home. You shouldn't be driving."

"I appreciate your concern, but I'm feeling a little better now. I'm sure I'm okay to drive myself home."

"At least sit here for another few minutes before you leave."

"I will. If I feel worse, I'll take you up on your offer. Thanks, Al."

"I'll be right down the hall in my office if you need me."

For the next ten minutes, Emma didn't move from the chair. Al poked his head in once to check on her. The waves of nausea were more infrequent and less intense. But even so, she decided he was right about skipping the meeting and going home for the day. Hopefully, the illness would turn out to be nothing more than a twenty-four bug, and she'd be ready to return to work tomorrow.

After a brief period of time, Emma no longer felt any significant dizziness, which left her reassured she'd be able to drive home safely. Coming to her feet, she walked back to her desk and removed her purse from the bottom drawer. It occurred to her that if she left through the front door, she'd probably run into some of her fellow attorneys and support staff. Having no interest in facing that prospect, she slipped out of her office and exited the building via the rear door into a windy and drizzly morning.

It was a short walk to her new coupe. Wasting no time, she unlocked the door and slid in behind the wheel. Before starting the engine, she looked at the image of her face in the mirror. With an inward groan, she conceded Al was right about her appearance. In addition to being sallow-faced, there was a subtle yellow tinge to her eyes that instantly reminded her of her college roommate's appearance when she first came down with hepatitis.

After taking a final few moments to boost her confidence that she was okay, Emma fastened her seat belt and pulled out of her parking space. She hadn't noticed it until now, but she had an undeniable salty taste in her mouth. Emma did her best to dismiss any further pessimistic thoughts regarding her unexpected illness, but as she pulled out of the parking lot, a sudden apprehensive chill penetrated to the depths of her marrow from the realization that, at best, the chances of her being behind her desk tomorrow were highly improbable.

Chapter 2

Not expecting much midday traffic, Emma estimated it would take her about twenty-five minutes to drive home. As she proceeded south on the interstate, her worst fear came true when her nausea and lightheadedness suddenly returned. It didn't take long for her symptoms to progress and become almost as unbearable as they were in the office. She considered pulling over for a few minutes, but since she was only a few minutes from her house, she decided to press on.

Exiting the interstate, Emma followed the loop ramp toward its termination at a main east-west boulevard. Drawing on every bit of concentration she could muster, she struggled not to drift out of her lane. Having to navigate the tightly curved ramp made her dizziness worse. When she finally realized the only sensible thing to do was pull over, it was too late. Her situational awareness had dwindled to a level that made it impossible for her to maintain control of the vehicle.

Emma suddenly panicked as the coupe began to swerve. Struggling to apply the brakes in a coordinated way, she prayed she'd be able to stop the vehicle from veering completely out of control and bring it to a safe stop. Despite her best efforts to prevent the inevitable, the car entered a hard pinwheel skid followed by a sideslip that carried it into a large retention pond. The coupe impacted the water at forty miles per hour, but the airbag didn't deploy, and Emma struck her head against the steering wheel and her shoulder against the dashboard.

The collision left her dazed and unaware that the car was beginning to take on water. Fortunately, within the space of a few moments, her mind began to clear, and she gained the presence of mind to try to unbuckle her seat belt. But the pain and loss of movement in her injured shoulder rendered her efforts futile. Her eyes flashed to the windshield. The vehicle was afloat, but the front end was being tipped forward by a steady rush of muck-laden water sloshing over the hood.

If the accident had one saving grace, it was that it was witnessed by dozens of motorists. Many had already pulled over and raced to the edge of the basin with their cell phones pushed against their ears. Among the first to reach the shore were Anita Chase and her seventeen-year-old-son, Brent. Being native Floridians, they were both proficient swimmers. After exchanging a confirming look, they ran into the basin, dove forward, and began swimming with all their power toward the submerging car.

Still struggling to unfasten her seat belt, Emma watched with heart-shaking terror as the front end became totally submerged. Whatever prayer she had that the coupe might remain afloat vanished. With one last tug, she succeeded in releasing the seat belt. She barely noticed the rising tide of water floating up her legs. Sensing the car was being engulfed by the basin's murky water, she thrust her left hand forward, searching for the power window switch. In the frenzy of the moment, her hand flailed, and she couldn't find it. Finally, she located the switch and lowered her window.

Her momentary sense of optimism disappeared when she felt a much larger rush of water spilling into the interior of the car. Filled with desperation, Emma mustered every particle of strength she could and managed to grab the steering wheel with one hand and the window pillar with the other. Tightening her grasp, she battled to pull herself out the window. But by this point, with water gushing in and her strength dwindling, she could barely pull herself forward. The water level inside the car was rapidly approaching the ceiling. Emma pushed her mouth against the headliner, gasping for the last few breaths of air that remained in the car.

By the time Anita and Brent reached the vehicle, the roof had fallen to just below the surface. Filling her lungs, Anita dove down to the driver-side window. Brent followed close behind. The water was muddy, obscuring her view, but Anita could see well enough to reach into the car and grab Emma's arm. With Brent's assistance, they pulled her out through the window. She wasn't free of the SUV for more than a few moments before it suddenly rolled to the side and plunged toward the bottom of the basin. Mother and son worked together to hook Emma under her armpits and start swimming upward. A few seconds later, the three of them broke the surface.

Emma's entire body was flaccid, but she was breathing. Two men were treading water a few feet away and assisted in bringing her to the bank. Removing her from the water, they carefully set her down. An off-duty paramedic was present, who immediately turned Emma on her left side. She continued to gasp for air while at the same time coughing up copious amounts of water. Two police cruisers followed by an ambulance pulled up to within a few yards of where the crowd had gathered.

Two paramedics jumped out of their rig and were instantly at Emma's side. The first one placed an oxygen mask on her face, while the second obtained a set of vital signs and assessed her ability to breathe on her own.

"She seems to be moving enough air," the first one said. "Let's hold off on an artificial airway for now."

They worked together to place cardiac and oxygen saturation monitors on Emma. They then inserted an IV. Just as they were finished preparing her for transport to the hospital, a TV news truck rolled to a stop. A reporter jumped out, followed by a burly cameraman, who hoisted his camera onto his shoulder as they weaved their way through the crowd to get as close to Emma as the police officers would allow.

The paramedics secured Emma in place on the stretcher, wheeled it to the ambulance, and loaded her into the back. With full lights and siren, they sped away from the scene. Not long after, the crowd began to disperse. After speaking to Anita and Brent and a couple of the bystanders, the TV news crew headed back to their truck.

"I'm a little more anxious than usual to have a look at the film you shot. I have a hunch about something," the reporter said.

"You and your hunches. What is it this time?" the cameraman asked, removing his EFP camera from his shoulder.

"Did the victim look vaguely familiar to you?"

"You mean with that big oxygen mask covering her face? I can't say she did."

"Well, I might be crazy, but the woman they just pulled out of the water sure looked a hell of a lot like Governor Collymore's daughter."

Chapter 3

COLUMBUS, OHIO

FOUR DAYS LATER

It was a few minutes past nine in the morning when Dr. Jack Wyatt strolled into his modestly appointed office. Normally, his busy schedule as the chief of neurology and the director of the Elusive Diagnoses Institute began at seven a.m., which made his late arrival today a rare exception. He had barely settled in behind his desk when his assistant, Meredith, appeared at the door.

"The dean wants to speak with you. She's on her way over."

"The dean of the medical school?"

"I think so. The dean of the College of Music rarely calls me to set up an urgent meeting with you."

A subdued grin appeared on his face. "You're a funny woman, Meredith. Do me a favor, please. When the dean arrives, try to keep the familiarity and sarcasm to a minimum, and try not to talk her ear off. And please, just show her right into my office."

"I'll do my best."

"Thanks."

For more years than he'd cared to remember, Jack had overlooked his practice manager's snarky persona because she was, hands down, the most efficient human being he'd ever worked with. It was her incomparable performance that allowed him to turn a blind eye to her Peck's Bad Girl behavior.

Jack was an enthusiastic tennis player and still fit and supple for a man his age. Owing to his ever-increasing clinical and teaching responsibilities, apart from racket sports, he had limited leisure time to pursue other pastimes or vacations. Left to his own devices, he might have arranged things differently—perhaps even chosen another career path—but he harbored no material regrets as to where his life had taken him.

Although he'd had ample experience with these types of last-minute meeting requests from the medical school powers that be and the direction they frequently took, he still wondered why the dean felt a pressing need to speak with him on such short notice. Assuming he'd find out soon enough, he turned his attention to reviewing his most recent emails.

He hadn't read more than a handful of them when he heard two sharp knocks at his door. Coming out from behind his kidney-shaped desk, he made his way to the center of his office to shake hands with Dean Blair Chaperlin. She had held the position of dean at the College of Medicine for thirteen years and had accomplished great things in the advancement of medical education and research. Having gooseberry-colored eyes that enhanced her soft facial features, she walked with a delicate gait and was always stylishly dressed.

"How've you been, Jack?" she asked him in a voice that betrayed her Oregon upbringing, blending classic pronunciation features from both Canada and the U.S.

"Never better," he answered as he escorted her to one of the two blue leather chairs that sat in front of his desk before moving back behind his desk. "We're very busy clinically, and all of our expansion and research initiatives continue to exceed our expectations."

"I'm not the slightest bit surprised to hear that. I remember the day I interviewed you for this job. Most candidates who sit across from me have the possibility of excellence. By the end of our interview, I was convinced you had the promise of it."

Not being one to field compliments with ease, Jack squirmed in his chair a little. "Thank you, Dean. Coming from you, that's quite a compliment."

"Please, call me Blair. I've never been much for formality. You know, Jack, whenever I ask Madison about her health, she tells me that she's never felt better. Excuse my trust-but-verify approach, but is she really doing as well as she claims?" Jack was aware that Blair and Madison served on several hospital and state committees together. Their excellent working relationship had provided an easy segue to a solid friendship.

"I wish I could respond positively, but whenever I ask her how she's feeling, I get the same never-better response she gave you." Jack knew Blair wasn't posing a random question. She was keenly aware that Madison had battled leukemia for more than three years, and even though she was currently in remission, the possibility of a relapse was ever-present. "I can tell you that she's been disease free for quite some time now. She goes to all her medical appointments without fail, and her team of hematologists have recently pivoted from cautious optimism to being openly encouraged that she'll continue to do well."

"That's wonderful to hear," Blair said, holding up crossed fingers. "Madison's always been a superstar. The medical staff and leadership at the children's hospital love her and the job she's doing heading up the perinatology center. I'd say you're a lucky guy to have found her, but I suspect you already know that."

Blair pushed her palms together, guarding her silence briefly as she tapped her fingertips together. Knowing her penchant for being frank, he wasn't surprised when she asked, "When are you going to persuade her to get off that fence and marry you?"

"It's certainly not due to any lack of trying on my part. If you have any tips on how to get her to pull the trigger, I'm all ears."

With a wafer-thin smile, Blair said, "Since I've always been single and happy to admit it, I'm probably not the one to ask." They shared a quick laugh. "Well, I should stop stalling and tell you why I'm here."

"By all means."

"I received a call from Governor Sam Collymore of Florida and his surgeon general last night. They told me they're facing an unusual problem that involves the governor's daughter, Emma, and were wondering if we might be willing to lend a hand."

"What type of a problem?"

"Evidently, Emma had a baby about a month ago. The delivery was uneventful, and she did great afterward until about five days ago when she suddenly became quite ill. She wound up being readmitted to Mothers and Infants Hospital in Palm Beach, where her condition has continued to worsen. What's got the governor on the edge of his chair is that the team of physicians caring for his daughter are all scratching their collective heads without a clue as to what's causing the illness or how to treat it."

Absently, Jack lightly drummed his fingertips on his charcoal-colored desk pad.

"Did the surgeon general share any of the details of the illness with you?"

"She did. Emma's an otherwise healthy thirty-three-year-old. Her pregnancy and delivery were uncomplicated, and she was discharged home the day after she gave birth. Five days ago, she was involved in a car accident. She was the only one in the car and somehow skidded off an exit ramp into a retention basin. Fortunately, she wasn't seriously injured, but not long after she arrived at the hospital, the attending trauma surgeon became concerned that Emma had signs and symptoms of an illness that were in no way attributable to the accident."

"That's interesting. Did she mention what those symptoms were?"

"Within a few minutes of her arrival, she vomited blood. It was also noted that she was jaundiced and had an extensive rash on her chest and neck."

"That would explain why the attending didn't suspect her illness was trauma related."

"He called Emma's obstetrician, and they decided to transfer her to Mothers and Infants, where she had given birth."

"Does Emma have a history of any liver problems or prior upper GI bleeding episodes?"

"No, and her father swears she's always been a teetotaler and that she's never had any significant health problems."

"Did she require surgery to stop her bleeding?"

"No, but she was about one step away from a trip to the operating room when the interventional radiologist managed to embolize the bleeding artery and stop the hemorrhage."

"I understand we're talking about a governor's daughter and that her symptoms are unusual. But when you're only dealing with one case of a perplexing illness, you have to remember that—"

"Forgive me for interrupting, but in the last three days the same physicians who are caring for the governor's daughter have admitted four other women with the exact same symptoms as Emma has."

"Even so, they're still only dealing with five random cases. Just because one of the women happened to recently give birth doesn't necessarily mean there's anything—"

"Unfortunately, they're anything but random," Blair said, moving forward in her chair and setting her eyes squarely on Jack. All five women gave birth within forty-eight hours of each other, and they all delivered at Mothers and Infants."

Jack's coincidence theory vanished from his mind as quickly as a shooting star disappears from sight.

"Just how sick are these women?" he asked.

"Sick enough to be admitted to their progressive care unit, which is one step down from their ICU. They've all been seen by a number of consultants from various specialties. I'm sorry to say that none of them seem to have the first clue as to what's causing the illness. As I'm sure you can imagine, the uncertainty of the situation in the face of these five women continuing to deteriorate is causing the anxiety level among the doctors, nurses, and administrators to skyrocket."

"How do the governor and surgeon general see us getting involved in this problem?"

"They're understandably getting more concerned with each passing day. They weren't specific, but their request came in the form of whatever you can do to help would be greatly appreciated. They also have no idea how many cases they may be looking at in the days to come in Palm Beach County, or worse if this becomes a statewide crisis."

"There're a few ways we can help, Blair. How would you like us to proceed?"

"I don't think we have much of a choice. Governor Collymore, the CEO of Mothers and Infants, and the surgeon general have all asked for our help. I think we should offer the services of our Elusive Diagnoses Center."

"I don't think a virtual or limited consultation will work in this case. We're probably looking at a boots-on-the-ground type involvement."

"I would agree with that assessment."

"Do we have any idea how the treating physicians at the hospital feel about the prospect of us consulting on these cases?" he asked.

"I haven't spoken to any of them directly, so I have no idea. But if we encounter pushback… Well, we'll just have to jump off that bridge when we get to it." After a quick grin, Blair added, "Being an out-of-town guest consultant, it's not like you've never seen that problem before. I'm confident you and Madison will be able to soothe the feelings of any physician with a bruised ego or ruffled feathers."

He chuckled. "Easy for you to say."

"From a legal and ethical standpoint, we're on solid ground sending you two down to Florida."

Jack smiled. "I was just about to ask you if the governor happened to mention Madison's name."

"There are plenty of folks in Governor Collymore's administration who well remember the role you two played in ending the GNS epidemic in Florida. The governor and the surgeon general didn't tap-dance around how pleased they'd be if Madison agreed to accompany you."

"I'll speak with her this morning. Assuming she can clear her calendar, I'm sure she'll agree to make the trip."

"If she should encounter any problems with the children's hospital's powers that be, have her give me a call. I may be able to help."

"Thank you," Jack told her, having no doubt Blair's offer wasn't an empty one.

"Please let me know as soon as you speak to Madison. I suspect I'll be hearing from the governor before lunch."

"As soon as I get the thumbs up, I'll call you. And, since time appears to be of the essence, I'll get going on our travel arrangements."

"Don't worry about the flight. The governor's brother offered to send his corporate jet for you and Madison. As soon as you give me a time that works for you, I'll let the governor's chief of staff know, and he'll arrange for the plane to meet you at Port Columbus."

"That'll certainly make things easier."

"Assuming Madison can make the trip, what are the chances you guys can be ready to leave by late this afternoon?"

"I'd say good."

Blair stole a peek at her watch. "I'd better get going," she said, coming to her feet. "Thanks for your cooperation, Jack. I've known Sam Collymore for twenty years. In addition to being a great governor, he's one hell of a family man. Emma's an only child. I suspect he's sitting in her hospital room right now with his cell phone clutched in his hand waiting for my call." They started down the corridor toward the elevators. "By the way, once you get down there and get the lay of the land, please keep me updated on the situation. If you can find the time to call every day or so, I'd very much appreciate it."

"Of course."

"One final thought—for obvious reasons, I think it's safe to assume you'll encounter a rather large amount of interest from the media."

"I think we can count on it," he said.

"It shouldn't be a problem. You and Madison are as experienced as any physicians I know in dealing with the media." The elevator doors rolled open "Any questions or requests?" Blair asked.

"It would help if the administration at Mothers and Infants could provide us with a physician contact."

"I'm sure they already have somebody in mind. Before you get on the plane, I'll make sure you have all the information you'll need to hit the ground running when you get to Florida."

"Thanks. I'll give you a call when our plans are set."

"Thanks, Jack. Maybe this will turn out to be an easy fix. Safe travels."

Making his way back to his office, Jack's mind filled with the flurry of details he needed to attend to before leaving Columbus.

"I hate to do this to you, Meredith, but I need you to start clearing my schedule. I have to go to Florida for a few days."

"I'm way ahead of you. I've already canceled your clinics and meetings for today and tomorrow. How far out do you want me to go?"

"How did you know to do that?"

"I was listening when you and the dean walked past my desk."

With a tolerant shake of his head, he said, "I'll be gone for at least four days. Anything beyond that, we'll handle on a day-to-day basis."

"Just to be on the safe side, I'll go ahead and cancel the rest of this week… and your pickle ball lesson. What about travel arrangements?"

"The flight's been arranged. I'm not sure about accommodations."

"Doesn't your mother live in the Palm Beach area?"

"Funny, I don't remember mentioning Palm Beach."

"I just naturally assumed."

"I don't know where Madison and I will be staying just yet. As soon as I've got it figured out, you'll be the first to know."

"The sooner the better, if you want me to find you a decent place."

Responding to Meredith's comment with an apathetic wave of his hand, he headed back into his office. The first thing on his agenda was to call Madison. It was a brief conversation, and he was unsurprised when she didn't bat an eyelash at the prospect of accompanying him to Florida and said that she could be ready to leave later in the day.

As he set the phone back on its cradle, his mind shifted to his meeting with Blair. In a way, and for reasons he couldn't quite get his mind around, he definitely felt leerier about consulting at Mothers and Infants than most of the other hospitals that had requested his help over the years. Perhaps he was feeling more apprehensive than usual owing to the added political issues that would be created by the predictable public curiosity over the governor's daughter being one of the affected patients.

Jack's other concern was that, in his experience, consulting at a highly specialized and prominent hospital oftentimes meant the attending doctors were significantly less interested in the opinions of an outside consultant than physicians who worked at less renowned medical centers. The degree to which those issues would complicate the medical challenges he and Madison would surely be facing at Mothers and Infants was anybody's guess. Being a naturally optimistic person, at least in his own mind, he hoped his concerns would turn out to be more imagined than real.

Chapter 4

Jack arrived home and stepped out of his newly purchased conversion van into an overcast and unseasonably chilly afternoon. He made his way up the flagstone path to the front door of his ivy-covered New England Colonial Revival home in the Upper Arlington area of Columbus. On his way home, he'd received a call from Blair advising him that Dr. Ely Stanberry, the vice president of medical affairs and chief of staff of Mothers and Infants Hospital, was looking forward to meeting with him and Madison tomorrow morning at nine in his office.

After stopping briefly in the foyer to set his umbrella in a ceramic stand, Jack strolled through the dining room and into the study where he found Madison tucked into the corner of her favorite couch with a mug of arabica coffee in one hand and her latest perinatology journal in the other. Moose, Jack's beloved bluetick hound, was curled up at her feet, sound asleep.

They had first met when she was a junior medical student rotating on the neurology service at Shand's Hospital where Jack was serving as the chief resident. She'd enjoyed the rotation, but when it came to an end and she received a failing grade, she'd held Jack completely responsible. When she confronted him, he categorically denied having anything to do with her failing grade, but his protests fell on deaf ears, leaving Madison to deal with the problem on her own. After a period of time, she successfully straightened out her academic crisis with the medical school, but along with the solution came her firm conviction that she never again wanted to speak to Dr. Jack Wyatt. Several years later, through pure serendipity, their paths crossed again when they were both asked to consult on a group of pregnant women suffering from an illness that came to be known as gestational neuropathic syndrome.

Time had done little to subdue her dislike for him, but after a heart-to-heart conversation, they'd agreed to set their differences aside in the interest of working together to discover the cause and cure for the illness. From that point on, their relationship steadily progressed from collegially distant to enjoyably platonic, and finally romantic. Madison eventually took a job at the Ohio Children's Hospital in Columbus. Over the years, she'd developed an interest similar to Jack's in the burgeoning specialty of elusive diagnoses and joined him on a part-time basis to consult on challenging cases around the country.

Jack cast an eye on Moose. His snoring was audible from ten feet away.

"He's quite the watchdog," he said. "I could be a deranged lunatic who broke into the house to kill you, and he'd sleep right through it."

"Nevertheless, I'd appreciate it if you'd try not to wake him. The only time I'm safe from his incessant slobbering and begging for dog cookies is when he's asleep."

"He's getting kind of old, Madison. He deserves your compassion."

"Which is why I'm happy to give him a pass on his poor behavior. I'll do the same for you someday," she added as she threw back her lightweight Columbus Blue Jackets blanket.

"Thanks. That's comforting to hear."

"So what's the update? When are we leaving?"

"Blair called me a little while ago. All the arrangements have been made. Our flight's at four out of Port Columbus. Tomorrow morning, we have a meeting with Dr. Ely Stanberry, the chief of staff at Mothers and Infants."

"Just him?"

"As far as I know." He noted the displeasure on her face.

"I'm sure it'll be nice to meet him for political reasons, but it would be even nicer to speak with a few of the key physicians who are actually involved in the care of these women."

"Blair didn't specifically mention who'd be there, but I wouldn't worry about it." Trying to overlook the predictable displeasure in her eyes, he went on. "It's our first meeting, and for all we know, there will be other physicians there. Even if there aren't, I'm sure there'll be adequate time later in the day for us to meet with the key people we'll be working with."

"What do you know about Mothers and Infants?" she asked him casually.

"Other than it's a highly respected women's hospital, not too much."

"There are a lot of highly respected hospitals in the country, Jack. But seeing as how we're going to be working there for several days, you should know that it's one of the most prestigious, state-of-the-art hospitals dedicated to the care of women and newborns in the country. It's a level four regional perinatal center. And, in addition to being recognized as providing the highest level of maternal-fetal care, the hospital also cares for women with cancer and all types of gynecological diseases. They've managed to recruit some of the most talented scientific investigators from all over the world, which has made their research center internationally renowned.

"For you to give a hospital a ringing endorsement like that, I'm sure it's a center of excellence."

"The quality of care they provide isn't what concerns me. Another thing you should know...," she said, folding the blanket and setting it on a glass side table. "I doubt whether the physicians at Mothers and Infants request help in the care of their patients very often."

"The same thing crossed my mind, and I suspect they didn't have much of a voice in the decision to ask us to consult. From what

Blair told me, I got the feeling the request came principally from the governor, the surgeon general, and Dr. Stanberry."

"That's kind of a no-brainer when you consider one of the patients just happens to be the governor's daughter," she said.

"I'm sure that's part of it, but there are probably a lot of folks down there who recall the GNS outbreak. The important thing is that we're going there for only one reason, and that's to help in the diagnosis and treatment of a vexing illness. That's where our focus has to be."

"I think I'm the one who's better at keeping her eye on the ball and avoiding any nonproductive political distractions. You're always too concerned about rubbing people the wrong way."

"By people, you mean our fellow physicians, Madison. And yes, I like to fool myself into believing that diplomacy still has a heartbeat."

"Your optimism never ceases to amaze me," she said, getting up and planting a kiss on his cheek. "I'm almost packed. What time are we leaving for the airport?"

"Ten after three."

"I hate flying, but isn't that cutting it kind of close for a four o'clock flight?"

"Actually, the governor's brother arranged a private flight for us."

"Private flight? If there aren't at least two pilots and two engines, I'll meet you in Florida."

"I suggest we take care of the medical aspects of the trip and let the aviation experts take care of our transportation needs."

Moose finally picked his head up, saw Jack, and instantly began wildly wagging his tail. He got off the couch a little more gingerly than in the old days, but he was still spry enough to jump up and plant his paws on Jack's chest.

"I assume Meredith's going to move in and watch Moose while we're gone," Madison said.

"We're taking The Moose Man with us," he stated, rubbing his beloved hound's ears.

"Tell me you're kidding."

"Nope. Blair inquired for me, and she was assured Moose the Goose is more than welcome to fly with us."

"In that case, I assume we'll be staying with your mother."

"Rather than call a million places to see if they're dog friendly, I figured it would be a lot easier to give Mom a call." Jack reached atop a hutch, plucked a sweet-potato treat from a plastic bag, and tossed it to Moose. "Knowing you and my mom are BFFs, I assumed you'd be okay with the idea."

"I love your mom. She's one of the brightest, most accommodating people I've ever met. We have a great relationship. I guess the question is how do you feel about staying with her?"

"Me? I'm thrilled," he said, pushing a sarcastic grin to his face. "I can't wait for you and Mom to gang up on me with all your suggestions on how I should run my life."

Madison couldn't contain a breathy chuckle. "Since when are you so sensitive? All kidding aside, Jack, calling your mom was the right thing to do. If she knew we were in the area and had decided to stay somewhere else, well, she'd probably find herself somewhere between devastated and mortified."

"I know. I'm going to take this guy for a walk and then pack." Moose heard the magic word and started turning tight circles in the middle of the room. "C'mon, buddy."

While Jack searched for the leash, Madison reached for her cell phone to call Dr. Charlotte Duffy to tell her how pleased she was to learn they'd be spending a few days with her.

Chapter 5

OUTBREAK—DAY FIVE

After an uneventful flight to Palm Beach International, Jack and Madison went straight to his mother's home in Lake Worth, dropped their suitcases in the guest room, and took her out to a leisurely and enjoyable dinner. The conversation was flowing, and by the end of the meal, they'd made a great start on catching up.

By eight the next morning, Madison and Jack were out of bed and dressed. As they came down the curved lightwood staircase, Jack detected the aroma of maple bacon coffee, a favorite of his mother's for as long as he could remember. When they strolled into the farmhouse-style kitchen with its antique designed cabinets and butcher-block countertops, they spotted Charlotte at the table sipping her coffee from a large ceramic mug and reading the morning paper. Since it had long been her custom to start her day at the break of dawn, Jack wasn't surprised to see her up and rolling. style

She moved her newspaper to the side, glanced at them over the top of her wire frame reading glasses, and smiled. Still spry and fit, with her seventy-fifth birthday only a few weeks away, her wide cheekbones and short eyebrows seemed to fit just right on her diamond-shaped face.

"Good morning. I hope you both slept well."

"We did," Madison said.

"Good. I was just beginning to wonder if you two were ever going to get up."

With a knowing grin on her face, Madison walked over to the table and kissed Charlotte once on each cheek. Having retired more than a decade ago after enjoying a long and distinguished career as an academic pediatric cardiologist, Charlotte continued her association with her medical school by coaching and mentoring students who were facing scholastic and personal problems. To all who knew her, she was a woman of unaffected grace who possessed the common touch.

Since the day she'd met Charlotte, Madison had adored her, always viewing her as one of the most erudite and insightful individuals she'd ever known. Although Jack playfully carped about his mother from time to time, they had a very special relationship as well. Nobody knew better than him that it was light-years apart from the one he had with his father—a man who'd departed the United States over three decades ago to live in Europe as an expatriot freelance writer. Charlotte made no secret of the fact that, once he'd made his decision, she had no further use for him.

After sharing a light breakfast with her, Jack and Madison left for their meeting with Dr. Ely Stanberry. Arriving at Mothers and Infants fifteen minutes early, they checked in at the guest center and were directed to take the elevator to the eighth floor. The moment they stepped into his outer office, his perky assistant walked over and greeted them with a Hollywood smile.

"You must be Doctors Shaw and Wyatt. Dr. Stanberry's expecting you," she said as she escorted them into his ornate Victorian-style office.

The moment they came through the door, he came out from behind his desk and joined them. An imposing man, he was stout and possessed a prominent chin that jutted out well beyond his bottom lip. After a four-year residency in general pathology, he'd gone on to complete a fellowship in neuropathology. His academic career was meteoric compared to most of his colleagues, but after sixteen years of peering through microscopes and earning a master's degree in healthcare administration, he'd decided to leave the world of clinical medicine and pursue a new adventure as a healthcare executive.

"Welcome to South Florida," Ely told them with a friendly smile as he shook each of their hands. "Before we go any further, I'd like to thank you both for agreeing to consult on these cases. I know we're early into this process, but I, for one, am happy to check my ego at the door and welcome two new sets of eyes, especially when they're as experienced as yours."

Madison immediately noted a sprinkling of formality in his manner and speech. "We're flattered that you asked us," she said. "I hope we can be of some help."

"We're all aware of your invaluable contribution to the diagnosis and treatment of both gestational neuropathic syndrome and leukemic malnutrition, not to mention your groundbreaking work on heavy metal toxicity. Much of what you've contributed has become required teaching in our medical school."

"That's quite a compliment. Thank you," Jack said.

"You're both very deserving of the praise." He removed a silver pocket watch from the waistcoat of his three-piece suit, flipped open the lid, and checked the time. "I'm expecting Dr. Josef Church to join us. He should be here at any moment. Josef serves as our director of obstetrical services and sits on our board of directors. I think you'll be quite impressed with him. His accomplishments have gone way beyond simply being an outstanding clinician. From the beginning, he was the one who breathed life into the concept of building a hospital in South Florida dedicated exclusively to the care of women. Without his inspiration and tireless efforts, this hospital never would've been built."

He gestured toward an oak trestle table. "Why don't we have a seat? I'm sure Josef will be here momentarily." As they walked across the office, Stanberry went on, "For reasons we'll discuss when he arrives, this illness has hit him very hard."

Just as they were about to sit down, Dr. Church came through the door. He was a man of average height who Madison guessed was in his mid-sixties. He had mild scoliosis and a slightly humped nose, and the charcoal gray in his receding crop of hair had made its first appearance twenty years ago.

He approached the table, where Ely took his time making the formal introductions.

"It's a pleasure to meet you both," Josef said. "I assume Ely's already thanked you for agreeing to help, but that won't dissuade me from offering my expression of gratitude as well."

"Thank you, Dr. Church," Madison said, having no difficulty noting his nervousness.

"Josef. Please, call me Josef."

"Before we get started, do either of you have any questions for me or Josef?"

"Not at the moment," Jack responded for both of them.

"In that case, I think it would be more helpful if I deferred to Josef to bring you up to speed regarding these patients."

With his steepled fingers revealing his pronounced knuckles and manicured nails, Josef set his hands on the table. "I suspect I could talk all day about what we don't know about this illness, so I'll concentrate on what we've been able to learn to this point. With the two additional women we admitted last night, we are presently treating seven postpartum women with what appears to be the same illness. All of them are between the ages of twenty-five and thirty-four. Each experienced an uneventful pregnancy and labor and delivered at this hospital about a month ago within a three-day period. They were all discharged the morning after they delivered. Until they recently became ill, they had all experienced a normal recovery from childbirth."

"Excuse me, Dr. Church," Madison began. "Were all these deliveries vaginal?"

"Yes, there were no C-sections."

"Have any of the other women who delivered during that same general time period become ill?" she asked.

"We've reached out to all of them, and our information is that not a single one of the others has suffered any significant health problem since giving birth," Ely said. "I should also mention that, during the three days in question, the hospital performed a total of a hundred and thirty-two deliveries."

Josef adjusted his gaze from Ely to Jack and Madison.

"I think it's important to point out that I was the attending obstetrician for all seven of the women who are now suffering from this disease. Irrespective of the cause, I'm ultimately responsible."

Chapter 6

"Josef was fully evaluated by Dr. Herbert Whiteacre, our chief of infectious diseases," Ely told Jack and Madison with complete conviction. "He personally informed me that, based on his examination of Josef and the laboratory tests he ordered, he finds no evidence to suggest Josef is either suffering from or transmitting an infectious disease to any of our patients. It's also worth mentioning that Josef performed seven gynecological surgeries on those same three days with no adverse outcomes. We made it a point to contact each patient. Not one of them has contracted an illness or suffered a complication related to their operation."

"How many separate delivery rooms were involved?" Jack asked, hoping to diminish the emotion of the moment and keep the focus of the conversation on the medical aspects of the illness.

"I performed all the deliveries using one of two birthing suites."

"Any concern that the problem might have come from a source of contamination in one of those rooms?" Jack inquired.

"Our infection control and facilities management teams have gone over every square inch of the rooms Josef used, and to this point, they've found nothing of a suspicious nature," Josef said.

"Do you always work with the same team?" Madison asked.

"For the past ten years or so, I've worked with the same anesthesiologist and OR nursing team."

"They too were evaluated by Dr. Whiteacre, and again, he found nothing to suggest they were a vector of some infectious disease," Ely said.

"To your knowledge, have there been any similar cases admitted to Mothers and Infants over the last several months?" Madison asked.

"None that we can identify," Josef answered with assurance in his voice. "We not only checked our hospital and practice records, but we also contacted every obstetrician who's delivered a baby here in the last twelve months and posed that very question to her or him. None had any recollection of a case that even remotely resembled the illness that we're currently treating."

"And to expand on what Josef just said—we deliver approximately thirteen hundred infants per month, which makes us one of the busiest maternity centers in the country. We also have an extremely committed quality assurance committee that carefully monitors our results. If there had been other cases, we'd have known about them."

Madison asked Josef, "Can you tell us a little more about the symptoms?"

"Of course. Each of the women presented with the same major symptoms: severe gastritis with varying degrees of vomiting blood, jaundice, and a rash. The less serious symptom they all report is a salty taste in their mouths."

"No fever or flu-like symptoms?" she asked.

"A low-grade fever maybe, but nothing beyond that. Dr. Whiteacre feels the absence of typical flu symptoms is significant."

"How long did it take for the symptoms to intensify following their onset?" Madison asked.

"Just a matter of a few days. All the patients were admitted to the hospital within a day or two of the illness's onset."

"It doesn't sound like you've noted any significant neurological symptoms," Jack said.

Josef shook his head. "Other than a general malaise, I'd say that's correct."

"What can you tell us about the jaundice and the rash?"

"The rash is maculopapular in nature, involving the neck and much of the torso," Josef answered. "It's pretty nonspecific, and unfortunately, according to our dermatology consultants, this particular rash has an endless number of possible causes."

"And the jaundice?" Madison said.

"Other than a mild elevation in their liver enzymes, there isn't an obvious explanation. If the jaundice and liver function worsen, we may need to consider obtaining a liver biopsy."

"I assume they've all undergone an ultrasound of their biliary tract?" Madison asked.

"Yes. gallbladder, liver, and pancreas appear normal in every case."

Ely spoke up. "Obviously, we have no idea how this illness will progress from this point forward. These young women are already pretty sick. And, as you can guess, the governor's daughter has thrown a rather large spotlight on us."

"You mentioned none of the patients underwent a C-section," Madison stated.

"That's right, although I did perform three sections during those two to three days."

"And I assume those women are fine."

"I've seen each of them as an outpatient and personally called them. They've all recovered without any difficulty. We've carefully reviewed each of the charts for both hospitalizations for all seven women. If there's some clue that links them together as to why they contracted IPS...well, so far we can't find it."

"IPS?" Jack asked, wondering why the acronym didn't ring a bell.

Ely and Josef shared a small smile. "You know doctors," Ely began. "As soon as a new or enigmatic illness is discovered, there's a race to name it. Not far behind is the inevitable clever acronym. It's not surprising that one of our physicians got the ball rolling by designating the illness inflammatory postpartum syndrome. Now, everybody's referring to it as IPS, as if the term has been well known to medical science for decades."

"I guess we should have known," Madison said. "Have any of the consultants on the cases come up with anything that might be helpful?"

"Our division of infectious diseases and our pulmonology, immunology, gastroenterology, and dermatology specialists have all been involved from the beginning. They've put forward some theories, but the reality is, they're basically stumped. We met as a group yesterday to go over the cases. Our differential diagnoses include illnesses stemming from autoimmune disorders, infectious diseases, environmental issues, drug reactions, and pre-cancer syndromes. We've also discussed the possibility of a remote vaccine side effect or a toxin."

"That's quite a comprehensive list," Jack said. "Have you given any thought to modifying or shutting down any of the hospital's services until the cause of the illness is determined?"

"We've discussed options that cover the spectrum from maintaining business as usual to indefinitely closing the birthing center," Josef answered.

Madison asked, "Just to verify—no caregiver, family members, or other hospital employees have contracted the illness?"

"Not to our knowledge. We've also spoken to every hospital from Orlando to Key West. None of them have seen any recent postpartum women with symptoms that resemble IPS."

Their conversation continued for the next thirty minutes. Madison was particularly interested in exploring the events of the final trimester. While she and Jack were impressed with the details that Ely and Josef provided, nothing they heard struck them as an eye-opening revelation that might turn out to be the promising first clue they were looking for.

"Are there any further questions we can answer for you?" Ely asked.

"For right now, I'd say no, but I suspect that'll change as we start looking into the cases," Madison answered, a little disappointed that their first meeting with the key members of Mothers and Infants Hospital had revealed so little about the illness.

"How would you like to proceed?" Josef asked, looking at Jack and Madison in turn.

Jack answered, "We'd like to begin by taking a careful look at each patient's medical chart. When we've completed the review, we'll make rounds on them. Hopefully, we'll be able to speak to a key family member in each case."

"That sounds fine," Ely said. "I'll give Teri a call right away. She's the nurse manager of the progressive care unit, and she has taken charge of the IPS patients' nursing care. If you're headed down there right now, I'll ask her to show you around. By the way, all the administrative arrangements have been made to designate you both as visiting faculty with unrestricted consulting privileges."

Josef checked his phone and stood up. "I apologize, but I'm late for my morning clinic." He turned to Jack and Madison. "It was a pleasure meeting you, and I look forward to working closely with you both. I'd appreciate it if we could sit down later this afternoon, after you've had a chance to review the charts and make rounds on the patients. I'm very anxious to hear your initial thoughts."

"Of course," Jack said, noticing a degree of relief in Josef's voice.

"I'll have my assistant reach out to you to set up a tentative time and place. If you don't mind, I'd like to ask my son, Zach, to join us. After he finished his ob-gyn residency at Northwestern, he came straight to Mothers and Infants to join our group. He's been involved with the IPS cases from the beginning and has been a tremendous help."

"We look forward to meeting him."

After Josef left, Jack and Madison spoke briefly with Ely before leaving his office and heading to the progressive care unit to meet Teri.

Waiting for the elevator doors to open, Madison asked, "What are the chances that seven healthy women select the same obstetrician, experience a normal childbirth, and then, a month later, develop the same serious illness that defies diagnosis?"

The doors opened and they stepped aboard.

"I don't know. But we're dealing with some pretty bright and talented physicians at this hospital, and I expect if they knew the answer to your question, you and I would still be in Columbus."

Chapter 7

After Jack and Madison stepped off the elevator, they crossed a windowed skybridge that looked out over the hospital's beautifully landscaped campus. From there, it was a short walk to the progressive care unit. The unit was designed for patients who weren't sick enough to require admission to the ICU but whose conditions were too serious for a regular hospital bed. It was a twenty-four-bed unit featuring the latest state-of-the-art technology. Its curved architectural style adhered strictly to a patient-centered design that included an attractive family lounge and ample natural lighting.

They hadn't taken more than a few steps when they were met by a young woman with an affable smile, sculpted arms, and shoulder-length, sandy-blond hair. Madison guessed they were about the same age.

"I'm Teri Woolf, the nurse manager. You must be Doctors Shaw and Wyatt."

"It's nice to meet you," Madison said.

"The pleasure's mine. Dr. Stanberry asked me to give you a tour of our PCU and get you set up on the electronic medical records system."

"We'd appreciate that."

Before Teri could continue, Madison noticed a limber woman wearing a Mothers and Infants purple lab coat approaching.

"This is Regina Leggett," Teri told them. "She's the supervisor of our birthing center. We'd all be spending a lot of time stumbling around in the dark if it weren't for her many talents."

"It's a pleasure," Madison said as she and Jack shook Regina's hand.

"The moment Dr. Church told me you'd be joining the team, I've been looking forward to meeting you," Regina said. "I was an assistant nurse manager at Southside during the GNS outbreak. I doubt if I'm the first person to tell you this, but anybody who was involved in those cases knows you two were clearly responsible for saving the day."

"That's very kind of you to say," Jack said.

"If there's anything I can do to help, please let me know."

Madison said, "I assume you took part in the evaluation of the two delivery rooms in which the IPS patients delivered."

"From top to bottom and every inch in between."

"Sometime at your convenience, Dr. Wyatt and I would be very interested in talking to you about your findings."

"I'd be pleased to meet with you, but I suspect it will be a rather short conversation. You see, to this point, we haven't found anything irregular or out of the ordinary, but our review is ongoing."

Madison nodded. "Even so, we'd be very interested in sitting down with you."

"Just let me know when," Regina said, again extending her hand to each of them. "I have a couple of patients to visit, so if you'll excuse me."

For the next half hour, Teri gave Madison and Jack a tour of the unit and an orientation to the electronic medical records system. When they were finished, she walked with them to the core desk.

"I'll be on the unit until late this afternoon. If you have any questions or need anything at all, please call me. Are you planning on seeing Emma Collymore right away?"

"We thought we'd take a look at her chart and then visit her,"

Madison answered. "We'd be interested in hearing any thoughts you might have regarding her condition."

An unsettled look instantly wrinkled Teri's face. "This is her fifth day with us. She came in pretty sick and hasn't shown any signs of improvement."

"Would you say she's worse?"

"She's definitely worse, Dr. Shaw."

"In what way?"

"Emma's clearly more fatigued, and we're starting to have trouble keeping her blood pressure up. Her jaundice and rash are more pronounced, and she's having more difficulty breathing. Except for the respiratory problem, I'd say the same is true for the other women with IPS."

"What's the word among the nurses—any ideas or theories about what's causing the illness?" Jack asked.

"At first, we assumed the women had picked up some weird bug during childbirth, but every test Dr. Whiteacre ran to identify it came back negative." From the way Teri kept looking up and down the corridor, Madison got the feeling she was intent on not being overheard. "I've been working here for nine years and believe me when I tell you that I can't remember a time when I've seen so much uncertainty and disagreement among our physicians."

"Most outbreaks of serious, unfamiliar illnesses affect the medical staff in just the way you've described," Jack stated. "The frustration among the doctors always seems to be a part of the total picture," he reassured Teri.

"All the nurses have their fingers crossed that with a little more time we'll have an answer."

Madison said, "Even though Dr. Whiteacre hasn't found a specific infecting agent, I'd be curious to know if you're using standard infectious precautions."

"Absolutely. We've instituted the use of full personal protective equipment, just like we did during Covid. Outside every room you'll find gowns, eye protection, gloves, and N-95 masks. One more thing—we adopted pod-nursing last year, which means that Emma has two nurses caring for her at all times. The other thing is that each pod has its own smaller satellite nursing station, which helps keep the staff separated from one another."

"Thank you for the information, Teri."

"If you'll excuse me, I have a meeting with some of our nurses. But if you ever need me for anything at all, just call me at 8918."

Jack and Madison made their way to the physician charting area and spent some time reviewing Emma's chart. In addition to studying the details of her history and physical examination, they scrutinized all her x-rays and laboratory results. There were also several consultation reports from various specialists that they read with extreme interest.

They were just about to leave and visit Emma for the first time when Jack's phone rang. "It's the dean. I'm sure she's calling for an update. I'd better take this."

"Tell Blair she needs to chill a little. We just got here and need a little time to make a meaningful assessment."

"I'm not sure I want to instruct the dean of our medical school exactly that way. She mentioned to me that she's known Governor Collymore for many years, which I suspect has made her a little anxious. I'd bet anything she got a call from our governor reminding her that, if this problem gets much larger, the nation's eyes will be on you, me, and the Elusive Diagnoses Institute."

"So now we have two governors instead of one raising the stakes of this situation."

"Take it easy, Madison. I'm sure Blair's just playing things on the cautious side. Nobody knows how to sidestep landmines better than she does. I suspect she assumes that once the media gets wind that we've been consulted, things are likely to heat up."

"That's exactly my point. From a medical standpoint, things are going to be challenging enough around here without having to deal with a lot of unnecessary political fanfare." Grim-faced, with severity in her voice, she added, "All I'm saying is that our focus has to be on IPS and not a bunch of distracting hospital drama."

"I'll tell you what. Why don't you go see Emma, and I'll join you as soon as I can?"

"Sounds like a plan, and don't forget to tell Blair I said hi," she told Jack as she strolled out of the physician's charting room and headed down the central corridor toward Emma's room.

If asked, even Madison would admit that nobody handled her better than Jack. Rather than viewing his skill as an annoyance, she looked at it simply as one of the many ways he'd been able to establish himself as the absolute love of her life.

Chapter 8

Not having the first clue how long Jack would be on the phone with Blair, Madison made

her way past the treatment room, continuing down the hall until she reached the last room of Pod B. After donning full protective gear, she slid open the glass door and stepped inside.

Emma's eyes were partially open, but she didn't seem to be aware of her surroundings. As she quietly approached the bed, Madison studied Emma's face. Her complexion was a washed-out shade of gray, while the sclerae of her vacant-appearing eyes were tinged a muted shade of yellow. But what sounded an instant alarm in Madison's mind was the labored nature of Emma's breathing.

The rate was entirely too fast, and with each shallow breath she drew, her chest wall expanded unevenly. Madison remembered reading one of the nurse's notes from the last shift indicating that the doctor had written an order for oxygen for mild respiratory difficulty. From what Madison was observing, the oxygen was doing little to improve Emma's breathing, and she was way past mild respiratory insufficiency.

When Madison reached the bedside, Emma's eyes seemed to focus on her.

"Good morning. I'm Dr. Shaw. I'm one of the doctors taking care of you. How do you feel?"

"I...I'm having...a lot of trouble...breathing," she said, scarcely able to get the words out between chopped breaths.

Before Madison could ask another question, Teri came through the door and wasted no time joining her at the bedside.

"I just thought I'd check to see if there's anything you need," she said in a quietly cautious voice as she leveled her eyes on Emma. From the look on her face, Madison assumed Teri shared her concern about Emma's labored breathing.

"Dawn's the nurse taking care of her. She must be looking in on her other patient. I was at the core desk and noticed Emma's oxygen saturation level had dropped to ninety-one. I thought I'd come take a look."

Madison looked back at Emma. From her appearance and her dropping oxygen saturation, she doubted whether she'd have the strength to answer any more questions.

"I'm more than a little concerned," Madison said to Teri, gesturing at the monitor. "She's breathing thirty-five times a minute, and her heart rate's one forty. The oxygen concentration in her blood is way too low. I'd get the respiratory therapist in here stat, and have them raise her oxygen to the highest concentration that can be given by mask. I'm not sure increasing the O2 will save her from being put on a ventilator, but it's worth a very brief trial."

"I was in here with her nurse right before I met with you and Dr. Wyatt. Her respiratory rate was seventeen, and her saturation was ninety-seven. Something happened, Dr. Shaw—she looks like a completely different patient."

"We have to assume that she's suffered some acute event that's severely compromised her respiratory status. When you call for the respiratory therapist, I'd also contact the physician on call and get them in here ASAP."

"Of course," she said, reaching for her hospital cell phone.

Madison began her exam by palpating the right side of Emma's neck. When she was finished, she gently felt her windpipe.

"Can I borrow your stethoscope?" she asked Teri.

"Of course." She slipped it from around her neck and handed it to Madison.

The first thing she did was listen to Emma's breath sounds on the right side of her chest. She then shifted the position of the stethoscope to auscultate her heart. It didn't take her long to make a diagnosis.

"Her right jugular vein's bulging, and the position of her trachea has shifted off the midline toward the left. She's also got no breath sounds at all on the right. Her heart and lung are being compressed by escaping air, severely affecting their normal function."

"You're saying she has a collapsed lung... a pneumothorax."

"I suspect it's the worst variety of a collapsed lung. I'm certain Emma has a tension pneumothorax."

"Her blood pressure's down to eighty over forty," Teri said in an anxious voice, just as the alarm on the cardiac monitor sounded.

"She needs a chest tube immediately. If we don't evacuate the trapped air from her chest cavity right now, she's going to arrest."

"I just saw Dr. Brandwyn on the unit a few minutes ago. She's one of our general surgeons. It's pretty rare for us to need a chest tube, but when we do, they're the ones we call to put them in. I'll page her stat."

"In the meantime, get me a fourteen-gauge angiocath as quickly as you can. If we insert it into her right chest, it'll relieve enough of the pressure and hopefully buy us the time we need until Dr. Brandwyn gets here."

Teri ran out of the room and was back in a flash holding the largebore IV catheter Madison had requested.

"Here's the angiocath you asked for, Dr. Shaw."

"Is Dr. Brandwyn on her way?"

"Not yet. I have one of the nurses working on it."

"And the physician covering the unit today?"

"He's in the middle of an emergency procedure. He said he'd be here as soon as he was able."

Two additional nurses and Olivia Phan, the respiratory therapist covering the unit, rushed into the room. With Teri and Olivia's help, they turned Emma on her left side and opened the upper portion of her hospital gown. While Madison was putting on sterile gloves, Teri was painting Emma's upper chest with an iodine solution.

"Okay, we're ready. I'll take the catheter," Madison said, reaching her hand out and sliding the catheter from its sterile package.

She leaned her lips close to Emma's ear. "You'll feel a needle stick in your chest, Emma. It'll help you breathe much easier," Madison stated, just on the off chance Emma could hear her.

Feeling the area under Emma's collarbone, she selected a spot between the second and third ribs and carefully slid the angio-catheter between them. The instant it penetrated the muscle layers and entered the chest cavity, there was an audible hiss as the trapped air compressing Emma's heart and left lung flowed out of her chest through the catheter. The characteristic sound of the air-rush was proof positive Madison's diagnosis of a collapsed lung was correct.

Pausing for a moment, she heaved a sigh of relief as she observed the improvement in Emma's breathing. But she was quickly reminded the catheter was only a stopgap measure. Once the chest tube was in, it would prevent any air from reaccumulating while the lung healed. Her decision to insert the angiocatheter had very likely saved Emma's life.

"Any word when Dr. Brandwyn will be here?" she asked, as she watched the steady rise in the blood oxygen level. Emma was instantly breathing easier. She opened her eyes briefly and sluggishly shifted her bleary-eyed gaze to Madison. The look of panic had fallen from her face. Madison responded with a subdued smile.

"How are you doing?" she asked, while she sutured the angio-catheter to the skin.

"I'm breathing better, but I still feel awful. What happened to me?"

"Your lung collapsed. We've been able to re-expand it with a small tube, which will take care of the problem temporarily, but you'll need a larger one put in."

"Do I have to go to surgery?"

"No. The surgeon's on her way. She'll numb up the area and give you some IV sedation in your vein. You shouldn't feel a thing."

Teri added, "Dr. Brandwyn should be here any minute to talk to you about the procedure."

Emma's eyes closed without any further response. Madison doubted she'd remember much of the life and death emergency she'd just been through.

"Great job, Dr. Shaw. Take a bow," Teri announced loud enough for everyone in the room to hear. Madison had been told more than once in her life that her cheeks and neck flushed quite a bit when she was lavished with praise.

Chapter 9

Just as one of the nurses was opening the sterile tray that contained all the instruments necessary to insert the chest tube, Dr. Brandwyn with her surgical intern in tow hurried into the room.

"Somebody tell me what's going on," she announced as she made her way to the bedside.

"This is Emma Collymore," Teri stated. "She was the first patient we admitted with IPS. A few minutes ago, she suddenly developed severe respiratory distress. Dr. Shaw came in to see her and diagnosed a tension pneumothorax, which she decompressed with a fourteen angiocath."

Brandwyn spoke as she examined Emma. "It's nice to meet you Dr. Shaw, and thank you for acting so quickly. Was there any doubt about the diagnosis?"

"No. She had all the classic signs. As soon as we inserted the angiocath, we got a noticeable rush of air with an immediate improvement in her respiratory status."

Emma was breathing better, but her level of consciousness remained blunted. Dr. Brandwyn spoke to her briefly to advise her she'd be inserting the chest tube. She then ordered some mild intravenous sedation, which Teri quickly drew up and administered. The oxygen saturation level had reached an acceptable level.

"Dr. Shaw's here with Dr. Jack Wyatt," Teri said. "They're consulting on the IPS cases."

"I think I heard something about that, but then again, so did everybody else who works here," Brandwyn said with a smile as she prepared to insert the chest tube. She turned to her nervous intern and asked, "Would you've ordered a chest x-ray to confirm the diagnosis before inserting a needle in this patient's chest?" He didn't answer immediately. Biting his lip, he stared across the room, taking a few moments to consider his attending's question. "I don't think you'll find the answer to my question written on that wall."

"No. I wouldn't have ordered a chest x-ray."

"You said that with extreme confidence. Can you back it up?"

"A tension pneumothorax is usually a diagnosis that can be made by the patient's history and physical examination. The delay in waiting for a chest x-ray to confirm could be costly and possibly even fatal."

"That's absolutely correct. It's refreshing to have an intern on my service who reads their textbook of surgery from time to time."

At that moment, Dr. David Phillips, the director of the Division of Intensive Care Medicine, entered the room. With rolled shoulders and a bristly red beard, he'd been on staff at Mothers and Infants since the day the ribbon was cut.

"Nice to see you, David," Brandwyn said. "Since when does the chief take first call?"

"I'm not ready to allow my junior colleagues to point to the privilege as an excuse to consider me over the hill."

"Sound thinking, Dave."

"I'm not as young as you guys, so I stopped running up three flights of stairs when I heard you were already here putting a chest tube in. To borrow from the British, *coals to Newcastle* summoned me here."

Brandwyn said. "I'm glad you stopped in. It's always nice to see you at a surgical emergency."

"I'd be lying if I didn't admit that I'm far more interested in the cerebral aspects of medicine than the procedural ones."

Having participated in the care of dozens of patients together, they knew each other well. They shared two things in common. The first was their same deadpan sense of humor, and the second was their staunch dedication to providing excellent care.

"Who's the patient?" he asked.

"This is Ms. Collymore, one of our IPS patients. Allow me to introduce you to Dr. Shaw. She's consulting on the case and happened to walk in just as Ms. Collymore was about to suffer a cardiac arrest. She was kind enough to save her life while I was sprinting over here."

"It's a pleasure to meet you, Dr. Shaw," he said. He then looked back at Brandwyn. "Since you seem to have things well in hand, as I assumed you would, I'll get back to the patient I was seeing and return after the chest tube's in. Do you think we'll need to put her on a ventilator?" he asked as he made his way back toward the door.

"I doubt that'll be necessary, but let's wait until we have a look at her post-insertion chest x-ray before we make that decision."

"Sounds like a plan. I'll see you in about twenty minutes."

After she'd anesthetized the area, Brandwyn picked up a scalpel from the tray and made a one-inch skin incision. "Do you have any idea what caused the pneumothorax?" she asked Madison, while she used a large hemostat to create a tunnel between Emma's ribs. When she felt it pop into the chest cavity, she reached for the chest tube and slid it into place. One of the nurses immediately attached it to suction. As was usually the case, the entire procedure took less than five minutes.

"I'm afraid I don't know what caused the collapsed lung. According to her chart, she's been having mild respiratory distress but nothing to suggest it would progress to an emergency," Madison answered. "It looks like you have things under control. I'm going to head back to the nursing station and take another look at Emma's chart. Maybe I missed something."

"It was certainly a pleasure meeting you. Hopefully we'll be able to chat again under less urgent circumstances."

"I'll look forward to that, Dr. Brandwyn."

"It's Elena."

"Thanks again, Dr. Shaw," Teri said.

"I'm glad things turned out okay," was all Madison could manage.

It had only been twenty minutes since she'd set foot in Emma's room. Everything had happened so quickly. But now she could take a breath and spend a few minutes going over things in her mind, trying to figure out why Emma had suffered a highly unusual and near-fatal complication from a disease that had some of the best and brightest medical minds in South Florida thoroughly baffled.

She lifted her eyes and saw Jack approaching. From the look on his face, she knew she wouldn't have to brief him on what happened to Emma.

"Tell me it's not true," he whispered to her.

"It's true."

"How's she doing?" Jack asked.

"The surgeon put a chest tube in. We got her lung back up. For now, she's stable."

"I just saw Josef. He requested we join him when he speaks to the governor and his wife about Emma's complication. They're pretty upset."

"Understandably so."

"Security has the meeting set up in the parent's lounge."

Even though she and Jack had barely arrived at Mothers and Infants, Madison was already consumed by a mounting uneasiness. She had very little to base the feeling on, but her instincts were telling her that a lot of undealt cards would have to be turned over if they had any chance of figuring out what was causing this terrible disease and how to treat it.

Chapter 10

Governor Sam Collymore was born and raised in Central Florida. In his whole life, the only appreciable time he'd traveled outside the state was when he spent his junior year abroad in England studying economics.

From the day he received his law degree from the University of Florida, he was committed, mind and body, to spending his life in service to the public. His road to the governor's mansion was a tireless one that included three terms in the Florida House of Representatives and a stint as Attorney General. Having recently attained his sixtieth birthday, he remained mentally agile, physically spry, and continuously brightly illuminated by the spotlight of success. A man who invariably had the courage of his convictions, he never forgot the importance of listening to the most informed sources on any issue that landed on his desk.

Seated on a couch with a coffee table in front of them, the governor and his wife, Carmela, sat with their hands clasped together waiting to speak with Dr. Church. Erudite and accomplished in her own right, Carmela was a distinguished high school principal. She and Emma had always had a natural mother-daughter chemistry. From the time Emma went off to college, a day rarely went by that they didn't speak.

The only information Carmela and the governor had was that Emma had suffered a serious setback in the form of a collapsed lung and that several doctors and nurses were in attendance trying to correct the problem. The assistant charge nurse had been in a few minutes earlier and informed them that Dr. Church would see them shortly.

The moment Josef, Madison, and Jack came through the door, the governor and Carmela stood up. The pure fear and uncertainty on their faces was undeniable.

"I'd like you to meet Doctors Wyatt and Shaw," Josef said to the Collymores.

"It's a pleasure," the governor was quick to respond. "I'd like to thank you for agreeing to come to Florida and consult on these cases."

Before they could respond, Carmela asked, "How's Emma doing? Why did this happen?"

"She suffered a collapsed lung that required an emergency procedure. Fortunately, it was successful, and she's stable," Josef said.

"Thank God," Carmela uttered as her eyes moistened with a drizzle of tears. "What kind of procedure was it, Doctor?"

Madison took the lead and spent a few minutes explaining every aspect of Emma's emergency treatment.

"You mentioned our daughter will require this tube until her lung recovers. How long will that take?" she asked.

"That's difficult to say, but a minimum of a few days."

With her lower lip quivering, Carmela asked, "Are there any other immediate problems we should know about?"

"Not at this time," Josef said.

"Apart from this sudden emergency," the governor began, "what can you share with us regarding Emma's general condition?"

"I'm afraid there's not much additional information since we spoke earlier. We continue to investigate every possibility, but we still haven't made a definitive diagnosis."

"But it's possible that Emma could recover on her own, even if you should never discover what's causing the illness?"

"That's definitely a possibility, Governor," Josef answered.

Collymore continued, "What specifically about her condition concerns you the most?"

"Her decreased level of responsiveness, impaired liver function, and risk of recurrent GI bleeding are particularly worrisome," Josef answered.

The governor was a man who understood the art of diplomacy and framing difficult situations as positively as possible. He also was well practiced at getting straight answers to his questions. It was his unique and perhaps God-given talent to do both at the same time that helped make him such an effective leader.

"I understand you haven't as yet identified the cause of IPS, but have you uncovered any promising clues?" Collymore asked, adjusting his gaze on Jack and Madison.

"Unfortunately, not yet. But we're still waiting for the results of quite a few tests," Jack responded. "As we progress through the process, our focus will be on narrowing down our list of diagnostic possibilities until we arrive at the correct one."

"I was Attorney General when you and Dr. Shaw came to Florida to consult on the GNS epidemic. I'm one of many who remember the terrible anguish so many Floridians suffered during the outbreak. I pray to God this isn't the beginning of a similar situation."

"The illnesses are quite different," Madison responded. "At least to this point, there's no strong indication that we'll be facing a widespread outbreak."

"Do you and Jack feel as if you've been here long enough to at least have a basic understanding of IPS?" he asked them.

"Doctors Church and Stanberry have done an excellent job of briefing us on Emma's and the other women's conditions. We've just started the process of evaluating the illness. Emma was the first patient we saw. We always begin with a broad view of the illness, which makes it too early to have any kind of a solid idea of what's causing IPS. The other problem when we start the process of investigating an elusive diagnosis is that we can't dismiss the possibility that we're dealing with a disease that medical science has never seen before."

"Are you at least reasonably confident that, given enough time, you and Dr. Wyatt will be able to make a diagnosis?" Carmela asked.

"That's a very difficult question to answer. I can tell you that I don't believe the diagnosis is going to jump right out at us, which means we have a lot of work to do in the days to come if we're going to be successful in figuring out what we're dealing with. I'm sorry for being so vague, but that's the most accurate and honest answer I can give you."

With a pained stare, the governor asked, "While you're looking for the answer, what will you do as far as treating Emma?"

Jack took this question. "We'll be focused on supportive care until we make a definite diagnosis."

"Emma's eyes seem to be getting more yellow every time we see her," Collymore said. "Are we sure she doesn't have hepatitis?"

Josef shook his head. "Her hepatitis evaluation was completely negative, but the jaundice and elevation in her liver enzymes indicate her liver isn't functioning normally. At its current level, we're still okay, but if there's further deterioration, we could be facing a major problem."

"Are you suggesting Emma might need a liver transplant?" the governor asked him.

"We're too early into the process to dismiss any possibility, sir."

Collymore said, "Excuse the simplicity and naiveté of my question, Doctors, but we live in a country where approximately three million women give birth every year. I'd hardly consider that a rare occurrence. My question is this: How could an illness like IPS that potentially affects so many women have escaped medical science's attention?"

"Your question's a logical one, but unfortunately, there's no good answer. We simply have to assume that IPS is an incredibly rare disease that has somehow eluded our recognition."

Holding onto Jack's words, Carmela averted her gaze in despair. "Do you feel there's a possibility we could lose Emma?"

"When we're dealing with cases like IPS, we try to remain cautiously optimistic regarding a favorable outcome, but the possibility of losing a patient always exists," Jack said, trying to maintain an honest balance between hope and reality. From the hopelessness that mirrored in her eyes, he sensed his words had done little to allay her fear of losing her daughter.

After a brief period of time, Carmela broke her silence. "There's something I'd like to share with you. Emma's an only child, and bringing her into the world was quite a struggle. Six months ago, her husband went out for his usual weekend bike ride, was hit by a drunk driver, and never came home. Emma and Rick started dating in high school. Since she lost him, she's had a terrible time trying to get over his passing. I guess what I'm trying to say is that Sam and I have seen Emma suffer more in the last six months than anybody should have to endure in a lifetime. From what you've told us, I'm terrified Emma's not going to survive this illness. All I can do is beg you to do everything in your power to find a way to bring her back to us."

Carmela could no longer contain her tears. She turned, slowly walked across the room, and looked aimlessly out the window.

"When do you anticipate we'll be able to speak with you again?" the governor asked.

"I'm going to stop back after my afternoon clinic," Josef answered. "Why don't we plan on talking at around four thirty?"

"Thank you. Do you think we can sit with Emma now?"

"We sedated her for the procedure, so I'm fairly certain she'll be sleeping for another hour or so."

"We just want to sit with her, Dr. Church. She hasn't been very conversant for the past twenty-four hours."

"I'll speak with Teri. She'll be out in a few minutes to escort you to Emma's room."

"Thank you."

Madison and Jack promised the Collymores they'd be back at

about the same time Dr. Church was planning on returning. With nothing more for the moment, they left the lounge.

The governor and Carmela retook their seats on the long leather couch. Sitting there in a bewildered hush, they gazed across the room through vacant eyes.

Chapter 11

After their meeting with the Collymores, Jack and Madison decided to grab some coffee in the staff lounge before starting rounds on the other IPS patients. Jack added a small amount of creamer to his brew, then took a couple of sips and immediately looked down at the cup, wondering why it was so much better than the usual flat, stale taste of staff-lounge coffee.

"The governor seems to be handling Emma's illness better than Carmela," he said.

"I think you may be relying too much on appearances. Maybe he's just very good at putting on a brave face. It can't be easy trying to focus on your severely ill child and run a state the size of Florida at the same time. Emma's an only child. I can't even begin to imagine how much they're suffering."

"I guess the fastest way to solve that problem is to figure out what's wrong with her and then come up with an effective treatment."

"I commend you on your aspirational thinking," Madison said.

"I know this is a long shot, but do you think it's remotely possible that all these women had already acquired the illness before they ever set foot in the hospital to deliver?"

Madison set her cup down. "We shouldn't dismiss any possibility, but I think it's highly unlikely. There aren't too many things that strike me as obvious, but I have to believe that whatever made them sick did so during that day or two that they were in Mothers and Infants having their babies."

"What's interesting about these cases is that there's a limited number of broad disease groups we'll need to consider."

"That may be true, but that still leaves thousands of possible diagnoses within those groups. I know we just got here, and I'm not trying to sound overly pessimistic, but I think we're in for a really tough one this time."

Jack rested his chin in his hands. "These patients were all healthy prior to giving birth."

"We already know that. What's your point?"

"It's impossible for me to imagine that they were unrelated, random victims of the same disease with nothing in common."

Madison said, "I don't think anybody would argue that the only things they shared in common were bad luck and giving birth within a few days of each other. Is some infectious cause your number one possibility?"

"None of them got sick for at least a month after they delivered. That would be a relatively long incubation period for most bacteria, viruses, and fungi."

"Which makes pathogens unlikely causes but not completely out of the question," she reminded him. "It's just a hunch at this point, but I'm also leaning away from an infectious disease."

"In that case, what are you leaning toward?"

"I've been thinking about the possibility of something noxious they acquired in the delivery room. Between medications, various types of anesthesia, and a host of environmental factors, a toxic exposure has to be on our short list."

"There's also the fact that Dr. Church had the same anesthesiologist and nurse assigned to him for every delivery and only used two delivery rooms. It's hard to dismiss that as an insignificant little detail."

Just then the door to the lounge opened, and Teri walked in. As she was making her way across the room to join them, she smiled and gave them a thumbs up.

"Emma's doing fine. Her parents are sitting with her now. Do you have time to stop in briefly before you start rounds to speak with them again? They have many more questions, and it would mean a lot to them."

"We were going to see them later this afternoon, but we can stop in now," Jack said.

"That would make them beyond happy. I may be speaking a little too soon, but from where I'm sitting, I'd say the Collymores are pinning their hopes for Emma's recovery squarely on you two." She glanced at her phone. "I'd better get back. I'll see you later."

Madison sighed dramatically. "Nothing like a little pressure from a famous governor to make things easier."

"He strikes me as a good guy. Plus, it comes with the territory. Think of it as just another distraction. You're the one who's always preaching to dismiss the inevitable political issues we face and stay focused on the medicine."

She grinned. "I'll remind you of that the next time I have to talk you off a ledge from everybody we meet trying to manipulate you." To dissuade him from responding and leading them into a conversation that would be better held another time, she wagged a finger his way. "We could talk about that all day, but it's not going to help us get to the bottom of IPS." She stood up and tossed her Styrofoam cup in the trash. "My suggestion is we get off our butts and go to work."

"I'm with you", he said, getting up and falling in alongside her as they headed for the exit.

Jack was quite familiar with Madison's propensity for diving headfirst into their cases with every ounce of energy she could gather. Even in the face of fighting leukemia, she was always on the attack, never retreating, always reloading.

Jack said, "Josef seems like a very competent and likable fellow, but at some point, irrespective of his friendship with Ely and Dr. Whiteacre declaring he couldn't possibly be a factor in the cause of

IPS, we're going to have to discuss Josef's possible role in the outbreak."

"I was just thinking the same thing myself. It's quite likely that many of the physicians will join ranks with Whiteacre and close their eyes to the possibility that Josef may be more involved than meets the eye."

"We're obviously not talking about negligence or willful intent."

"Of course not," she said.

"We should have it front of mind that delving into Josef's possible role in all this could be a very prickly undertaking. I'm not saying we should abandon the issue. I'm simply pointing out that we should tread lightly."

"I'm not proposing a call to arms, Jack. I'm merely suggesting we don't turn a blind eye to the possibility that Josef might be a clue to the cause of IPS." He sensed her patience fading rapidly. "We can't be dissuaded from pursuing it for fear of stepping on a few bigwig toes."

"I'm only advocating for courage with courtesy."

With squinted eyes, she said, "C'mon, buddy. Let's go to work."

Chapter 12

The final patient on Jack and Madison's list was Samantha Manion, who also happened to be the last patient admitted to Mothers and Infants with IPS. Sammie, as her parents lovingly dubbed her in early childhood, was a healthy twenty-seven-year-old who presented with a symptom complex identical to the other IPS patients.

Jack and Madison having lost track of time, it was almost five o'clock when they approached Sammie's room. Just as they were about to step into her room, Madison spotted Dr. Elena Brandwyn coming down the hall.

"Hi, Elena. How's Emma doing?"

"For what she's been through, she's doing great. The chest tube's working perfectly, her lung is well expanded, and her respiratory status is remarkably better." She turned to Jack. "You must be Dr. Wyatt."

"I am. It's a pleasure to meet you. Please, call me Jack."

"From all the buzz around here about you and Madison, I'd say the pleasure's all mine."

"Thank you," he said with a smile. "But the buzz I've been hearing all day has been about how you and Madison saved Emma's life."

"My part was easy. All I had to do was put a chest tube in. An intern could have done it. You guys, on the other hand, are facing one hell of a diagnostic challenge trying to figure out IPS. I don't envy you." She checked the time on her cell phone. "I told Madison if either of you needs me for anything—and I mean twenty-four seven—please don't hesitate to call."

"Thanks," Madison said. "But I hope we won't have to take you up on your offer."

"Are you guys finished for the day?"

"One more patient," Madison said. "Would you mind if we touch base with you tomorrow to get an update on Emma?"

"Not at all. I look forward to hearing from you," she told them as she again started down the hall.

When Jack and Madison went into Sammie's room, they found her sleeping on her back with the same pale, clay-colored complexion as the other IPS patients. Her rash was somewhat different, being more patchy and shrouding a greater area of her neck and upper chest. Jack studied her breathing. It was only slightly on the labored side—nothing to worry about.

Tony, the nurse taking care of Sammie, walked over and introduced himself. He mentioned he'd worked the day shift for the past three days and had been assigned to Sammie for the entire time.

"How would you say she's doing now, compared to when she was first admitted?" Jack asked.

"She's sleeping more. And when she's awake, she's definitely not as alert as she was when she first came in. She vomited again this morning, but for the first time I didn't see any blood. Except for her worsening liver function, everything else is about the same."

Just then the door opened, and a young man with his hair cropped to the scalp, dressed in an army-green service uniform, walked in. The inverted three chevrons on his left sleeve identified him as a sergeant in the United States Army.

"Good morning. I'm Mason Reed. I'm Samantha's fiancé."

"I'm Dr. Shaw, and this is Dr. Wyatt. We've been asked to consult on her case. Would you mind answering a few questions for us?"

"Dr. Shaw, there's nothing I wouldn't do to help Sammie."

"Let's talk on the other side of the room," she suggested. "Were you with Sammie the first day she got sick?"

"We were together from the time we got up until the paramedics took her to the hospital."

"What do you remember about that day, especially when she first began to get sick?"

"Sammie's been in the market for a new car, so we spent the entire day shopping for one. To know Sammie is to know that she's not exactly known for making snap decisions. I'm an Army recruiter now, and I've had men and women who enlisted in less time than it takes Sammie to pick out a new toothbrush." He hesitated briefly as the corners of his mouth turned up into an affectionate grin.

"Do you remember at about what time she started to feel ill?" she asked.

"She didn't mention anything about feeling sick until we were in the car on the way back to our townhouse."

"What was the very first thing she complained about?"

"It was kind of all of a sudden—she just said she was feeling washed out and sick to her stomach. The other thing was that she asked me if I had any gum because she had an awful taste in her mouth."

"What time was that?"

"I'd say about six o'clock. When we got home, I asked her if she was getting her appetite back. She told me she was feeling sicker and went into the living room, curled up on the couch, and fell asleep for about an hour. My sister was watching the baby. I called her and told her what was going on, and she said she'd keep him as long as we needed her to, especially if Sammie was getting sick."

"What happened when Sammie woke up?" Madison asked.

"She looked terrible. All the color had drained from her face, and she told me she had to throw up. She rushed into the bathroom, and I could hear her vomiting. The next thing I knew she was yelling for me to come help her. When I got there, I saw a lot of fresh blood and clots in the commode. After two tours in Afghanistan, I'm familiar with the sight of blood."

"What happened next?"

"By this time, she was hysterical from fear. I grabbed my phone and called 9-1-1. When the paramedics arrived and started working on her, I told them she'd just given birth a month ago. They said she had to go to the emergency room, and the next thing I knew, they loaded her on a stretcher and wheeled her outside to the ambulance. I followed them, and fifteen minutes later we pulled into the emergency room here at Mothers and Infants."

"Mason, is there anything about Sammie's health you can think of, from the time she got home from the hospital after she delivered until she got sick, that struck you as unusual?"

"Sammie and I go back a long way, Dr. Shaw." He lowered his head in disbelief. In a shaky voice, he added, "I can't even remember her having a bad flu. She's as healthy as they come."

"What about new medications or supplements?"

"Sammie won't take any meds. I could barely get her to take her vitamin pills when she was pregnant."

"I know you've probably already answered this, but has she traveled recently or been around anybody who's been ill?"

"No."

He sat down in one of the club chairs, inclined his head forward, and rested his chin on this chest. "We have a one-month-old baby, Doc. Sammie already has our life completely planned out, down to the month, for the next twenty years." He paused to exhale a bottomless breath. "I've been visiting her twice a day. Every time I see her, she looks worse, and not a single one of her doctors has the first clue what's wrong with her." His face was filled with fright. "I'll tell you Dr. Shaw, I'm really starting to get scared."

Chapter 13

"We're just beginning to look into this illness," Jack said, trying to quell Mason's fears. "Today's the first time we've seen Samantha. I promise you that we're going to do everything we can to get her through this, but we need more time. I know that's not what you want to hear, but for now, you're going to have to do everything you can to remain calm and patient."

"I understand."

It was at that moment that Sammie slowly began to open her eyes. They all walked over to the bedside. Tony helped her push herself up a little higher in the bed.

"Hi, Sammie. I'm Dr. Shaw, and this is Dr. Wyatt. We were asked by your doctors to consult on your case."

"You must be the two doctors from out of town Dr. Church told me about," she said softly. "He told me you'd be stopping in to see me."

"Congratulations on the birth of your son," Madison said. "How's he doing?"

"He's so cute, I can't stop kissing his toes." Even though Madison had heard the expression countless times before, she couldn't contain a grin.

"Is it true you're studying to be an ultrasound tech?"

"A few more months and I'll be certified."

"Congratulations. Do you feel up to answering a few questions?"

"I'm pretty tired, Doctor, and still kind of sick to my stomach, but I'll do my best."

Madison began by repeating some of the questions she'd just posed to Mason. After a few minutes, it became obvious that Sammie's answers were becoming affected by her increasing fatigue. Madison asked one last question and began a physical examination. By the time she was finished, Sammie had drifted back to sleep.

They spoke briefly to Mason, assuring him that they'd be seeing Sammie daily and that they would make themselves available, along with her other doctors, to answer any questions he might have. Madison was a firm believer in first impressions. She found Mason to be bright and was reasonably certain he had the emotional strength to deal with the trying situation he'd be facing in the days to come.

"I don't know how you feel about it," Madison said as they made their way back to the core desk. "But for a first day and a first set of rounds, we didn't exactly hit the ground running."

"I'm not sure we know anything more about IPS now than we did when we got up this morning, but let's not get too dispirited about it."

"How much time until we meet with Josef?"

"We have exactly ten minutes."

"I suspect he's not as convinced as Ely is that he's not responsible for IPS. I think he loves being a doctor, and right now he's feeling the weight of the world on his shoulders."

"Hopefully, when the smoke clears, we'll be able to prove that he played no role in causing this illness. Once this is all behind him, he strikes me as the type of person with the wherewithal to be able to pick up where he left off."

"I hope so. So what's our next move in trying to get our heads around this illness?"

"The most obvious thing we can do is carefully monitor all the new test results and round on the patients at least once a day. We'll keep speaking to all the key family members and wait for the first real clue that will point us in the right direction. I wouldn't know of any other way to approach things."

"I agree, but I do have one suggestion," Madison said. "Rather than waiting, I think we should set up the meeting with Regina Leggett as soon as possible. Nurses in a supervisory role can be a treasure trove of information."

"Not to contradict you, but my experience has usually been exactly the opposite. I've found that they're usually very loyal and discreet employees who don't go around expressing any boat-rocking opinions."

"We'll just hope that Regina is the exception to your observation. After we meet with Josef, I'm going to give her a call and set up a meeting. Any objections?"

"None at all," he said.

A knowing smile took shape on her face. "Since you're the guru of hospital politics and appropriate behavior, are we going to speak to Regina alone, or are we obligated to invite Josef, Ely, and God knows who else to sit in? Before you answer that, I'll remind you that she might be a lot less forthcoming with two of the most important physicians on staff at Mothers and Infants seated across from her. On the other hand, if it's just the two of us, we can promise her confidentiality."

Jack dwelled on Madison's take on things briefly before answering. "Since we have the governor's and the surgeon general's green light to do whatever it takes to figure out what's causing IPS, I don't see why we'd be obligated to include anybody else when we meet with her."

"Are you implying that we have a little extra wiggle room as far as sidestepping accepted protocols?"

"I am. I think we should be as professional and diplomatic as possible, bearing in mind that we weren't invited down here to win a popularity contest. I agree with you that it would be helpful to meet with Regina alone. If Josef, Ely, or anybody else is offended that they weren't invited…well, I guess we can jump off that bridge when we get to it. This may be one of those times when it's better to beg for forgiveness afterward than ask for permission ahead of time."

"I'm really glad to see we agree on this one," she said. "It doesn't happen that often."

"I'm starting to wonder if you and my mother graduated from the same charm school."

Truth be told, Jack was unconvinced that meeting with Regina wouldn't result in some dicey consequences. Despite the confident way he'd voiced his opinion to Madison, he hoped that such a conversation wouldn't get them summoned to Ely's throne room to explain their poor manners.

Chapter 14

At a few minutes before six, Madison placed a call to Regina, hoping to set up a meeting for the following day.

"I was just finishing up some last-minute administrative things. I'm happy to meet with you and Dr. Wyatt now if you're available," she told Madison.

"That's very kind of you. That would be great."

"We can talk in the birthing center. There's a seminar room on the second floor directly across from the elevators that should be available. Can you be there in fifteen minutes?"

"We'll see you then."

Ten minutes later, Jack and Madison walked into the large, nicely appointed conference room that was used principally by the nurses for committee meetings, interviews, and continuing medical education lectures.

Regina was already present, seated at a small keystone-shaped table, leafing through the pages of a spiral-bound notebook. Before they set foot in the room, Madison and Jack had decided that he'd take the lead.

As they were sitting down, Jack said, "Thanks for agreeing to speak with us on such short notice. This shouldn't take too long."

"There's no reason to thank me, Dr. Wyatt. We're all deeply concerned about these women, and we understand the urgency of the situation. We're ready to help in any way we can."

From the amiable look on her face and the easy tone of her voice, Jack didn't sense any unspoken annoyance at being delayed from going home for the day. "I'm happy to answer any questions you may have. Or, if you prefer, I can brief you on what we've looked at to determine whether IPS is the result of some environmental or system-related problem that occurred in the birthing center."

"I think a good place to start would be if you'd share your general impressions of what your investigation has yielded to this point," Jack stated.

"We began by forming a task force. It was at about the time when the third patient was admitted with IPS. The team includes five key individuals with upper-level positions in various phases of the birthing center's operations. We've looked at every detail, from staffing assignments and patient profiles to operative protocols and departmental procedures. We've enlisted the aid of the hospital's infection-control team and environmental services and interviewed every staff member who worked during the three days in question. We're still going over our results, but so far we've been unable to identify anything out of the ordinary that would give us a clue as to the cause of IPS."

Regina was moving along at a fairly brisk pace. Jack was duly impressed by her on-point presentation. She was obviously bright and confident, and she had excellent organizational skills. Most obvious in her manner was her avoidance of any evasive tap dancing or finger pointing. "I could continue with a lot of the details, but those are the basics in a nutshell. I'd be happy to try and answer any questions you may have," she added with no false ceremony.

"Can we assume there were no incident reports filed by the staff for those two days?" Jack asked.

"There were no unusual incidents, so there were no reports. As I said before, we checked every medication, piece of equipment, and patient issue for the entire three days and came up with nothing. We're not finished yet, but I'd be pretty surprised if we should suddenly discover something of importance that we missed."

"Dr. Shaw and I feel it's highly unlikely that these women contracted IPS prior to coming into the hospital. Would you agree?"

"I would. We don't feel they brought the disease into the hospital with them or somehow acquired it after they were discharged."

"Was there anything at all that you and your committee came across in your initial review that even in a small way raised an eyebrow?"

Regina didn't answer at once. Sitting back in her chair, she took a long hard look at him. It wasn't his intention, but he felt as if his question had struck a chord with her. Rather than move off in another direction, he remained silent.

She finally spoke. "If we're going to be successful in figuring out this disease, we're going to have to check our egos at the door and accept the fact that something or somebody at Mothers and Infants is responsible for causing IPS. If somebody made a mess of things…"

An intrigued glance passed between Jack and Madison. If his contention was that nurses in leadership roles tended to be diplomatic and reserved, Regina Leggett could not be counted among them. Her statement was about as subtle as a wrecking ball.

"Do you truly think that somebody making a mess of things could be at the heart of the problem?" he asked.

"That's difficult to say. But it would be natural enough for people looking into this terrible disease to lose their objectivity."

"In what way?"

"Put simply, if anybody dismisses the possibility of an intentional act or hospital error, I'd invite that individual to take a step forward and speak right up."

Jack was getting a peculiar vibe from Regina. He suspected Madison was sensing the same thing. He was more than a little taken aback by her candor and wondered if she had real concerns that a hospital mistake or worse had segued into the IPS outbreak.

Chapter 15

While Jack was being cautious in thought and word, Madison was experiencing no such inhibitions.

She said to Regina, "I know you haven't gathered facts that would definitively identify a cause, but I'm getting the feeling you have an… unproven theory as to what may have happened to these women to make them so ill." Her voice was flat, with no hesitation.

"I'm here to report the facts as best as I can to you and Dr. Wyatt, not to make speculations that would be light-years above my pay grade."

"We're just talking, Regina, and it's just the three of us. Nothing's going to leave this room."

"I've spent a lot of time at Mothers and Infants without cracking out of turn, as my grandfather used to call it. Beyond that, you're free to draw your own conclusions."

Madison stared at her for a moment. "The smallest observation might seem like an insignificant detail at first but later turn out to be the key to making a diagnosis. What I'm saying is, to hell with being a good soldier, Regina. Tell us what you think, not what you're positive of. If there's something you think you know, even if there's no proof, we'd like to hear about it."

Madison was quite self-aware about her penchant for being blunt. She was waiting for Jack's usual response of clearing his throat when he thought she was going a little overboard, which was his subtle way of suggesting she tap on the brakes a little before she said something she wouldn't be able to take back or apologize for.

"I have a question I'd like to pose to you, Dr. Shaw," Regina said, looking at her with a bit of a sour face. "Do you believe that all adverse hospital events are either unavoidable or an act of God?"

"That's an intriguing question," she said, beginning to feel as if she were sitting across the board from a chess grandmaster. "If you don't mind me saying so, Regina, you seem to keep coming back to a possible hospital error as the cause of this illness."

"Mistakes can include all manner of sins, Dr. Shaw. Different people have different ways of connecting the dots." Before Madison could respond, Regina fired another question at her. "What I may or may not know is irrelevant. The real question is whether you and Dr. Wyatt will be able to open your minds sufficiently to make a correct diagnosis."

"All I can tell you is that we're cautiously optimistic. But absent a significant clue that puts us on the right track, the odds of identifying the cause of IPS and how to treat it go way down."

"For the sake of those poor women, I certainly hope you uncover the elusive clue you're referring to." The room sank into silence. Regina came to her feet. "Do you have any further questions for me?"

"Not at the moment," Madison answered. "Thanks again for taking the time to meet with us. If we have any other questions or concerns, would you mind if we reach out to you?"

"Not at all," she answered as she exited the room as if her car was double-parked.

As they moved down the hall and made their way toward the birthing center's exit, Madison said, "If I've had a stranger conversation than that one with anybody recently, I'm hard-pressed to remember it."

"I wonder what Regina thinks she knows," Jack said. "She sure seemed to be a master at dropping hints, but leaving things unsaid."

"I think something's bothering her about all this, and she really wasn't interested in sharing it with us. Did you get the feeling she might have been a little frightened?"

"It's possible. I'm still trying to figure out why she agreed to speak with us. She could have dodged our request fairly easily."

Continuing to discuss their chat with Regina, they took the elevator down to the lobby of the birthing center, exited the building, and made their way to the parking lot.

"Your mother mentioned she has dinner plans tonight with some friends," Madison said. Why don't we find some quiet place to eat, enjoy a glass or two of a nice wine, and put a moratorium on discussing anything to do with IPS or what's going on at Mothers and Infants for a couple of hours? What do you say?"

"I think that's a great idea."

While Jack and Madison's conversation shifted to non-medical topics, Regina had already returned to her office. Seated at her desk, lost in thought, she stared at her phone. The mantel clock she'd received as a Christmas present from her brother chimed its quarter-hour melody. Finally, she disposed of whatever remaining doubt was still swirling around the edges of her mind, reached for her phone, and made a call.

Chapter 16

SARASOTA, FLORIDA

OUTBREAK—DAY 6

For their entire lives, Scarlett and Nell Thacker had lived within a few miles of each other. Only thirteen months apart in age, they'd learned at an early age what Irish twins were.

It had been almost four weeks since Nell, a certified instructor and owner of a local flight school, gave birth to her first child, Emeline, at Caring Hearts Medical Center. She came through her labor and delivery without a hint of a complication. Nell was a single mom, and when she came home with the baby, Scarlett had moved in, making herself available to help with Emeline's care around the clock.

It was Saturday morning, and Scarlett, a registered nurse, had fed Emeline at four a.m. She'd checked her again at seven and found her sleeping contentedly. Knowing her sister wasn't always an early riser, she left the nursery and walked down the hall to the master bedroom. Quietly, she opened the door and took a peek inside. Nell wasn't in bed, but she noticed the door to the bathroom was open. She was a little surprised, because ever since they were kids, Nell had been a fanatic about privacy and always keeping the bathroom door closed.

"Nell, are you in there—are you okay?"

When there was no response, Scarlett's first thought was to give her a little more time before checking on her again, but when she realized she didn't hear the shower running, she decided not to wait.

"Nell?" she repeated as she took her first step into the bathroom. The instant her eyes fell on her sister slumped over between the sink and toilet, she gasped. In the flash of an eye, she was at her side. She placed her hands on Nell's shoulders, gently turned her upper torso, and eased her a few feet away from the toilet. She was pale and semiconscious but breathing normally. "Oh my God," she muttered to herself. "Nell, can you hear me?" Nell opened her eyes about halfway and managed to nod once, with obvious difficulty. "What happened to you? Did you fall?"

"I… I think so."

Her words were still hanging in the air when Scarlett noticed the copious dark reddish-brown blood clots in the toilet. She was consumed with disbelief, and it was only her years of training and experience that enabled her to stay focused on the emergency at hand. She reached for Nell's wrist and checked her pulse. It was rapid and thready. As a nurse, Scarlett had been in similar positions before when every second of delay could be critical to the patient's outcome.

"If I help you, can you get up?"

"I… I think so."

"Let's see if we can get you into the chair. It's only a few feet away."

"How's Emeline?"

"She's fine. I just fed her, and she went right back to sleep. C'mon, let me help you," she said, kneeling down on Nell's left side.

Supporting her by reaching around her and clasping her hands in front of Nell's midsection, Scarlett was able to help her to her feet. With one guarded step at a time, they made it to the upholstered club chair located just outside the bathroom door. Once she had Nell securely in the chair, she wiped the perspiration from her sister's brow and rechecked her pulse. It was at that moment that she saw her sister's yellow sclerae.

"It can't be," she whispered to herself, fearing Nell had somehow contracted hepatitis. Scarlett wasted no time in reaching for her phone and calling emergency medical services.

She hung up after being assured an ambulance was on the way, then checked to make sure the baby monitor was on before placing a call to their mother who lived a few miles away.

"I need you to come over to Nell's right now. She's sick, and I just called the paramedics. I'm positive they'll want to take her to the emergency room. I need you to watch Emeline so I can go with her." She listened impatiently for a few seconds. "Mom, now's not the time for questions, just get over here. I'll fill you in when you get here. Right now, I need to focus on Nell."

She grabbed the blanket from the bed and spread it around Nell's shoulders.

"I'm so dizzy."

"Do you have to vomit again?" Scarlett asked, fearing blood loss had put Nell into the early phases of shock.

"No... No, I think I'm okay for now."

"When did you get sick?"

"I woke up feeling dizzy and sick to my stomach. I made it to the bathroom, but after I threw up, I didn't think I'd be able to make it back to bed, so I just stayed where I was. But the dizziness got so bad, I slowly lowered myself to the floor. I didn't have my phone with me, and I couldn't even find the strength to yell for you." Scarlett noted Nell's words were slurred, and her eyes had rolled up slightly.

"I'm going to go with you to the hospital. Mom's on her way over to take care of Emeline."

"Do I really need to go to the hospital?" Her question prompted Scarlett to wonder if she knew she had vomited blood.

"It's not up for discussion, Nell. We're going to the ER."

"I'll go with Mom. I'd rather you stay with Emeline."

"Mom's perfectly capable of watching her. Are you forgetting who raised us?"

Scarlett heard the doorbell and rushed to the front door, returning with the paramedics. After assessing the situation, they advised that Nell be urgently taken to the hospital.

Ten more minutes came and went as they worked quickly to prepare Nell for transport.

"Do you have any idea what the problem is?" Scarlett asked the more senior-appearing paramedic.

"Being postpartum opens up a lot of possibilities," she answered. "After the ER staff has had a chance to fully evaluate her, they'll be in a better position than we are to let you know what's going on."

"Which hospital are you taking her to?"

"Caring Hearts. That's where she delivered, and they're the only hospital in the area equipped to handle a problem like this."

They checked the monitors and the IV one last time before snapping the gurney into its upright position.

"I don't like the looks of her," the second paramedic whispered to his partner as they loaded Nell onto the stretcher, secured her in place, and headed toward the front door.

"I don't know how much blood she's lost or how much time we have before something bad happens. We need to get her to the ER ASAP."

Scarlett escorted them out of the house and stayed with Nell until the ambulance pulled away from the curb. Just as it did, her mother pulled up.

"What in God's name is going on, Scarlett?"

"Nell's been vomiting blood and is very weak. She needs to be in the hospital for IV fluids and a thorough workup."

The color drained from her mother's face. "Will she need a transfusion?"

"I don't know, Mom, but it's very possible. Don't worry. She's going to be fine," Scarlett added, trying to avoid answering her mother's litany of questions. "I should get going. After they've had a chance to have a look at Nell and brief me, I'll call you."

"But what if—"

"I promise, Mom. As soon as I know anything, I'll call."

"What about Emeline?"

"As of five minutes ago, she was asleep. She'll be due to eat again pretty soon." Without waiting for a response, Scarlett quick-walked to her car.

Fifteen minutes later, she arrived at Caring Heart's emergency room. She was about fifty feet away and able to see the ambulance with its lights flashing had backed into the ER's loading dock. A team was gathered at the back of the vehicle and were just beginning to offload the gurney. Scarlett recognized the paramedics.

As she got out of her car, she inhaled a generous breath of the damp morning air. Consciously slowing her breathing, she said a short prayer and hurried toward the entrance.

Chapter 17

In his final year of medical school, Dr. Mel Slocomb had applied to ten emergency medicine residencies. He was offered an interview at each of them, but after the one at Rush Hospital in Chicago, he'd decided he was a perfect fit for their program. The teaching faculty felt the same way about him, and when match day came, he was informed that he'd be moving to Chicago in June to begin his residency.

Three years later, when he'd completed the program, he'd felt well prepared to begin his career as an attending emergency room physician. Between medical school and residency, he had endured enough of the big-city experience for a lifetime and decided to accept a job in Sarasota at Caring Hearts Medical Center. Within a few months, he was recognized as an outstanding doctor by his colleagues, the ER staff, and the administrative leadership. After ten years as an attending, he'd been offered the position of chief of emergency services, which he proudly accepted.

On this particular Saturday, he was working the day shift. It was early and still relatively quiet. He was sitting in his office attending to a few administrative responsibilities when the charge nurse, Kace Ellsworth, walked into his office.

"Sorry to bug you, Dr. Slocomb, but we need you right away."

Noting the look on Kace's face, Mel wasted no time grabbing his stethoscope and getting up from his desk.

"What's going on?"

"The paramedics just brought in a woman who's about a month postpartum who is vomiting blood and is jaundiced," he answered as they hurried out of his office, crossed the hall, and entered the emergency room's treatment area.

"Where is she?"

"We put her in the critical care room."

Slocomb walked into Nell's room, put on a pair of gloves, and went directly to the bedside. The moment he laid eyes on her waxen, sweat-soaked face, his level of concern skyrocketed.

"What are her vital signs?" he inquired as he began his examination.

"Her blood pressure's a hundred over sixty and her pulse is one twenty-two," Kace responded, holding up an emesis basin that contained a large amount of bloody vomitus for Mel to see."

"Nell, I'm Dr. Slocomb. I'll be looking after you. How are you doing?"

"I feel awful," she answered with a vacant stare, rocking her head sluggishly from side to side.

Mel took another quick look at her monitors. The oxygen level in her blood was a little lower than he liked.

"How much oxygen is she on?" he asked.

"Just two liters," the respiratory therapist replied.

"Let's up it to four and see how she does. If her sat doesn't come up, we may need to change to a mask."

"What else do you need?" Kace asked.

"Send off a complete set of labs. Make sure we get a type and screen, a coag profile, and a tox screen. Also, let's get a chest x-ray, an EKG, and a set of blood gases…and put in another large-bore IV. Any fever?"

"No, she's afebrile. What about the IV rate? It's currently wide open."

"Finish up the liter of normal saline, and then slow it down to a hundred an hour."

"Got it. How about a nasogastric tube?"

"She'll probably need one, but let's hold off for now. Is any of her family with her?"

"Her sister."

"Let me take a quick look at the squad's run report, and then let's get her in here."

While a second nurse began implementing Mel's orders, Kace stepped outside the room to get Scarlett.

In the interim, both Nell's vital signs and her oxygenation had improved, and most of the lab tests were still cooking. For the moment, Mel was satisfied Nell's condition was stable enough to spend a few minutes speaking to her sister.

"Let me see her blood count the moment you get it from the lab," he called out, not speaking directly to any of the other four people in the room. A couple of minutes later, Kace returned with Scarlett.

"I'm Dr. Slocomb. I understand you're Nell's sister."

"Scarlett Thacker. That's correct."

"I have a few questions I'd like to ask you."

"Of course."

"Do you have a fairly good idea of your sister's medical history?"

"For most of our lives, we've lived within shouting distance of each other. We're very close, and I probably know as much about Nell's health as I do about my own. She's always been incredibly healthy."

"By that I assume she's not currently being treated for any significant illnesses?"

"No."

"Has she ever vomited blood before?"

"No...never."

"Are you aware if she has a history of stomach ulcers, gastritis, bleeding problems, or liver problems?"

"No. As I said, she's always been very healthy."

"What can you tell me about her alcohol consumption?"

"She has an occasional glass of wine."

"So nothing to excess, including in the past?"

"My sister's not a drinker and never has been, Dr. Slocomb."

"Does she have any orthopedic problems related to physical activities?"

"She swims laps several times a week and is an avid walker. If you're asking me if she takes NSAIDs, the answer's no." He raised his eyes. "I'm a nurse."

"In that case, why don't you just fill me in on what happened this morning?"

"A month ago, she delivered her first baby after a normal thirty-nine-week pregnancy. She spent one day in the hospital. Since they were discharged, she and the baby have done great—no problems. I've been spending some nights at her house helping to care for the baby. About an hour ago, I found her collapsed in the bathroom. She had vomited a large amount of clotted blood. She was semiconscious. She looked pale and had a rash on her chest and neck. Her eyes were jaundiced. The paramedics arrived, took one look at her, and transported her to the ER."

"Has she been around anybody who's been ill?"

"Not that I'm aware of, but she's a flight instructor and went back to work last week. It's possible one of her students or somebody she works with was ill. I see her every day, and until this morning, I haven't seen any signs of illness."

"The paramedic's run report indicated she was afebrile. Did she feel warm to you?"

"No. I'm certain she didn't have a fever."

"From what you said, I presume your sister hasn't traveled since the baby was born."

"She's been in Sarasota the entire time."

"Do you have any siblings who are chronically ill?"

"No. It's just me and Nell."

"And your health?"

"Very good."

"Is there anything you observed that I didn't ask you about specifically that might be important?"

"No. So where do we go from here, Dr. Slocomb?"

"I'm going to get our critical care team involved and have them admit Nell to the ICU. After we have a look at all her lab studies and x-rays, we'll ask GI to consult to deal with the vomiting. I'm fairly certain they'll want to scope her today."

"Do you have any idea what's causing the illness?"

"Not at this point. Based on Nell's past medical history, there's no explanation for the sudden development of upper GI bleeding. Once we can get her scoped, we'll probably have a better idea as to what's going on."

"Thank you." Considering the information the doctor had given her and his frankness regarding the uncertainty of Nell's diagnosis, Scarlett decided to do everything in her power to remain calm until the lab and x-ray reports were back and they had the opinion of the gastroenterologist. "Thanks again, Dr. Slocomb. Would it be okay if I sit with Nell until she goes to the ICU?"

"Of course. We're going to have one of our ER nurses stay with your sister until she's transferred to the unit."

"Do you think she'll need a blood transfusion?"

"I'm waiting for her blood count before making that decision. It all depends on how much blood she's lost and if she's still bleeding," he answered. "I'll be back as soon as I can with an update."

"Thank you."

For the next twenty minutes, the staff instituted the therapeutic measures Dr. Slocomb had ordered. As soon as he walked out of the room, he called the intensive care physician on call and fully briefed her on Nell's condition and the urgency of the situation. A few minutes later, Dr. Jayne Goldsmith appeared in the ER and undertook a complete evaluation. When she was finished, she told Mel she was in complete agreement with his assessment and would make the arrangements to get Nell admitted to the ICU.

Prior to her being transferred, they met with Scarlett and updated her on her sister's condition and what her realistic expectations should be for the next twenty-four hours. Some of the results of the blood tests were back, but none shed any light on the exact nature of Nell's illness.

"Are you planning on having her scoped?" Scarlett asked Dr. Goldsmith.

"I'm leaning that way, but the ultimate decision will be up to the gastroenterologist."

Scarlett's eyes dropped away briefly as she felt the emotion of the day beginning to catch up with her. She struggled to put on her calmest face and not come unglued right in front of the doctors. Five minutes later, the transport team arrived. Scarlett walked along next to the gurney, accompanying Nell to the emergency elevator and then to the third-floor ICU.

Chapter 18

Marcus Parry stood on one side of LeJune Road with his eyes fixed on a quaint coffee and snack shop across the street. He ignored the earsplitting whine from the powerful engines of a wide-body passing overhead on its final approach into Miami International Airport. After a time, when he didn't see the man he was waiting for, he ventured across the street to wait for him inside.

The café was bustling with customers. Marcus spotted the only unoccupied table toward the back and immediately walked to the rear and claimed it. He had always considered himself a rather lucky person, although the events in his life that had convinced him of his good fortune had been a lot riskier than simply spotting an empty table in a busy coffeehouse.

He selected the chair facing the entrance and sat down. After a few minutes, a young barista wearing a black apron appeared and took his order for a wet cappuccino. Wondering if his time calculations had been correct, he removed his cell phone from its leather case on his belt and checked his airline travel app. The man he was waiting for, Milan Leki's, plane had landed a little over an hour ago. As they always did, they'd agreed there'd be no status reports from either of them by text or phone on delivery day.

Marcus reasoned that by now Leki should have cleared Customs and arranged transportation, and he should be coming through the door at any minute. If an additional thirty minutes passed and Leki didn't make an appearance, he would conclude that something unexpected had happened, the meeting was off, and new arrangements would have to be made after seven days of no contact between them.

The server returned with his cappuccino, and for the next five minutes Marcus sipped it while keeping his eyes trained on the café's entrance. Leaning back in his chair, he felt no particular uneasiness. Regardless of what occurred or didn't occur in the next several minutes, he'd deal with it. If Leki didn't show, it would only amount to an inconvenience. Marcus's plan would move forward and not be affected in any significant way.

Finally, a pudgy man with sagging jowls to match came through the door. He was wearing the same ragged carpenter jeans and snug-fitting charcoal-gray work shirt he always did. Marcus wondered if his choice to never alter what he wore was evidence of Leki's superstitious nature. Even though they'd done quite a lot of business together, he knew very little about Leki. It was simply the way of things between them, and it never occurred to him to mind.

Watching as Leki methodically scanned the restaurant, Marcus didn't gesture, stand up, or do anything to attract any attention to himself. Finally, Leki spotted him and made his way over to the table. He removed his backpack, set it down on the empty chair next to him, and took a seat.

"How was your flight?" Marcus asked, noting Leki's clothes reeked of stale cigarette smoke.

"Okay, I guess," the man said in a glib voice, setting his elbows on the table.

"I'm glad I chose to provide you with a first-class ticket."

Leki chuckled. "You chose to? You'll forgive me if I don't say thank you, but my first-class ticket's always been a condition of our business agreement."

Ignoring his quip, Marcus asked, "Did you have any trouble getting through customs?"

"Do I ever? I mean, I'm here, aren't I?"

"And I assume you've already been to the cargo area."

"Another rhetorical question." Leki's tone grew impatient.

From the beginning, Marcus had accepted the cloak of secrecy that Leki insisted on. The two men shared a similar and essential knowledge base, although Marcus viewed himself as intellectually superior. He had no intention of allowing Leki's flippant nature to provoke him.

"I have a schedule to keep. We've discussed the details of the product. Is there anything else I need to know about the shipment?"

"If there was, you'd already know about it. I'm certain you'll find everything precisely as you requested." Leki removed his sunglasses and slipped them into the arm pocket of his shirt. "You surprise me."

"In what way?" Marcus inquired.

"I'm not some dimwitted buffoon stumbling around in the dark. Why do you think you pay me an obscene amount of money to get you what you want?"

"It must be nice to operate with such a high level of self-assurance."

"It's only bragging if you can't do it, Marcus."

Having had just about enough of Leki's incessant prattle, Marcus said, "Where did you park the van?"

"A few spaces away from your SUV. Just like always."

"Let's go make the transfer." He came to his feet. When Leki remained seated, Marcus folded his arms in front of his chest. "Is there something wrong?"

"Aren't you forgetting something?"

With a faint smile and a quick shake of his head, Marcus reached into the pocket of his olive-drab field jacket and removed a thick envelope. He casually tossed it on the table. Leki wasted no time picking it up and taking a discreet peek inside. Appearing satisfied, he pushed the envelope into the front pocket of his pants and got up from his chair.

After a short walk, they reached the parking lot where both the rented white panel van and the SUV were parked. After surveilling the area briefly, Leki opened the side door. Marcus couldn't help taking the liberty of gazing into the cargo area. What he saw prompted him to shoot Leki a judgmental look.

Leki scoffed at Marcus. "Did you think you were my only customer?" He reached inside and handed Marcus a very specially constructed wooden crate. "That should do it. Let me know when I can be of service again."

"I assume the shipment didn't suffer any ill effects from the trip."

"I never have and never will make that guarantee. I thought you'd know that by now."

"Any problems with the paperwork?"

"No. Private charters help with that. What's with all the questions?"

"I'm a man who prides himself on paying meticulous attention to detail."

After a telling pause, Leki said, "All sales are final, Marcus. There are no refunds, no returns."

"I'm aware of that. I was just checking to make sure there wasn't something you inadvertently forgot to mention."

Without so much as another word or a casual look Marcus's way, Leki slid the door closed and made his way to the driver's-side door.

By the time Marcus had walked to his vehicle and placed the crate in the rear storage area of his SUV, Leki was gone. Adrift in thought, he climbed in behind the wheel and sat there for a short time, staring out the windshield.

With the knowledge that he'd just accepted Leki's last delivery, a self-satisfied smile came to rest on his face.

Chapter 19

As Dr. Mel Slocomb usually discovered when he worked a weekend day shift, the number of patients coming through the door of his emergency room increased exponentially with each passing hour. He'd been on his feet for almost twelve hours, having attended to a wide variety of patients, ranging from a three-year-old boy who had swallowed a lithium battery to a sixty-year-old woman with her third kidney stone in as many months.

It was approaching six o'clock when there was finally a break in the action. Taking the opportunity to catch his breath, Mel sat down at the nursing station. After a couple of minutes, he picked up the phone and called Dr. Goldsmith to check on Nell Thacker.

"How's she doing?" he asked.

"She's stable. We still haven't transfused her. Her vital signs are okay, and she's making adequate urine."

"Anything helpful in her lab results?"

"Not really. I can't say I'm any closer to making a diagnosis than I was when I first saw her with you this morning."

"What did GI think?"

"They scoped her at the bedside and found diffuse gastritis with no evidence of ongoing bleeding."

"How's her sister holding up?"

"She's pretty shaken."

"Jayne, if you can, please keep me in the loop."

"Will do. I'll be here until tomorrow. I'll give you a call later."

Mel slowly set the phone down and leaned back in his chair. Working through lunch, he'd almost forgotten how hungry he was.

Kace walked over and handed him a mug of black coffee. "It doesn't get much busier than it's been so far today. How are you holding up?"

"I'm okay. I think I'll go over to my office. I have a giant Snickers bar sitting on my desk with my name on it."

"Another weekend gourmet dinner. We can order you something from the cafeteria."

"Thanks, but I'd prefer to remain the doctor on duty rather than one of the patients."

"At least the fatigue hasn't affected your sense of humor. Actually, we share your concerns and always order out. Let me know if you want something."

"Thanks." Mel came to his feet and headed across the hall to his office. Settling in behind his desk, he made quick work of the candy bar. He turned his attention to his emails and was doing his level best to get through them when Kace popped his head in.

"Hey, boss. You'd better get out here."

"I knew this lull was too good to be true. What do you have?"

"You're not going to believe it."

"Try me."

"The squad just brought in a twenty-six-year-old woman with the exact same symptoms as Nell Thacker."

"I've had a long day, Kace. I hope you're not…"

"I'm as serious as a heart attack."

Mel immediately raised his eyes from his computer screen. He pushed his chair back, stood up, and came out from behind his desk.

"This could be a blessing in disguise. Let's talk to the families and see if their paths have crossed or if there's some other common factor."

"I don't think that'll be necessary."

"What do you mean?" he asked, concern gathering in his eyes.

"I already know where their paths crossed."

When Kace paused, Mel's impatience got the best of him, and he opened his palms to the ceiling.

"About a month ago, both of them were admitted to our maternity service on the same day. They each delivered a healthy full-term baby and went home the next morning. Like Nell, the patient who just arrived was recovering uneventfully until about an hour ago, when she developed upper GI bleeding."

"What else, Kace? You have that look on your face."

"I saw her briefly. She's jaundiced."

As Mel walked out of his office, his mind filled with a mixture of uncertainty and uneasiness about Caring Hearts Medical Center being the best hospital to manage Nell and the new patient who had just arrived with the same symptoms. While he hurried with Kace to the critical care room, he gave serious consideration to calling the Mothers and Infants transport team and arranging for both young women to be transferred to their care.

Chapter 20

OUTBREAK–DAY 7

As Josef Church drove home from work, the difficulties IPS was creating weighed heavily on his mind. With the pressures and anxiety of his professional life rapidly approaching a red line, he made an uncharacteristic last-minute decision to take tomorrow off.

The plan was made easier when he realized his entire day's schedule had been set aside for administrative matters, which meant he had no operations to perform or office hours to attend. His day would be filled with a long line of boring meetings—the type of meetings he could politely beg off without raising too many eyebrows. To avoid creating any significant problems, Josef would send out an email as soon as possible informing his colleagues that, regrettably, he'd be unable to attend any of the next day's meetings.

Josef was well aware of the stress and burnout many busy physicians faced on a day-to-day basis. But perhaps more than his colleagues, he felt capable of coping with the expected stress of being a hardworking obstetrician. Unfortunately, that conviction had been recently shaken to its core by the undue anxiety created by the IPS crisis. For the first time in his career, he had to admit his work was being adversely affected by the emotional issues confronting him.

He had just parked his car in the driveway and was heading into his two-story colonial home when it dawned on him to give Zach a call and invite him to join him for a day of sailing. Catching the breeze was a passion he and his son had shared ever since he was a small boy.

As soon as he walked through the door, he grabbed his phone and made the call. Zach understood his father's unexpected and last-minute invitation to join him was prompted by more than a perfect weather forecast for sailing. Despite being faced with the same problem of having to clear his own schedule, Zach didn't hesitate to accept his father's invitation, but with one condition. Before they got off the phone, they'd agreed the topics of IPS and the recent events at Mothers and Infants Hospital would be strictly off limits.

For many years, Josef had owned a vacation home in Key Largo that he and the family visited whenever the opportunity presented itself. The home with its large beachfront was a perfect location to dock their twenty-six-foot daysailer.

Early the next morning, Zach picked up his father, and they made the two-and-a-half-hour drive to Key Largo. The day couldn't have turned out better. As promised by the Maritime Weather Service, the weather was ideal, and they enjoyed an extraordinarily beautiful day of sailing. Their conversation encompassed a host of topics without violating their pact to avoid anything work-related. The several hours of escape did wonders to ease Josef's angst.

At four p.m., they called it a day.

During his last two years in high school, Zach had expressed a passion for flying. He'd obtained his private pilot's license but only had time to fly intermittently. When he'd entered his father's practice, he'd decided to buy a floatplane, which he kept docked behind the house.

"When are you going to sell that airplane of yours?" Josef asked as they docked their boat alongside the plane.

"Never. You know, Dad, you haven't really experienced fishing until you cast your line into some undiscovered spot on a lake or river you can only reach by floatplane."

"You sound like a travelogue, son."

"One of these days you'll change your mind and join me on one of my trips."

"Don't hold your breath. C'mon. Let's finish up here and get on the road before I catch hell at home from your mother."

"Stepmother."

"Sorry, I see you're still a little sensitive about that."

"It is what it is, Dad. C'mon, let's get the boat tucked away.'

After they'd cleaned and secured the sailboat, they went inside and tidied up a little before heading back to Palm Beach. And making the perfect day even better, there was none of the usual annoying northbound traffic.

They'd already covered the gamut of topics from college football to the best restaurants in New York. For the last year or so, Josef had found Zach's die-hard preference to remain a confirmed bachelor fertile ground for conversation.

"Are you seeing anybody?"

"Yes."

"Does she have a name, or is that a matter of national security?" Josef asked.

Zach chuckled. "You wouldn't know her."

"So she doesn't work at the hospital?"

"Never again. I learned that lesson the hard way."

Before Josef could tease his son about his overly cautious position, his phone rang. It was Ely Stanberry.

"Good afternoon, Ely."

"How did you two enjoy the day?"

"Our whereabouts were supposed to be top secret," Josef joked.

"Don't worry. Your little escape is safe with me. So how was it?"

"I think we'd both agree it was a perfect day to be on the ocean. If we could have figured out a way to extend our time away from the hospital, we'd have made a real father-son vacation out of it."

"I'm glad you guys had a great day."

Josef sensed his good friend was stalling. "As much as I enjoy hearing from you, your call's a little unexpected, which leads me to believe that you're a man with something on his mind."

"I won't deny that there's been a development here at the hospital that I'd like to discuss with you, but if this isn't a good time, you can call me when you get home."

"Zach and I don't have any secrets from each other. Go ahead and tell me what's on your mind."

"Earlier today, our transport team got a call from Caring Heart in Sarasota requesting we accept two of their postpartum patients in transfer."

"There's nothing unusual about that," Zach said. "One of our most important functions is to serve as a regional referral center to handle high-risk, complicated obstetrical patients that smaller hospitals aren't comfortable caring for."

"I fully understand that, and nobody's done more to promote those types of relationships with our referring hospitals than your father."

Suspecting there was more to the story, Josef inquired, "What was the nature of the transfers?"

"I personally spoke to the referring intensivist. She told me that both women are about a month postpartum. Their recoveries had been totally uneventful until yesterday, when they each developed symptoms remarkably similar to our IPS patients. Our transport team has already picked them up, and both ambulances are on their way back."

Josef was a man of integrity and a dedicated doctor who always had the best intentions, but for understandable reasons, there was a part of him that was relieved to hear that IPS had surfaced at another hospital.

Ely went on, "We're designating a second pod in the PCU to accommodate the new admissions. As you can imagine, the impending arrival of these two new patients has stirred up considerable apprehension among the staff."

"Is the governor aware of what's going on?" Zach asked.

"Technically, the patients' right to privacy is still protected under HIPAA. But we did send our transport teams to Caring Hearts. So, practically speaking, it's hard to imagine the addition of these two women to our list of IPS patients will evade attention for very long. I have to assume some type of conversation with the governor is on the horizon."

"I assume Jack and Madison are aware we're expecting two new patients with possible IPS," Josef said.

"Yes, they've been briefed and are standing by."

"Being that these patients are from a different part of the state, maybe they'll help us clarify what this illness is all about," Josef said.

"You may be right, but, unfortunately, I have concerns they may add to the problem."

Josef and Zach exchanged a look. "I'm not sure I understand what you mean."

"Both women gave birth on November fifteenth. If you recall, Josef, that's the same day you visited Caring Hearts as part of our educational outreach program. You gave a couple of lectures in addition to touring their labor and delivery suites."

"That's obviously nothing more than a coincidence," Zach was quick to note.

"I'm aware of that, but I'm concerned about perception."

"What are you trying to say, Ely?" Josef asked.

"As it turns out, you were physically present in the delivery room observing when both women delivered."

Chapter 21

"My God," was all that Josef could manage. He took a few moments to collect his thoughts. The relaxed expression from the calming day on the water vanished from his face.

"Are you positive it was the fifteenth?"

"I'm afraid so. I had my assistant double-check the date and Caring Heart's medical records. Your name's included in the delivery room record as being present for both deliveries."

"I recall observing at a few of the deliveries. Were there any others I attended?"

"I'm afraid not. It was just those two."

Josef found himself dumbfounded. Ely's shocking news left him speechless and unable to keep a clear thought in his head. He struggled to come up with a rational explanation to account for how two random women from Sarasota could present with IPS on the same day a month after they'd delivered. With the knowledge he attended both deliveries, the entire scenario became inconceivable.

After a brief but stunned silence passed, Zach let his displeasure be known. "I don't mind telling you, Ely, that I find what you're telling us impossible to understand. Dad's been thoroughly evaluated by two infectious disease experts who both stated categorically that he's not the cause of this illness. The same experts also went on record that there's no evidence to support that IPS is even an infectious disease. Why are we ignoring the conclusions of our consultants who feel strongly our focus should be on an autoimmune cause or some anesthesia or delivery-room mishap? I hope what I'm about to say never goes beyond the three of us, but why aren't we focusing our efforts on discovering the true cause of IPS instead of blaming somebody who's already been ruled out as the problem?"

"I don't think that's the case, Zach, and I'd hope your father would agree with me."

Zach wasn't appeased. "I'm trying to remain restrained and cooperative, but I'm starting to get the feeling that the finger of accountability is being pointed squarely at my father. I know we're facing a difficult problem, but matters like this can have a funny way of taking on a life of their own. And sometimes that life can include a nasty witch hunt. I pray that's not the case here."

When Zach had first arrived at Mothers and Infants, he was a bit of a loose cannon. Both Ely and Josef were aware of the issue but realized his intentions were genuine. They'd agreed that he'd benefit from some mentoring and coaching when it came to his communication skills. After he'd completed his first year as a medical staff member, they'd reevaluated the issue and agreed Zach had made measurable progress toward being viewed as a physician who was a calm and engaged team-player.

Ely said, "Every problem has a solution, but we have to be patient and remember this is a time for cooler minds to prevail."

"I agree," Josef said. "And I understand that the circumstances demand that my role in the care of these patients be just as closely scrutinized as any other possible cause."

"I understand the importance of diplomacy and process in this matter, Dad. On the other hand, most of our colleagues view you as the most important doctor on the medical staff. Regardless of appearances, you deserve to be treated with respect. You've earned it."

Ely stated, "I assure you, Zach, that's exactly the way we're going to move forward. There's not a particle of scientific evidence that links your father to this illness, but we do have the appearance of a possible connection, and like it or not, that's what we have to deal with. Right now, we're in damage-control mode, which means conducting ourselves in a way that reflects our overriding goal of patient safety and finding a cure for IPS."

"It's hard for me to remain completely objective, especially when I know the accusation doesn't even graze the truth," Zach said. "What happened to innocent until proven guilty?"

"You're speaking from your heart, Zach, and that's admirable, but we're not in a court of law—we're in the court of public opinion. None of us in leadership feel that moving to center stage bellowing protestations and denials is the way to go. I suspect your dad agrees with us. It bears repeating that the problem will take care of itself as soon as we figure out the indisputable cause of IPS." Ely's tone turned cautionary. "But if we're not smart about this thing now, we may not get another swipe at the piñata."

"Ely, what you're saying makes perfect sense to me," Josef said. "I suggest we talk about what our next step should be."

"Whatever we believe, the fact remains that we're currently caring for nine women with a serious new illness. Josef, you were either the attending obstetrician or an observer for each of their deliveries. It's our mission to provide excellence in medical care in the safest possible environment. And it's not only our responsibility, it's an operational imperative to convey that mission to the community we serve."

"Do you think it would be advisable for me to modify my clinical responsibilities?"

"I do, but only temporarily," Ely said calmly. "Once we've resolved the issue, we go right back to business as usual."

Zach jumped in. "When you say modify, I assume that means Dad should stop delivering babies."

"I think that would be the wisest thing to do, but we don't need to work out the specific details now."

"I'm largely agreeable to that, but I'd like a little time to think about all this," Josef said with caution in his voice.

"That's fine, Josef."

"Have you spoken to our public relations department? What can we expect from the press and other media?" Josef asked.

"I spoke to them earlier today. Right now, even though this involves the governor's daughter, the media has only had a moderate interest in the story. Our people are fairly certain that's not going to last much longer. With the addition of the two new patients from Sarasota, we can expect to become the focus of a bigger story."

"Is there any fear that it could go national?" Zach asked.

"We expect it to. And when it does, we're concerned that we'll see an avalanche of our current patients shifting their obstetrical and gynecological care to other doctors and hospitals."

"So, like most things, money becomes a major consideration," Zach said.

"There's an enduring expression in hospital administration: *no margin, no mission*. We can't naïvely ignore the reality that we have to keep the hospital financially viable," Josef said.

Josef asked, "When do you suggest we meet to nail down the specifics of how we'll be

proceeding?"

"Why don't we get together for lunch tomorrow? We can each use the time to take a closer look at things and organize our thoughts."

Zach was suddenly conspicuously silent.

"That sounds fine. If you don't mind, I'd prefer to meet outside the hospital," Josef said.

"I was just about to suggest the same thing. How about Prestin's?"

"I'll meet you there at twelve."

"Good…and, Josef, we've been friends and colleagues for a long time. I want you to know how sorry I am about all this. You're a key member of our medical staff and our franchise player. Believe me when I tell you that I'm going to do everything in my power to get this situation behind us as soon as possible."

"Thank you. I look forward to seeing you tomorrow." Josef hung up.

For the next few minutes, a strained silence descended on the car.

Zach was the first to speak. "I understand Ely's in a tough spot. I know he's trying his best to help, but that doesn't change the fact that what's happening to you is totally unfair."

"Fair is like beauty; it's in the eye of the beholder. You'll come to learn that solving every hospital challenge eventually comes down to focus and perspective. That's what I need to remember if I'm to weather the storm and put this entire unpleasantness in my rearview mirror."

For Zach's benefit, Josef did his best to project optimism and confidence. But inwardly his spirits were severely dampened. He realized Ely had done his best to paint a positive picture, but a lot of what he'd heard were drumbeats of disturbing things to come.

"I think we both know you're more than capable of handling emotional turmoil. I'll never forget what you went through when Mom committed suicide and everything that followed. I don't know how you did it. Nobody can question your emotional mettle, Dad. The police had no right to launch that investigation into her suicide."

"She killed herself with my gun, which I'd absentmindedly left unsecured in my desk drawer because I received an emergency call and had to run to the hospital. The authorities followed proper procedure. They were only doing their job."

"C'mon, Dad. They weren't making you stay after school for forgetfulness. They were threatening to charge you with reckless and negligent homicide, Dad, and as we both know, they almost did. Charging you of all people with any kind of crime? It's absurd."

"But in the end they didn't."

"That's true, but they tortured you for a month until they finally decided there wasn't enough evidence to warrant an indictment. That's not the same as them patting you on the back and saying, 'We believe you.'"

"Your mom was a tragic figure, Zach. She was a wonderful woman, but she was terribly depressed for many years."

"You did everything in your power to get her the help she

needed. My most vivid memory of the whole thing is how difficult and stressful the investigation was for you."

Josef nodded. "How much do you remember of those days?"

"I remember Mom's long history of severe depression and the few times you had to insist that she be hospitalized because of it."

"A couple of those hospitalizations resulted directly from her suicidal ideations. I was the one who left her alone in the house with a loaded handgun in an unlocked desk drawer."

"It was an accident. Your mind was elsewhere because of an obstetrical emergency."

Josef slowed the car and parked it on the side of the road. "You've spoken about my strength in dealing with personal problems, but you didn't mention anything about yourself."

"What do you mean?"

"The way you dealt with Mom's passing. You acted way beyond your years. I'll never forget it."

"It wasn't easy. Maybe some kids deal better with traumatic events and the grieving process than adults do. I guess, after enough time passed, I found a way to deal with her loss. I've never looked at that difficult time in my life with a lot of introspection." Zach turned and looked out his window. "I don't know. Maybe that makes me a little on the shallow side."

"First you lost your sister to meningitis and then your mother a few years later."

"I always assumed Sarah's death contributed significantly to Mom's unhappiness."

"I've seen a lot of little-sister/older-brother families in my life, Zach. I don't recall ever coming across a more devoted older brother than you were."

"That's quite a compliment, especially coming from you. Sarah and I were pretty close. I still miss her."

"First you had to deal with her loss, and then a few years later Mom dies, and you find yourself going through the same grieving process all over again." Josef cleared his throat. "I want to ask you something that I've never asked you before, and I'd appreciate a frank answer."

"Sure, Dad."

"Did you ever wonder if the police got it wrong?"

"What do you mean?"

"I'm asking you if you've ever wondered if I intentionally left the gun where Mom could get it?"

"My God, Dad. Of course not. How could you possibly think something like that could even cross my mind? It was a tragic accident. I know how much you loved Mom and how much you struggled to protect and help her. "Placing his hand on his father's shoulder, he added, "The answer to your question is that there's not an iota of doubt in my mind that the police got it right."

"Thanks, Zach. With the way things have been going for me lately, I needed to hear that."

Without either of them having to make the suggestion, for the remainder of the ride back to Palm Beach County, Zach and Josef limited their conversation to topics that had nothing to do with Mothers and Infants Hospital or the IPS crisis.

Chapter 22

As soon as Zach arrived home, he grabbed a shower and went straight to the hospital to check on the status of the two new admissions from Sarasota.

At about the same time Zach was pulling into the doctors' parking lot, Jack and Madison were finishing up seeing Nell Thacker and Mary Charles, the other patient from Caring Hearts. When they'd completed their initial evaluation, they were in complete agreement that both women were suffering from IPS. Because they hadn't been symptomatic from the illness as long as the other IPS patients, they weren't as sick. They had spoken with Scarlett at length, providing her with a thorough briefing on what they'd learned about IPS so far, the state of their ongoing evaluation, and their guarded outlook for the patients. Scarlett did the best she could to control her emotions, but it was obvious to Madison and Jack that she was visibly shaken about the possibility of losing her sister.

Before calling it a day, they decided to visit Emma. They reviewed her chart and spoke briefly to Teri about her condition. She informed them that, for all intents and purposes, Emma had remained stable since they'd seen her that morning. In speaking with the Collymores, Jack and Madison continued to ask for their patience, assuring them that they were doing everything they could to discover the cause of the illness that was threatening to take their daughter from them. The governor and Carmela continued to be polite and respectful, but Jack and Madison both left Emma's room with the same impression—their well-intentioned words were falling on unconvinced ears. Jack and Madison promised the Collymores they'd continue to monitor Emma's progress through the night and return the first thing in the morning.

Jack and Madison were heading for the elevator when they saw Zach coming toward them. Their eyes all met at the same time, prompting them to walk over and join him. Even though they hadn't gotten to know Zach very well yet, they were impressed with his demeanor and fund of knowledge as an obstetrician. Teri had mentioned to them that he was held in high esteem by the nurses and other ancillary healthcare providers for his unshakable dedication to his patients.

"You two are here kind of late," Zach said.

Jack nodded. "We wanted to be here when the two new patients from Sarasota arrived."

"So you've already seen them?"

"Yes."

"I was going to visit them after I finished rounding on my current patients. What was your impression?"

Jack said, "Based on their symptoms, if we didn't know they were transferred in from another hospital, we'd have assumed they gave birth right here at Mothers and Infants a week or so after our other IPS patients did." Jack was aware of the connection between Zach's father and the two patients from Sarasota, but he saw no reason to mention it.

"If we look on the bright side of things," Madison began. "Maybe we'll discover something about our two new patients that'll give us some insight or new information about IPS."

"That would certainly be a nice break. I'm a little worried about my father."

"That's understandable," Jack assured him. "How's he doing?"

"I wouldn't say he's holding on to the bottom rung of the ladder just yet, but since the outbreak, he definitely hasn't been himself."

"Hopefully, when we figure this disease out, things will improve quickly for your father. He's a fine man, Zach," Madison said.

"That's what most people say about him. He doesn't deserve any of this, but I suspect spending my time begging at the top of my lungs for basic fairness would probably be about as successful as shouting at the rain. The fastest way Dad's problem will be resolved is if we can figure out what's causing IPS and how to cure it. Once we've done that, I'm certain it'll become clear to everybody that he had no role in causing it."

"Jack and I only wish him the best."

"Thank you. I hate to impose on you like this, but would you mind taking a look at Sammie with me? I'm concerned about something, and I'd really like to get your opinion."

"No imposition at all," Jack said. "We saw her early this morning, and other than a general decline in her overall condition, we didn't note any new signs or symptoms."

As they started to make their way toward Sammie's room, Zach said, "I'm hoping I'm just overreacting a little, and what I observed won't turn out to be anything of clinical importance. Even so, I'll feel better about it after you've taken a look and agree."

Madison stopped in the middle of the hall. "If you guys don't mind, I have a call I have to make. Would it be okay if I meet you in the room in a few minutes?"

"Of course," Zach said.

When they entered Sammie's room, besides the nurse, who was adjusting the IV rate, there was nobody else present. They approached her bed, and the moment Jack's eyes came to rest on her face, he had a pretty good idea of why Zach was worried. She was in a restless sleep and demonstrating a slight increase in her breathing rate. He wondered if her depressed level of consciousness had worsened since he saw her earlier in the day.

Taking a few steps closer, Jack took a brief period of time to study her face. He then motioned to Zach to accompany him to the far side of the room. By the way Zach had drawn his lips into a tight line and was frowning, Jack guessed he suspected he was about to get some unfavorable news.

Even though they were on the other side of the room, Jack spoke in a muted voice. "She clearly has a facial droop on the right side that wasn't there this morning. I assume that's what you're concerned about."

"To me it looks most obvious at the corner of her mouth."

"I agree. Obviously, her right facial nerve isn't functioning properly. Let's get an update from Sujin."

Zach raised a hand and got the nurse's attention. He closed his laptop, came to his feet, and joined them.

"Have there been any significant changes since you started your shift this morning?" Jack asked him.

"I've been assigned to her for the past two days, so I feel like I know her pretty well. She's been less alert since this morning, and earlier this afternoon she began complaining of a headache behind her right ear. And then, at around two, I noticed she was drooling a little from the right side of her mouth."

"Can you expand a little on the change in her level of consciousness?" Jack asked.

"I'd say she's definitely more lethargic and sleeping more, but she's not out of it by any means. Actually, I was talking to her a few minutes before you came in."

"Thank you," Zach said before turning to Jack. "Would you agree that she has a Bell's palsy?"

"She definitely has a facial nerve abnormality, with the most likely cause being a Bell's palsy. Its occurrence during pregnancy and the postpartum period has been well described. Some clinical studies have actually reported a higher incidence in these women when compared to the general population. I've consulted on several women with a Bell's over the years. Most were postpartum, but a few were in their final trimester."

"From a nursing standpoint, is there anything I should be doing?" Sujin asked.

"Most patients with Bell's palsy have a hard time closing their eye on the affected side. To prevent discomfort and the eye getting dry, we should start her on some eyedrops every few hours," Jack answered. "Let's see if we can speak with her," he said, just as Madison walked into the room.

Jack quickly briefed her on Sammie's facial nerve paralysis. Sujin was the first to reach the bedside. He gently awakened her. Jack observed she was able to open her right eye, but not without some degree of difficulty. There was also no question that the muscles controlling her right eyelid and mouth were paralyzed.

Zach said, "Sammie, I'm here with Doctors Shaw and Wyatt. We'd like to ask you a few questions. Do you feel up to it?"

"I think so," she said with a lopsided smile. "Is Mason here?"

"He said he'd be back at about eight," Sujin informed her.

"Are you having any facial pain?" Jack asked.

"Just a little along my jaw and behind my ear."

"What about ringing in your ear?"

"Yes, a little, and it's hard to close my right eye," she said softly. "I don't remember having any of these problems yesterday."

"We think you've developed a weakness of your facial muscles," Zach said. "We sometimes see this within the first month or so after a delivery."

"Will it be permanent?"

Zach looked to Jack. "I'll let Dr. Wyatt answer that question. He's a neurologist and an expert in these types of problems."

"The vast majority of people who have this problem make a complete recovery," Jack stated.

"How long does it take?"

"The best we can hope for is a few weeks, but sometimes a full recovery can take several months. We should be able to take care of your symptoms until the problem resolves."

They took another few minutes to finish up their examination and ask Samantha a few additional questions. It quickly became obvious that she was becoming drowsier and having difficulty following the conversation. They all agreed the best thing to do was allow her to go back to sleep.

"We'll stop back and see you in the morning," Madison told her.

"Thank you. I think Mason will be here then. Do you think you'll be able to speak with him?"

"Of course."

After touching base with Sujin, they stepped out into the hall.

Madison was the first to speak. "I wonder if her Bell's palsy is a coincidental event or if it's a late entry into the IPS symptom complex. I haven't seen it in any of the other patients. Have you, Zach?"

"No. That's why I was so anxious to have you and Jack take a look at her."

"I think we're going to need a little time to determine whether Sammie's an isolated case or her Bell's is part of IPS," Jack said.

Zach asked, "What about systemic treatment?"

"Usually, steroids are prescribed for Bell's palsy. Some physicians are adding antiviral drugs, but most of us feel the jury's still out on their effectiveness. Since we know nothing about IPS and have no way of predicting how she'll react to steroids or antiviral drugs, my recommendation would be to hold off."

"We can discuss treatment options at our case conference tomorrow morning," Zach pointed out. "Any physician who has a material role in the care of the IPS patients will be there."

Zach removed his glasses, took out a fiber cloth from his pocket, and began cleaning the lenses. "You're the neurologist, Jack. Without pinning you down, what's your gut feeling about Sammie's Bell's palsy?"

Jack responded, "I doubt it's simply a coincidence, and I wouldn't be surprised if we saw some additional cases in the next few days. Whether these types of changes in the disease's natural course will ultimately help us figure out the cause…well, I don't know. At least for now, the answer to that question is another undealt card."

Chapter 23

At six o'clock, Regina Leggett walked out of her last meeting of the day. The choice before her was to return to her office and spend another hour or so answering emails or head home. Reminding herself that she'd arrived at work eleven hours ago was enough to convince her to call it a day. The only challenge facing her was how to slip out of the hospital without running into any of her staff who'd suddenly remembered a pressing question or problem that couldn't wait until the morning. On this particular evening, good fortune was hers, and she managed to make it to the parking lot without a single *by-the-way* conversation.

Living alone, Regina's custom was to eat dinner at home, but tonight she had a craving for chicken piccata prepared to perfection by her favorite neighborhood Italian restaurant. When she considered the added benefit of not having to clean up her kitchen, she went straight to Donella's, where her dinner was prepared in a way that more than lived up to her expectations.

Twenty minutes after Regina paid her check, she pulled into the driveway of her two-story townhouse. Four years earlier, when she'd finally brought her only marriage to a merciful end, she'd chosen an existence that favored solitude over a bustling lifestyle. She maintained a social life of sorts, but with the condition that she'd never again share her life or bathroom with a man. Her friends and family questioned the wisdom of her decision, but since the day she'd made it, she hadn't regretted it one iota.

Once she had closed the front door behind her, she wasted no time heading upstairs and preparing her evening bath—a pleasure that had become a routine part of her nightly schedule. While she was running the water, she thought about her conversation with Doctors Wyatt and Shaw and the rising tension-filled atmosphere that IPS was creating in the hospital. After a couple of minutes of dwelling on the problem, she began feeling a noose tightening around the top of her stomach. The annoying discomfort prompted her to dismiss any further thoughts of the hospital and do everything in her power to clear her mind and enjoy her bath.

She added a couple of capfuls of the homemade vanilla extract bubble bath she'd taught herself to make, put on her preferred eighties playlist, and turned off the main lights. The last thing she did before climbing into the tub was light a lavender-scented candle. Gently setting her head and neck on the tub's oval rim, she closed her eyes and listened to one of her favorite Elton John songs. She let her mind go blank, and the first five minutes led to the next five. She soon found herself in a blissful state of relaxation.

At first, Regina didn't notice the subtle sweet citrus aroma of the man's aftershave. But as the scent thickened the air, she was suddenly whisked back to the here and now. Her eyes snapped open, but the only light in the room radiated from the single decorative candle. Just as she was reaching for a towel, the music stopped, and the candlelight died. In the barely perceivable illumination that remained and with her glasses out of reach on the granite countertop, Regina's ability to see anything with clarity was extremely limited.

Within the silence of the room, she thought she could make out the melodic breathing of somebody who couldn't be more than a few feet away. Before she could react or investigate her hunch, Marcus's muscular hand seized her around her neck. Clutching it with more than sufficient force to squeeze her windpipe closed, he cut off the flow of air into her lungs while at the same time rendering her unable to scream.

Filled with panic, Regina flailed and spun her upper body back and forth, frantically trying to free herself from his iron grip. His strength far exceeded hers, allowing him to keep her head and neck pinned against the back of the tub. Terrified to her core, her mind shut down. A surge of adrenaline shot into her bloodstream, triggering an intense fight-or-flight reflex. More out of instinct than calculated thought, she grabbed his wrist, trying desperately to tear his hand from her throat. Despite using every ounce of strength she could gather, she couldn't break the unyielding hold.

Regina suddenly thrust her legs upward while at the same time violently twisting her lower body as far as she was able. But the result was the same—Marcus kept her head and neck pinned to the tub's rim. On her second attempt, she was able to turn herself toward him enough to reach over and dig her fingernails into the fleshy underside of his forearm. Swells of water splashed over the sides of the tub as her nails penetrated into his soft tissue causing a slow drip of blood down his arm. The blows from her leg struck his torso but did little to affect his stance. The pain from his grip on her neck was intense, and she could feel herself weakening as her oxygen supply was rapidly consumed.

Chuckling for a few seconds, Marcus suddenly plunged her head below the surface of the water. Regina did everything in her power to push back against the force of his hand, but her efforts were futile. She was on the verge of inhaling a lungful of water when he suddenly yanked her head out of the water and relaxed his grip. As she spun her eyes toward him, she took an enormous gasp of air followed by one choked breath after another. While he waited for her to recapture her breath, he relit the candle.

"Beg me," he told her plainly.

"What?" she asked, still violently hacking water from her lungs.

"I want you to beg me to let you live."

"I'm begging you. Please don't kill me. Just leave, and I swear I won't call the police."

He pressed his lips together and shook his head slowly. "That was unconvincing."

"Just take whatever you want. Don't hurt me," Regina pleaded in a horror-struck voice. For a moment she thought she noticed a ring of familiarity in his voice, but she couldn't put a face to the dim recollection.

He spoke softly. "You'll have to do better than that, Regina—a lot better."

"What the hell do you want from me?" she sobbed as she felt the force of his hand again beginning to crush her windpipe.

"I was thinking of making this look like some kind of an accident or perhaps even a suicide or robbery, but the more I think about it, the more I realize that's completely unnecessary. It even crossed my mind to try and come up with some way to spare your life, but I just don't see how that'll work either."

"For God's sake, don't."

"If it helps, I'm sorry."

With no hesitation he thrust Regina's head back under the water. This time, he pinned the back of her skull flush against the bottom of the stone resin tub. With the last fragment of strength left to her, she battled for her life, desperately trying to escape the inevitable, but what little oxygen remained in her lungs went to zero.

Marcus kept her head submerged for a full five minutes. Finally, he slid his hand up and grabbed a generous fistful of Regina's hair. With a single yank, he pulled her up until her shoulders broke the surface. Rolling her to the side, he eyed her lifeless face. Using his index finger, he flicked away some of the bubbly lather that was fixed to her nose and mouth.

After a time, he simply released his grip and allowed her entire body to slip below the surface. He felt detached from the situation, but he wasn't surprised. Regina Leggett wasn't the first human being he'd killed. With the job well done and feeling no remorse, there was nothing left for him to do. He already had a plan for disposing of his latex gloves and clothing.

And then, without so much as a backward glance, Marcus strolled out of the bathroom and made his way down the stairs.

Chapter 24

OUTBREAK–DAY 9

As Josef Church stepped off the elevator and made his way down the hall toward the hospital's administrative offices, he was uncertain of several things. But one thing was crystal clear, and that was that he had no illusions that his impending meeting with Ely was going to drastically change his professional life. Josef could only hope it would be temporary.

Based on their long relationship, Josef knew his close friend and colleague would do everything in his power to cushion the blow. But in the end, Ely had a job to do—a job he took as seriously as any physician Josef knew. For him to expect Ely to compromise his principles to assist an old friend would be naïvely optimistic.

Ely met him at the door to his office with a contained smile.

"Come in and have a seat. Thanks for coming over on such short notice," he said, as he retook his seat behind his large mahogany desk while Josef sat down across from him. "The first thing I'd like to share with you is that, as you probably expected, we made the decision last night at a special risk management meeting to report the IPS cases to the Agency for Healthcare Administration as Code 15s. Florida law only gives us fifteen days to officially report a wide variety of adverse clinical events. We're convinced that what occurred to these women definitely meets the definition of a Code 15 and must be reported to AHCA."

"I was expecting that, and I agree. We'd be setting ourselves up for some pretty serious consequences from the state if we failed to report."

"Unfortunately, the speed AHCA will move forward with their investigation is entirely in their hands and unpredictable."

"I understand," Josef said, following his plan to keep his answers short and sweet.

"I assume you also realize it's a near certainty their team will want to interview you."

Josef nodded.

"Tom's the chair of the risk management committee, and I've asked him to keep you in the loop as to the progress of their investigation and be involved in your preparation process. Next on the agenda is something rather concerning, and something you may not be aware of yet. I received a call while I was driving in this morning that we've admitted another postpartum patient with IPS."

"No. I hadn't heard. From Sarasota?"

"No, she's one of our patients."

"Did I do the delivery?"

"Yes. You were the attending physician."

"What's her name?"

"Wendy Bealer."

Having no difficulty remembering her, Josef nodded.

Ely continued. "She delivered about a week after the governor's daughter and our other patients. Without getting into a lot of the details, her clinical course has closely mirrored the others, and we're confident she has IPS."

"Where do we go from here, Ely?" Josef inquired in a monotone.

"I was hoping we could find another way to handle the current situation, but I don't think that's going to be possible. As you're aware, we've already received dozens of phone calls from patients and their families requesting their care be transferred to another obstetrician. Many of them have gone a step further and elected to deliver at another hospital. What's particularly upsetting is that we've had several of our own employees who've made similar requests."

"I can't say that surprises me. I know you understand better than most the significant amount of personal pain this problem has caused me. But I haven't lost sight of the fact that the most important aspect of all this is the well-being of this hospital." With a despondent sigh he added, "That being said, what can I do to help the situation?"

Never being one to mince words, Ely said, "In my mind, the only sensible thing to do until we can find a solution to this problem is for you to step back from your clinical practice and attend only to your administrative responsibilities. Obviously, the hospital board's keenly aware of the crisis we're facing and has made it crystal clear they want us to proceed with an abundance of caution. They're convinced our patients and their families aren't going to understand or care about the medical nuances or the circumstances surrounding IPS. Everything will be about appearances and perceptions. And as more details of the illness reach the public, it would be naïve of us to assume they'll retain enough confidence in us to stop them from transferring their care to other providers and other hospitals. I firmly believe this problem is much bigger than just you, Josef—and by the way, so does the board. We're faced with having to deal with an unfavorable public opinion, not reality," Ely stated with impunity. "I know this is a tough blow for you to take, but we're dealing with basic human nature, and that can be a tricky challenge."

"My intent is to fully cooperate with the board's wishes. So, as of right now, I won't go near another patient until I hear otherwise in an official manner from you and the board."

"The other option open to you is simply to take a few weeks off. It might be a little easier on you."

Josef held his next comment while he considered Ely's words. He wondered if he should view his advice as a suggestion or as his strong preference that Josef disappear until the storm passed.

"What are your thoughts on the matter? Would the board prefer that I geographically remove myself from the situation?"

"I'm confident they'd be fine with either approach. It's your choice, Josef. I promise, there's no hidden agenda."

"In that case, I'd prefer to stand down from my practice responsibilities and attend only to my administrative duties."

"Then that's exactly the way we'll play it."

"I would also ask that I be allowed to attend our scheduled clinical conferences," Josef added, with some trepidation that his request might be turned down.

"I see no problem with that," Ely answered without delay. "The other matter I'd like to mention to you is our enormous concern about the media. We're going to schedule a public briefing for tomorrow morning. The governor's considering attending."

"No need to worry. I won't be there, nor will I have any contact with the media in any way moving forward."

"I thank you for that. As you've aptly demonstrated over the years, you're very skilled when it comes to dealing with the media, but in this case, keeping a safe distance may be the smarter way to go."

"I'll make the necessary arrangements for my partners to begin covering my patients immediately." Josef appreciated Ely's diplomatic manner and optimism. He had always been a valued friend and colleague. He felt comfortable he'd never allow anything unjust to befall him. "What else is on the agenda?"

"I've covered everything that I wanted to talk with you about," Ely responded, coming out from behind his desk. Placing a reassuring hand on Josef's shoulder, he escorted him across his office. "This hospital owes you a debt of gratitude that it'll never be able to repay. All I can say is that I truly believe that, in time, we'll find a cause and a cure for IPS and that you'll be totally vindicated. Once this is all behind us, I'm certain you'll be more admired by your patients and the hospital staff than ever before."

Josef reached out to open the door. "I hope with all my heart that's the case." He pushed a faint grin to his face and raised a hand. "You're a good friend, Ely. I'll give you a call tomorrow."

As Josef made his way down the hall toward the elevator bank, he couldn't help but face the obvious. Ten women he'd cared for within a brief period of time were all suffering from the same novel illness. Despite the unconditional assurances he was receiving from his friends and colleagues, it was inconceivable to him that they could look at the crisis objectively and not have even a sliver of doubt that in some way he was responsible for the illness.

Chapter 25

OUTBREAK – DAY 10

Jack and Madison arrived at the hospital at seven thirty. Their preference before starting morning rounds had always been to meet with the nurse manager for an update on how the patients had fared overnight. They stopped at the core desk, where the health unit coordinator informed them that Teri was working the day shift and that they could find her at the far end of the hall speaking with a few of the other nurses.

When Teri spotted them waiting, she quickly brought her conversation to an end and walked over to join them.

"Good morning," Madison said. "Do you have a few minutes to give us a quick patient status update?"

"Sure do. We finished sign-out rounds about thirty minutes ago, and I got a report on each patient's condition. The nurses are pretty much in agreement that their conditions are worsening, especially their liver function and neurologic status. They're less responsive, more confused, and sleeping more."

"What about their vital signs?" Madison asked.

"Several of them are showing an increasing instability of their patient's blood pressure. Another reason for concern is that this morning's labs showed a further deterioration in their liver function, as evidenced by rising levels of hepatic enzymes and more pronounced jaundice." Pausing briefly, she added, "And if you haven't heard, three additional patients have developed a Bell's palsy."

"No, we hadn't heard," Jack said with a dispirited shake of his head, but he was no more surprised than Madison to hear the news.

Teri went on. "We all had our fingers crossed it wouldn't happen. Any idea why Bell's palsy would be part of IPS?"

"Other than some type of associated neurological inflammation, I'm afraid we're as much in the dark as anybody. What about their respiratory status?" he inquired.

"I'd say that's about the same. All of them are having some difficulty, but no one has required a ventilator…at least, not yet. So where do we go from here?"

Jack answered, "There's only one option I know of. We keep following each patient and stay hyper-focused on every detail, looking for any changes or new information that gives us a clue that will point us in the right direction."

"I know the docs are a little at odds about what's causing IPS, but most of the nurses are convinced that something went wrong in the delivery room, either with a med or maybe a toxic exposure. Yesterday, one of the physicians told us that he was pretty sure IPS is an autoimmune disorder, maybe similar to preeclampsia. Do you think that's possible?"

"I hate to be the one to splash mud on anybody's theory, but at this point, I don't think anyone has the inside track on what the most likely cause is," Madison answered.

"It seems like the only thing the doctors, nurses, and family members can agree on is that every patient is getting worse. The conversations between the families are practically nonstop. From what I can gather, they're getting more and more nervous that we'll never find the answer and the outcome is inevitable. They've lost hope that some patients will survive IPS on their own. And the growing dismay among the family members isn't helping my nurses' morale either, which I'd say is in a tailspin."

Jack decided to take the conversation in another direction. "How's Emma doing?"

"About the same as the others—clearly worse but holding on. Dr. Brandwyn has already been in to see her and said it's still too early to remove the chest tube. Are you going to see her first?"

"Probably. Thanks for the update."

"I'd appreciate it if you'd get a hold of me after you've finished rounds. I'd like to know what you think."

"Of course," Jack said.

He had little doubt the information the nurses had provided Teri was entirely accurate. He wasn't encouraged that after they finished making rounds he'd have any heartening news to share with her. Jack considered himself a relatively patient person, but he was beginning to fear the disease would get so far out in front of them that they'd lose any chance they still had of helping these women.

Chapter 26

Jack and Madison took their time making morning rounds. When they visited Sammie, there was no doubt her Bell's palsy was still present. Fortunately, the nursing staff had done an excellent job of controlling her symptoms. As was the case with most of the other patients Madison and Jack had seen so far, Sammie's overall condition had worsened a little.

After seeing her and briefing the nurse on the plan for the day, they made their way to the adjoining pod and into Emma's room. Her nurse, Annella, was at the bedside checking on the medication she'd just started administering intravenously. The governor and Carmela were not in the room.

Emma was asleep. Madison studied her face for a few moments and concluded that it lacked any animation and had lost a significant amount of its ruddy appearance since the first time she'd seen it. Both she and Jack agreed with Teri that the jaundice had progressed. It was becoming no secret that the key to recovery would likely boil down to their liver function. If it continued to deteriorate and progress to frank liver failure, it would almost certainly foretell a grave outcome. Madison checked the monitors for the second time. Emma's vital signs were barely in an acceptable range.

"How's she doing?" Madison asked.

"She's hanging in there, but I haven't seen any signs of improvement," Annella said, voice just above a hush.

The cardiac monitor alarm suddenly sounded. The loud blaring prompted Jack and Madison to exchange a surprised look as to why the volume had been set so high. Madison checked Emma's heart rate. It was high enough to trigger the alarm, but certainly not a life-threatening change that required urgent treatment.

Annella hurried to the bedside, silenced the alarm, and turned down its volume.

"I don't know why the night staff sets the alarm volume so loud. I'm starting to wonder if they're all hard of hearing."

Madison walked over to the bedside. Emma's eyes were wide open and unblinking, an odd mixture of astonishment and fear reflected in them.

"Emma, it's Dr. Shaw. Can you hear me?"

"Yes."

"How are you feeling? Are you in any pain?"

"No. I just feel a little jumpy."

"Do you feel that way often?"

"From time to time, I guess," she said. Her words were shaky.

Madison moved in closer and examined the rash, finding it basically the same as it had been on her prior exam. But when she turned her attention to Emma's hands and arms, Madison was surprised to see classic-appearing goosebumps carpeting her arms from her fingertips to above her elbows. She looked at Jack. From the expression on his face, she suspected he'd made the same observation. Still somewhat taken aback, Madison continued her exam. She noticed at once that Emma's arms were covered with perspiration. When she shifted her gaze to Emma's legs, she identified significant muscle spasms, especially in the calves.

Madison signaled Jack and Annella to take a few steps away from the bed.

"Have you seen this before?"

"No. I've been at her bedside for the past half an hour, and there were no signs of any abnormalities of her arms or legs."

"And you're positive of that?" Jack asked.

"As I am of my own name."

"Thanks, Annella," Madison said. "We'll speak with you again after we're done seeing Emma."

"It's a classic pilomotor reflex," he said quietly.

"I agree. But the question is, what triggered it? It's a rather uncommon phenomenon."

"I have no idea, but it's probably something we should do our best to figure out. Most pilomotor reactions are associated with an abrupt change in skin temperature or a stressful emotional stimulus," he said, checking the monitors again. The mild increase in her heart rate was still present.

"Are you feeling any better?" Madison asked Emma as they returned to the bedside.

"A little calmer maybe."

"Have you ever had panic attacks?"

"No, never."

"Are you having any other symptoms now, other than feeling a little jumpy?" Madison asked.

"I feel pretty itchy, and my legs are cramping."

"Have you ever had symptoms like this before?"

Emma tilted her head slightly. "This is the first time."

Madison noticed that she was fighting to keep her eyes open. "We can give you something to help with the itching," she assured her. "Do you have any questions for us?"

"No…I don't think so."

"We'll let you get some sleep. We can talk more later," Madison said.

Jack and Madison finished up quickly, touched base with Annella, and left the room. Once they were out in the hall, Madison wasted no time diving into what they'd just observed. "Have you ever seen a pilomotor reaction in a hospitalized patient?" she asked, as they made their way back toward the nurse's station.

"No, but something tells me if we can figure out why Emma all of a sudden became prone to one, it might give us a helpful clue about IPS."

"Do you think we could've missed something in the latest lab or x-ray reports? Maybe one of the other patients had the same reaction, but it went unnoticed or uncharted."

"I doubt it," he said. "These nurses are pretty sharp, and a pilomotor reflex isn't exactly subtle. If they'd observed the same thing that just happened to Emma in one of the other patients, they would have reported it immediately."

All of a sudden, Jack slowed his pace. It didn't take him long before he came to a complete stop. Madison couldn't help but notice the gratified look on his face that always seemed to appear when he was having a flash of genius. He turned and looked back down the hall in the direction of Emma's room.

"Okay, Jack. What's going on?"

"Let's go back to Emma's room. I have an idea about something, but it's a long shot. C'mon. We have plenty of time, and it'll only take a few minutes. If I'm right about what caused Emma's pilomotor reflex, we may have already made a costly mistake in trying to figure out what's causing IPS."

Chapter 27

As soon as Madison and Jack walked back into Emma's room, they noticed the distressed look had vanished from her face, and she seemed to be resting comfortably. Jack was also pleased to see the monitor showed slower heart and breathing rates.

"She certainly looks better," Madison said.

Annella was sitting on the far side of the room with her laptop open, trying to get caught up on her charting.

She looked up at them. "I didn't expect to see you again until tomorrow."

"We decided to stop back to check something," Jack said, as he began to repeat his examination. "We'll just be a couple of minutes." When he was finished, he turned to Madison. "Try not to wake her, but have a look and tell me if you agree that she doesn't have any residual signs of her pilomotor episode."

"Don't wake her?" she asked as she began her exam.

"I think you'll see why in a minute."

Madison spent a couple of minutes repeating her examination. "The goosebumps are gone, she's no longer sweating, and I can't detect any muscle spasms. I agree, the episode has passed."

Jack motioned to Annella. "I wonder if you could help us for a moment."

"Sure." She came to her feet and joined them at the bedside.

"I'd like you to intentionally set off the alarm on the cardiac monitor at the exact same volume it was set at when we first came into the room earlier. Can you do that?"

"I don't see why not," she answered, with a modicum of hesitancy creeping into her voice. She reached up, silenced the alarm, and lowered the pulse rate required to activate it. Before turning the alarm back on, she increased the volume to where it had been.

"It's ready—how long should I let it go for?"

"Let's try ten seconds," Jack said.

As expected, the moment Annella activated the alarm, Emma's eyes snapped open. She appeared to be in a hyper-alert state, her gaze flashing around the room as if she were desperately searching for something. Her frenzied eye movements were accompanied by a shocked expression. Jack pointed at the monitor as her blood pressure and pulse skyrocketed.

"You can turn off the alarm," he told Annella. He then turned to Emma. "You're fine. Your heart rate went up a little and set the alarm off," he told her while Madison repeated an examination of her arms and legs.

The findings were hardly subtle. "Her arms are diaphoretic and covered with goosebumps." She reached down and palpated her legs. "Same finding—cramped muscle groups."

"How are you feeling?" Jack asked.

"Just like before, except my calves are cramping more," she responded, in a voice choked by apprehension.

"The symptoms should pass in a few minutes. You'll be fine," Jack assured her.

"I'm... I'm getting a little scared. How often is this going to happen?"

"Hopefully, that's the last time," Jack told her. "It's a type of panic attack probably caused by the cardiac alarm startling you. We'll make sure it doesn't happen again."

"Are you sure that's all it is?"

"I'm certain. We'll stay here with you for a few minutes, just to make sure your symptoms completely go away."

Similar to the first episode, it didn't take long for Emma's goosebumps, sweating, and muscle cramps to resolve. When they were certain she was fine and had dropped back off to sleep, they briefed Annella to make sure she understood that all measures should be taken to ensure that Emma was not subjected to any form of extreme auditory stimuli.

"Let's find a place to talk," Jack said as they made their way down the hall. "I want to bounce something off you."

"Sure. How about the walking path alongside the hospital?"

"Perfect."

"I'll meet you back here in…say in a half an hour," she said.

"What's wrong with now?" he asked her.

"I want to go check out a few things first."

"In that case, I'll find Teri and double-check, just to make sure none of the other patients have experienced a pilomotor response."

"Good idea. And Jack, I may have a theory that you'll find a little out-there."

"So?"

"Well, sometimes you can be unnecessarily skeptical about my ideas."

"Unnecessarily skeptical? I've never heard you use that term before."

"Nevertheless, try and open your mind in the next thirty minutes," she told him as she hurried down the hall.

Chapter 28

Having just returned from lunch, Detective Paul Allensworth of the Palm Beach County Sheriff's Office sat at his desk going over a recent arrest report. He'd been promoted to the rank of detective nine years earlier and had flourished in the position since day one. From a personal standpoint, his many years of tracking down murderers had somewhat eroded his faith in humanity. Fortunately, the core principles that led him to pursue a career in law enforcement easily trumped his occasional misgivings about the type of people he was sometimes forced to deal with.

He was just about to refill his coffee mug when his partner of three years, Libby Rafferty, strolled into his office. She had toned arms from her minimum of five weekly workouts, and wore her medium brown hair pulled back in a low bun. Ten years younger than Paul, she was well aware that his expertise as a homicide detective surpassed hers. Instead of being threatened by his added experience and insight, Libby viewed it as an opportunity to cultivate her skills and grow as a police officer.

"You got a sec?" she asked him.

"Sure. What's up?"

"The Regina Leggett case. The one we got the other day

involving the woman from Wellington who was killed in her bathtub."

"She was the nurse in charge of the labor and delivery unit at Mothers and Infants, right?"

"That's her." Libby sat down, stretched out her legs, and crossed her ankles. "What do you know about this group of women who gave birth about a month ago and were readmitted to Mothers and Infants, all apparently suffering from the same mysterious disease?"

"Other than what I've heard on TV and read in the papers, not too much. Why? Do you think there's some connection between Leggett's murder and these women?"

"Maybe. I got a call from Drew Crossfield a little while ago. It seems Ms. Leggett called our offices the day she was killed, wanting to speak to someone about certain bothersome circumstances surrounding the cases at Mothers and Infants."

An intrigued look appeared on Paul's oblong-shaped face. He leaned back, resting his clasped hands on his ever-enlarging midsection.

Libby went on, "Drew said that when he called her back, she sounded anxious. He asked her a few questions, but she dodged his inquiries, insisting the only way she'd talk to him was face-to-face. They set up a meeting for the next day, but for obvious reasons, it never happened."

"What do we have on the case so far?"

"Not much. It's still pretty early. The medical examiner hasn't even released her autopsy report yet. I've done the usual preliminary work. I figured I'd brief you today and we'd begin diving into things. So what do you think?"

Pushing himself up in his chair to better position himself in front of his monitor, he brought up Regina Leggett's case file. "As you said, from what we have here, there's no way of knowing what Ms. Leggett had on her mind. What do you suggest we do?"

Libby suspected he knew the answer to his question and was simply interested in finding out if she did as well. "I spent some time this morning trying to find a coworker at the hospital or someone in her personal life she might have confided in."

"And?"

"I really didn't come up with anybody, so I was thinking maybe if we just took a ride over to Mothers and Infants and knocked on a few doors, we might find somebody worth interviewing. Maybe we'll even get lucky and come across somebody who knows something."

"Sounds like a decent enough plan to me."

"Great, let's go."

He rolled his chair back far enough to give his spare tire sufficient room to clear the edge of his desk as he came to his feet. Libby thought to herself that he was probably the only person she'd ever met who frequently furrowed his brow and grinned at the same time.

"The only thing we might want to do before heading to the hospital is speak to the lieutenant to brief him on what's going on. There are times when these little information-sharing sessions are just a formality, but you never know when one of them will keep your ass out of the boss's briefcase."

"You certainly have a way of sidestepping whatever land mines you encounter, Paul."

"Experience is a wonderful thing, Libby. C'mon, let's see if he's in his office."

Chapter 29

Jack and Madison rode the elevator down to the lobby, exited the hospital, and made their way around to the back of the building. At the insistence of the founders, the landscape architects had been tasked with providing a generous amount of greenspace around the hospital. What they'd accomplished was exemplary. A total of six acres were beautifully landscaped with abundant greenery and maintained with meticulous attention to detail.

They reached the threshold of the red cedar–colored granite path. Because their walk was intended to provide a quiet and secluded place for them to talk and not be a workout, they made their way around the path at a relaxed pace.

"Obviously, you've had one of your lightbulb moments," Madison said. "I can read it in your eyes. I think we both agree that it was the earsplitting shrill of the cardiac monitor alarm that triggered Emma's pilomotor reflex."

"That type of reaction to a harsh sound would be more accurately defined as an auditory hyperacusis episode."

"As I recall, hyperacusis reactions usually occur in conjunction with a psychiatric disorder, trauma to the ear, or sometimes surgery," Madison said. "What's the connection to IPS?"

"You've just listed the more common causes, but there are some other, less common ones. For instance, there have been reports of patients with Lyme's disease having hyperacusis episodes."

With her eyes fixed on his, she asked, "What are some of the others, Jack?"

He cleared his throat. "Some individuals with certain viral illnesses like Covid and mononucleosis have been known to experience them."

"So we're back to a possible viral cause?"

"Perhaps we dismissed it too soon," Jack said.

"But there are also hyperacusis theories suggesting a connection to autoimmune diseases and certain surgical procedures. What I'm saying is, I don't see how this new finding gets us any closer to the IPS finish line."

Waiting for Jack's response as they strolled past a long row of flowering lantana shrubs, Madison said nothing further.

Jack finally spoke. "I think it does get us closer, because the evidence tying auditory hyperacusis to a viral syndrome is real, not theoretical. A few years ago I participated on a panel in Copenhagen where one of the participants presented a strong argument that a cause-and-effect relationship does exist between certain rare viruses and auditory hyperacusis reactions."

Madison said, "Before you totally embrace the hyperacusis-virus idea, I'd like to remind you that we have ten patients with IPS, and to the best of our knowledge, only one of them has had a hyperacusis episode."

"I guess this may be one of those events where only time will tell. For all we know, it could be just the beginning." Slowing his pace, Jack pointed to an eight-foot-long teak bench.

They sat down, and even though Madison already had an idea of where he was about to take her, she guarded her silence. Jack's style was to move forward cautiously, but he wasn't given to vague answers or deliberate stalling. She adjusted her gaze. While she watched him, something in his face changed.

"Okay, Jack, let's dive a little deeper into the viral theory."

"As I was saying, I'm wondering if we were a little trigger happy when we dismissed the idea that the cause of IPS might be either a very rare or novel viral infection."

"We talked about this yesterday morning, and we agreed the ID consultants did an exemplary job in ruling out any and all infectious diseases, which definitely includes viruses. You said it yourself that it was so unlikely that we could practically eliminate it from consideration."

"I know what I said. Am I not allowed to change my mind?"

"Of course you are, but then there's the small matter of Dr. Whiteacre."

"What do you mean?"

"C'mon, Jack. He's the head of infectious diseases, an expert in virology, and practically a god around here. He's come out firmly in the opinion that IPS is not a viral illness."

"Which challenges us to change his mind."

"Your level of optimism is inspiring," Madison said.

"I'm aware of what we discussed yesterday, but things can change. Sometimes a new clinical finding can prompt you to go back and reconsider possibilities you've already ruled out. Closing a diagnostic door prematurely can be a fatal error. Do you agree?"

With a subdued grin, Madison confessed, "I've kind of been playing devil's advocate with you."

"What do you mean?"

"The same concern regarding a viral cause crossed my mind."

"Because of Emma's hyperacusis or something else?"

"Something else. I noticed it on rounds yesterday afternoon and again this morning. I didn't want to say anything too soon, but I think we're dealing with a new finding."

"I'm all ears."

"Three of the patients, including Emma, have swollen tongues. I'd say the finding was a little less obvious yesterday than it is today, but I'm sure it's definitely present. What's interesting about it is that, similar to hyperacusis reactions, the finding of a swollen tongue has been seen in several different viral infections. Herpes is probably the best example, but there are others."

"So we're in agreement that the dice are still rolling on the chance that IPS is a viral infection," Jack said.

"I'm agreeing with you that taking another look at the possibility is not an unreasonable thing to do. I suspect some of the physicians we're working with might call it a vast waste of valuable time."

"Which begs the next question: Should we spend more time looking for supportive evidence regarding a viral cause or share our suspicions with the other physicians sooner rather than later?"

"We're supposed to meet with the treating physicians this afternoon," she said. "Ely told me the division chiefs from immunology, anesthesiology, and infectious diseases will all be attending. I think it would be a good idea to get his input about sharing that we think we should take another look at a viral cause today at the meeting or wait a little bit longer to see if we can build our case."

"I agree," Jack said. "Let's see if we can track him down and talk with him."

"Do you think he'll be in favor of us sharing with the group what we know today?"

"I suspect he'll give us the green light. I'll give him a call as soon as we return to the hospital. Let's finish up this last lap and head back."

"It might be a good idea to have another look at the patients to see if any more of them have developed either a hyperacusis episode, a swollen tongue, or both," Madison said.

As they picked up their pace and tackled the last hundred yards of the walking path, Madison admitted to herself that, looking at things logically, the chance IPS was being caused by a virus was remote at best. She certainly didn't consider herself to be clairvoyant, although she'd always relied heavily on her intuition. Setting logic and probability aside for a moment, she felt as if she had a lot more than an inkling that they may have stumbled onto the cause of this dreadful disease.

Chapter 30

At five minutes to four, Jack and Madison walked into the hospital's executive conference room. Being a few minutes early, they were surprised to see so many of the treating physicians already seated at a large boat-shaped glass conference table. The room was decorated with refined taste and featured a plush gray carpet, a dark wood sectional wall unit, and a large bay window that overlooked the entrance to the hospital. Jack and Madison had managed to speak with Ely prior to the meeting. After briefing him about the latest patient findings and their renewed concern that a virus might be the cause of IPS, he'd encouraged them to share the information with the other physicians as soon as possible.

Ely was seated in the middle of the table. He had spoken with Josef earlier about attending the meeting, but he declined. For obvious reasons, Ely agreed with the wisdom of his decision and made no attempt to change his mind. By this time, Madison and Jack had met all the physicians in attendance and, at a minimum, had spoken with each of them at least once about the IPS cases. Based on first impressions, they both felt that, for the most part, they were cordial team players committed to finding the cause and a cure for the illness. A bit of subtle resentment was present among a few of them regarding Jack and Madison's presence at Mothers and Infants, but to this point, the negative feeling hadn't created any material problems.

Another ten minutes came and went. Ely was just about to get the meeting under way when Dr. Herbert Whiteacre strolled nonchalantly into the room. With an unapologetic look on his face, he offered no greetings as he selected a seat at the end of the table. Madison may have been imagining it, but she felt as if he'd intentionally avoided making eye contact with either her or Jack. It reminded her of the only time she'd spoken to him, when she'd found him cordially distant and a little full of himself.

"I believe we're all present now," Ely said, looking up and down the table. "I'm certain everybody in the room knows each other and has had the opportunity to meet Jack and Madison. I'd like to begin by thanking everybody for attending this crucial meeting. I think we'd all agree that our current situation has reached a crisis level. Despite our best efforts, we still haven't identified a cause for IPS. Making matters more worrisome is the ongoing deterioration of our patients' conditions."

He stopped, raised his eyes, and again scanned the faces of his colleagues. "I realize the communication between all of us has been adequate, but we've reached a point where impromptu hallway conversations, reviewing each other's progress notes in the charts, and cursory phone calls simply aren't enough. I think it's high time we sit down regularly as a team and focus on this illness until we figure out what in perdition is causing it."

He paused to slide his eyeglasses higher up on the bridge of his nose. "It's of paramount importance that we all get on the same page regarding a specific plan for moving forward," he explained. "If there are no questions, what I'd like to do is begin by going around the table and asking one of the physicians from each specialty to provide us with their current assessment of the illness."

When nobody in the room requested recognition, Ely went on, "Do we have a volunteer who'd like to kick things off?"

Rosabel Chalmers, the chief of immunology, raised her hand. One of the younger department heads, she had four immunologists in her division reporting to her. With her limited experience in a significant leadership role, she still had a lot to learn about bringing out the best in her partners and determining which battles needed fighting. But she was a quick study and for the most part was thought highly of by those she worked with.

"Since I suspect my report's going to be short and sweet, I'm happy to go first."

"The floor's all yours."

"We discussed each of the IPS cases in extreme detail at our division meeting this morning. We can't totally rule out an autoimmune disease, but our minds remain open to the possibility that we may be dealing with a disorder like preeclampsia that could be an inflammatory response to an undefined cause. If IPS does turn out to be an autoimmune illness, the consensus of our team is that it's very likely one that's never been seen before. Unfortunately, we don't have the first clue what might have triggered it. That being said, I'm happy to answer any questions."

"How will you be moving forward?" Ely asked.

"Our plan is to continue to see each patient on a daily basis to monitor her progress, hoping that new clinical evidence will surface that will either confirm or rule out an autoimmune origin for the illness." A few moments of side conversations passed before the room faded to silence in anticipation of Ely's impending remarks.

"Thanks, Rosabel. If anything changes from your team's perspective, we'll be anxious to hear about it."

"Of course."

Madison stole a peek at Whiteacre as he pushed his palms together and rested his elbows on the table. The unsatisfied look on his face spoke volumes. He looked to her like a man who was having difficulty remaining silent.

Ely turned his attention to Dr. Parker Armondy, the venerable chief of anesthesia. "I know we've all read your report, but if you have an update for us, I'm sure we'd like to hear it."

"Thank you," he said, electing to come to his feet to address the group. "We continue our intensive study of the entire delivery room environment. To this point, we have nothing significant to add to our original findings. We can identify no specific cause or condition that might have contributed to this outbreak. That being said, we'll continue to examine and reexamine all aspects of the birthing center's operation that might provide a clue as to how the IPS patients contracted the illness."

"Any questions for Parker?" Ely asked. When there was no response, he added, "I scheduled this meeting for an hour. The way we're flying through the agenda, we'll be out of here long before that." He thumbed the bottom of his chin a couple of times before going on. "Before hearing from Jack and Madison, I'd like to give Herb Whiteacre an opportunity to bring us up to date on any ideas the division of infectious diseases might have."

Whiteacre was a potbellied, high-minded man, who had served with distinction as the chief of infectious diseases since the day of the hospital's ribbon cutting. He was no stranger to hard work, nor was he averse to tackling challenging cases. At times his pride and stubbornness teamed up to frustrate the nurses and other hospital staff, but most would agree his value to the hospital outweighed his annoying faults.

Whiteacre waited a few moments before raising his eyes to address the group.

"Ely, would you mind if I begin by posing a question to Doctors Shaw and Wyatt?"

Ely looked surprised by the request, but after a few moments he looked across the conference table at Jack and Madison, offering them the opportunity to respond for themselves.

"That would be fine," Madison said. "We'd be happy to try to answer any question that you might have, Dr. Whiteacre."

"As everybody present knows, based on the information we've gathered to this point, it's the opinion of my group that IPS is not a viral illness. Because we're the recognized authority in this area, I was under the impression that Doctors Shaw and Wyatt were in agreement with us. But when I looked at today's meeting agenda, I discovered my impression couldn't be further from the truth." He reached for his agenda and held it up. "I was hoping one of you might be able to enlighten us on this infectious disease decision that you've suddenly done a one-eighty on."

Madison looked at Whiteacre as if he was somebody who'd been raised someplace that good manners were unknown, where smug and condescending were the coin of the realm. From the expression on Jack's face, she assumed he agreed.

Ely was quick to say, "As you mentioned, Herb, the prospect that we're dealing with a virus is an agenda item, but my plan was to cover it later in the meeting. However, if there's no objection from anybody in the group, we can discuss it now."

"I don't see why anybody would object to a slight change in the agenda, Ely. I, for one, see no reason to wait," said Whitacre.

From where Madison was sitting, it wasn't hard to see that Ely was doing his level best to keep the meeting as productive and noncontentious as possible.

"I'm happy to respond to Dr. Whiteacre's question," Madison stated. "Jack and I are well aware of his view on the possibility that IPS is a viral illness. However, we've just come across two new clinical findings that question the accuracy of his opinion. We felt we should bring the information to the group to see if there was sufficient interest to take a second look at the possibility."

"I'm sure we've all read your notes in the charts regarding auditory hyperacusis and macroglossia," Whiteacre said. "If those are the two findings you're referring to…well, the only thing I can say is that I hope you're not pinning our hopes of curing this illness on a couple of obscure findings that have been linked to many more nonviral illnesses than viral ones."

"As I said, We're not proposing these symptoms constitute indisputable proof that IPS is being caused by a virus," Madison stated not in a patient way. "As I've already said, Jack and I thought it was appropriate to bring this information to the group to allow our colleagues the opportunity to draw their own conclusions."

Leaning back in his chair and crossing his arms in front of his chest, Whiteacre said, "I'm sure we all appreciate your diligence, Dr. Shaw, but I would remind you that four fellowship-trained, board-certified infectious diseases specialists have basically taken a viral cause for IPS off the table. Our decision is based on a considerable amount of testing in addition to the patients' clinical histories and symptoms. I would remind you, Dr. Shaw, that we are the experts in this area. I'd also like to inform you that I have an extensive amount of clinical experience in the field of virology."

Madison was prepared for a reasonable amount of pushback, but Whiteacre was coming at them locked and loaded. He was an articulate individual who clearly had no problem standing by the courage of his convictions.

Owing to the nature of their consulting practice, Jack and Madison had found themselves in many prickly discussions with self-assured physicians representing a variety of specialties who saw things differently than they did, but today's situation involving Dr. Whiteacre was a little different. Nobody in the room would question that clinical issues relating to viruses would fall more appropriately within the purview of an infectious disease expert than a neurologist and a perinatologist. Regardless, Madison and Jack were trying to convince Dr. Whiteacre that, even though he was a recognized expert in the area, he wasn't the voice of God, and perhaps he'd rushed to judgment on the cause of IPS. Despite feeling comfortable posing the question to the group, she still had a sinking feeling she had just waded into an ocean that was overflowing with box jellyfish.

She said, "We understand the viral workup has been negative to this point, but there are still test results that are still pending. And it's worth mentioning that if we *are* dealing with a rare or novel virus, the currently available standard tests could fail to identify it."

"Now it's suddenly a novel virus," he said, cupping his chin. He exhaled a maddened breath and went on, "Isn't it fascinating how history so often repeats itself in the practice of medicine? I'll never understand why, every time a physician is faced with a challenging diagnosis, he claims the patient has contracted some mysterious, unidentifiable virus. I'd like to know when viruses became the doctor's whipping boy and default diagnosis whenever the cause of an illness escaped them."

There was a light chuckle in the room as everybody realized

there was a degree of truth in Dr. Whiteacre's assertion. Almost since their discovery, viruses had been accused of causing a wide variety of illnesses, only for medical science to eventually discover their assumptions were wrong.

"Dr. Whiteacre," Madison began in her most polite voice. "Just to make sure we're all on the same page, is it your recommendation that, in view of these new clinical findings, a viral cause for this illness should still be categorically dismissed?"

"In view of the rapid progression of this illness, my answer to your question is a resounding yes, Dr. Shaw. The reason I say it with such confidence is that, in addition to our own resources, we've had two other very sophisticated labs working with us that haven't uncovered a scintilla of evidence that we're dealing with a bacteria, fungus, or virus. Our team is leaning more toward some event that triggered an overwhelming inflammatory reaction. It's even possible there was more than one trigger. What we think is key and should be a major focus of our attention are the hormonal shifts of the postpartum state. The condition or toxin that triggered this illness is in the hospital environment—we just have to be smart enough to find it."

"Can you be more specific as to what those triggers might be?" Zach was quick to ask.

"I'm afraid I can't, but based on the fact that all these women presented within a day or so of each other, I'm convinced that whatever sparked this illness happened during childbirth."

One of the other doctors said, "But, Herb, we all just listened to Dr. Armondy's report regarding the delivery room environment, and nothing abnormal was found."

"All that means is that we haven't found it yet," Whiteacre said.

"If you suspect that, Herb, we'd welcome whatever assistance you'd be willing to offer us in locating the problem," Armondy said, more as a challenge than a request.

"I'm sure you have an excellent team in place, Parker. I'd prefer to leave the nuts and bolts of the investigation in your capable hands."

"So you're saying you have no idea about a possible trigger or cause, other than that it occurred in my delivery room while I was providing the anesthesia."

"I didn't say that."

"Then what are you saying, Herb?" Armondy inquired, now with a noticeable edge to his voice.

"If you're asking me directly, my answer is that I do have an idea of what may have caused IPS, but since I've just started investigating the possibility, I'd prefer not to discuss the specifics at this time. I think it would be premature."

"But, Herb," Ely began, "don't you think it—"

"I'm sorry, Ely. My decision is firm. Hopefully, in the next few days I'll have something of substance to share with the group." He paused and pinched the bridge of his nose. "I wonder if any of you are as worried as I am that, in a matter of days or weeks, we could be dealing with a hundred cases of IPS instead of only ten," Whiteacre said, raising a restraining hand to dissuade anybody from responding to his rhetorical question. "Excuse me, Ely, but I'd like to cut to the chase. How many of you seated here today share my opinion that an untoward event during delivery is the most likely cause of IPS?" When several moments passed and only a small minority responded positively to his question, a hardened look took shape on his face. "I'll take your response to mean we're light-years apart on how to approach diagnosing and treating this disease."

Considering her role was that of a consultant, and suspecting Whiteacre was spoiling for a fight, Madison didn't respond to his comment.

"Let's all take a breath for a moment," Ely said. "We can't allow this frustrating clinical problem to become contentious. We have two operational imperatives: The first is to stay open-minded about IPS, and the second is to behave professionally and keep the lines of communication open between us."

"I'm sure we're all in agreement with your recommendations, Ely, but it seems we've gotten a little sidetracked," Rosabel said. "I, for one, would very much like to hear more of the details of what Jack and Madison have uncovered."

"I agree," David Phillips said.

For the next few minutes, Jack joined Madison in explaining in extreme detail what they'd discovered. Their presentation sparked a number of questions, which they fielded.

When the last question had been answered, Ely asked, "I'll begin by asking if anybody feels strongly that we shouldn't pursue any further investigations regarding a viral cause for IPS?"

Dr. Elena Brandwyn said, "I think it's reasonable to take another look at the possibility. This would be a good time to check our egos at the door and not commit a drastic error of omission."

"Spoken like a true surgeon," Dr. Phillips said. His modest attempt at humor successfully eased the tension in the room.

"I agree with Elena," Zach said. "We're not suggesting abandoning our other attempts to find a cause for IPS. We're just going to double back in one specific area to make sure we haven't fallen victim to an oversight."

The murmur in the room seemed to be in support of Madison and Jack's recommendation.

"Is anybody opposed to that plan?" Ely asked. When there were no negative responses, he added, "In that case, we won't drop a viral illness from our differential diagnosis list."

"I know when I'm fighting alone. My group and I will continue to assist in the care of these patients, but from this point on, I'll assume I'm a one-man team."

Above the whispers in the room, Ely said, "All I can say to you, Herb, is that I hope in time you'll reconsider your decision." He shifted his eyes to Madison. "Thank you for your comments. At this time, I'd like to ask Zach Church if he has anything to share with us from an obstetrical standpoint."

"I don't believe we have anything new to add. But on another note, I'd like to suggest we begin meeting on a daily basis to ensure we're all on the same page regarding diagnostic studies and possible treatment plans."

"That's an excellent idea. I assume we're all in agreement with Zach's suggestion," Ely said, looking around the table.

Whiteacre spoke up. "Schedule all the meetings you please, but allow me to warn you of one thing. The day may soon be upon us that we're caring for an untold number of IPS patients. When that time comes, you may discover that, because we negligently went down a dead-end rabbit hole, it'll be too late to help any of these poor women."

He came to his feet, stepped away from the table, and took a first step toward the exit. He was just about to push open the door when he turned and added, "God forgive us all if I'm right."

Chapter 31

Marcus spent the majority of his morning relaxing on his farm. After a light lunch, he went to his office in the barn where he worked at his computer, continuing his research on Doctors Madison Shaw and Jack Wyatt. Having a natural aptitude for information technology, he had done a yeoman's job in gathering considerable information on them in a relatively short period of time.

Getting lost in his work, he was surprised when he checked the time and discovered it was almost four o'clock. He shut down his computer and exited the barn into a drizzly afternoon. Making his way around to the back of the building, he stopped at the modest grove of palm trees. As he always did, he glanced at the clay pots he'd hung from a dozen or so of their trunks to collect the trees' sweet sap.

From the grove, he made his way to the barn-house, changed his clothes, and grabbed a snack of mixed fruit and nuts. When he was finished eating, he got into his truck and headed to Mothers and Infants Hospital. He was pleased to encounter no traffic delays, and forty-five minutes later, he drove onto the hospital's campus. Facing the main entrance was a small parking lot that had a couple of designated accessible-parking spaces. They were ideal for his purposes, as they provided him an excellent view of the hospital's exit. Marcus understood the value of patience but was introspective enough to admit that he sorely lacked it at times and that it was a character flaw he needed to work on. For what he hoped to accomplish by coming to the hospital, the annoying possibility of a long wait lingered in his mind.

But on this particular evening, his natural good luck was with him, and he spotted Doctors Shaw and Wyatt as they exited the hospital and headed toward the doctors' parking lot. When they were about fifty yards away, he backed out of his space, followed them, and watched them get into their rental. The moment they pulled out of the parking lot, he fell in behind them, keeping a safe distance to avoid detection. He thought about the many hours he'd spent at his computer gathering every bit of information he could about the celebrated physician team. Ever since he was a child, Marcus had been excessively curious about other people, prompting his mother to affectionately call him her *chismosito*, little gossip in Spanish.

Marcus's major interest in the doctors was to acquire detailed information about their daily schedules and determine if they'd formed any patterns, even though they'd only been here a relatively short period of time. This was the second time he'd followed them to Jack's mother's house after work. On a separate day, he'd surveilled them on their way to the hospital in the morning. He'd realized from the first day he learned of their presence at the hospital that acquiring information about them could be invaluable if extreme measures suddenly became necessary. Not having a trigger-happy mentality at key moments, for now he remained comfortable merely keeping a watchful eye on them, ever mindful that he wouldn't hesitate for an instant to act if it became necessary.

As he continued to follow them, he thought about how easily he'd handled the Regina Leggett problem. When it was over and done, the entire operation had been little more than a walk in the park. He couldn't help but believe that assuring a permanent solution to ending Doctors Wyatt and Shaw's interference would be infinitely more challenging than eliminating a meddlesome nurse.

As soon as they pulled into Charlotte Duffy's driveway and got out of their car, Marcus noted the time in a small notebook and watched how they gained entrance to the house. Once they were inside, he turned around and headed home. He was well on his way when he thought back to the way the two doctors had walked up Wyatt's mother's driveway. The image reminded him of a lesson he'd long ago learned—more often than not, the best way to deal with a troublemaker is to bypass them entirely and focus your attention directly on somebody they dearly loved.

Chapter 32

OUTBREAK—DAY 11

Jack and Madison pulled into the hospital parking lot and for the first time had little to no problem finding a space. They had eaten a light breakfast at his mother's house, prompting them to skip a stop at the lobby coffee shop and head straight to the PCU. Following the decision the physicians had made at yesterday's meeting, they were both in a good mood. All that came to an end as soon as they stepped onto the unit and observed a sizable commotion outside of Nell's room, several nurses and ancillary personnel rushing in and out.

Teri spotted Madison, signaled to her at once, and wasted no time walking over to join her and Jack. As she came closer, Madison could see the demoralized look in her eyes.

"We've had one hell of a night. Three of the IPS patients started having major blood pressure instability and other manifestations of shock. Nell is one of them, and she's barely holding on. We had to call a code blue on her a few hours ago. Fortunately, the docs were able to resuscitate her, but she's on a ventilator now and not doing well."

She hesitated momentarily. Madison gave her the few seconds she needed to compose herself. "Emma Collymore's not doing much better than Nell. Zach Church has already been in to see her and spoke with her folks. Both of them have been here all night. Carmela finally went downstairs about fifteen minutes ago to get something to eat, but the governor stayed to be with Emma and to be sure he didn't miss you two when you made rounds. He's already asked me twice if I knew when you'd be in."

"Has Emma had any more pilomotor responses?"

"No. Everybody who's taking care of her has been briefed not to create any loud noises."

"We'll have a look at her chart and then go speak with the governor," she told Teri.

"All the nurses are terrified that this is the beginning of the end and that we're within a few days of losing all the IPS patients. The family members are collectively starting to believe that none of their loved ones are likely to recover. We're having a hell of a time trying to keep them calm."

"Other than talking with the governor, is there anything else you need us to do right now?" Jack asked.

"Dr. Church is still on the floor. I'm sure he'll want to speak with you about Emma."

"We'll track him down as soon as we take a look at her and speak with her parents."

Just then, one of the nurses' aides hurried over and stopped right in front of Teri. "I'm sorry to interrupt, but we need you in right away in Nell's room."

"Please come see me before you leave the floor," Teri said to them as she hurried away.

Seeing little else they could do, Jack and Madison made their way to the physicians' charting area and spent the next twenty minutes reviewing every detail of Emma's clinical course for the past several hours. Teri was right. Every aspect of her condition had worsened appreciably overnight.

They left the charting area and headed down the large central corridor to the last patient pod. The moment they stepped into

Emma's suite, Governor Collymore jumped up from his chair and met them in the middle of the room.

"I was hoping you and Dr. Shaw would stop in," he said. "Carmela and I are very worried. We have a few minutes before she returns, so now would be a good time for us to have a frank conversation," he said, glancing toward the door. "I hope you'll take this the right way, but all day I deal with people who speak to me in sugar-coated code. With all due respect, I'd appreciate straight answers. Now just how bad is this?"

"She's battling, Governor," Jack said. "We've just finished speaking with Teri and reviewing Emma's chart. We're extremely concerned. We're dealing with a highly unpredictable and aggressive illness. For right now, she's holding on, but for the next day or so, the situation's going to be an hour-to-hour one."

"Thank you for the candid answer, which brings me to my next question: How close are we to a possible treatment?"

Madison answered, "We have some reasonable leads but nothing that looks encouraging."

"Based on what you're telling me, it seems my wife and I should hope for the best but prepare for the worst."

"If you hadn't just said that yourself, it's the advice Jack and I would have given you."

"It's not my intention to put you on the spot, but I'd like to ask you a question as the governor of this state. I won't hold you to your answer. I'm just looking for your best guess."

"Go ahead, sir," Jack said.

After a long moment, he inquired, "I'm aware we already have two cases that didn't occur in this hospital. What's the chance we'll be facing a statewide crisis?"

Jack answered, "Governor, all we can say with certainty is that, at this particular point, we have no strong evidence pointing to that possibility. What makes your question incredibly difficult to answer is that, since we don't know the natural history of IPS, we have no reliable way of predicting how many new cases we'll see or where those cases might occur."

"With the continued attention of the media, I'm sure you can guess that our phones in Tallahassee are ringing off the hook with calls from concerned healthcare providers, pregnant women, and those who are postpartum. I don't think we can keep simply putting them off with one nebulous and evasive response after another. Our plan has to be to take a more proactive and detail-oriented approach. With each passing day, IPS is getting more and more media coverage. We'll be creating a task force, and I'd be grateful if you two would agree to attend the meetings."

"Of course," Madison responded with no hesitation.

Collymore walked back to Emma's bedside and took her hand in his.

"I don't mean to come across as a heartless father, talking to you about issues other than my daughter's illness. Believe me when I tell you that I'm grief-stricken and terrified about Emma's condition. Unfortunately, I don't have the luxury of losing focus on my responsibility as the governor of this state. My personal issues and problems don't afford me a pass on my gubernatorial duties." His lip curled for a few moments.

"I wish there was something we could tell you that would sound more optimistic, but at this point I don't think we have any solid medical evidence that might help to allay the family member's fears," Jack said. "The only thing I can say on a positive note is that, sometimes when you least expect it, the first key clue to making a tough diagnosis hits you smack in the face and opens the door to an effective treatment plan."

With an exasperated sigh, the governor responded, "That would be a great relief, Jack. To the limits that your professional ethics will allow, I'd appreciate it if you'd keep me personally informed of the progress you and the other physicians are making. I have an abiding confidence in my healthcare team, but this is one of those rare circumstances when I'd prefer to get my information straight from the horse's mouth, which means you two." Collymore paused long enough to turn his gaze back to Emma. For a moment, he said nothing. "I think I'm a pretty good father, and at the risk of sounding a bit full of myself, I think I'm also a hell of a fine governor. It's trying to do both at the same time that's got me pulling my hair out."

"That's perfectly understandable," Madison said, watching Collymore as he averted his eyes.

"If the disease turns out to be untreatable, how much time would you say Emma has?"

"I'm afraid that's an impossible question to answer, sir."

"C'mon, Jack, save the crap for the customers," he said, looking at him through sorrowful eyes.

"A week or two at the most," he replied.

Chapter 33

After their meeting with the governor, Madison and Jack spent some time going over each of the IPS cases with Zach Church. Just as they were finishing up, Teri called and asked them to sit in on an emergency meeting she was having with the nurses. Jack gathered the information regarding the time and place and told Teri he and Madison would be there.

As soon as they were done reviewing the last case, Zach left the core desk.

"What was that call all about?" Madison asked him.

"Teri asked if we could attend an urgent meeting with the nurses to discuss the IPS cases."

"Did you tell her we'd both be there?"

"Yeah... is that okay?"

"Actually, do you think you could represent us? I'd like to find a quiet place and spend some time going over the charts again," Madison said.

"That's no problem. But how many times are you going to go over them?"

"I had an idea about something. I want to change my focus and go back to the month before they delivered," she answered.

"Do you have a legitimate hunch we missed something, or is this a Hail Mary?"

"Probably a little of both. Ask me again in a couple of hours. After you sit in on Teri's meeting, go ahead and start rounds. I'll give you a call when I'm finished."

"Sounds good. Will do."

Jack watched her start toward the exit and was just about to call out to her and ask her about having lunch together when he quickly dismissed the idea. She was in her maximum-effort mode, and the chances of her stopping for lunch were nil.

At a few minutes past eleven, Ely called Jack to see if he could come to his office to bring him up to speed on the patients' conditions. After their meeting, Jack returned to the unit and picked up where he'd left off, which included another conversation with the governor, this time with Carmela present. Considering the circumstances, it went as well as Jack could have hoped. He guessed the governor had done the best he could to prepare her. Carmela said very little, giving Jack the impression she was close to giving up.

He was just about to reach out to Madison when his phone rang.

"Where are you?" she asked him.

"I'm still in the unit waiting for your call."

"C'mon up to the library. There's something I want to show you."

"I was just about to call Columbus and update Blair on how things are going. Give me about twenty minutes."

"Listen, Jack. Unless you're performing CPR on somebody, come now. Blair can wait."

"You sound so serious. What the hell's going on?"

"Just get up here."

Sensing the urgency in her voice, he caved in and told her he was on his way.

Chapter 34

Jack stepped off the elevator on the seventh floor and went straight to the library, where he found Madison in one of the private study rooms. When the hospital was being designed, it was decided to designate the entire seventh floor as a nonclinical area. The layout included many of the hospital's administrative offices, the executive conference room, and a state-of-the- art medical library and teaching center for the residents and medical students.

"What's going on?" he asked, as he took a seat across from her at a rectangular wooden study table.

"I think I may have come across something that skipped our attention."

He removed a Granny Smith apple from his lab coat's pocket and took a generous bite. "Let's hear about it."

"Let me start with the basics," she said, closing her laptop's lid. "On the days in question, the hospital performed seventy-one vaginal deliveries. Obviously, that number includes all the IPS patients we're currently treating except the two from Sarasota. I've spent a lot of time reviewing every detail of those deliveries, looking for a common factor among the eight of our patients who delivered here at Mothers and Infants."

"A lot of people, including us, have already spent a lot of time doing that."

"Nevertheless, I'd like to go over it again. The most obvious thing is that they were all delivered by Dr. Josef Church. There are a bunch of other common factors, but they're pretty obvious as well and have all been dead ends to this point."

"From the gleam in your eye I'm going to assume that's all changed now."

"And you'd be correct."

"Don't stop now."

"It's fairly routine for women in labor, whether it's induced or natural, to receive a medication that neutralizes the acid in their stomach—the idea being to prevent aspiration pneumonia." Madison reached for the legal pad she'd been making notes on. Using her finger as a pointer, she ran it down the first page to make sure she didn't omit anything. "Various types and brands of acid blockers are available to the anesthesiologist in charge of a delivery. Mothers and Infants happens to have two different ones on its formulary. One is oral; the other is given IV."

"How is it determined which acid blocker a particular woman in labor receives?"

"Basically, it's the anesthesiologist's choice, but sometimes the obstetrician puts her or his two cents in. Almost all of them strongly prefer the intravenous choice. The anesthesiologist Dr. Church works with only uses sodium citrate, which is the one taken by mouth." She stopped, lifted her eyes from the legal pad, and raised her index finger. "All eight of our IPS patients who were delivered here at Mothers and Infants received sodium citrate."

"How many total deliveries did Dr. Church do during the days in question?" he asked.

"Ten vaginal deliveries."

"That leaves two other women."

Madison nodded.

"But neither of them contracted IPS—at least up until now."

"Right again."

Jack allowed a lengthy breath to depart his lungs. "So, just so we're completely clear on this, you're proposing a possible cause-and-effect relationship between the sodium citrate and IPS."

Madison nodded again.

"I'm just guessing, but there must be thousands and thousands of doses of sodium citrate ordered for women in labor every year in this country."

"No doubt about it."

"But to the best of our knowledge, none of them has ever become a victim of IPS."

"That's correct. And before you ask me why, I don't have the first clue to explain that."

"Okay. The other thing I'd ask you is this: Unless patients nine and ten were from the planet Krypton, how did they escape contracting IPS?"

"I said ten patients had an order for sodium citrate. I didn't say they all received it."

"That's interesting. Do you know for sure they never got it?"

"Being treated for leukemia, I'd venture to say that I've spent a lot more time in a hospital as a patient than ninety-nine percent of the doctors and nurses I work with, and I can tell you for certain that not every oral medication that a nurse or pharmacist charted as given was actually swallowed by the patient."

"Okay, but do you know that's what happened with Dr. Church's other two patients?" he asked.

Flipping to the next page of her notes, she answered, "I called Ellie Parrise, the ninth patient. She's an elementary school teacher who just had her third baby. She had an uneventful labor and delivery and went home the next day. She's been fine ever since."

"So did she or didn't she take the sodium citrate?"

"When I spoke with her, she told me she was quite familiar with its awful acidy taste from her prior two deliveries and reluctantly confessed to me that her nurse in pre-delivery was very busy caring for other patients. Sometimes it's kind of an honor system as to whether a patient actually swallows the medication. In Ellie's case, when her nurse was looking the other way, she sweet-talked her husband into dumping it into the sink."

"You're kidding me...right?"

"Do I sound like I'm kidding?"

"What about number ten?"

"That answer's in her chart. She too wasn't a fan of sodium citrate and begged the anesthesiologist to give her something in her IV instead, which he did, but not until she was in the delivery room."

"How do you happen to know all this, Madison?"

"It's all in her chart. The nurse anesthetist made a note in the anesthesia record that stated, at the patient's request, the order for sodium citrate was canceled. The nurse in the pre-delivery area didn't know anything about it, so she assumed her patient drank it, prompting her to chart that it was given."

"That's a little frightening," he responded. "And do we know for certain she's also doing well?"

"I called her. She told me she's doing great."

"Of course you did—why did I bother asking? This certainly begs some interesting questions," Jack said.

Madison held up her hand. "I know what you're going to ask me —how did our two patients from Sarasota contract IPS?"

"The question did cross my mind."

"I called the medical records department at Caring Hearts Medical Center, and they checked the two charts for me. Neither of them received sodium citrate. But I'm not sure how much that proves. We're talking about a different hospital with entirely different lot numbers of medications."

Jack said, "Let's take a look at the big picture. Just because all eight Mothers and Infants patients with IPS were given sodium citrate doesn't mean that's definitely what caused the disease, and—"

"But don't you think that, at a minimum, we should—"

"Take a breath and slow down," he said, pushing his palms together in front of his chest. "Let me finish. The two patients from Caring Hearts didn't receive any sodium citrate, so it seems pretty clear that they contracted the disease in a different way than the eight women who delivered right here at Mothers and Infants."

With a lazy shake of his head, he asked, "Would you agree that makes sense?"

"It would seem to, but what occurred to me is that, if we're truly relooking at a viral cause, doesn't the fact that we have cases from two separate hospitals a hundred miles apart strengthen the argument?"

Jack thought for a few moments. "It certainly does. I hadn't thought about it that way until you just mentioned it."

"We also can't forget that we just formally pitched to all the physicians involved in caring for the women with IPS that we should take a longer and harder look at IPS being a viral disease."

"Now that I think about it," Jack began, "many viruses are transmitted orally, which lends credibility to the contaminated sodium citrate argument. And even though the women in Sarasota weren't given sodium citrate, who knows how many other oral preparations are out there that the virus can survive in that they could have ingested?"

"All good points, Jack. But somebody's going to say it's still very coincidental that ten patients from two hospitals would just happen to become infected at the same time with a disease that's unknown to modern medicine."

"Well, I hate to be the one to say this, but maybe it's time to consider the possibility that this disease didn't just happen by chance."

"I think the possibility has crossed both our minds," Madison said. "But if somebody caused this illness intentionally, that person would not only have to be familiar with a disease that probably hasn't been discovered yet, but they'd also have to figure out a way to infect ten women with it without getting caught." With a casual shrug of her shoulders, she added, "I guess that would make him or her the smartest person in the room."

Chapter 35

Jack and Madison stayed in the library another few minutes discussing the new developments relating to the IPS patients before wrapping things up and heading back to the progressive care unit. They were walking across the skybridge when Jack's phone rang.

"Dr. Wyatt, this is the hospital operator. I have a doctor on the line who'd like to speak with you or Dr. Shaw. His name is Jordan Sturgess . He asked me to tell you that he has important information regarding IPS, and it's of the utmost importance that he speak with one of you."

Before answering, Jack thought about getting Dr. Sturgess' contact information and calling him later, but after a few extra moments of hemming and hawing, he asked the operator to put the call through.

"This is Jack Wyatt."

"Hello, Dr. Wyatt. My name's Jordan Sturgess. I'm an internist in Dade County. Thank you for taking my call."

"It's my pleasure. I'm here with Dr. Shaw and have you on speaker. How can we help you?"

"I admitted a patient yesterday whom I'd like to discuss with you. My wife's a nurse at Mothers and Infants, and she's currently involved in the care of the IPS patients. I wasn't sure if I should bother you with this, but when I told her about the patient, she strongly encouraged me to give you and Dr. Shaw a call."

"Why don't you go ahead and tell us a little about the case?" Madison suggested.

"Thank you. The patient's a thirty-two-year-old with a two-day history of bloody vomiting, jaundice, and a fairly distinctive neck and chest rash."

Jack's stomach instantly rolled with apprehension, thinking they might soon be dealing with a new admission of an IPS patient. He and Madison traded a cautious look. He assumed Dr. Sturgess' patient had given birth at Mothers and Infants but wanted to confirm it to rule out the possibility they might be dealing with a woman who gave birth at a third hospital.

"Do you happen to know the exact date and the hospital where your patient gave birth, Dr. Sturgess?" The call suddenly went silent. Jack was surprised by Dr. Sturgess' hesitation in answering a rather straightforward and simple question.

"That's what has me so worried, Dr. Wyatt" he finally said. "The patient I admitted—the one I'm calling you about—is an otherwise healthy thirty-two-year-old man from Bangladesh."

Jack and Madison had just reached the halfway point of the skybridge. They stopped and sat down on matching wicker chairs.

"We certainly appreciate your call, Dr. Sturgess," Jack said. "We'd very much like to hear about the case."

Chapter 36

Jack and Madison hung on his every word as Dr. Sturgess briefly presented Mr. Abul Kahn's clinical history.

"We're somewhat shocked to hear that we may be dealing with a man with IPS," Madison told him. "Based on the cases we've been consulting on, we assumed the illness only affected women."

"If I'm right about my suspicion, Dr. Shaw, I'd say, as of right now, there's considerable evidence to the contrary."

"What else can you tell us about him?" she asked.

"As I mentioned, Abul's thirty-two years old and has lived right here in South Florida with his wife and two children for several years. He works as a roofer and has been in excellent health until a few days ago."

Jack was still having difficulty believing his own ears, but his inner voice was warning him not to dismiss Dr. Sturgess' concerns as an overactive imagination or a grave misdiagnosis.

"In addition to the symptoms you mentioned, does he have a swollen tongue? Has he demonstrated an auditory hyperacusis reaction?" Jack asked.

"No. I haven't observed macroglossia or any distinct neurologic symptoms—not as of yet, anyway."

"Did he report any unusual abnormalities regarding his taste?" Jack continued.

"Yes. He said one of the first things he noticed was an unfamiliar salty taste in his mouth."

Madison asked, "From the workup you've done to this point, do you have a diagnosis that would account for his symptoms?"

"Other than IPS, I'm afraid not, Dr. Shaw. As of today, our evaluation remains entirely negative. I understand the significance of Abul being the first male to have IPS. As I mentioned, I considered not calling you but then decided you'd be in a far better position than I to decide whether he could possibly have the illness."

Dr. Sturgess' comment gave Jack reason to pause. It was obvious he was being as diplomatic as possible, but at the same time he was warning Jack and Madison not to assume his patient wasn't suffering from IPS based solely on gender. Jack found himself reminded of a nugget of wisdom passed on to him from his mother when he was a neurology resident. Her advice echoed in his mind: "Don't be too anxious to dismiss any diagnostic possibility based on an extremely low likelihood. To the contrary, everything in medicine is fifty-fifty—it's either the case or it's not; and it will either happen or it won't."

"What hospital did you admit him to?" Madison asked.

"Lakeside in Hialeah. If you and Dr. Shaw would like to take a drive down here and have a look at Abul, I can easily clear it with our administration. I'm sure you don't recall, but I had the pleasure of meeting you both briefly when you were in South Florida consulting on the GNS cases. My niece was one of the patients you were asked to see."

"How is she now?" Madison inquired.

"She completely recovered and to this day has done extremely well. She studied to become a chef, and now she and her husband are just about to open their third French restaurant."

"That's certainly wonderful to hear."

"Our entire family is very grateful to you both."

"Madison and I appreciate your kind words, and we'd be

pleased to see your patient. Does late this afternoon work for you, say at around five?"

"I'll make it work. I'll meet you in the lobby at our welcome center." They took a minute to exchange phone numbers. "I appreciate your willingness to have a look at Abul. I look forward to speaking with you later today."

Jack and Madison sat in silence looking out the skybridge's window wall toward the beautifully landscaped back of the hospital.

Madison finally broke the silence. "This illness is starting to get awfully daunting," she said in a dejected voice. "I prefer diseases to be more like an uninspired crossword puzzle—dull and easy to solve."

Chapter 37

Jack and Madison had promised to take Charlotte to one of her favorite restaurants for a late lunch. It was a few minutes past two when they entered the dimly lit Thai restaurant. Charlotte had arrived a few minutes earlier and was already seated. She spotted them at the welcome area and waved. The hostess escorted them to her table and placed an additional two menus on the table. Traditional Mahori-style music played softly in the background.

Madison kissed Charlotte once on each cheek, and Jack gave her a hug around her shoulder.

"It's been a long time since I've eaten here," he said. "Is it still as good as ever?"

"Maybe better."

After a few minutes of casual conversation, Jack said, "Madison and I got the strangest phone call a couple of hours ago."

Charlotte set her menu down and looked at him briefly before responding. "You have an ever-so-subtle tremor to your voice when you're feeling stressed. I doubt anybody even notices it."

"Except you."

"I've known you the longest."

"You've never mentioned it before," Jack said.

"Why would I disclose something that frequently helps me understand you better? Tell me about the call."

Jack and Madison spent the next few minutes recounting their conversation with Jordan Sturgess. Just as they finished, the server came over to the table and took their order.

After he left, Charlotte asked, "So what are your thoughts? Do you think this man has IPS?"

Madison pointed at Jack. "You first, buddy."

"I think I was more concerned about the possibility when I first listened to Dr. 's case presentation. I'm trying to keep an open mind, but the more I think about it, the more I'm leaning toward two different illnesses that share some symptoms in common."

"What do you think, Madison?"

"As much as I dislike disagreeing with Jack, my sense is that Abul Kahn is suffering from IPS, which I fear will make finding the cause of the illness and an effective treatment even more difficult."

"Interesting," Charlotte said. "So what will you do next?"

"We're going to see the patient later this afternoon," Jack answered. "That should give us a lot more information, which will help in making an accurate diagnosis."

Charlotte spoke directly to Jack. "It sounds to me like you've already made up your mind that this man's not suffering from the same illness as the women."

Jack was quite accustomed to his mother's fondness for playing devil's advocate. He always felt it was her unique way of encouraging him to slow down and think beyond the obvious.

"I guess I'm somewhere in the middle," he said to them both. "We have ten cases of an illness that exclusively affects postpartum women. That's a pretty small carve-out of the entire female gender. Common sense would dictate that it's unlikely Dr. Sturgess' patient is suffering from IPS."

With a coy grin, Charlotte said, "You're choosing your words carefully."

Charlotte said nothing further. When her silence became conspicuous, Madison was prompted to say, "I'd be very interested in hearing what your impression is."

"I'm thinking back to a time when Jack's Uncle Dave told me about an experience he had when he was a medical student in Burlington doing a rotation in the emergency room. He said it was at the tail end of a bitterly cold winter, even for New England. In the first four weeks, he saw eight hip fractures. They were all in elderly men who had slipped on an icy sidewalk within a block or so of their homes." Jack fidgeted in his chair for a few seconds before uncrossing his ankles and pulling his legs in. A look of impatience settled on his face as he swallowed another forkful of his Thai fried rice.

"I'm getting the feeling there's a lesson to be learned from Uncle Dave's clinical experience," he said.

"Have a little patience, dear. I'm coming to that. The next hip fracture he saw was in a twenty-year-old beer-soaked sophomore who hit a tree while she was sledding down a hill at night." Her eyes moved across her son's face. "If his emergency room rotation ended on the night he saw the last hip fracture in a man, he would have spent his entire career believing broken hips occurred only in elderly men who lived in icy climates."

Jack looked at Madison again, seeing her lips pushed together to prevent another grin.

"That's an interesting slice of medical wisdom, Mom, but there's also truth in the time-honored diagnostic tenet that advises young doctors to remember that *the most common things occur most frequently*. I've always taken that to mean that common sense and laws of probability come first." He paused long enough to dab the corners of his mouth with his napkin. "And, just for the record," he began with a playful uptick in his voice, "Uncle Dave went to med school in Dallas."

"I know, but the story works much better if it all happened on a snowy New England night."

"You two are really something," Madison said.

"I appreciate your insight, Mom, but I think you may be over-thinking the problem."

"Or you're oversimplifying it," she said.

For the remainder of the meal their conversation returned to more innocuous and pleasant topics, but it wasn't as if her advice had fallen on deaf ears. When they finished lunch and Jack had paid the check, they walked Charlotte to her car.

"I'll see you and Madison at home later. I have dinner plans, so you're on your own."

"Okay, Mom. Thanks for joining us."

Madison gave her a hug. "We enjoyed our lunch very much."

They waited until she got into her car and pulled away.

"She's incredible," Madison said.

"I guess that's one way of putting it."

"I know it was a little corny, but I suspect there was a nugget of wisdom in what she

said. And cut out the big act, trying to hide how much you love her. It isn't working."

"Is it that obvious? Since she knows the truth about how I feel about her, I've never given it much thought."

Chapter 38

Palm Beach Sheriff's Office Detectives Paul Allensworth and Libby Rafferty entered the lobby of Mothers and Infants Hospital and went directly to the information center where an elderly volunteer clad in the hospital's emblematic pink and blue vest provided them with directions to the Carlisle Birthing Center.

"What's your gut feeling," Libby asked as they stepped off the elevator on the third floor.

"What do you mean?"

"I know it's just a field interview, but do you think we're wasting our time?"

"I'm not sure, but let's keep an open mind. If it looks like we've hit a dead end, we can wrap things up quickly and move on to something else."

They made their way down a wide corridor with its walls nicely decorated with Anne Geddes baby portraits. They were almost at the end of the hallway when they reached the birthing center's administrative office. When they entered, they were greeted by a young woman wearing large rimless eyeglasses and an easy smile. They each pulled out their badge wallet and presented Kimberly Benavides with their credentials.

"I'm Detective Allensworth, and this is Detective Rafferty. We're investigating the murder of Regina Leggett."

"Everybody's totally horrified by what happened," Kimberly said. "We all loved her."

"We understand Mila Jennings is the administrator in charge of the birthing center. If she's available, we'd like to speak with her," Libby said.

"I'm afraid she's out of the hospital at a conference in Miami for the day."

"I see. Is there somebody else of authority we could talk with? We just need some general information. It's all pretty routine."

Just at that moment, a young man with scruffy brown hair dressed in light blue scrubs under a lab coat walked into the office.

"Sorry to interrupt," he said, quickly setting a manila envelope on the corner of Kim's desk. "This is the report Mila wanted." He wasted no time turning and heading back toward the door.

Kim reached for the envelope and called out to him, "Gil, this is Detective Rafferty and Detective Allensworth with the Palm Beach Sheriff's Office. They're investigating Regina's death and wanted to speak with Mila, but she's out of the office all day. Would you happen to have a few minutes to talk with them?"

With a forced smile, he responded, "My brother's a detective in Los Angeles. I mention that only because I suspect these detectives didn't come all the way over here to take no for an answer."

"What's your position here at Mothers and Infants?" Libby asked.

"I'm the chief nurse anesthetist."

"How well did you know Ms. Leggett?"

"Fairly well. We were casual friends outside the hospital, but both of us served on the birthing center's executive committee, which meant we worked together quite a bit."

"If you have a few minutes, we'd appreciate your cooperation," Paul said.

Gil looked back at Kim and pointed down the hall. "Is the conference room available?"

"It's free until late this afternoon."

Gil escorted them into the conference room and gestured toward an ultramodern stone conference table. He sat down first and watched as the detectives each took a seat directly across from him. Being no stranger to these situations, Libby reached into her purse and removed a notebook and a pen. As was their custom prior to any interview, Paul and Libby had decided on which one of them would take the lead. On this particular day, it was Libby.

"I didn't get your last name," she said.

"Hornbeck."

"Well, Mr. Hornbeck, how long have you been the chief nurse anesthetist?"

"It'll be seven years next month."

"Did you report directly to Ms. Leggett?"

"Regina and I reported up the chain through different pathways."

"Could you be more specific?"

"As the vast majority of my responsibilities are clinical, I report directly to the chief of anesthesiology. Regina's position was more of an administrative one. Her role was to oversee the day-to-day operations of the unit. She reported to the administrator of the birthing center. As I mentioned, we both sat on the executive committee. Are you here because you think she knew the person who killed her?"

Libby had conducted enough field interviews to know that most people were inquisitive by nature. They were usually able to stem the tide of their curiosity, but when they couldn't, she was adept at politely evading their questions.

"As I mentioned, Mr. Hornbeck, at this point, we're just trying to gather some basic information." Libby could see the doubt in his eyes as he responded to her comment with only a nod. "Would you say that Regina was easy to work with?"

"Yes, I would. She was a person of uncompromising integrity who understood the meaning of being fair. She was experienced, tireless, and totally dedicated to her job, but she was a no-nonsense person. She made it clear to everybody that what we do here every day is serious work—it's not a pajama party. She had no patience for people who had attitude problems or who weren't fully engaged."

"Were you aware of anybody she had a problem with?"

"What kind of problem?"

"Maybe somebody she tended to lock horns with for either a work-related or personal reason."

"Not that I was aware of. But I can tell you that those kinds of employees don't last very long around here. It's usually as obvious to them as it was to Regina that working in the birthing center probably isn't the best job for them, and perhaps they'd be happier employed somewhere else."

"So you know of no disgruntled employees who might have been upset enough with Regina to take matters into their own hands?"

"No."

"Would you say for the past several weeks Regina had been acting herself?"

"I saw no changes in her behavior, if that's what you mean. She seemed fine to me."

"Were you here the day she was murdered?"

"I was."

"Did you speak with her that day?"

"I did."

"You seem quite sure."

"We had our monthly resource utilization meeting right after lunch. It lasted about an hour, and Regina seemed totally normal to me. If she had an inkling she was in danger, she didn't act like it."

Libby cocked her head. "That's an interesting comment, Mr. Hornbeck. You said in danger. I asked you if she was acting herself. I mean, there are all kinds of things that could have been bothering her without her feeling she was at risk of bodily harm."

"I naturally assumed you were asking the question with her murder in mind. I guess if I were feeling threatened, I'd assume I was in danger. Wouldn't you, Detective Rafferty? But to clarify, I'd say Regina was acting pretty normally that day. She didn't strike me as somebody who was wrestling with a personal problem."

"How friendly would you say you two were?" Libby inquired.

He grinned. "I'll answer that question if you clarify it."

"Did you ever see her outside the hospital…maybe at a time when she let her hair down. Sometimes people are one person at work and somebody entirely different when it comes to their personal life."

"We didn't have that kind of relationship. As I said, we were casual friends outside the hospital. Other than our yearly holiday party in Key Biscayne, we rarely socialized."

"There have been several stories in the media about a number of women suffering from a strange illness who've recently been admitted to Mothers and Infants. I believe it's being referred to as IPS."

"Anybody who works in this hospital is well aware of that."

"Did you discuss the illness with Regina?"

"It's been the major topic of conversation among the staff since the first case was admitted—especially since one of the patients just happens to be Governor Collymore's daughter."

"What was Regina's take on the illness?"

An inquisitive look appeared on his face. It wasn't hard for Libby to guess that Hornbeck was wondering why she'd broached the topic of IPS. Whatever direction her question took the interview, she had no intention of informing him of Regina's call to their office.

"The illness has hit us all pretty hard. I don't believe anybody in the hospital's ever seen anything quite like it. I can tell you with complete certainty that Regina's feelings about the disease were no different from any of us who work here."

"What were those feelings?"

"We're all praying the doctors will be able to figure out what's causing IPS and how to cure it. Nobody wanted to see that more than Regina."

Even though she sensed some mild resentment in the tone of his voice, Libby pressed on, spending the next twenty minutes asking Hornbeck questions. While Paul posed an occasional one of his own, he stuck to their plan of allowing her to conduct the interview.

Finally, after exchanging a nod with Paul, she said, "Thank you for taking the time to speak with us, Mr. Hornbeck."

As they pushed back their chairs to stand up, Gil said to them, "All of us who work in the birthing center admired Regina enormously. I assure you that nothing would please us more than seeing this vile psychopath brought to justice and get what's coming to him."

"Rest assured, Mr. Hornbeck, we feel the same way," She said, handing him one of her cards. "If you hear or think of anything else that might help us in the investigation, please give us a call."

"Of course."

They exited the conference room, thanked Kim on their way out, and headed down the corridor toward the elevators.

"What do you think?" Paul asked.

"It's hard to say. Hornbeck's a bit of a wiseass. I don't think he either suspected or was aware that Regina had information she was anxious to bring to our attention."

"I agree. If Regina did suspect something, she didn't share it with him." They reached the elevators, and Paul slapped the button a couple of times. "So what do you want to do?" he asked her.

"If we're trying to rule out that there could be a connection between Regina's death and this mysterious illness, we haven't done that."

"Do you think Regina really knew something of importance?" he asked.

"Hard to say, but my gut's telling me she's not the type of person who suffers from a wild imagination. Bottom line—I don't think she would have called us unless she had a damn good reason."

Chapter 39

After answering a couple of pages he'd received while he was talking with the two detectives, Gil Hornbeck emerged from the conference room. Before heading back to the birthing center, he stopped at Kimberly's desk. They had known each other for several years, and both were chin-wagging gossips with a robust interest in hospital politics.

"That was interesting," he said with a smirk as he sat down on the corner of her desk.

"What do you mean?"

"They told me the only reason they wanted to interview me was to get some general background information on Regina."

"And?"

"Well, that's hardly the way it turned out." With a penchant for the dramatic, he paused briefly to sneak a peek over his shoulder at the door. He then leaned in and said in just above a whisper, "I think they're suspicious that somebody who works here had a hand in Regina's murder."

Wide-eyed, Kim said, "Your imagination's getting the best of you again, Gil. They're cops. They're looking into every possibility. They're just doing their job."

"Maybe, but I think there's a lot more to it than that." He slid off the desk and headed for the door. He was just about to leave when he stopped and raised his index finger to his lips. "Let's keep our little conversation between you and me."

"Of course, and you don't need to tell me that."

"We can all use a reminder from time to time. I'll see you later for coffee."

Kim shifted her head back behind her monitor. She waited a minute to make sure he was gone before reaching for her cell phone.

"Hi, Kiara. It's Kim. How are you?

"I'm fine. How about you?"

"Good. How's that annoying baby brother of mine that you foolishly agreed to marry?" Kim asked.

"I wish I could be more generous, but I'd have to say no improvement. He's still impossible to live with, but, as I recall, he was the pick of the litter at the time, so what's a girl to do? But I will say this: After ten years of marriage and two great kids, I guess I could have done a lot worse."

To her family and those who counted her among their friends, Kiara Das, with her large hazel eyes, rounded lips, and athletic physique, was one of the most kindhearted, diligent women on the planet. Some would affectionately add she had the unique ability of dovetailing her traditional Indian culture with the modern realities of living and working in a bustling American city.

"What's going on?" Kiara asked. "You never call me from work."

"I have a question."

"Shoot."

"Are you currently working on an earth-shaking piece?"

"Actually, I finished a story on some of South Florida's less hygienic hotels a few weeks ago that the magazine loved. Instead of jumping right into my next story, I decided to take some time off."

"Define some."

"Well, until the end of the month, my plan is to continue playing pickleball, spinning, attending ceramics classes, and catching up on all the streaming series my friends have been raving about."

"It's hard for me to believe that the hardest-working investigative reporter in the free world's taking such an extended break. Who's watching the kids?"

"They're on autopilot, and why the sudden interest in my life's agenda?"

A self-satisfied grin came to rest on Kim's face. "I have something that I think may be of interest to you."

"Personal or professional?"

"Strictly professional."

"I can't say I've ever gotten a lead on a story from a family member before, but I'm willing to listen."

"Have you heard about the group of postpartum women at Mothers and Infants being treated for this weird disease that has every doctor in the hospital stumped?"

"I'm on vacation, Kim, not in a coma. Of course I've heard about IPS. The governor's daughter's one of the patients. It's all over the news."

"The nurse administrator who ran the birthing center here at Mothers and Infants was also recently on the news. It seems some lunatic broke into her home and drowned her while she was taking a bubble bath."

"I think I also saw something about that in the papers."

"Two detectives from the Palm Beach Sheriff's Office just left here after interviewing our chief nurse anesthetist, Gil Hornbeck. They didn't confirm it, but he thinks they're suspicious that there's some kind of a connection between Regina's murder and IPS."

"And you know this how?"

"Because after the detectives left, Gil told me about the interview."

"I don't suppose the detectives told him why they suspect there's a connection."

"No, it was just his impression. But Gil's a pretty sharp guy who has a gift for connecting the dots in all types of situations," Kim answered. "What do you think?"

"I don't know. It depends on how much truth there is to the

theory. Do you think Gil would be willing to speak with me about the interview?"

"I don't know. Especially since I'm telling you about all this after I swore to him I wouldn't breathe a word of it to anybody."

"Try telling him you won't contact me without first getting his approval. If you tell him he'd be an anonymous source, at least to start with, he'll probably agree to meet with me."

"I'm not so sure."

"I'm an investigative reporter, Kim. I don't cover high school football games where all the pertinent information's right there on a scoreboard at the end of the game. For me to write a good story, I have to convince a lot of reluctant people to speak to me."

"Okay, Kiara. I'll give it a shot. I'm meeting him for coffee later. I'll ask him then."

"Thanks. And if this looks like it may be going somewhere, I may need more of your help."

"Regina was my boss, but we were also friends. If there's one chance in a thousand somebody in this hospital was responsible for her death, nothing would make me happier than helping to nail them. I might not be able to step across any red lines, but if I have to, I'll be happy to move a couple."

As Kiara listened, her interest in pursuing Kim's lead increased. Parading back and forth in front of her leather loveseat, she realized that the last week of her vacation was about to slip away.

"So what do you think?" Kim asked.

"This story may be a long shot, but I don't think I can pass on it without at least taking a look."

"Which entails what?" Kim asked.

"I'm going to spend a couple of days gathering as much information as I can and then make a decision about proceeding, which would mean starting to talk to people. I'll probably want to begin with Gil. If I can't get anything out of him, it'll probably be a no-go."

"As soon as I speak with him, I'll let you know what he says."

"Thanks. Give me a couple of days after that, and I'll give you a call with an update—and Kim, thanks for the tip."

"No problem. Just don't forget about me when you get that huge check from whatever magazine you sell the story to."

"I hope we can speak about that in the future. I'll call you soon."

Kim set her phone down on the desk. Her idea to tell Kiara had certainly looked good in the store window…but now that she'd gotten it home and given it another look, she wasn't so sure.

Chapter 40

As promised, Dr. Jordan Sturgess met Madison and Jack at the visitor's welcome center in the lobby of Lakeside Hospital. After they'd dispensed with the formal reintroductions, they took the elevator to the seventh floor and made their way to Abul Kahn's room.

Before entering, Sturgess again went over the specifics of the timeline of Abul's illness with Jack and Madison. He also informed them that, after his arrival in the United States, he'd joined a small Bangladeshi community who welcomed him with open arms. Four years later, he met Nadia, and after a short courtship, they married and wasted no time becoming the proud parents of two daughters.

The moment they walked into Abul's room and approached the bed, Jack and Madison noted his whitened face, distinctive neck rash, and jaundiced eyes. His look was identical to that of the IPS patients being treated at Mothers and Infants.

Sturgess took the lead. "Abul, I'd like you to meet Doctors Shaw and Wyatt. I've asked them to consult on your case. They'd like to ask you some questions and do a physical examination."

"Of course, Dr. Sturgess," he said, turning his glazed eyes toward them. "I appreciate you taking the time to see me." He was awake but just barely alert enough to politely answer their questions. He informed them that he had become ill three days earlier and had experienced a rapid progression of his symptoms. He'd always been a healthy, stoic individual, but his level of fear and concern reached a point where he finally acquiesced to his wife, Nadia's, relentless insistence that he allowed her to call Dr. Sturgess, and take him to Lakeside's emergency room.

The ER physician, Irene Holling, who was the first doctor to see Abul, knew enough about IPS from all the alerts they'd received from Mothers and Infants to be concerned. After completion of her evaluation, she'd called Dr. Sturgess to share her findings with him. He'd come to the ER immediately, where he did his own history and physical on Abul. When he was finished, he met with Dr. Holling to discuss the most appropriate next steps in his care. They agreed with very little discussion that Abul should be admitted to the hospital for further evaluation and treatment. After two and a half days of watching Abul's condition worsen, and at his wife's behest, he'd called Jack and Madison for assistance.

They spent thirty minutes with Abul, and Jack and Madison concluded that, despite his gender, he was suffering from IPS. Even though he was growing more ill by the hour, they felt he was still in the relatively early phases of the disease. Owing to the rapidly rising media attention, Dr. Sturgess and the administrator at Lakeside decided not to admit Abul with the diagnosis of inflammatory post-partum syndrome until they had more input from their medical consultants and Lakeside's CEO.

Jack and Madison spent a few extra minutes answering Abul's questions, but they both sensed his mounting fatigue as his responses became more clipped and his breathing more labored.

Dr. Sturgess intervened. "Do you have any further questions for Doctors Wyatt and Shaw?"

"Not at this time."

"We'll discuss our findings with Dr. and stop back and see you in the next day or so," Madison said.

"Thank you again for coming to see me."

The three physicians exited the room and walked down a short hallway until they reached the staff lounge. They stepped into the nicely appointed room and found seats at a table toward the back.

"What do you think?" Sturgess asked.

"I know this is only his third hospital day, but do you have any test results that point to a diagnosis?" Jack asked.

"So far, no. But some of our test results are still pending. Other than an abnormal chest x-ray and some mildly elevated blood inflammatory markers, we really don't have anything else to hang our hats on." In a flat, calm voice, he continued, "I haven't seen the IPS patients at Mothers and Infants, so I don't have a basis for comparison. Just how certain are you that he has IPS?"

"If he were a woman who'd just had a baby a month ago, I'd answer your question with an unqualified one hundred percent," Madison said. "It still may be too early, but I didn't notice any signs of a swollen tongue or any other significant neurologic finding."

"How would you like to handle this moving forward?" Sturgess asked.

"The Florida Department of Health is already involved. Since you're the attending physician, it may be a good idea for you to notify them," Jack said.

"I'll take care of that first thing in the morning."

"I assume, other than Mr. Kahn, there are no patients in the hospital with similar symptoms."

"Not to my knowledge."

"For now, I'm not sure where all this leaves us, but let's keep the lines of communication open," Madison suggested.

"I agree," Sturgess said as they came to their feet and walked out into the hall. "Thank you again for agreeing to consult."

"Of course."

As they headed back in the direction of the elevator bank, an alluring woman with light-toned brown skin wearing a pink chiffon saree approached. Sturgess smiled and took a few steps forward to greet her.

Chapter 41

"Mrs. Kahn, this is Dr. Shaw and Dr. Wyatt. They're the physicians I spoke to you about earlier who agreed to consult on Abul's case."

"It's a pleasure to meet you both," Nadia said, shaking each of their hands. "Dr. Sturgess mentioned to me that my husband's condition is quite similar to the women who are being treated at Mothers and Infants. Are you aware of any cases of IPS that have affected men, or is Abul the first?"

"If we confirm that your husband has the illness, to our knowledge, he'd be the first," Madison answered.

"Which I assume would only complicate matters more regarding making an accurate diagnosis," she said, her perceptive eyes fixed on Madison. "Is that correct?"

"Possibly. On the other hand, it might provide a clue that would bring us to the diagnosis sooner. It's very hard to say."

"What should my expectations be, Doctors?"

Jack said, "We can't provide you with any more information than Dr. Sturgess has already shared with you. In the hours and days to come, we'll be watching Abul's condition very closely for any clues that might reveal the cause of his illness. Hopefully, from there we can find an effective way to treat it."

"I watched yesterday's news conference from Mothers and Infants. It seems as if the women are getting worse and that no treatment plan has been identified. Can I expect the same regarding Abul?" she asked, her words suddenly becoming choked with fear. Madison had just met her, but she was already impressed by her agile mind and not surprised she was beginning to display some emotion. "We have some ideas regarding a treatment, but I'm afraid the information released in the news conference is accurate."

"I was afraid you might say that."

"Would you mind if we asked you a few questions?" Madison inquired.

"Of course, Dr. Shaw. I'd be happy to answer any question that I'm able to."

"Is there anything about your husband's recent activities that has been in any way different from his normal routine?"

"No. He works six days a week on a roofing crew, and I can't say he's changed any of his basic personal or work habits of late."

"His medical record says he takes no medications. Is that true?"

"It is, Dr. Shaw."

"What about over-the-counter vitamins, herbals, or other supplements of that nature?"

Shaking her head slowly, she responded, "None that I'm aware of."

"Has Abul done any traveling recently?"

"We traveled back to Bangladesh with our children about three months ago for a couple of weeks."

"Did anybody get sick while you were there or since you've been back?"

"No. It was a wonderful trip…no problems at all."

"Does your husband have any unusual dietary habits?"

She smiled. "We've clung to some of our traditional Bangladeshi foods, but our entire family has become surprisingly Americanized with respect to our diet—probably more than we'd like to admit."

"Does your husband consume any alcohol?"

"He'll enjoy a very occasional toddy, but other than that, he doesn't drink any alcoholic beverages."

"I assume that nobody else in your family or any of his acquaintances are ill with similar symptoms."

"None that I'm aware of."

"Is there anything at all you can think of that could have possibly made him ill?"

"I've been asking myself that same question for three days, Dr. Shaw. And my honest answer is that I simply cannot. I wish I could recall something…anything that might help him."

"I think that's all the questions we have for now, Ms. Kahn. If anything should come to mind that you feel might help us, please let Dr. Sturgess know at once."

"Of course," she said with downcast eyes. "If you should wish to speak with me again, please call me."

"We will," Madison said.

"I'm going to walk Doctors Wyatt and Shaw to the elevators, Nadia. I'll be right back to give you an update on Abul's condition."

"Thank you, Dr. Sturgess." She turned to Jack and Madison. "I'm a very spiritual person, Doctors. I appreciate everything you're doing, but I'm going to rely very heavily on my God to get my beloved Abul through this." She paused momentarily to collect herself. Struggling to get the words out, she finally added, "My husband's a good man. He deserves to live a long and happy life."

"Along with Dr. Sturgess, we're going to do everything in our power to help make that happen," Jack said. "We'll let him know when we'll be returning to see Abul, so he can let you know."

"Thank you."

"I'll be right back," Sturgess said as they made their way toward the door.

They spoke briefly as Jack and Madison waited for the elevator. All they could do was reassure Dr. Sturgess that they'd remain actively involved with Abul's case.

They rode the elevator to the lobby in silence. The moment they stepped off, Madison said, "You have that look on your face."

"Really? What look is that?"

"The one you get when your mind's madly chopping away but the wood chips aren't flying."

"As terrible a metaphor as that is, it pretty well sums up the way I feel."

"Do you think he has IPS?"

"I sure do," he answered. "What are your thoughts on the possibility?"

"I think so, but I'm probably not quite as positive as you are. I'll become more convinced if he continues to progress in the same manner our IPS patients have."

They crossed the lobby and exited the hospital. They had only taken a few steps toward the parking lot when Jack casually said, "The question is, how much does Abul Kahn's illness help us? With some luck, maybe it will turn out to be the undealt card we've been waiting for."

Chapter 42

OUTBREAK—DAY 12

Jack and Madison were up with the sun. They put on their sweatsuits and drove to Mullins Park with the plan of taking Moose for a power walk. They started out with the wind at their backs, watching the last vestiges of a vivid red-sky sunrise.

Jack finally felt the time was appropriate to broach the question that had been on his mind for the past couple of days. Most of his delay was related to his concern regarding what Madison's reaction to his inquiry would be.

"Is it today that you're supposed to check in with your hematologist?" he asked in a casual manner.

"I think we both know you're aware of the answer to that question."

"I was just making conversation."

"Sure, Jack. You have to stop worrying about me so much. I'm doing fine. Lea and I are going to talk at around noon." She handed the leash to him because Moose was pulling too hard.

"I mention it only because, as physicians, we tend to view our own health issues with less concern than most normal people."

"Can you name anybody we know who's been more attentive to his or her illness than I have?"

"Maybe not, but that doesn't change the fact that, as doctors, we allow ourselves to get lulled into a mindset that we're immortal."

"Where did you get that from?" Madison asked. "I've survived a life-threatening illness, and I hardly feel that I'm laid back about keeping an eye on things. For God's sake. Since the day Lea told me I was officially disease free, have you ever known me to miss a follow-up appointment with her?"

"Not that I can remember, off the top of my head. You're getting the wrong idea. I'm quite confident that you'll never have another day's problem with leukemia."

"If you pretend you're telling the truth, then I'll pretend I believe you. C'mon, Jack. We both know you're a card-carrying Nervous Nellie."

"Perhaps that's a conversation for another time. But since you answered my question and confirmed you'll be talking to Lea later, I'm happy to change the topic."

"I promise you, Jack. If I get a twinge of anything, you'll be the first to know. We've been over this ground. I won't keep anything from you." Before he could say anything in response, she said, "Since you offered to change the topic, and we're on family matters, what have you heard from Anise?"

"She's doing great. Her grades are superb, and she loves everything about Vanderbilt."

"Are you still planning on going to Nashville for a family weekend?"

"I certainly am. There's no way I'd miss that."

"What about Nicole? How's she doing?"

"She's been totally back to normal ever since she recovered from her bout with heavy metal poisoning."

"She's a nice person and a great mom to Anise. Most men aren't as lucky as you are to have such a pleasant ex-wife."

"We've had our moments, Madison."

It took them another thirty-five minutes to finish their walk.

During that time, they talked about a host of topics, all unrelated to Madison's health or IPS.

On arriving back at Jack's mom's house, they still had plenty of time to shower, get dressed, and share a light breakfast with Charlotte before leaving for the hospital. During the drive, their conversation was strictly confined to the IPS patients. They had met with Ely yesterday and briefed him on Madison's sodium citrate theory.

He expressed his opinion that the likelihood the medication was responsible for IPS was remote, but he felt the smart thing to do was file a report with the FDA and seek their input. From an internal standpoint, he decided making a referral to the hospital's Pharmacy and Therapeutics Committee was the best way to pursue the possibility of a medication irregularity. Ely felt strongly that, until they had meaningful evidence of a cause-and-effect relationship, there was no reason to discuss the possibility with the other physicians. Jack and Madison weren't totally in agreement with his decision, but they saw no reason to make an issue of it—at least not for now.

Once they entered the hospital's lobby, they went straight to the progressive care unit. They hadn't been there for more than a few minutes when they saw Zach coming toward them. Since his father had taken a step back from his clinical practice, he had become the designated member of their medical practice to keep the other physicians apprised of any new developments regarding the IPS patients. Seeing as Josef had been the original treating physician in each case of IPS, Zach was flattered that his partners had chosen him to represent the group.

Grateful for the vote of confidence, he'd soon discovered his role gave him the opportunity to keep the lines of communication open between his father and the hospital administration. It also allowed him to continue to voice his conviction to all concerned that Josef's treatment of the IPS patients exceeded the accepted standards of care and that his father was in no way responsible for the IPS outbreak.

"Good morning," Zach said. "Have you already made rounds?"

"Actually, we just got here," Jack responded. "Are you already done?"

"Since I haven't been sleeping too well lately, I got here pretty early. I saw all my patients plus my dad's. I also met with Teri for an update." His voice was understandably discouraged, and the look on his face betrayed deep disappointment.

"How's your dad doing?" Jack asked.

"He's lost a lot of his confidence that we'd quickly find the cause of IPS and figure out how to treat it. It was his hope that he'd be quickly vindicated of having done anything negligent. The stress on him has been significant, and I'm concerned he's started into an emotional tailspin because he feels powerless to do anything about the current crisis."

"I hope you can convince him not to wave the white flag just yet," Jack said. "Madison and I are basically strangers here, but everybody we speak to feels he's a talented obstetrician with a lot more to give. The other physicians hold you in high regard too. You're the one in the best position to keep them thinking positively."

"Don't confuse my venting with surrender. I have no intention of giving up until all these women are cured and back to their normal lives and my father's held blameless of any wrongdoing." Zach said nothing further as he tapped absently at his cleft chin.

"You mentioned you just finished rounds. What were your thoughts?" Madison asked.

"They're worse, and I'd say we're no closer to figuring out this disease than we were the day we admitted Emma Collymore. I could go over every vital sign, lab report, and x-ray with you, but I'm sure you have a pretty good idea that there's been no improvement in any of them. Ultimately, what may mark the end of things is rapid liver failure. Gastroenterology broached the topic of liver transplantation as a desperate heave, but the logistics of anything like that are mind boggling. To make matters worse," he went on, "I got a call from Ely, who informed me that the drop-off in new-patient appointments for obstetrical care is getting worse, and there have been many more requests from patients wanting to transfer their obstetrical and gyn care to other doctors and hospitals. All of this is largely due to the way the media is really beating up on us."

Before Jack or Madison could respond, Zach's phone rang.

"This is Dr. Church." For a few moments, he listened calmly. With a downward gaze and speaking in a monotone, he said, "Thank you for the call. I'll be right down." He replaced his cell phone in his pocket and blew out a short breath. "That was the ER. They've just started treatment on a young lady who has all the symptoms of IPS. I'm going to head down there and have a look."

"I know it's the last thing we wanted to hear, but I guess we shouldn't be shocked," Madison said. "When did she deliver?"

"She gave birth to her last child two years ago in Iowa."

"Does she live in the area?" Madison inquired with a wrinkled brow.

"She moved to South Florida six months ago," Zach answered.

"From what we know about the illness, there has to be something else going on," Jack said. "How sure is the ER that the patient has IPS?"

"From what they just told me, there's not much doubt about it."

Trying to sound as positive as she could, Madison said, "Well, we'll just have to figure out how she contracted the illness."

Zach pushed his hands into the pockets of his white coat. "That may not be as difficult as you think. It seems that she had a radio frequency ablation of uterine fibroids done right here about four weeks ago. Her recovery until two days ago was uneventful. I guess that makes number eleven, not counting the patient you're seeing in Dade County."

"Who did the procedure?" Jack asked, afraid that he might already know the answer.

Zach looked directly at him before lowering his head. "She was my dad's patient. I'd better go down to the emergency room and see her."

"Just when I was thinking that things couldn't get any worse, Madison said with a slow shake of her head."

"Maybe they haven't."

"What do you mean?"

"Our victims of IPS now include a man and a woman who isn't postpartum," he answered.

"And that doesn't complicate matters?"

"Well, it does and it doesn't."

"C'mon, Jack. What are you trying to say?"

"I'm worried that the harder we look for some medical factor that these patients share in common, the less likely it is that we're going to find one. So maybe it's time we began looking for a non-medical one."

Chapter 43

With his intent being to conduct a calm interview as opposed to an intense interrogation, Detective Paul Allensworth extended Ely Stanberry the courtesy of a phone call to arrange a time that he and Libby Rafferty could discuss the murder of Regina Leggett with him.

The first thing Ely did after the meeting was arranged was call his brother, an experienced prosecuting attorney in Milwaukee, who advised him to be cooperative and to respond to the detectives' questions truthfully, but in a way that avoided volunteering any additional information beyond the scope of the question. Ely appreciated his brother's guidance but wondered if following it was easier said than done.

It was one p.m. when Detectives Allensworth and Rafferty arrived at Ely's office. As soon as they identified themselves, his administrative assistant escorted them into the office, where Ely had already come out from behind his desk to greet them. After introductions and an exchange of a few customary niceties, Ely gestured toward his meeting table, and they all sat down.

On their way to the meeting, the detectives had decided that

Paul would conduct the interview. "Thank you for taking the time to speak with us," he said as they were settling into their chairs.

"Of course. How can I be of help?"

"As I mentioned on the phone, we're looking into the death of Regina Leggett. We've reason to suspect that she may have had critical information about the women you're treating for IPS that she was anxious to share with us."

"Would you mind telling me what prompted you to believe that?"

"The day Ms. Leggett was killed, she called our office to arrange a meeting to discuss the matter with us. Unfortunately, she was murdered before we had the opportunity to talk with her. Did she mention anything about her concerns?"

"Not a word."

"Is there anybody you can think of whom she might have reached out to with her concerns?"

Ely guarded his silence, slowly shaking his head in thought. "I'm sorry, Detective, I don't have the first idea if she had any concerns or who she might speak with if she did."

"It's our understanding that, as the birthing center's director of nursing, she was very much involved in the investigation into IPS."

"Yes. Regina and I both served on the root cause analysis committee."

"Can you share with us your impressions of how she felt the inquiry was going?"

"I'm not sure I fully understand your question, Detective. Perhaps if you could be a little more specific."

"We're trying to determine whether Ms. Leggett believed these women acquired IPS by anything other than natural causes."

"Natural causes?" Ely asked with a bit of a head tilt. "Let me be sure I understand you. Are you asking me if Regina or any of us suspect that IPS was intentionally inflicted?"

"That would be one possibility. Another might be a tragic medical error that nobody's aware of or wants to talk about."

"On an official level, I'm completely unaware of any such theories; on an unofficial one, I'm sure there's been the usual far-fetched hallway chatter that goes on in any hospital that's facing an enigmatic and highly publicized clinical problem."

"So you don't think it's likely that Regina either suspected or knew a hospital error had occurred that might have caused this terrible disease?"

"That's correct. I don't think it's likely."

"What makes you so sure, Doctor?"

"If what you're suggesting were the case, Regina would have reported it through normal channels. It's inevitable that patient errors occur in hospitals, but we don't run from them or cover them up. Our response is to do a root cause analysis on the incident and formulate strategies to ensure the problem won't happen again."

"I see."

"By the way, Detective, contacting the police is generally not the path we choose to report our findings."

"The same thing occurred to us, Doctor. That's why Detective Rafferty and I are sitting here talking with you." When Ely didn't respond, Paul changed directions. "Was Dr. Church present at these meetings?"

"Josef or Zach?"

"I'm asking about Dr. Josef Church," Paul said in a voice that revealed his hunch that Ely knew which Dr. Church he was asking about.

"Yes, he attended. He was a member of the committee."

"That must have been a little uncomfortable for him."

"I think that's a question you'd have to ask Dr. Church directly."

"How did the other committee members react to the attending physician for all these women being part of the committee trying to figure out how they came down with the same illness?"

"Again, I'm not in a position to speak for other members of the committee. I can tell you that Dr. Church submitted himself to extensive medical testing. It was the opinion of the doctors who conducted the evaluation that there was no evidence suggesting he was either directly or indirectly responsible for IPS. Unless new information to the contrary comes to our attention, we're considering the matter a coincidence."

"That would amount to quite a coincidence, Doctor, don't you think?

"Excuse me?"

"Well, we're talking about eleven women, all of whom had the same doctor, and all of whom became ill with the same mysterious disease. That's quite a coincidence—don't you think?"

"I'm a physician, not a statistician, Detective. I answered your question—the finding of the committee was that there was no credible evidence that Dr. Church caused or contributed to IPS."

"Assuming Dr. Church isn't the direct or a contributing cause of this illness, what are the other possibilities?"

"That's the unanswered question we've all been asking ourselves since the first woman with IPS was admitted."

"If it was something contagious, wouldn't you have been able to determine that by now?" Paul asked.

"Not necessarily."

"How well do you know Dr. Church?"

"We've worked closely together for many years," he answered, reminding himself of his brother's advice.

"Do you know if he's suffered from any significant psychological problems during that time?"

"None that I'm aware of, Detective," Ely said, with an annoyed wringing of his hands. "His record as a medical staff member at Mothers and Infants has been exemplary. If it weren't for Dr. Church, it's quite likely this hospital wouldn't exist."

"That's high praise. Has he ever faced any disciplinary actions?"

"Never," Ely answered with impunity, beginning to feel more annoyed at the detective's bluntness and interview style with each question. Ely considered himself a charitable man, but reminding himself that Allensworth was just doing his job wasn't working for him. "Detective Allensworth, Josef Church is a pillar of our medical staff. Beyond that, I'm sure you have access to the Florida Medical Board's records. I suggest you check with them."

Paul pushed a half smile to his face. "I already have. But sometimes delicate or embarrassing matters between colleagues and friends get handled unofficially and leave no paper trail."

"That may be the case where you work, Detective, but not here. Let me assure you again that Dr. Church is emblematic of what every physician should strive to achieve. He's incapable of deliberately harming anybody. Nobody in their right mind would entertain the possibility he'd be capable of the type of behavior you continue to allude to."

"It's my job, Dr. Stanberry, to entertain possibilities when everybody around me is assuring me those possibilities are absurd and not worthy of taking a look at," he explained. "Are your inquiries into the circumstances surrounding this illness concluded?"

"Our investigation is an ongoing process."

"We did some checking and discovered that Regina Leggett didn't call any of the state healthcare agencies—she only called us. We found that kind of unusual. Can you offer an opinion as to why she might have done that?"

"I don't have the first clue. But as I recall, Regina was murdered at home at night, which means she almost certainly called your office much earlier that day."

Paul's expression changed, reflecting his annoyance at Ely's not-so-tacit criticism of the sheriff's department's relaxed approach to setting up a meeting with her.

Ely said, "I'm getting the impression you're considering formally investigating Dr. Church."

"Detective Rafferty and I always do our best never to get ahead of ourselves."

"I see."

Allensworth continued to ask questions for the next fifteen minutes before polite parting words were exchanged.

"Thank you again," he said.

Ely shook their hands. "If there's any further information you might require, please feel free to call me."

As soon as they were out of his office, Ely sat down behind his desk. Ignoring the messages that had come in while he was talking to the detectives, he thought about his conversation with them. In the end, there was only one conclusion that made any sense to him. Detectives Allensworth and Rafferty's main focus was on trying to determine whether the IPS patients had been the victims of a cold-hearted crime or a negligent hospital mistake that was now the center of a conspiracy to cover it up.

Chapter 44

OUTBREAK—DAY 13

After two conversations with Dr. Jordan Sturgess during which he painted a rather bleak picture of Abul's condition, Jack and Madison decided to make another trip to Lakeside Hospital. Based on their lack of success at Mothers and Infants, their level of optimism wasn't very high that they'd be able to make a meaningful contribution to Abul's care.

The moment Jack and Madison entered his room and laid eyes on him, they noted a striking change in his appearance. His complexion was powdery, and his yellowed eyes were sucked in and hollow. There was hardly a speck of animation in his face, and the rash across his neck had gotten worse.

Jack couldn't remove his eyes from Abul's face. There was something unique in his appearance that he found reminiscent of an illness he'd seen before. It was a faint recollection that prompted him to spend a few extra moments drilling down on the dim memory. After a brief period of time passed and nothing specific came to his mind, Jack gave up and took a few steps closer to the bedside.

"How are you feeling, Abul?"

It took a few moments, but he slowly opened his eyes. "Not great, Doctor."

"Are you having any pain in your face or eyes?"

"No. I'm just very weak."

"Can you open your mouth for us a little?" Madison asked.

"I think so." As soon as he opened his mouth sufficiently, she noted the swelling of his tongue. Jack also took a look, confirming her finding of macroglossia. They both were well aware that the abnormality hadn't been present the first time they'd examined him.

After completing the examination, Jack said, "Why don't you try and get some sleep. We're just going to have a word with Dr. Sturgess."

"Thank you, Doctor," he said. His eyes closed almost before the words were out of his mouth.

"What are your thoughts?" Sturgess asked them.

"The continued downward spiral of his condition is the same as we're seeing at Mothers and Infants," Madison said.

"What concerns me the most is Abul's worsening liver function and his decreased level of consciousness," Sturgess said.

"Which is also exactly what we're seeing with our patients," Jack stated.

"Have you come across any clues or ideas regarding a possible cause?"

"Nothing that has created a consensus of opinion. Although, there's a feeling among several of the physicians that IPS is being caused by some obscure autoimmune phenomenon," Jack answered.

Sturgess stood there looking more than a little discouraged. "Since autoimmune responses can be caused by anything from foods to stress to strange drug reactions, I don't envy you trying to pinpoint the specific trigger. I'm probably not in the best position to say this, but for Abul and the other IPS patients, it looks like the luxury of time is not something they have."

Before either Jack or Madison could respond, Nadia Kahn came through the door.

"Good afternoon," Sturgess said. "Doctors Wyatt and Shaw have just finished their examination of Abul."

"Thank you for coming to see my husband again. How's he doing?"

Madison smiled sadly. "I wish we had better news for you, Ms. Kahn, but Dr. Wyatt and I both feel his condition has worsened."

"Are you convinced that he's suffering from the same illness that the women at Mothers and Infants are?"

"Yes, we are," she answered.

Despair creeped into Nadia's voice. "I don't mean to sound like the voice of doom, but do you feel there's any possibility that a treatment may become available?"

"We continue to explore various possibilities, but so far, I'm sorry to say that everything's still theoretical at best." Madison continued, "Since the last time we spoke, has anything else occurred to you regarding Abul's health or lifestyle over the past few months?" She was doubtful her question would provide any new information.

"I wish I could say there was. As I mentioned to you, Abul is a simple man. He puts in long days, sometimes working on the weekends. Whatever leisure time he has, he spends with our children, gardening, or watching British football."

Since it had been in the front of her mind since Nadia mentioned it, Madison decided to dive deeper into the family's trip abroad.

"You mentioned you traveled to Bangladesh a few months ago."

"We went with our daughters to attend a wedding and to visit our family."

"Did you travel to any other countries?"

"No. We stayed in Bangladesh."

"Have you or Abul done any additional traveling since your return?"

"No."

Madison considered not overwhelming Nadia by repeating questions she'd already asked her, but she decided it was worth the risk, just in case it sparked something in her memory that she'd overlooked the first time they spoke.

"I'm sure I asked you this, but your husband's not a drinker or a smoker?"

"Abul doesn't have any vices, Dr. Shaw. He smoked cigarettes when he was a teenager, but only for a couple of years. He's not a drinker, except for his occasional weakness for a toddy."

"So other than whiskey, he consumes no alcohol."

"I doubt my husband has ever tasted whiskey, Dr. Shaw."

"But you mentioned he enjoys a toddy from time to time. As I recall, a toddy's made from whiskey, lemon, and honey."

"I'm sure you're right about a traditional American toddy, but the ones we enjoy in Bangladesh are made from the fermented sap of date palm trees."

"Date palm trees?"

"Yes. And the freshly harvested unfermented sap is also a popular drink across most of Southern Asia."

They continued speaking for a brief period of time, the three physicians answering the few additional questions Nadia posed to them. Madison and Jack reiterated their pledge to continue working diligently on Abul's case and to stay in close touch with Dr. Sturgess.

"We've just spoken with your wife," he said. "We'll stop back tomorrow."

They started toward the door, but Jack glanced back at Abul and decided to return to the bedside. He was awake, and he noticed his gaze was fixed straight ahead, a finding he hadn't previously observed. After a few moments, Abul began struggling to shift his gaze in a horizontal direction to make eye contact with Jack. Finally, he managed to turn his head a couple of inches, which allowed him to look more directly at him. There was no question in Jack's mind—Abul's gaze was dramatically uncoordinated.

Stepping away from the bedside, he walked to the other side of the room.

"Abul clearly has a gaze palsy," he told Madison and Sturgess.

"Are you sure? I didn't notice it," Madison said with a sudden intensity in her voice.

"It's not the most obvious one I've ever seen, but I'm pretty sure. Take a look and tell me what you think."

Madison stepped away, crossed the room, and began studying Abul's gaze and head movement.

"I'm a little rusty on my unusual neurological findings," Sturgess said to Jack. "I've heard the term, but I don't remember too much about it."

"It's the inability to move both eyes in the same direction in a coordinated manner," he explained. "It can be in either a horizontal or vertical direction. Instead of tracking a person or an object with their eyes, an affected patient turns their head."

"What causes it?"

"The most common causes are brain tumors, strokes, and certain serious neurologic diseases. Less common causes include trauma and infection."

Madison rejoined them. "What do you think?" he asked her.

"I agree."

Their conversation was brought to a halt when Nadia joined them. Seeing that she was struggling to put on her bravest face, Madison placed an arm around her shoulders.

Nadia listened in silence as Jack made her aware of Abul's gaze palsy and what it might mean. When he was finished, she asked no questions.

"I pray you and the other doctors will find a way to help my husband. If... if anything should happen to him, our family will be lost forever."

"Dr. Wyatt and I have faced a lot of perplexing cases in our careers, and we're not ones to give up easily. As I promised you the day we met, we'll do everything in our power to help Abul recover."

Nadia's eyes swelled with tears. "Thank you, Doctor," she managed to say. "I'm very grateful to you and Dr. Wyatt."

Madison appreciated Nadia's kind comment, but she was left feeling unconvinced that any words of hers had done much to allay Nadia's fear of what the future portended for her beloved husband.

Chapter 45

It was after six, and Madison and Jack decided to head home. They exited the hospital and made their way to the visitor's parking lot without discussing any of the details of their visit with Nadia and Abul Kahn.

"I have to tell you something," Madison said.

"Go ahead," he said, noting the rising intensity in her voice.

"You know how you're always talking about that undealt card and unexpected key clue when we're trying to nail down an elusive diagnosis?"

"I do."

"What do you think the significance of the gaze palsy is?"

"I'm not sure, but it's probably the result of the same problem that's causing the Bell's palsy in our other patients. My best guess would be some type of neurologic inflammation."

"I have an undealt card theory I'd like to bounce off you."

"Sure thing," he said. "Go ahead."

"When I was a third-year med student, I rotated on the infectious diseases service. I had to present a rather complex patient for grand rounds. I'd never done it before, and I was so nervous and over-prepared that the patient and the illness left an indelible memory in my mind. The patient was a middle-aged man who lived in a rural area of Malaysia. He was in the United States visiting his family when he became ill. His symptoms were on the baffling side, to say the least, but what I remember most clearly about him was his general gray appearance and his unmistakable gaze palsy. It wasn't until after you mentioned it and I went back and looked at Abul again that the lightbulb came on and reminded me of the case. I don't know why I didn't connect the dots sooner, but I remember the appearance of his face and his gaze palsy vividly. I've never seen anything like it since—until today." Madison paused and looked over at Jack.

"Don't stop now," he told her.

"I remember distinctly that the patient had had a fondness for drinking the fresh sap of date palm trees. For at least a year prior to coming to the United States, he was consuming it with regularity."

"Was the ID team able to establish a diagnosis?"

"The practice of drinking date palm sap has been linked to viral infections. We couldn't prove it beyond a shadow of a doubt, but since that time, the laboratory tests available for confirming viral infections have become much more specific and sophisticated." Pausing for a few moments, she added, "The Nipah virus is now considered the pathogen responsible for severe outbreaks in individuals who drink fresh sap from the date palm tree. At the time I was a medical student, Nipah was a relatively new diagnosis. Not very much was known about it."

"And now?"

"The virus was first isolated from a group of patients in Malaysia in 1990. Since then, several outbreaks have occurred in South Asia and Africa. One of the more notable ones took place in Bangladesh in 1993. In general, the reported mortality rate can be anywhere from forty to a hundred percent, and to this day, there's still no effective treatment."

"Do you recall when effective testing for Nipah became available?"

"I'd say not until around 1999 to 2000, and the test was only sensitive to certain strains."

"Do the victims of Nipah virus generally develop a Bell's palsy?"

"I only found one case report of the association, but Nipah can cause a number of different neurologic abnormalities," Madison answered. "I don't know if anybody's ever reported a patient with Nipah who developed auditory hyperacusis, but as we discussed, hyperacusis has been linked to other viral infections."

"I'm vaguely familiar with Nipah infections. From what I remember, our IPS patients' symptoms are somewhat different."

"I agree, but I don't think that, in itself, excludes the diagnosis. Nipah's a viral species with new strains being discovered all the time. The spectrum of symptoms can be quite varied, not only from strain to strain but from patient to patient."

He asked in a flat, calm voice. "How long does the virus survive in the sap?"

"A few days."

"Assuming Nipah's the cause of IPS, how do you explain the ten cases we have at Mothers and Infants, where it's highly improbable that these women attended the same party where fresh palm date sap was served. Do you see what I'm getting at? Your theory could be right for Abul, but beyond that, it's not much help."

"I don't think they transmitted it to each other. Nipah mainly causes infection by being ingested, which introduces all kinds of possibilities...including sodium citrate."

"None of this explains why every patient stricken with IPS was under Dr. Church's care."

"Maybe it does."

"Excuse me?"

"C'mon, Jack. You yourself suggested a possible mechanism a couple of times in the last few days." Just as Madison finished expressing that thought, they pulled into Charlotte's driveway.

"I think it might be a good idea to just enjoy dinner and not get into all of this with my mother. After we're done eating, we can spend a little time with Mom. As soon as she decides to call it a day, we can take Moose for a walk and pick up the conversation where we left off."

"I'm not sure that's the smart move. Your mom may have some

helpful ideas; she usually does. It sounds like you're trying to exclude her."

"In a way, I am. I'm not sure why, but my gut's telling me tonight's not the right time."

"Your call."

"As I mentioned, I don't remember much about Nipah infections, but what I do recall is that it's basically incurable," Jack said.

"I guess we're just going to have to see about that."

Chapter 46

"C'mon, Jack. Let's hear about it," Charlotte said as she was setting the salad course on the table.

"What do you mean, Mom?"

"You guys have been home for over an hour. The entire time, you've been out in the den behind the computer monitor. The way you're distracted now, and trying to make idle chitchat, I have to assume you have something major on your minds." She stopped to take the first bite of her chopped salad before continuing. "My first and only guess would be you've stumbled across some new information on IPS." She looked up at them. "If I wanted to have dinner with two Cheshire cats, I would've contacted Lewis Carroll."

Jack and Madison exchanged a surrendering nod.

"Okay, Mom. But since this is mostly Madison's brainchild, I'll let her tell you about it."

"That sounds fine, dear. We might as well eat while we're talking, so give me a moment

and I'll put the main course on the table." Charlotte excused herself, went out to the kitchen, and returned with the puff pastry–wrapped pork tenderloin she'd prepared. Setting it on the table, she said, "Okay, dear. You're up."

Madison took her time explaining to Charlotte what they'd learned when they'd visited Abul and the many questions the new information had raised. She provided her with a thorough review of the key factors known about the virus.

"How does the sap become infected with the virus?" Charlotte asked.

"It's a common custom for local inhabitants in the rural areas to harvest the sap by wedging out a piece of the tree trunk and then hanging a clay pot from a nail. The sap can either be consumed right away as a sweet nectar or as a fruit wine after it ferments."

"What about person-to-person transmission?" she asked.

"It's possible, but it's not as common as drinking contaminated sap. Outbreaks involving beef have also been reported."

"What's the mechanism that allows the virus to contaminate the sap?"

"Unfortunately, humans aren't the only species who find the sap appealing. Fruit bats regularly drink it as well, which leads to Nipah contamination via their saliva and urine. Because of the bats' unique immunologic system, they're unaffected by Nipah. They're the number one animal reservoir for disease-causing viruses known to modern medicine. The reason they're such an important research tool is because of their uncanny resistance to a multitude of severe viral infections."

Charlotte said, "Wouldn't it be a rather simple matter to cover the pots so the bats don't have access to them?"

"It would seem, and when the harvesting process involves individuals who are aware of the health risk, that's exactly what they do. Unfortunately, the vast majority of people who enjoy date palm sap are extremely provincial and unaware of the risks. Most of them either harvest it themselves or purchase it locally from equally uninformed suppliers. Legitimate companies are far more interested in selling the fermented fruit wine rather than bottling the pure sap."

"What's the incubation period?" Charlotte asked.

"Generally two to five weeks, but it can be much longer. The other interesting fact about these infections is that other animals, such as pigs, can infect humans. There've been many outbreaks reported from the ingestion of contaminated pork where the pigs were initially infected by bats."

"Tell me about the treatment options," Charlotte said.

"Several medications have been tried but, unfortunately, none have proven to be effective. The drugs that are currently available are basically still embryonic, and the best anybody can say is that a few have shown limited success."

"I would assume from what you're telling me that these fruit bats aren't indigenous to North America."

"There are fruit bats in some areas of South Florida, including the Keys, but none that have been shown to carry Nipah. What's interesting is that bats have an enormous ability to transmit viruses from one species to another."

"All of this makes for an interesting topic for grand rounds, but as you said, the bats are found exclusively in Asia and Africa, which is why that's where all the outbreaks have occurred. But for the sake of argument, let's say all your theories are true and that this patient in Dade County somehow contracted a Nipah infection with a particularly long incubation period while he was in Bangladesh. Even if that's what happened, it doesn't explain how our postpartum patients at Mothers and Infants contracted the illness."

Not anticipating that the topic of Nipah infections would come up at dinner, Jack and Madison hadn't discussed just how much information they would share with Charlotte when the time was appropriate. Jack felt that suggesting that the IPS patients had been the victims of an intentional act would not be a wise thing to do. He was certain from the look on her face that Madison agreed with him.

He said, "The other interesting thing worth mentioning is that the laws regulating the transportation of bats into the U.S. are very strict. Even so, there's only so much the authorities can do to prevent illegal shipments of live bats across U.S. borders. And as Madison mentioned, bats are very capable of transferring many strains of virus from one species to another."

"Where do you two go from here?" Charlotte asked.

"I think it would be helpful if we took a step back and looked at the big picture," Jack said. "Everything we've discussed may or may not be true, and I'm not suggesting it's unworthy of consideration, but as a diagnosis for IPS, it's still pretty far-fetched."

"Far-fetched or not, any rational scientist who just listened to your account of things would tell you that dismissing out of hand the possibility that IPS is caused by a Nipah virus would not only be counter-intellectual but also quite dumb."

"Thanks, Mom."

"So what will you do next?" she asked him.

"I'd say the most important thing is to confirm or rule out that the IPS patients are suffering from a Nipah-related infection. Once we've done that, we can tackle the problem of our limited treatment options."

"I couldn't agree more," Madison said.

A voilà smile came to rest on Charlotte's face at Jack and Madison's agreement.

"What are the diagnostic tests available for proving whether Nipah's the culprit?" she asked them.

"Nipah assays aren't routinely included in the currently available, basic viral panels that we ran on Abul and our IPS patients. However, PCR and ELISA blood tests are available by special request that will reliably detect Nipah. We came across four labs while we were researching Nipah infections earlier. We can easily choose one and send off blood and spinal fluid samples to see if we're dealing with a Nipah infection."

"Would that be a hundred percent definitive one way or the other?" Charlotte asked.

"I'm afraid not. There are strains of Nipah and novel viruses that even the most modern and sophisticated tests won't pick up," Madison said. "We'll just have to accept the small possibility that the test results could come back negative, even in the face of an active Nipah infection."

A thoughtful look crossed Jack's face. "I think we should remember that the current situation's a little prickly, so it might be a good idea to proceed cautiously."

"Was that code for treading lightly for political reasons?"

Madison asked him. "Because if it was, there's a simple enough solution that will guarantee we won't bruise any of our colleague's egos. In order to avoid offending Dr. Whiteacre or anybody else at Mothers and Infants, why don't we bring Dr. up to date and ask him to order the Nipah studies on Abul?"

Charlotte played devil's advocate. "Suppose the PCR and ELISA assays both come back negative, but you're still not ready to dismiss the possibility that you're dealing with a never-before-seen virus. Then what?"

"In that case, I guess we're just going to have to convince our colleagues at Mothers and Infants that it's essential we send off the same tests on the IPS patients as we did on Abul," Jack said. "But, to start with, I still feel we're better off avoiding that dicey situation, and the only way I can see that happening is if Abul's tests are positive for Nipah."

Madison chuckled. "That sounds like one of your *we'll jump off that bridge if and when we get to it* philosophies."

"My experience is that it works every time."

"Sounds like you two have hatched a hell of a plan," Charlotte said. "With that out of the way, let's eat the brownies I baked for dessert."

Chapter 47

OUTBREAK—DAY 14

When Kiara walked through the door to Kim's office, she spotted her sister-in-law sitting at her desk with a mug of coffee in one hand and her cell phone in the other.

"Hey."

"Hi, Kiara. I didn't expect to see you until dinner on Sunday."

"I have an interview in a few minutes, and I thought I'd stop in and say hi to my favorite sister-in-law."

"Good. You'll save me a call."

"About what?"

"I heard something that I wanted to share with you." Even though they were the only ones in the office, Kim glanced in the direction of the door. "There's a rumor in the hospital that there's another case of IPS."

"When did the patient come in?"

"That's just it. The patient's been hospitalized at Lakeside."

"Did she give birth here?"

"The patient didn't give birth at all."

"Excuse me?"

"Evidently, she's a he. And yes, you heard me correctly. The patient's a man. Supposedly, he's in his early forties and is pretty sick."

"Why do they think he has IPS?"

"Because his symptoms and everything else are identical to our patients here."

"Do you know anything else about him?"

"Only that he's from Bangladesh."

"Could all of this just be hospital gossip? I mean, where's it coming from?"

"What I heard was that the patient's doctor is married to one of our nurses. And don't bother asking me for the patient's or the doctor's name, because I don't have the first clue," Kim told her in no uncertain terms.

"You may not know now, but I'm sure somebody as crafty and connected as you are could find out."

"I hope you're kidding."

"Do I sound like I'm kidding?"

"Have you ever heard of HIPAA?" Kim asked. "They frown on the practice of obtaining or disclosing unauthorized and confidential patient information."

"If I didn't bend a rule from time to time, I'd never sell a story."

"That might work for you, Kiara. But in this particular case, you're not the one doing the bending, I am. Plus, this isn't bending a rule, it's fracturing it. If I get caught illegally helping myself to sensitive medical information, I could wind up spending some time in a gated community, if you know what I mean."

Kiara took a couple of steps closer and sat down on the corner of the desk.

"If people already know about this patient way up here at Mothers and Infants, how much of a secret can it be? I'm not asking for copies of anybody's medical records. All I want is a name, which I highly suspect is already out there. I'm not talking about breaking into Fort Knox here."

"I don't know," Kim responded, her voice fading in conviction.

"C'mon, Kim. You're the one who lit the fuse on this story. I'm just trying to shorten it. There's a chance that what I discover could help the cops nail Regina's killer."

After an inward groan, Kim said, "Okay. I know some folks here and at Lakeside—no promises, but I'll see what I can do. But before you ruin my life, let me verify that the rumor's true and this new mysterious patient really exists."

"Great idea," she said, quickly kissing Kim on each cheek. "I have to get going." She jumped off the corner of the desk and headed for the door. "Say hi to that brother of mine."

"No can do. I'm not speaking to him."

"I'm kind of in a hurry now, but when you call me later with the name of the Lakeside patient, I'd love to hear what he's done this time to deserve the silent treatment."

"It was his crowning achievement of rudeness."

Kiara couldn't contain a chuckle. As she reached for the handle, she glanced over her shoulder.

"You know you're the love of his life. Why, he couldn't get from one day to the next without you."

"What's your point?" Kim asked with crossed arms.

"My point is, that no matter how much you deny it, you adore him just as much as he adores you. And irrespective of what harebrained thing he did this time, you're going to let him off the hook. I'm simply suggesting you do it before Sunday, so we can have a pleasant evening."

"Okay," Kim said with a wag of her finger. "But until then, it's the West Point silence. I want to enjoy this for another couple of days before I cave in."

"Sound thinking and very mature, all in the same breath," Kiara said in a voice overflowing with sarcasm.

Chapter 48

OUTBREAK–DAY 15

After a long morning of making rounds on the IPS patients, Jack and Madison decided to take a break and grab a quick lunch in the doctors' dining room. Despite what they'd hoped to see on rounds, none of the patients were showing any signs of improvement.

The first thing they'd done when they'd arrived at the hospital that morning was call Jordan Sturgess to see if he'd heard anything about the special Nipah tests he'd ordered on Abul. He told them he'd already been in touch with the lab, and they anticipated having the test results by mid-afternoon.

Jack and Madison had discussed when might be the best time to inform Ely of their suspicion that IPS was caused by a Nipah virus and that they had asked Jordan Sturgess to send off blood and spinal fluid specimens to confirm the diagnosis. They'd finally decided to bring Ely into their confidence the moment they heard anything from Dr Sturgess. Until then, anything they were aware of or suspected was to remain a tightly guarded secret.

"What time are we supposed to meet with Ely for our daily

patient-update conference?" Madison asked, as they made their way toward exit.

"He texted me about half an hour ago confirming two o'clock."

"Is there anything else on his mind, other than getting an update on the IPS patients?"

"Not that I'm aware of."

"Ely strikes me as a little on the chatty side."

"Which is a topic you know something about," Jack teased.

"Watch it, buddy," she said with a smile and a cautionary finger wag.

Before Jack could respond to her jab, his phone rang. It was Sturgess "Good morning. I'm standing here with Madison. We're both hoping you have information to share with us."

"I just got off the phone with Dr. Douglas Jones. He's the director of the virology lab in Philadelphia. Unfortunately, he can't give us a definitive answer if the samples we sent him are positive for Nipah."

"Were all the tests inconclusive?" Jack asked with disappointment. "Of all the possible answers, that's the one we least wanted to hear. Did he give you any details of why the tests weren't conclusive?"

"No, but they ran both the PCR and ELISA twice with the same result. Dr. Jones told me the lab ran a few additional tests that were more sophisticated, and while they were highly suggestive of a viral infection, they weren't specific for Nipah."

"It's still helpful information," Madison said. "At least we have a high probability of knowing in general terms what's wrong with the IPS patients."

"Dr. Jones wanted us to know that over the past few years they've seen a steady increase in new viral strains of Nipah. He cautioned us against dismissing the possibility of a Nipah infection based solely on the results of the tests his lab ran. So where do we go from here?"

"I was just asking myself that same question," Jack said. "Madison and I will give you a call later today, after we've had a chance to digest all this and figure out what to do next."

"Thank you both. And I hope you'll take this in the spirit it's intended, but we're running out of time. Abul's liver function is getting worse. His bilirubin is going up more rapidly, and his level of confusion from the buildup of ammonia in his blood is increasing. He can't be too far away from a major hepatic crisis."

"We understand. We'll get back to you later today," Jack said. He ended the call and looked directly at Madison. "I can't remember a time when we were so unsuccessful in trying to figure out a disease."

"We can't be thinking about things like that right now, Jack."

"I know." He straightened his shoulders. "The timing isn't great but we agreed that as soon as we got the lab results, we'd bring Ely up to speed. We're due to meet with him shortly. Let's hope we catch him in the right mood, and he agrees it's time to speak with the other physicians."

"What about Dr. Whiteacre?" she asked. "He'll be a madman about all this."

"Let's let Ely worry about him. We have patients to take care of."

Chapter 49

Ely welcomed Jack and Madison into his office and escorted them to the leather guest chairs that faced his desk. For the next half hour, they went over each of the IPS patients with him. As he listened, his face remained bathed in concern. They then took a few extra minutes to advise him of their suspicion that IPS was very likely a viral illness.

"I'm not surprised by anything you've just shared with me, although I was hoping for better news. This couldn't have come at a worse time. Morale among the nurses and staff is at an all-time low." He cleared his throat and took a swallow of ice water. "Since it's pretty obvious our backs are up against the wall, we have to come up with an action plan immediately. Is there any chance this Wistar Institute could be wrong?"

"I don't think so," Jack told him.

For the next hour, the three of them went over every aspect of the disease and what they'd learned since the first IPS patient was admitted.

"Before I put my two cents in, what do you and Madison think is the smartest thing to do?"

Madison said, "Jack and I think it's essential to locate an ace virologist and a highly sophisticated research laboratory that specializes in identifying never-before-seen viruses."

"Kind of the top gun of viral research?" Ely asked.

"In a manner of speaking, yes. There are several we can choose from."

Massaging the bridge of his nose, Ely asked, "Are you limited to institutions in the United States?"

Jack suspected his question wasn't a random one. "I don't see why we should be limited by geography."

"I'd like to do this without having our efforts splashed across the media. I think I know a way we can pursue your complex novel virus theory both expertly and discreetly." His face relaxed and a genuine smile appeared.

"Who or what facility do you have in mind?" Madison asked.

"I did my pathology training with Dr. Archibald Dankworth. Our time together led to a solid friendship that's endured for many years. Archie was an academic prodigy who achieved triple-board status in internal medicine, pathology, and infectious diseases. After he completed his training, he was highly recruited by a dozen or so major research centers from around the world. Having been raised in England, he decided to return to Britain and took a position at the highly respected Pirbright Institute, where he established himself as a gifted virus researcher at their Plowright Building. He's now the director and continues his work on new viral diseases that spread from animals to humans. His achievements have been lauded on a global scale." Ely paused long enough to flash them a satisfied grin. "Does Archie sound like the type of ace we might be interested in talking to?"

"He sounds perfect," Madison said with no reluctance.

"So let's do this," Ely suggested. "I'll give him a call immediately and share our problem with him. As soon as I have his thoughts and recommendations, I'll give you two a call."

"That sounds great," Jack said.

Ely came to his feet. When Jack and Madison didn't follow suit, he slowly sat back down. "Why am I getting the feeling there's something else?"

"Dr. Whiteacre has made it abundantly clear he doesn't believe IPS is a viral infection. We've already gotten off to a rocky start with him, and we'd like to avoid upsetting him any further," Jack said.

"Which will absolutely occur the moment he finds out we've gotten Dr. Dankworth and the Pirbright Institute involved."

"That's what I'm worried about," Jack said.

"And you and Madison would like me to foam the runway for you," Ely stated. "Herb's a bit of a stubborn old curmudgeon, but we've known each other a long time, and I suspect if we handle him with kid gloves, we'll be okay."

"If we get a reasonable amount of positive input from Dr. Dankworth, it'll give Madison and me considerably more credibility when we take the matter to the other physicians," Jack said.

Ely again came to his feet. This time Jack and Madison followed.

"It could also have the opposite effect, Jack. If Archie's assessment isn't an encouraging one, I'm afraid the path ahead could be a very slippery slope. Without an expert's blessing, nobody's going to be interested in following your recommendations." He tapped his bottom lip a couple of times. "If we can't get the medical staff's approval, you two will almost certainly be forced to abandon the notion that these women are suffering from a viral infection of any type."

Chapter 50

After their meeting with Ely, Jack and Madison spent the remainder of the afternoon rechecking a number of the sicker patients and meeting with Teri to go over the IPS patients from a nursing perspective. The meeting lasted about half an hour. There were no revelations or plans to make any major care plan changes. Afterward, before heading home, they decided to take a couple of brisk turns around the hospital's covered footpath. The weather had substantially improved from earlier, when a stubborn Scottish mist had produced a damp chill in the air.

They were about halfway around their first lap when Madison's cell phone rang.

"Good afternoon, Ely," she said. "Yes, Jack and I are still here. We decided to take a walk before leaving for the day." As she listened, Madison slowed their pace by placing a hand on Jack's shoulder. "Of course. We'll meet you at the beginning of the walking path in fifteen minutes."

"What's going on?"

"Ely spoke with Dr. Dankworth. He's on his way here. I've got a feeling we're about to get some bad news."

"Let's hope that's not the case," Jack said.

They resumed a more energetic pace. When they made the final turn, they caught sight of Ely standing at the head of the path. He casually waved at them.

"Thanks for meeting me." He pointed at a nearby wooden bench, and the three of them sat down.

"Archie called me a few minutes ago. After I briefed him on our problem, he told me his lab would be happy to help in any way they could. He said they're currently doing quite a bit of investigative work on innovative techniques for identifying and classifying novel viruses."

"That's great news," Jack said.

"What kind of innovative techniques?" asked Madison.

"For one thing, they've moved away from electron microscope work and are focusing on developing unique new culture media to grow the latest strains of viruses. They're also using some groundbreaking genetic techniques."

"How would he like us to proceed?" Jack asked.

"He wants us to send him some samples. He provided me with clear instructions on the types of specimens he wants and how to send them. I've already done some checking. If we draw the blood and spinal samples in the next couple of hours, we can arrange for them to be on a flight to London tonight. As soon as Archie gets confirmation that they're on their way, he'll arrange for a courier service to meet the flight and transport them to his lab."

"That's really something," Jack said. "Did he give you any idea when we might get some results?"

"He was purposely a little vague on that topic, and I didn't push him. But I got the impression it could be as soon as the next couple of days. Regarding the other physicians, I see no reason to conceal what we're doing. On the other hand, I don't think we need to arrange an urgent meeting to announce things."

"Perhaps we should agree upon an explanation if any of the physicians or nurses ask us if we know anything about sending blood samples to Europe?"

"The simple answer to that is, make me the bad guy. I'll use my relationship with Archie to explain why the specimens are being sent. I'll emphasize that I have confidence in the labs we're using, but because of my relationship with Dr. Dankworth and his relationship with a world-class resource like the Plowright House, we'd be foolish not to verify our lab's findings," Ely proposed. "Before you ask about Herb Whiteacre, I'll do my best to handle him. I'm cautiously optimistic I'll be able to keep him from blowing his stack."

"And in the event he corners Jack, me, or the both of us?"

"If Herb wishes to speak with you, be honest and treat him with the same degree of respect and professionalism we'd extend any colleague."

"Sounds like we have a plan," Jack said.

As they made their way back to the hospital, Ely said in a guarded voice, "As long as we're on the topic of IPS, I'd like to talk with you about Josef Church."

Chapter 51

OUTBREAK—DAY 16

Dr. Amy Lukes was a skilled gastroenterologist with a particular interest in liver diseases that affected pregnant women. Ely had personally recruited her five years earlier to a full-time position at Mothers and Infants.

The first IPS patient she was asked to consult on was Emma. Since that time, she'd been involved in the care of every woman suffering from the disease. Based on what she'd observed for the past three days, she'd placed a call to her transplant colleagues in Miami to brief them on the situation at Mothers and Infants and broach the topic of emergency liver transplantation. Her first objective was to get their thoughts on IPS, and the second was to advise them of her concern that several, if not all, of the patients might require an emergency liver transplant.

On this particular morning, she was called urgently to see Nell Thacker. She responded immediately and spent considerable time reviewing her chart and doing an extended physical examination. In a relatively short period of time, Nell's bilirubin level had soared to seventeen, and it was becoming more difficult for her to produce the proteins her body needed to clot her blood and prevent hemorrhage.

Amy was in the middle of her examination when Dr. David Phillips entered the room.

"Good morning."

"Hi, David."

"I just heard. Are things as bad as I think?"

"Probably worse."

As they spoke, two nurses were giving it their all, trying to implement all the measures Amy had ordered to help support and stabilize Nell's vital functions.

"Nell's really taken a turn for the worse over the past twenty-four hours. She's acidotic, and her encephalopathy has gotten much worse. Her Meld score for liver failure is now thirty-six. To give you an idea how serious that is, the highest severity score is forty. I don't think there's a hepatologist in the country who wouldn't consider her to be in fulminant liver failure. The Organ Procurement and Transplantation Network would designate her status as 1A, which puts her at the top of the transplant priority list."

"What does all this mean in practical terms?"

"It means that I've placed a call to the transplant department at the university and requested Nell be transferred to their transplant unit ASAP for evaluation to undergo an emergency liver transplant. Without one, I wouldn't expect her to survive more than five days."

"It's your call, Amy. What can we do to help?" he asked.

"Anything and everything that will expedite her transfer. Hopefully, they'll be able to locate a liver for her within the next twenty-four hours."

"I'll make a call to the university as well. I've sent them several transplant patients over the years. I can't say it will help, but it can't hurt. What are Nell's chances?" he asked.

"Well, if they can find a donor within the next day or two, she's got a reasonable chance of having a successful transplant."

David looked at her through searching eyes. "I'm getting the feeling there's something you're not saying."

"If the liver transplant team at the university feels her underlying disease is incurable, they'll probably turn her down."

"That's an uncertainty at this point," David said. "I'm not sure there's any way we can get around that."

"If you convince them we've found a treatment that has a reasonable likelihood of leading to a cure, they might agree to a transplant, viewing it as a possible lifesaving bridge to therapy."

David checked his watch. "We have a rather important meeting on treatment options in about thirty minutes. Hopefully, I'll know more then. If you can spare the time, you may want to sit in."

"I'll try to make it. I'm going to stay here with Nell for a while to review all the new meds she's getting and other things we're doing. If I can't make it to the meeting, give me a call and brief me on what was decided."

"Will do," he promised, as he turned and headed for the door.

Chapter 52

OUTBREAK – DAY 17

At a few minutes before three, Kiara entered Lakeside Hospital's lobby. Kim had called her earlier that morning to inform her she had experienced considerably less trouble finding out about the mysterious patient at Lakeside Hospital than she'd anticipated. As it turned out, she had no difficulty confirming he existed, and she'd also managed to discover his full name and that of his attending physician.

After taking a look around, Kiara made herself comfortable on an upholstered couch that she'd chosen for its excellent view of the elevators. As it turned out, Jack's and Madison's visits to see Abul hadn't gone unnoticed by many of the staff members, which had eliminated any possibility of keeping his hospitalization a tightly guarded secret. Kim had even managed to find out Nadia's general appearance and approximately what time every day she visited her husband.

Kiara's plan was to take her best shot at identifying Nadia, introduce herself, and hopefully convince her to discuss the circumstances surrounding her husband's illness. She knew it was more of a shot in the dark than a carefully conceived strategy, but her only price for failing would be Nadia's refusal to give her the time of day, so she'd decided to take a stab at it.

Twenty minutes later, a woman who fit Nadia's description stepped off the elevator. She crossed the lobby and exited the hospital with Kiara trailing behind at a safe distance. She continued to follow Nadia, using the time to decide upon the best way to strike up a nonthreatening conversation. After considering her options, she decided this was one of those times when the simplest way was probably also the best way.

Kiara only had to pick up her pace briefly before she caught up to Nadia. "Nadia?" she asked with the type of casual smile she hoped might make her wonder if they'd ever met.

Nadia stopped. "Good morning," she said, observing Kiara through hesitant eyes. "I'm sorry. Have we met?"

"My name's Kiara Das."

"Are you a member of the Bangladesh Association of Florida?"

Her inquiry gave Kiara an idea. "Actually, I'm Indian," she answered, speaking in fluent Bengali. "My entire family is from West Bengal. Many of them still live in Calcutta."

"Have you lived here your entire life?" Nadia answered in the same language.

"No. My parents came to the United States when I was fifteen." Pausing momentarily, she added, "I apologize for my unorthodox introduction, but I'm hoping to speak with you briefly about your husband."

"Abul? Are you a well-wisher?"

"Yes, but I'm also a freelance investigative reporter. I'm writing a story about the ten women who are currently hospitalized at Mothers and Infants suffering from a serious undiagnosable disease. I expect you've been following the story in the media?"

"I'm an educated woman, Ms. Das. IPS has attracted quite a bit of attention, both on TV and in the papers. I also suspect we wouldn't be here talking if you weren't already aware of my husband's possible diagnosis and why he's in the hospital."

"Please call me Kiara, and yes, I assumed you were well aware of the other IPS patients. In researching the story, I recently learned that Dr. Sturgess asked Doctors Wyatt and Shaw to consult on your husband's case. As I'm sure you know, they're also assisting in the care of the women with IPS. I've been told that your husband's symptoms and those of the IPS patients are very similar, which is giving the doctors cause to wonder if there might be a connection."

"Since you already seem to know quite a bit about my Abul's illness, I'm not sure I'd be of much help to you. More importantly, and as I'm sure you're aware, our shared culture is one of prudence and conservatism. We're provincial people who don't sensationalize our personal lives. Seeing our names splashed all over the newspapers or on TV is not something my husband or I would approve of."

A young mother pushing a twin stroller walked by, affording Kiara the few seconds she needed to gather her thoughts as to how to remain respectful in her response.

"The type of information I'm looking for would be basically non-medical in nature. I wouldn't violate your privacy or your husband's by printing your names without your permission. If you agree, I can approach this one question at a time. If you're comfortable answering that way, we can continue. If not, we'll skip that question and try a different one, or simply stop altogether. It's totally up to you."

"I get the feeling you could charm the birds out of the trees, Kiara. You strike me as a decent person, but even so, I'm still not sure how I feel about providing you with any information about my husband's situation."

"My concern is this, Nadia—the doctors are justifiably hyper-focused on the medical issues. I'm wondering if there's more to this illness than meets their eyes."

"I'm not sure I understand what you mean."

"Suffice it to say that my intuition and instincts are God-given gifts, and there's something about IPS that's setting off alarms in my head."

"Are you saying that, if you should come across information that you believe might be helpful to the doctors treating these cases, you'd make them aware of it?"

"That's precisely what I'm saying."

"Even if it had a negative impact on your story?"

"My desire to see all the victims recover from this terrible disease far exceeds any personal gains I might realize from writing this story."

"And you're pledging Abul's name and mine will never be disclosed."

"Only if you should change your mind and provide me with written authorization. I'll also put that in the form of a solemn promise."

Nadia replaced her key in her handbag. "Let's try it your way. Ask me a question, and I'll consider whether I have any qualms about answering it."

"Fair enough," Kiara said, removing a small orange notebook from her purse. "Just to confirm, am I correct in assuming Doctors Wyatt and Shaw are consulting on your husband's case at his physician's request?"

"Yes, they are."

"Have you spoken directly with them?"

"Yes, on more than one occasion."

"And they agreed that Abul and the women at Mothers and Infants are suffering from the same illness?"

"They said there was a very high likelihood of it."

"The media's reporting that the physicians at Mothers and Infants don't have any idea as to the cause of the illness. From speaking with Doctors Shaw, Wyatt, and Dr. Sturgess did you get that same impression?"

"Yes, I did."

"What I'd like to talk to you about are the circumstances surrounding Abul's illness. As I mentioned, I'm far more interested in the events leading up to him getting sick than the medical aspects of it. Can you tell me a little bit about your husband's work?"

"He's a roofer. It's the only job he's had since coming to the United States."

"Are you aware if any of his fellow roofers have become seriously ill recently?"

"None that I'm aware of. Many of them have reached out to Abul to wish him the best. He's quite popular at work and due to be promoted to be one of the foremen soon."

"Has Abul said anything to you that may have suggested it was something at work that made him sick?"

She thought for a few moments. "Nothing that I recall, but Abul has never been very talkative about his work. Once he gets home at the end of his day, his focus is on the family. The doctors have been very thorough. They've asked me many questions about our life in Bangladesh."

"Would you be able to help me contact his boss? I'd like to see if I can arrange to speak with one or two of his fellow workers."

"If you think it could possibly help Abul, I'll be happy to give you the information you need to reach out to the owners of his company." Nadia swept a few tears from the arches of her cheekbones.

Having no interest in upsetting Nadia any more than she already had, Kiara decided not to ask her any further questions. "I'm so sorry for your husband's illness, Nadia. I pray the doctors can find a way to help him and that he fully recovers. If you're agreeable, I'd like to exchange contact information with you and keep you updated if I come across anything important."

"I would very much appreciate that."

After they traded contact information and said goodbye, Nadia got into her car and pulled out of the parking lot. Kiara watched until the white sedan was out of sight. Her conversation with Nadia couldn't have gone better, which pleased her to no end.

Kiara was generally comfortable in her own skin. What she'd told Nadia was the absolute truth. At the moment, doing everything she could to help Abul and the ten innocent women battling IPS trumped anything related to the journalistic reward of writing the story.

Chapter 53

Jack and Madison entered Emma's room as scheduled to brief Governor Collymore and Carmela on their daughter's condition. It was a meeting Jack had been dreading since they made rounds on her a couple of hours ago. As was the case with the other IPS patients, Emma's jaundice was worsening, and she was less responsive.

Looking into the eyes of her two dismayed parents, Jack said, "I wish we had better news for you, but Emma's condition hasn't shown any signs of improving during the past twenty-four hours."

"Would you say she's worse?" Carmela asked. At the same time, the governor got up from his chair and walked to the bedside.

"In one or two areas, her condition has gotten a little worse, but fortunately, her cardiac and pulmonary function remain acceptable," Jack said.

"We understand one of the IPS patients was transferred to Miami for an emergency liver transplant," the governor said.

Jack was reticent to disclose any medical information about another patient, but under the circumstances, he didn't see the point in denying what the governor obviously knew.

"Yes, I'm afraid that's true."

"I apologize in advance for continuing to pose the same question," Carmela said. "But have any of the physicians come across any promising leads that could possibly lead to an answer?"

"We have a couple of ideas we're pursuing," he said, "but I wouldn't feel comfortable telling you that either of them will materialize."

The governor chimed in. "My surgeon general tells me that, in medicine, physicians successfully treat many illnesses with various medications and other techniques without having the first clue as to what's causing the illness. If we shift our focus away from a specific cause, is there some treatment out there that Emma and these other women might respond to?"

"That's always a possibility. But that method can be fraught with possible adverse outcomes," he answered.

"Can you expand on that for me, Jack?"

"If we're dealing with an illness that these patients will recover from without medical science having a hand in things, but we choose to use an uncertain treatment plan, and it turns out that it's not only of no help but could possibly make the situation worse… well that could be a fatal error."

"I see. So what's your plan moving forward, Doctors?" he inquired.

"To continue following any leads that arise from the new clinical information we gather every day."

"That sounds logical—it doesn't sound hopeful."

"I'm afraid it's the best we can do for now, Governor," Madison said. "We've been in this position before. Sometimes it just takes one break, and it's a straight shot to the finish line."

Returning to his wife's side, the governor wrapped an arm around her, and said, "I guess that's what we'll have to pray happens this time. Thanks for taking the time to speak with us."

Chapter 54

OUTBREAK—DAY 18

Jack and Madison were on their way to meet with the radiologist regarding the latest patient films when his phone rang. He glanced at the caller ID and saw the phone number was formatted with a 44—the country code for England.

"This must be Dr. Dankworth." They stepped into the atrium at the end of the hall to take the call. "This is Jack Wyatt."

"Good morning, Archie Dankworth calling from the Pirbright Institute in Britain."

"Thank you for calling, sir. I'm here with Dr. Shaw. We have you on speakerphone."

"It's good to speak with you. Ely was extremely complimentary about the job you two are doing."

"We haven't known him as long as you have, but we already hold him in pretty high regard," Madison said.

"I have no doubts. So let's talk about your problem, shall we?"

"Were the specimens satisfactory?" Jack asked.

"As a matter of fact, whoever prepared and sent them did an

excellent job. It greatly expedited our analysis. Let me begin by inquiring as to how familiar you two are with the Plowright Building and the techniques we're currently using to identify suspected novel viruses."

"In all honesty, Dr. Dankworth..."

"Archie...I'd be much more comfortable if you called me Archie."

"Thank you. Ely gave us some insight into your work, and Madison and I have done some reading on your research center and the projects you've taken on."

"It's a fascinating area of study, and I'm proud to say that, on a global basis, we're one of the institutions that's leading that charge. When we received your specimens, we began with routine diagnostic testing like cell culture–based assays, immunological testing, and molecular techniques, such as PCR analysis. As we suspected, the classic methods we employed weren't too helpful, so we shifted to more sophisticated means to increase the likelihood we'd identify a novel virus if one were present. Of all our cutting-edge diagnostic techniques, we're most excited about our next-generation DNA sequencing of randomly amplified DNA."

As Archie droned on, Madison swung her most impatient look at Jack, screaming on the inside for Archie to stop the mini course on big-time virus hunting and get to the point.

"Did any of the more sophisticated techniques you used yield any encouraging results?" she finally asked, prompting Jack to glare at her for interrupting him. Offending Dankworth was the last thing he wanted to do.

"In a word, yes, Dr. Shaw. We have strong reason to believe that your patients are suffering from a novel viral infection. We think the strain has a strong resemblance to Nipah, but it doesn't meet the strict criteria for being included in the same species. One thing's for sure, it's definitely a strain we've never seen before."

Madison asked, "Is it possible it's been identified in another laboratory?"

"It's possible, but unlikely. Those of us doing this kind of work get the word out pretty quickly when we come across something new."

"Please excuse this question, but just how certain are you of your findings?" she asked.

"When dealing with the identification of new strains and species of viruses, I rarely offer a categorical opinion, but in this case, I'll give you a ninety-eight percent chance that our findings are accurate. We'll of course back that up with an official written report that you'll be receiving from us later today."

"I know this may be a little outside of your purview," Jack began, "but would you have any suggestions regarding possible treatment options?"

"Since the virus is close in appearance to Nipah, I'd suggest you review the current literature. It's still considered basically untreatable, but over the past couple of years there's been some promising research using certain antiviral agents and monoclonal antibiotic therapy."

Jack said, "Because of our location in North America, we've ruled out the possibility that a bat's the vector of transmission. Based on your findings and the possibility the virus is not one of the Nipah strains, would you agree?"

"That's a tough one. There's never been a serious outbreak of Nipah in North America. Anything's of course possible, but by the natural laws of nature, I don't see how you could be dealing with a bat problem."

"If you were facing the same problem we are, who would you reach out to for assistance regarding the latest, most effective treatment for Nipah infections?" Jack asked.

"You'll have to forgive me for this, but I've already reached out to an individual who is a world leader in the field. Her name's Elsa Ahlberg. She's at the Karolinska Institute in Sweden. She's dedicated her career to novel viruses and has been an innovator in the treatment of severe viral infections. She spent quite a bit of time on the phone with me and was quite helpful."

"Would this be a good time for you to share the information with us?" Jack asked.

"It would indeed."

For the next hour, Archie went to extreme lengths to supply Madison and Jack with a detailed approach to a treatment plan based on Dr. Ahlberg's recommendations. It involved some creative ideas, with some suggestions that might not hold up to FDA guidelines and requirements. When he was finished, they asked him some very pointed questions that he fielded with an honest, no-holds-barred assessment of the crisis that Mothers and Infants was facing.

"I know this must sound hopeless," he said, "but you have to understand that Nipah infections are still considered incurable. We can support these patients when they become critically ill, but those who survive probably do so thanks to their own immunological systems."

"We understand," Madison said. "If you'd like, we'll keep you advised of things as they unfold."

"I'd appreciate that. And we very much appreciate your display of confidence in asking for our help. I'll be sure to get a report out to you within the next twenty-four hours. Please reach out to me if you have any questions at all. And if you ever have the opportunity to visit England, I'd be proud to show you around the Plowright Building."

"We appreciate your kind offer," Madison said.

Jack slowly replaced his phone in its holder.

"What do you think?" Madison asked him. "Are you convinced we finally have a working diagnosis?"

"There are so many questions and uncertainties rattling around in my head at the moment that it's hard to say. The important thing is that I'm not sure it matters, because if there's one thing I'm convinced of, it's that we have more than sufficient evidence that IPS is a viral illness to strongly recommend treatment. Do you agree?"

"I do. And obviously I think we should formulate a treatment protocol based on Dr. Ahlberg's suggestions and institute that therapy ASAP," she said. "I don't know how you feel about it, but I'd like to see us get this plan off the ground without another touchy-feely meeting where there's a lot of ideas and no implementation. That kind of approach isn't going to get us where we need to be."

"I tend to agree with you."

"To what degree, Jack? I'm looking for specifics here."

"There's no reason to recommend a meeting, especially one that lacks teeth."

"What convinced you of that? How would we deal with the potential uproar?"

"By politely ignoring it."

"Excuse me?"

"All of the IPS patients are in the ICU or PCU, both of which are in the critical care area. Technically, every one of them is on Dr. Phillips's service. He's the attending physician of record. Every other doctor involved, including Herb Whiteacre, is only a consultant. Whether they like it or not, Dr. Phillips has the final say in all treatment decisions."

"You seem very certain that he'll share our opinion."

"You're damn right I am," he said to her with the confidence of a hardened warrior.

"What about Dr. Whiteacre?"

"We'll ask Ely to speak with him personally before the meeting and give him a choice—he's either in or out."

"It makes sense on paper, I guess."

"Let's go find Ely," he said, rising from his chair.

After checking with Ely's administrative assistant and being informed that Ely was attending a robotic surgery presentation in the birthing center, they made their way to the auditorium. There were about fifty people watching the presentation, but they had no trouble spotting him toward the back. Jack waited until he caught his eye and then signaled to him they'd like to speak with him outside in the hall. Once they were outside, they took a few minutes to brief him on their conversation with Archie.

"I'm on board," he said with very few questions. "When do you want me to set up the meeting?"

"The sooner the better," Madison answered.

"I'll invite all the physicians who've been involved in any way in the care of the IPS patients, the nurses, and the key leadership of administration. I'll try to get it set up for tomorrow morning." He stopped and fidgeted with his wedding band before adding, "I'd recommend you two come to the meeting well prepared, because something tells me this is going to be the only shot you're going to get."

Chapter 55

Nadia Kahn turned her tear-drenched eyes away from the ventilator that was keeping Abul alive. As his liver function became progressively worse and Dr. Sturgess painted a gloomier picture each time they spoke, every fiber of her being kept praying for a miracle that would save his life. Seven hours ago, she'd received a call from Dr. Sturgess that Abul had suffered a major stroke and that he didn't expect him to survive.

The metronome-like whoosh of the ventilator continued at a steady rate of eighteen breaths per minute as Nadia sat there motionless. Watching Abul steadily decline since the day he'd been admitted had eroded her spirit, but somehow she continued to cling to hope. She tried to dismiss it from her thoughts, but she couldn't help but wonder what hers and the children's lives would be like without him.

When Nadia heard the glass doors slide open, it took her a few seconds to raise her eyes and look across the room. When she did, she saw Dr. Sturgess walking toward her.

"I'm so sorry, Nadia."

"Thank you for everything you've done. What happened to Abul, Doctor?"

"We can't be entirely sure, but the most likely explanation is that his compromised liver function affected his ability to clot his blood normally, and that's what led to the severe bleeding in his head."

"Has the neurologist come to see him yet?"

"Yes. I met her here a couple of hours ago."

"Does she hold out any hope at all for him?"

"Unfortunately, her examination was very suggestive that the pressure created by the accumulation of blood resulted in a fatal injury to his brain."

"Is she absolutely certain? You hear stories of conditions like Abul's that sometimes have ended in a miraculous recovery."

"Some of those accounts may be true, but, unfortunately, most of them are related to an inaccurate assessment of the presence of brain death. We test for certain reflexes, such as how the pupil reacts to light, to accurately determine if there's any brain function at all. The neurologist found all the reflexes were negative, which means, from a clinical standpoint, his brain has no function. We also did an assessment to see if Abul was able to breathe on his own. He showed no signs of being able to initiate a breath, which is another indication the brain tissue has been deprived of oxygen for too long and is no longer alive."

"Is there anything further that should be done?"

"We'll arrange for Abul to have a brain scan and an ultrasound. If those confirm our other findings, I'm afraid the evidence will be conclusive that we've lost him."

"But his heart is still beating, Dr. Sturgess."

"That can happen in any severe injury to the brain. People have different definitions of death, depending on spiritual and moral beliefs. There's also the area of what constitutes brain death from a legal standpoint."

"I see."

"I'd suggest we hold off on any of those types of conversations at this time. Let's complete our evaluation first." Grim-faced, he continued, "We have several individuals on staff who can help you if you'd like. I'm sure you'll be relying heavily on family support as well."

"Thank you, Dr. Sturgess, I know you've done everything in your power. You've been a great source of comfort to both Abul and me."

"I appreciate those kind words. I'll stop back in a few hours, after the ultrasound and scan have been read. Is there anything we can do for you in the meantime?"

"What happens after Abul is declared legally brain dead? How much time will it be until they withdraw life support?"

"It depends on the family and their requirements for making the appropriate and necessary arrangements. Other considerations such as the family's spiritual and religious beliefs can come into play as well," he explained. "But as a general rule, most hospitals in Florida, including ours, extend a three-day compassionate grace period to loved ones before discontinuing all life support measures."

"Dr. Sturgess, I'm certain I will request the three-day period. Also, would it be possible for the next few days that we keep Abul's passing as confidential as possible? I'd like some time with my family before I share the news of his death."

"Of course. Would you like me to notify Doctors Wyatt and Shaw?"

"Yes, and please thank them again for me."

"If you need me for anything, just call my office and they'll get in touch with me." Nadia responded with a forced smile and a quick nod.

Sturgess quietly exited the room. Nadia turned in her chair, her eyes, flooded with tears, fell on Abul's face. All she could do was keep asking herself what horrible deed she'd committed that had resulted in life treating her family so cruelly.

She was at Abul's side twelve hours later when he was pronounced dead.

Chapter 56

Making their way across the skybridge that connected the hospital to the medical office building, Jack and Madison talked about the best way to approach Dr. Whiteacre.

"Polite and professional," Jack suggested.

"Just like he'll be, I'm sure."

"Try to dismiss his demeanor as unimportant. All we need from him is an answer. No matter how we perceive him, it might be nice to have him on board."

"He's so full of himself, Jack."

"It's only bragging if you can't do it, and there's no doubt in my mind he's the smartest guy in the room when it comes to virology."

They arrived outside his office and found the door open. Whiteacre was on the far side of the room, staring out the window toward the hospital's modest research facility. Jack knocked a couple of times. Whiteacre turned, set his eyes on them very briefly, and returned to gazing out the window.

"Excuse me, Dr. Whiteacre," Jack said. "We'd like to speak with you briefly. If this isn't a good time, we can stop back later."

"Now's fine. How can I help you?" He returned to his desk and sat down in his executive chair.

"We've come across some new information on IPS that we're anxious to share with you."

"We?"

"For now, I'll say Ely, myself, and Madison."

Herb fixed his impatient eyes on his uninvited guests. Remaining plain-faced, he gestured toward the chairs in front of his desk.

"Ely mentioned to us that you were aware that we'd sent several blood and spinal fluid samples for verification to the Plowright Building in England."

"I know where the Plowright Building is, Dr. Wyatt. And I'm familiar with the research they conduct in the area of viral zoonotic infections. I'm getting the feeling that you two keep forgetting that I'm a virologist of some renown myself."

As I recall, Archie and Ely are old friends. When I first heard about this, I assumed he was involved. Archie's a solid researcher, but he sometimes gets ahead of himself and winds up displaying more flash than substance." Whiteacre reached forward and picked up his cell phone to check his text messages. Without raising his eyes, he continued, "If you're here to get my endorsement for whatever it is you're planning, you'd better get comfortable in those chairs, because you're going to be here for a while."

"We were hoping you'd listen to what Plowright reported before making a decision," Madison said.

"It wouldn't change my thoughts on the matter. To put it bluntly, I'm not buying what Archie's selling. By the way, I've read their report. You look surprised. Allow me to remind you this is a hospital, not the CIA. Reports of diagnostic tests our patients undergo are not a matter of national security. There was a time when I believed that Ely was running a transparent organization. Obviously, I was mistaken."

Jack sensed the apparent futility of the meeting and was tempted to call an end to it, but after some thought, he chose to press on a little further before waving the white flag.

"I'd be interested to know your reasons for being so skeptical of Plowright's findings."

"A novel virus similar to or one that closely resembles the Nipah family? Archie works in a lab, Dr. Wyatt; you and I are in the real world of medicine. Have you ever seen a patient with a severe Nipah viremia?"

"No."

"I have," Madison stated.

"I have too, Dr. Shaw, and the hallmark of the illness is profound respiratory failure and generally the absence of severe liver impairment." With a smug grin, he added, "Unless I'm missing something, that doesn't seem to be the case here."

"No, but if we accept that it may be a different strain, then we have to accept the possibility the symptom complex could be dissimilar to Nipah. I'm not sure the difference in symptoms is sufficient evidence to dismiss Plowright's findings," she pointed out.

"Maybe, but that's one hell of a reach, young lady," he said. "Let's speak hypothetically for a moment. Let's assume Plowright's correct in their results. They're reporting they've identified evidence of this… this phantom virus in every spinal fluid sample you sent them. I'm sure you're aware that such a finding in Nipah infections is a strong predictor of a dismal patient outcome. There've been Nipah outbreaks that have resulted in a mortality rate of a hundred percent. It seems to me that with each passing day we're plunging deeper into this crisis." He stopped for a moment and tossed his phone on his leather desk pad. "Since all three of us know there's no effective treatment for Nipah infections, and you seem to be leading the charge in the care of the IPS patients, what are your treatment recommendations going to be?"

"That's why we're here talking to you about this," Jack said. "Dr. Dankworth gave us several recommendations. We were hoping you'd be willing to sit in on the meeting and assist in creating a detailed treatment plan."

"I'm not sure that's a role I'd like to take on. At this point, my strong preference is to assign the position to one of my junior partners. They're all board certified in internal medicine and infectious diseases, and no matter who I select, he or she will be the most qualified person at the meeting to deal with this problem." He turned his eyes to his computer monitor and added, "Was there something else you wanted to speak with me about?"

"No," Madison said as she and Jack came to their feet and left Whiteacre's office without so much as another word. "He's some piece of work," she said, not in a kind way, as they made their way back toward the skybridge.

Jack's cell phone rang. He placed it on speaker

"Hi, Jack. It's Jordan Sturgess. I'm afraid I have some sad news for you and Madison."

Jack exhaled a solemn breath. "When?"

"He had a major cerebral hemorrhage several hours ago. He has no clinical evidence of brain function. We're going through the checklist now to officially diagnose brain death."

"How's Nadia doing?" he asked.

"Not well. She's been with him most of the time."

"We're so sorry," Madison said.

"I thought you'd like to know that we lost him. Nadia asked me to again convey her thanks to you."

Madison moved closer to the phone. "We appreciate you letting us know, Jordan."

They reached the skybridge and crossed it in silence, both wondering how much time was left to the other victims of IPS.

Chapter 57

OUTBREAK—DAY 19

By twenty-five minutes after eight, most of the attendees were seated in Blankenship Auditorium anxiously waiting for the meeting to get under way. Last evening, Ely had provided each of them with copies of Archie Dankworth's reports and narrative impressions. Because of the guarded outlook of the report, many of the physicians were feeling more defeated than ever. Predictably, Jack and Madison had been barraged with calls for further information. They did their best to be responsive but intentionally avoided any detailed conversations regarding treatment options until today's meeting. It was their general impression that, except for Herb Whiteacre, there weren't any dyed-in-the-wool skeptics or naysayers regarding the accuracy of Archie's conclusions.

At precisely eight thirty, Ely asked all those present to end their conversations and those who weren't as yet seated to please do so.

"In view of the fact that we have a large number of physicians and representatives from other areas of the hospital joining us today, I thought it might be a good idea to begin with a brief review of the IPS patients' status. To that end, I can't think of anybody more qualified to do that than Dave Phillips, our chief of critical care services." He turned to Dave and nodded. "The floor's yours."

"Thank you, Ely," he said, coming to his feet. "I wish I had better news, but as you all know, none of our patients are showing any signs of improving. We continue to face liver failure, increasing neurologic impairment, and progressive cardiovascular instability, to the point of impending collapse. To put it frankly, we're probably within hours or perhaps a few days of facing a series of cardiac arrests. Unfortunately, we still find ourselves with many more questions than answers." He stopped briefly to reach for a large tumbler and take a swallow of ice water. "That's our situation in a nutshell. If anybody has something specific they'd like to ask, I'll do my best to answer your questions."

Ely waited for a few moments to recognize any attendee who wished to ask a question. A little to his surprise, there were none.

"Thank you, Dave. You've all had an opportunity to review the material I sent you yesterday. Since Jack and Madison were the ones to speak with him, I'd like them to go over Dr. Dankworth's findings and recommendations. Before they begin, I'd like to mention that Dr. Dankworth consulted with Dr. Elsa Ahlberg to discuss possible treatment options for a Nipah virus–related infection. Dr. Ahlberg is a world authority on the treatment of novel and severe viral infections. Dr. Dankworth informed us that she was extremely informative and helpful. He also made it clear that she didn't pull any punches regarding what we're up against. Some of the treatment modalities she went over with him are still in the experimental stage."

Ely paused and swung his gaze to Madison. "Dr. Shaw spoke directly with Dr. Dankworth, and I'd like to ask her to brief us on their conversation. I suggest we make this meeting an interactive one. Let's discuss issues and pose questions as we go along instead of holding them until the end."

Madison was accustomed to addressing large groups and being a key participant in a wide range of medical discussions. She felt well prepared and wasn't a bit nervous. Prior to the meeting, Jack, Madison, and Ely had met with Dr. Phillips to emphasize the critical role his opinions and treatment plans would play in the care of the IPS patients.

"Thank you, Ely," Madison began. "I think we should keep in mind that the novel virus Plowright has identified is, in all likelihood, not a new strain of Nipah, although it does closely resemble it. So, for the purposes of creating a treatment plan, both Jack and I would advise following Dr. Dankworth's suggestion that we rely heavily on what's known about treating Nipah virus infections."

Raising her eyes before continuing, she was pleased to see no visible objection on anybody's face. "I'd like to begin with what we know from Dr. Dankworth's report and build on that information." Madison then spent a considerable amount of time going over the spectrum of antiviral treatment options, from conventional therapy to the few drugs that were in the early phases of approval in both the U.S. and Asia. From time to time, she glanced down at her notes to make sure she wasn't omitting any key information. "Almost all the commercially available antiviral drugs that we're familiar with have been used to treat severe Nipah infections. Unfortunately, the success rate has been disappointing. But considering everything, we believe the best of the group is ribavirin."

"We currently have all the patients on favipiravir," Dr. Phillips pointed out.

"Which brings us to the first decision facing us. Our recommendation is to switch over to ribavirin. Dr. Dankworth agreed with the change."

"Speaking for the critical care team, we'd have no objection to making that change," Dr. Phillips said.

"I think we're all in agreement with beginning ribavirin and discontinuing favipiravir," Ely said. Madison was pleased he didn't put the matter to a vote.

"I'll take care of it as soon the meeting's over," Phillips said.

Dr. Rosabel Chalmers stated, "I understand there's work currently being done on a Nipah vaccine. Did Dr. Dankworth have any thoughts on its use?"

Wanting to get Jack involved, Madison nodded at him to field Rosabel's question.

"Several countries, including the United States, have entered into phase one trials, but because of the increased number of outbreaks in Bangladesh, the majority of the work is being done there," he said. "Dr. Dankworth mentioned one Asian company whose vaccine has just moved into phase two trials. Unofficially, they've reported encouraging results, but you have to remember that most vaccines in development are directed only at prevention. There's very little known about the potential of the Nipah vaccine's benefit in patients who already have the disease. I suggest we keep the idea of using any experimental vaccine on the back burner for now. We're not dismissing the possibility, but with so little known about their ability to help with existing infections, I think there are other treatment possibilities that warrant our attention."

Sliding her legal pad a little closer, Madison was just about to add to Jack's response when she caught sight of Herb Whiteacre slipping into the auditorium via the back entrance. She continued to watch as he took a seat in the last row. She traded a dubious glance with Jack. From his quizzical expression, she assumed he'd seen him as well.

She continued, "There are some interesting studies and human trials going on in certain areas of immunotherapy we should consider. There are two areas that seem to be the major focus: the first is allogenic T-cell therapy, and the second is viral-neutralizing monoclonal antibodies. Both of these targeted techniques are currently being used primarily to treat cancer patients. More recently, their indications have broadened to include combating viral infections."

"What's the theory behind how they work?" Teri asked.

"They're both capable of targeting specific viral cells and killing them. The main difference is that T-cells are obtained from human donors, while monoclonal antibodies are produced in a laboratory. Dr. Dankworth feels, and we agree, that for our situation, monoclonal antibody therapy would be a better choice."

"How are they administered?" Teri followed up.

"There's quite a bit of variation in both dosing and the way they're administered. Many are simply an intravenous two-dose protocol."

"I assume these drugs are FDA approved for the purpose we'd like to use them," Clayton Rice, the chief legal counsel of the hospital, said.

"It's a mixed bag. Certain monoclonal antibodies are approved for the treatment of specific viruses. The best example would be in the treatment of Covid. But most of the research and clinical experience using monoclonal antibodies to treat Nipah infections has been in India, Bangladesh, and Malaysia. England has also recently started some studies. Unfortunately, the results to this point haven't been extremely encouraging."

Ely said, "Before we get into the specifics of monoclonal antibody use, are there any other treatment areas you or Jack would like to mention?"

"Chloroquine therapy was tried many years ago in a few of the larger outbreaks. There was no hard scientific evidence to support its effectiveness. The final possibility is Ephrin-B2. It's a protein that seems to block the entrance of the Nipah virus into the human cell, but the research projects looking at it are still in their infancy. Dr. Dankworth doesn't feel enough is known about either its efficacy or side effects to recommend it."

Without being recognized, Dr. Elena Brandwyn stood up. "I realize I'm the only surgeon in the room, and perhaps as a specialty we reduce problems to their simplest form, so I'd like to pose the following cut-to-the-chase question to our visiting consultants: After being presented with an enormous amount of material and options, what conclusions can we take away from today's meeting, and what's our next step?"

Jack took the opportunity to answer Elena's pointed question. "Considering what we've learned about IPS and what Dr. Dankworth has contributed, Madison and I feel the best approach would be to use a viral-neutralizing monoclonal antibody. The problem before us would be to select the best one to use. That decision would involve choosing between an FDA-approved monoclonal, which has no proven track record against Nipah or one of the experimental ones we might be able to obtain that has a greater chance of specificity against the virus that's causing IPS."

Elena said, "I'd just like to be absolutely sure of something you mentioned earlier. It's your feeling and Madison's that using one of the vaccines in development is a long shot at best."

"That's correct. But by no means are we recommending that we take it off the table as a future option. We just feel it's not a decision we need to make right now. We think it's best to see how the patients respond to a monoclonal antibody before seriously considering using one of the vaccines."

By this time, Madison and Jack had shared the key points of what they believed should be the treatment plan. They knew from a prior conversation that Ely was a hundred percent on board.

"We're up against a ticking time bomb that mandates action," Ely said. "It's imperative that we create a detailed treatment plan and start therapy as soon as possible."

Ames Saylor, one of the attendings from the infectious diseases department, raised his hand and was recognized by Ely.

"With all due respect, Ely, there may be physicians present in this room who feel the best option is to continue watchful waiting. I believe it's the concern of several of us that our zeal to intervene with unproven methods may prove fatal to a group of patients who could possibly recover spontaneously."

"I'll respond to that," David Phillips said. "We've carefully considered continuing with supportive therapy and surveillance, but we dismissed it because we feel it's in the best interests of our patients to proceed with a more aggressive treatment plan."

Saylor shook his head. "It sounds to me like you made that decision in a vacuum."

"I'm the attending physician of record, Ames. Ultimately, it's my responsibility to direct the care of any patient who's hospitalized in a critical care area. I greatly value the opinion of my consultants and colleagues and consider their input vital in managing our critical care patients. But in the end, it's me and my fellow intensivists who write the orders."

Now Saylor looked angry. "What you've just told us begs the question: What's the purpose of this meeting?"

"To choose the best course of active therapy. I've decided that it's time to act. Watchful waiting is no longer an option. My decision was solidified when I learned that, even as we speak, arrangements are being made for one of our patients to be transferred to the University to undergo an emergency liver transplant. I'm sorry, Ames, but I can't imagine the other IPS patients are far behind."

Above the murmur in the room, Ely asked, "Are there any further questions?"

For the next thirty-five minutes, Jack and Madison fielded one question after another. They were both quick to note that Dr. Whiteacre conspicuously clung to his silence.

Rosabel said, "Purely for the sake of conversation, if a healthcare team was facing a desperate situation and wanted to administer a monoclonal antibody that's not as yet approved by the FDA, a case could be made for doing it under the umbrella of compassionate use."

"That's true," Evan Saunders, one of the senior administrators said. "We've done it before on a couple of occasions. And I guess the same could be said for the Nipah vaccine undergoing trials in Bangladesh that Dr. Shaw mentioned."

"By the way," Madison began, "I'm sure Dr. Dankworth would assist us in acquiring the monoclonal antibody or the vaccine if we should decide to go in that direction."

"I see that Herb Whiteacre has joined us," Ely said. "Herb, I think we'd all appreciate your opinion."

Apparently for dramatic effect, Whiteacre said nothing for a few moments. Finally, in a grand gesture, he slowly came to his feet, looking at those seated in the room as if they were inmates of an insane asylum instead of attendees at a critical medical meeting.

"To put it simply, I'm very skeptical. Most of what I've heard here today regarding therapy is a wellspring of conjecture, faulty thinking, and unproven theories, especially on the topic of monoclonal antibodies. I'm surprised that nobody mentioned the striking number of serious complications associated with their use. The same could be said for experimental viral vaccines, especially when administered intravenously—the ones being used in several Asian countries have barely started phase one trials."

A severe expression came to his face. "We're in the business of saving lives. It's one thing to take a calculated risk with a reasonable chance of helping a patient. It's quite another to take a blind plunge into a pool when you don't have the first clue if there's any water in it or not. It's a grave disservice to our patients to behave as if we can't be bothered by the facts." With his harshly critical words still hanging in the air, he got up and exited the auditorium without so much as a glance behind himself.

Ely said, "With that, I'd like to adjourn the meeting and move immediately to formulating a specific treatment plan. We'll be reaching out to the key consultants to assist in the initiative. If anybody has any further questions, please direct them to Dr. Phillips. Thank you again for attending."

With the participants in stunned silence, the room emptied fairly quickly. Madison and Jack stood up and made their way toward the exit.

"Whiteacre's really something," she said. "It's bad enough what he said, but his level of condescension was inexcusable."

"We were attending a scientific strategy session, Madison. It wasn't a pajama party. He's entitled to his opinion."

"I don't dispute that. What I'm saying is that he should have checked his pomposity and arrogance at the door and shared his ideas with us in a professional manner."

"I've dealt with plenty of physicians like him, so I guess I'm not as shocked as you are. I was surprised he even showed up at the meeting. I suggest we consider Whiteacre a lost cause for now and stay focused on everything we can do to give these patients their best shot of being cured."

Madison didn't respond.

Jack gestured to the doors. "C'mon, let's find Ely and go over our next steps with him."

Chapter 58

When Madison and Jack left the conference room and walked out into the foyer, they noticed several of the attendees had remained and were talking in small groups. They opted to avoid any protracted conversations with the other doctors and headed back to the unit to see a few of the patients. They were making their way across the marble floor when they saw Herb Whiteacre chatting with a few of the other physicians.

"During the meeting, he was silent as a stone until Ely asked him directly for his opinion. Now he's out in the hall acting like he's running for mayor," Madison said.

As they walked past him, he looked up and spotted them. He gestured to them by raising a hand, excused himself from his group chat, and started toward them.

"This should be interesting," Madison muttered under her breath, wondering what was on his mind.

"Keep your cool," Jack warned.

"Do you two have a couple of minutes? I'd like to have a word with you."

"Certainly," Jack said.

They strolled over to the opposite side of the foyer, where they found a small grouping of club chairs.

"Procole Health Solutions," Herb said.

He didn't utter another word, just looked at them as if he'd presented them with the Holy Grail.

After an awkward few moments, Jack said, "I beg your pardon?"

"Procole Health Solutions is a small pharmaceutical company in the Pacific Northwest. Their main area of interest is cutting-edge immunotherapy. It appears that you and certain others who are standing shoulder-to-shoulder with you in the wheelhouse have made a definite decision to treat the IPS patients with a broad monoclonal antibody. I'm simply suggesting you contact Procole."

"For what purpose, if you don't mind me asking?" Madison said.

"They keep a relatively low profile, and I think it's safe to say that the corporate executives don't count themselves among the Big Pharma elite."

"Why are you sharing this information with us?" Madison asked, unconcerned if her snarky tone offended Herb or made Jack wince. Herb extended his legs and crossed them at the ankles.

"I may disagree with your medical opinions, Dr. Shaw, but since you've made the irrevocable decision to move forward with monoclonal antibody therapy, I feel it's my ethical responsibility to make you aware of certain facts that you appear to be oblivious to that could prove to be detrimental to our patients. And for that reason alone, I'm alerting you to the existence of sintenimab. What you do with the information is entirely up to you."

"What don't you tell us a little more about it?" Jack suggested, trying to learn about the drug while at the same time bring down the temperature of the conversation.

"About five years ago, Procole started a research initiative to produce a broad-spectrum monoclonal antibody that specifically targets viruses. Except in the area of Covid, no other pharmaceutical company has chosen to go in that direction. Procole's original target was the Ebola virus, but early on they decided to include the Hendra virus as well, which, as I'm sure you know, is in the same genus and species as Nipah. They completed all three phases of the FDA approval process and submitted their new drug application for formal approval last year. After reviewing it for six months, the FDA granted it."

"Wait a minute," Madison said. "Are you saying this monoclonal antibody is FDA approved?"

"That's what I'm saying."

"And that it's probably more specific for the type of virus that's causing IPS than the others we're considering?"

"Very good, Dr. Shaw."

"What's the name of the drug again?"

"Sintenimab."

"And it's completely legal for distribution and administration?"

"I believe I've already answered that question, but, yes, it's every bit as legal as penicillin."

Madison asked, "How come Dr. Dankworth and the experts he consulted were unaware of this drug?"

"You'd have to ask them that question."

"What kind of results did they see in their trials?" Jack asked.

"I don't have that exact data at my fingertips, but I think it's safe to say they were a hell of a lot better than anything you presented this morning."

Jack frowned. "I don't recall seeing any advertising or scientific articles in our journals about the drug."

"That's because there haven't been any yet. Procole rejected the crash-release approach that the pharmaceutical giants generally use. They're intentionally moving slowly. It's not unusual for the smaller companies to delay submitting scientific articles while the drug is under development or going through the FDA's approval process. I am aware of a few articles that have appeared in the medical literature about the drug."

Looking him straight in the eye, Madison said, "Excuse me for asking, Dr. Whiteacre, but do you have more than a passing interest in seeing us use Procole's monoclonal antibody?"

"Are you asking me if I have a financial interest in the company?"

"Yes, I am."

"I've consulted on a few of Procole's studies, but I have no financial interest in the company. And none of those studies involved sintenimab. I guess I'm aware of the drug because I'm the type of doctor who keeps up with the newest drugs and innovative medical procedures."

"Dr. Whiteacre, with all due respect, you've made it crystal clear that you're opposed to the use of a monoclonal antibody."

"That's partially correct, Dr. Shaw. What I said was that I considered it premature to use a monoclonal antibody at this time but that my opinion could change at any time." He paused to take a few calming breaths, then went on. "I'm savvy enough to see that no words of mine are going to stop your group from pursuing a plan that, in my opinion, has little to no hope of helping these women. It would be nice if my colleagues would act in a professional manner and extend me the courtesy of allowing a dissenting opinion."

"Dr. Whiteacre, we greatly appreciate you providing us with the information on sintenimab," Jack said. "I think we should brief Ely and David Phillips as soon as possible."

"If you do decide to use it, I'd be willing to make a phone call to Procole to help expedite the process."

"Thank you," Jack said.

"Whichever monoclonal antibody you select, I'll support your choice, and if called upon, I'll offer an opinion on any matter related to the recovery of the IPS patients."

"Why do we have to choose?" Jack asked, pausing to look at both Madison and Whiteacre.

A confused look appeared on Whiteacre's face. "Excuse me?"

"It's something I've been thinking about since we started discussing monoclonal antibody therapy. What's to prevent us from using both of them? I'm certain that dual therapy of monoclonal antibodies has been used."

"Actually, you raise an interesting point," Whiteacre said. "There have been limited studies where dual therapy using two monoclonal antibodies has been tried. In some of those cases, a clear-cut advantage was documented."

"How can I persuade you to speak to Ely with us?" Jack asked.

Turning his head, Whiteacre gestured to Ely, who was on the other side of the foyer speaking with two other physicians.

"You just did."

When Ely saw the trio standing a few feet away with impatient expressions on their faces, he ended his conversation and joined them.

"I assume the three of you have something on your minds you'd like to speak to me about."

"We do," Jack said. He spent the next few minutes going over the new information that Herb had thrown into the mix and the idea of using dual monoclonal antibody therapy.

"It sounds reasonable to me, but the one you have to speak with is David Phillips."

"If Dave approves," Jack began, "I think we should send an email to all the IPS consultants that our plan is to proceed with a two-drug monoclonal antibody approach, plus ribavirin, and that we'll hold the vaccine in reserve for now. We should include that we'll be using sintenimab."

"We might want to consider contacting Dr. Dankworth immediately to see if he can help us get the other monoclonal antibody shipped to us ASAP," Madison said.

"I'll take care of that," Ely stated. "Herb, your thoughts?"

"I haven't changed my mind. I still think it's an impulsive move. So for now, I'm going to sit in the cheap seats and just watch."

Ely turned to Madison and Jack. "Last chance, guys. Is this the direction you two think we should go in?"

"Absolutely," Madison said, confident that she was speaking for them both.

"That's it, then. Let's see what David thinks. If he's on board, we're officially a go."

Chapter 59

At eleven p.m., Jack and Madison were still sitting at home impatiently waiting for Ely's call. Jack was watching an old Errol Flynn swashbuckler movie, and Madison was thumbing through her latest pediatrics journal.

"Maybe we should call him," she suggested.

Without diverting his gaze from the television, he answered, "I'm sure Ely's busy enough without having to deal with us bugging him. He said he'd call us as soon as he had any news. I don't think it's a promise he's likely to forget."

"Okay, but if he doesn't call by eleven thirty, I'm going to call him."

"Try to be a little patient, Madison. Think about something else."

"Did you hear from Anise today?"

"Of course. She's getting ready for finals and loves college."

"What about her choice of major?"

"It changes weekly."

"I think I was the same way until I was a junior," Madison said.

Before Jack could respond, his phone rang. "It's Ely." He answered and put it on speakerphone.

"Hi. Is Madison with you?"

"She's right here. I've got you on speaker."

"I never know which one of you to call. Is there some protocol I should be following?"

"We're not that sensitive," she said.

"It's official. We're good to go. I spoke to David earlier. He had a lot of questions, but he agrees fully with proceeding with dual monoclonal antibody therapy. I also reached out to Archie and got an email back letting me know he received a positive response from the research team in Bangladesh about sending us their monoclonal antibody on an urgent basis."

"Did Archie mention anything about the interval between the two drugs?"

"He suggested we begin with sintenimab and follow up twelve hours later with the second monoclonal antibody from Bangladesh. Twelve hours later, we repeat the entire process. Barring any complications, if we begin early tomorrow evening, the entire treatment plan should be complete on the morning of the third day." For a second time, Ely paused.

"Will we have the drugs by then?" she asked.

"As he promised he would, Herb intervened and arranged for us to get the sintenimab by tomorrow afternoon at the latest."

"That sounds perfect," Jack said. "And the drug being trialed in Bangladesh? Will we be able to get it in our pharmacy in time to administer the first dose twelve hours after the sintenimab?"

"We got a break there. As it turns out, it's being manufactured in Canada, which makes the logistics of us getting it a heck of a lot easier. The information I have is that we'll have it in time if we make the formal request early tomorrow morning."

"We should probably get the key players together early tomorrow and create our treatment protocol in detail," Jack said.

"There's also the matter of meeting with the family members, which I assume we can do after the meeting Jack just suggested," Madison added. "Jack and I are fairly certain all of them will want to proceed, but we may want to give them a few hours to think things over, just to make sure they're comfortable with our recommendations. And, if you'd like, we'll be happy to help with those conversations. We've gotten to know most of the family members pretty well."

"Thanks, Madison. That will be helpful."

"Where do we stand with getting official approval for using a monoclonal antibody that's not FDA approved?" Jack inquired.

"I spoke with Legal and Evan Saunders. Since we're facing a life-threatening situation, we can proceed without obtaining formal FDA or Institutional Review Board consent."

Jack asked, "If our treatment plan goes south, what kind of a reaction do you think we can expect from Herb?"

"As you've probably noticed, Herb can be pretty inhospitable at times, but I've never known him to be much of an I-told-you-so-type person. Let's hope we don't have to address your concern," Ely answered. "Off the record, Archie mentioned to me that Herb called him to brief him on the patients from a virologist's point of view."

"Wow," Madison said, more to herself than anybody else.

"You can say what you want about Herb, but he's an extremely bright and experienced physician. I know you two have had a clash of ideas here and there, Madison, but we're better off having him in our camp."

"I agree," she said. "I'll make it my business tomorrow to find him and extend an olive branch."

"Thanks. You've just saved me five minutes trying to persuade you to do just that. The final thing I'd like to mention is that it might be a good idea if you two meet with the Collymores to brief them on our new treatment plan for Emma."

"We'll be happy to."

"I don't want to sound pushy, but I'd appreciate it if you could meet with them before we speak to any of the other family members. I'd like to make sure they're fully informed before bits and pieces of the plan reach them via the gossip mill."

"We'll head over to Emma's room right after the physician meeting," Jack assured him.

"Thanks, and please give me a call afterward and let me know how they reacted."

"Of course."

"It looks like we're good to go," Ely said. "We're getting to the point of no return, so if you two have any last-minute concerns, call me... And I mean at any time between now and the meeting tomorrow morning."

"Will do," Jack said.

As soon as they were off the phone, a cautionary glance passed between them.

"Ely doesn't sound as convinced as I hoped he might be," she said.

"To tell you the truth, neither am I. This one's a long shot, even for you and me."

"Have some faith, buddy. How about joining me in a glass of wine?"

"I was just about to make the same offer. I'm not sure about you, but I'll probably need it to help me sleep."

Chapter 60

INFUSION–DAY ONE

Changing their minds, Jack and Madison decided to speak with the Collymores before the physician meeting to formalize the dual monoclonal antibody therapy protocol. When they entered Emma's room, the governor and Carmela were standing on either side of the bed, hovering over their daughter. They both looked up at the same time. The dismay that lay across their faces was becoming a permanent part of their appearances. Because of Emma's deteriorating liver function and the buildup of ammonia in her blood, she had become unresponsive to any stimuli in her environment.

"Good morning," Madison said.

"I don't even think she knows we're here anymore," Carmela uttered in a monotone.

"Jack and I would like to talk to you about a change we're proposing in Emma's treatment protocol. We've discussed it with Dr. Phillips, and he agrees."

"We'd very much like to hear about it," the governor said.

Jack took the lead. "After quite a bit of discussion with our consultants and several experts outside of the state, we're going to recommend what's termed dual monoclonal antibody therapy. The protocol will consist of two new drugs in addition to the new antiviral medication Emma's presently receiving. One of the monoclonal drugs is still in trials, which means it's not as yet approved by the FDA."

"I wasn't even aware that was permitted," the governor was quick to say.

"Hospitals and physicians do have the option if they deem the patient's condition to be life or death and no other therapy exists," he explained.

Madison and Jack then took some time to go over every step of the treatment plan with the Collymores. They were careful to include the possible risks and complications of each monoclonal antibody. Without extinguishing all hope, they were candid about the chances of Emma having a favorable outcome from the new treatment plan.

The governor posed the first question. "But until a few days ago, you hadn't identified the virus that's infected Emma. If these monoclonal drugs are produced to attack specific viruses, why would you be hopeful they'll eradicate this virus?"

"We're fairly certain the strain that has infected Emma closely resembles a virus that we do have some experience in treating. We're also hopeful that using two viral-neutralizing monoclonal antibodies together will give us a greater chance of success than using just one."

"Has that been tried?" he asked.

"Not in this setting—not to our knowledge," Madison said.

"Dr. Shaw, are you saying this new combination of drugs could totally wipe out the virus?" Carmela asked, with the first speck of hope in her voice that Jack had noted in several days.

"We think there's a chance. That's the most we can say."

She looked over at her husband. Doing her best to fight off a faltering voice, she said, "If they think there's any chance at all that this might work, we have no choice, Sam."

He put a comforting hand on her shoulder. "If we do decide to go ahead with your recommendation, when do you anticipate beginning the treatment?"

"By late this afternoon or this evening," Jack answered.

"How long will the treatment last?"

"We anticipate three to four days. We haven't set the exact schedule yet."

"Do you have any way of predicting how long after you've given the monoclonal antibodies before you'll have an idea if they're working?" Carmela asked.

"That's one aspect of this that could be in our favor. When monoclonal antibody therapy is used to treat Covid, some patients experience positive results almost immediately."

"That's certainly encouraging to hear," he said. "If this treatment fails, will there be any other options available to us?"

"There's a vaccine being trialed overseas, but our knowledge of its efficacy and risks is limited, and we haven't made a decision yet if we're going to recommend its use to the family members."

Carmela gradually raised her eyes and focused them squarely on Madison and Jack.

"Sam and I have come to believe that, absent a major breakthrough or miracle, Emma's not going to survive this illness. I speak for the two of us when I say we'd like to proceed with your proposed treatment. We'll sign whatever consent forms you ask us to."

"I'm very impressed with the medical staff here at Mothers and Infants, but there aren't two doctors in the world I trust more than you two. If you think it will help with the other families, you have my permission to share with them that Carmela and I have consented for Emma to be treated."

Carmela moved forward and put her arms around her husband. Her eyes moistened as a sudden new strength found its way into her voice. "Don't you worry, Sam. Our Emma's not going to die."

Chapter 61

One of Kiara's favorite restaurants for lunch in Palm Beach County was Alexandra's Bistro. With its open kitchen and brick and glass facades, the restaurant featured a contemporary American menu in a modish environment. She'd be hard-pressed to remember the total number of people she'd interviewed there over lunch or dinner.

On this particular day, she had set up a meeting with Detective Libby Rafferty. Over the years, the two had crossed paths more than a few times. Although they were generally investigating the same crimes, their reasons for doing so were distinctly different. Once they were able to see beyond the natural conflict between their respective professions and what separated them, they'd realized they shared many of the same likes, dislikes, and life outlooks. Although they didn't see each other all that often, their friendship was a solid one.

"Detective Libby Rafferty," Kiara said as Libby approached the booth. "How long has it been?"

"I believe it was about three articles ago, when you did that riveting exposé on credit card fraud and referred to the sheriff's office as oversupplied with idle officers who were prone to look the other way when it came to unexciting, routine crimes like identity theft."

"That doesn't sound like something I'd say," Kiara said with theatrical sarcasm. "Are you sure I used those exact words?"

"You might have put a little lipstick on it, but that was pretty much word for word."

"Truth be told, it was only out of my deep respect for your department that I reported the story with such restraint."

Libby grinned and gazed upward for a few seconds. "I've been racking my brain trying to figure out what I owe this unexpected lunch invitation to."

"That's the trouble with you cops—you're suspicious of everything."

"And freelance writers don't usually have hidden agendas? How was your trip to California?"

"We had a great time. How are Ron and the kids?" Kiara asked.

"I organized a garage sale recently and almost put price tags on all three of them, but in the end, I managed to somehow suppress the urge."

They were still sharing in the laugh when a server wearing a red vest walked over and handed them each a menu. They spent the next few minutes catching up and keeping the conversation to harmless small talk. When the server returned, they each ordered a Cobb salad.

"I heard you're investigating the Regina Leggett murder," Kiara said.

"How did you know that? Is there anybody in South Florida you don't know well enough to pump for information?"

"It seems like I spend my whole life making friends with people. But if it's a confession you're looking for, I did hear you and Paul were at Mothers and Infants snooping around."

"Maybe I know somebody who had a baby there, and I had a sudden urge to visit her. Anyway, I'm a homicide detective. What's so unusual about me investigating a murder?"

"Nothing, if it was just a routine homicide investigation. But if the murder was possibly tied to a bunch of women all suffering from some odd disease that none of the doctors can figure out, that might be a little unusual."

"Why do I get the feeling that if I shake your family tree, somebody who works at Mothers and Infants will fall to the ground," Libby said. "Why the big interest in the IPS cases?"

"Just a feeling that I'm not the only one who thinks there could be a connection between the murder and the illness."

"Maybe it's just that wild imagination of yours, Kiara."

"I'm an investigative journalist, not an author of sword-and-sorcery fiction. I've trained myself to keep my imagination reined in."

Libby leaned in, and with a tilt of her head, she asked, "C'mon, Kiara. What's on your mind?"

"I was thinking that this might be the perfect time for us to break the glass on tradition."

"Which tradition are we talking about?"

"I was thinking maybe we could be a bit more relaxed about sharing information."

"Is that a serious suggestion? Do I need to remind you that I'm a police officer? We don't collaborate with freelance writers on matters of official police business."

"It's only official if we make it official," Kiara said.

"Not everybody works for themselves, and this may sound a little self-protective, but I'd rather not do anything that could get me busted to the school crosswalk patrol."

"So, you're saying…?"

"I'm suggesting you work your side of the street, and I'll work mine."

"You could at least listen to what I've found out."

"Listen, Kiara. A woman's been murdered. If you have information that could assist the police department in solving a crime, you shouldn't need a deal to disclose it."

"And that's exactly what I'm talking about."

"I'm not getting any of this," Libby said. "You're usually more into writing hair-raising exposés than vanilla healthcare stories."

"There's nothing vanilla about what's going on at Mothers and Infants, and you know it."

The conversation came to an abrupt halt when the server strolled over to the table and placed their salads in front of them. The moment he was two steps away from the table, they picked up where they left off.

"We both know you've always been pretty good at connecting the dots, so if you're trying to get me to confirm or deny what's keeping you up at night, I can't do it."

"But you wouldn't mind hearing anything I might have discovered about IPS."

"That's my job, Kiara. I'm in the business of protecting people," she said, straightening her napkin on her lap and reaching for her fork. "I assumed you knew that. It seems to me that you have more than a passing interest in the Regina Leggett murder. I'm just trying to figure out what convinced you there's more of a story here than a routine murder. Why don't you tell me what you think you know?"

"The gossip in the hospital is that Dr. Church is somehow involved."

"Are you now relying on hospital chitchat as an authoritative reference source for your pieces? By the way, and off the record, Dr. Church is a good man."

"I know that. He delivered both my kids," Kiara said.

"That's a funny thing to say when you just asked me about his possible involvement. I'm still trying to figure out what's really going on here."

"We're both women and mothers. A lot of pretty smart doctors are convinced all ten of the women with IPS are going to die. If sharing information can prevent those deaths and make sure there aren't any future victims, either from illness or violence, I don't give a damn about bending a few rules or regulations."

Libby set her fork down and met Kiara's eyes. "Just what exactly do you have in mind?"

"To start with, I've got an interview late this afternoon that could provide some information that might be helpful in your investigation. If I'm right, I'll be happy to share the information with you. Maybe, if we put our heads together, we can figure some things out that neither of us can do alone."

"I assume you're suggesting we do this completely unofficially."

"I am. As far as I'm concerned, you're just interviewing me."

"I'm probably out of my mind for agreeing to this, but let's meet back here tonight at seven. We can talk about the interview and see where we stand."

"Sounds good," Kiara said, removing her orange spiral notebook from her purse and making a note in it.

"I have two conditions," Libby said.

"Let's hear them."

"Number one: You don't publish anything until all this is over. And two: We never disclose that we talked about this to anybody for any reason. It remains a deep dark secret that we both take to our graves with us."

"I agree completely."

"Perfect. Can we now change the topic of conversation to something unrelated to our work?" Libby asked.

"I was just about to suggest the same thing."

Over the next half an hour, their conversation flowed easily, talking about everything from their kids to future vacations.

As they were paying the check, Libby said, "By the way, I love your perfume. What are you wearing?"

"When I was a teenager, I fell in love with the fragrance of sandalwood. I've never worn anything else. A few years ago I had a fleeting urge to try something different, but as soon as my husband got home, he took one sniff and threatened to divorce me."

"Obviously, you caved in on that one," Libby said with a chuckle.

"It's just perfume," she responded with a light shrug of her shoulders. "I'm a big believer in picking your battles, and I'm pretty sure I'm still way ahead on the scorecard."

"I always knew you were the one in charge in your marriage."

"I am. And to tell you the truth, I wasn't crazy about that new perfume anyway. I'll call you after the interview when I'm on my way to the restaurant."

They said goodbye outside the restaurant and went off in different directions to where they'd parked. Before Libby reached her car, she had ample time to think about her intriguing lunch date. Kiara was right about one thing. She'd always followed police procedures to their strictest interpretations. But Libby's slant on Kiara's proposal was that it didn't necessarily violate any ethical rules of her profession. All she did was agree to one meeting where she'd be in a position to acquire important information pertaining to an ongoing murder investigation. Part of her deal with Kiara was a rather large back door she could stroll through at any time she wanted, which included after their first meeting. She saw what she'd agreed to as, at worst, a minor bend of the rules that she could easily justify when she considered its possible benefit.

Chapter 62

Kiara hadn't published a dozen blockbuster articles by being bashful about pursuing interview opportunities. After lunch with Libby, she wasted no time contacting the owner of Quality Choice Roofing. To her delight, he didn't hesitate for a moment in granting her request to speak with Pintu Nundan at their current worksite. Pintu was one of three names of Abul's coworkers Nadia had given her. Each of the men knew him well, although Nadia felt he would be the most forthcoming and helpful.

It was a short drive to the job site, and she had no trouble finding a parking spot across the street from the one-story house that was in the early stages of having its roof replaced. After speaking with the foreman, Al, briefly, she was escorted to a dump truck parked in the driveway where Pintu was shoveling fragmented tiles to be discarded.

"Pintu, c'mon down here," Al hollered above the crash of the tiles slamming against the floor and walls of the dump box.

Pintu stopped what he was doing, acknowledged his boss with a smile and a wave, and climbed down from the truck. Wearing the company's bright orange polo shirt, he was a trim, middle-aged man with tightly cropped black hair.

"This is Kiara Das. Bryan sent her over to speak with you about Abul. He said to make sure you know that it's entirely up to you if you want to talk to her or not."

"It's nice to meet you," he said to Kiara.

"I'll leave you two to it," Al said as he strolled away.

Kiara wasted no time. "I'm a freelance writer doing a story on Abul. His wife, Nadia, told me you were one of his closest friends and suggested I speak with you."

"We heard he's pretty sick. I visited him in the hospital a few days ago. Has there been any improvement?"

"I don't have any information on his current condition, but my understanding is his doctors are hopeful."

"Why are you doing a story on Abul?" The light-toned skin of his brow wrinkled, and a guarded look came to rest on his face.

"I'm writing a piece on patients with mysterious illnesses, and Abul could certainly be counted as one of them. Since nobody can figure out what's wrong with him, the question's been raised whether the illness he's suffering from could be a hazard to other people."

"Has he required any surgery?"

"I really don't have any of the details of his condition or the treatment he's undergoing."

He scrubbed his hands briskly to knock the dirt from them.

"I see. I came to this country seventeen years ago, Ms. Das. When I left Bangladesh, I was a fully trained nurse. Excuse me if I have an added interest in his condition."

"I see," Kiara said, pulling out her orange spiral notepad and pen.

"You said you'd like to ask me some questions."

"I'd like to hear about the recent work you and he did to see if there might be a clue as to what's causing his illness. How well do you know him?"

"I'd say we're casual friends."

"Do you two socialize together when you're not at work?"

"Sometimes after work we go for a drink with some of the other crew."

"I didn't know Abul was a drinking man."

"He isn't. I never saw him drink anything with alcohol in it."

"Has there been an unusual amount of illness among your crew the last few months?"

"Nothing out of the ordinary that I've noticed."

"Anything about Abul specifically that you're aware of that could have gotten him sick?"

"Not that I saw or heard about, Ms. Das."

From the look in his eyes, Kiara got the feeling he was holding back something. For the moment, she'd leave her inquiry alone, but she fully intended to circle back to the question. "To your knowledge, did he have any unusual habits that might have endangered his health?"

"Abul's the most regular guy you'd ever want to meet. He's an honest, hardworking man. The only things he cares about are his kids, Nadia, and providing for them."

"His wife mentioned to me that the family recently visited Bangladesh. I assume you talked with him about the trip."

"Quite a bit."

"Did he mention anything he did that might have struck you as unusual or out of character for him?"

Pintu grinned. "No, nothing that I can think of."

"Did he mention to you that he hadn't been feeling well before he went into the hospital?"

"No, he got sick pretty quickly. We didn't know anything. He just didn't show up for work one day."

"There's one thing I want to make sure of. I kind of already asked you this, but like I said, I just want to be certain."

"Sure."

"Sometimes people can do the most innocent-appearing things that can get them hurt or sick. Take a minute and think back to your last few jobs with Abul, just to make sure you don't remember anything like that."

Pintu bent his head forward in thought. "I just thought of something, but I doubt it's anything."

"Tell me about it."

"We did a job about a month ago out in the west part of the county. The owner had a small grove of date palm trees and was harvesting the sap from several of them. He was never home, and Abul couldn't resist sampling the sap a few times."

"I'm familiar with its popularity in India and Bangladesh, especially among the rural population."

"I remember Abul telling me that he drank it quite frequently before coming to this country. Are you aware that if the fresh sap becomes contaminated, it can make some people very ill, Ms. Das?"

"I have some vague recollection of the possibility. Did you see any cases when you were a nurse?"

"Yes, a few. It was a small outbreak."

"How sick were these patients?"

"Some were very sick."

"What about you, Pintu? Did you sample any of the sap?"

He smiled. "I assure you, I did not, Ms. Das. I lost my taste for the sweet nectar of the date palm when I moved to this country."

"What about the other roofers? Do you know if any of them tried the sap?"

He shrugged his shoulders. "Not that I saw. There's only a few of us in the company from that part of the world, and none of them were on that job except me and Abul. The rest of the crew wouldn't know what they were looking at if they saw a bunch of clay pots hanging from palm tree trunks."

"From what you're saying, it doesn't sound like the owner caught Abul sampling the sap."

"I don't think so, and I guess Abul didn't mind taking the risk of sneaking a little."

"Do you know if Abul ever ran into the owner of the farm?"

"Not that I saw, and not that he mentioned."

"Did you ever see the owner…even from a distance?"

Pintu didn't answer immediately. "Yeah, I saw him once."

"Did he look Asian or Indian?"

"No way. He was American."

"Would you be comfortable sharing the address of that job location with me?" Kiara asked, taking her time scribbling a few notes in her notebook.

"I'm sorry, I don't remember the address. I might be able to give you a rough idea how to get there, but it might be a better idea for you to call Bryan. I'm sure he can give you the exact address."

"Thanks. I'll do that," she told him. "Is there anything else you can think of that might help me? Anything that happened on one of the other jobs?"

"Nope, not off the top of my head."

She opened her purse and handed him one of her business cards. "Thanks. My cell phone number is on the back. If there's anything else you can think of that might give me added insight into Abul, please call me. Thanks for taking the time to speak with me."

"You're welcome. Please tell Nadia that I'm praying for Abul."

"I will."

On her way back to her car, Kiara took the time to locate Al and thank him. As she crossed the street, she thought about her interview with Pintu. Her general impression was that, while he'd mentioned some interesting things, there were no shocking revelations. Though she viewed going out to the location he'd mentioned as a one-in-a-hundred shot, Kiara still had every intention of going.

"Ms. Das," came a voice through the open car window. Inhaling in surprise, she turned her head.

"I'm sorry to have alarmed you," Pintu said.

"I'm fine. Just a little startled."

"A couple of minutes after you walked away, I remembered something about the owner of the farm. That one time I saw him, he was wearing hospital scrubs."

Chapter 63

Because of the distinct absence of any dissent or naysaying, the meeting to finalize the precise IPS treatment protocol lasted only thirty minutes. Ely limited the group of invitees to ten physicians and nurses in order to facilitate a more productive session. The group decided to go along with Jack and Madison's recommendations, administering two rounds of each of the monoclonal antibodies and continuing the ribavirin. Emphasis was placed on careful observation of each patient with no changes in the protocol, which included the use of the experimental vaccine, unless absolutely necessary.

As soon as the meeting was over, the principal physicians began meeting with each of the women's healthcare proxies to carefully explain the proposed treatment plan. Added attention was placed on alerting the family members to the risks, complications, and alternatives to dual monoclonal antibody therapy. As Jack and Madison had anticipated, every proxy gave consent to administer the monoclonal antibodies.

It was twenty past four when Madison and Jack stepped off the elevator and made their way to the progressive care unit. They had spoken with Teri an hour earlier and requested she meet them in the staff lounge to brief them on each patient's status prior to administering the first dose of sintenimab. As soon as they came through the door, they spotted her sitting on a gray wool couch with a Mothers and Infants Hospital coffee mug in her hand.

"Are we ready to go from a nursing perspective?" Madison asked.

"We're all set. There've been no acute changes in any of the patients' conditions since nine this morning. I've been over the pre-infusion checklist with all the nurses. They're all clear on the IV infusion procedure. I just checked with the pharmacy. They informed me that nine doses of sintenimab are ready for infusion. I assume we're still a go for four thirty."

"That's the plan," Madison said.

"I called the pharmacy, and they confirmed the second monoclonal antibody arrived from Canada an hour ago, so we should easily be ready to infuse it early tomorrow morning. I assume you're going to be in Emma's room at some point during the first round of treatment."

"We plan on spending a little time with each patient while the drug's being infused," Madison said.

"I should get going to see if my nurses have any last-minute questions. I guess I'll see you in a little bit. It sounds like all three of us will be circulating around the rooms during the infusions."

"I assume Dr. Phillips is on the unit too," Jack said.

"He's been here all day with three other intensivists, poring over the charts and making rounds on the patients. Elena's also here, in case we have any unexpected surgical problems."

"You seem a little nervous," Madison said.

"And proud to admit it," she said heading for the door. "I wouldn't want to be working with anybody who wasn't a little bit nervous."

Jack and Madison followed Teri out of the lounge and made their way down the central hallway to Emma's room. When they walked in, Avery, the nurse assigned to her care, was just finishing up checking the plastic infusion bag that contained the sintenimab and the IV pump. David Phillips was at the bedside.

Because of all the activity in the room, the governor and Carmela had chosen to sit down on the opposite side of the room.

"I'm ready whenever you are, Doctor," Avery said. Phillips looked at the group around Emma's bed, checked the time on his phone, and nodded. The Collymores got up and approached the bed.

She took her husband's hand. His head was bowed in sorrow. "She's going to make it, Sam."

"It's four thirty," Phillips said. "Let's get started."

Silence fell on the room as they all watched the first drops of the orange solution depart the infusion bag, course down the clear plastic tubing, and disappear into Emma Collymore's bloodstream.

Chapter 64

From the address given to her by the owner of the roofing company, Kiara was able to research the property's demographic data from the Palm Beach County website. She discovered the farm had been purchased for cash by a corporation registered in Delaware three years earlier.

Using her GPS for guidance, she had no difficulty locating the farm. Once she arrived at the property, Kiara followed the circular driveway to the front of the barn. She stepped out of her late-model SUV into a pleasantly temperate late afternoon with the sun burning through a narrow stack of broken gray clouds. Taking a minute to have a look around at her surroundings, she noticed a well-detailed late-model black pickup truck parked next to the side of the barn by the small grove of palm trees Pintu had told her about. She considered walking over to get a closer look and perhaps grab a picture of the truck's license plate, but her concern that she might be observed prompted her to dismiss the idea. When she looked beyond the truck to the far side of the grove, she noticed a dozen or so of the trees had clay collecting pots hanging from their trunks. So far, Pintu's account was accurate.

Kiara walked up to the barn-house, following a bluestone path that led to an ornate Dutch door. She reached for the arm of a large brass knocker and struck it twice. When after a minute or so there was no answer, she did it again.

This time, a man with an unrevealing expression dressed in jeans and a flannel work shirt appeared at the door.

"May I help you?"

"My name's Kiara Das. I'm a freelance journalist working on a story. I was hoping you'd be able to answer a few questions for me."

"I guess that would depend. To start with, do you have any identification?"

"I do," she answered, gratified by his request, as she assumed it ruled out a categorical no. to her request Wasting no time, she reached into her purse and produced her press pass.

"Would you mind telling me what you're writing about, Ms. Das?" He continued to study her credentials.

"I'm working on a story about individuals with strange illnesses that seem to defy diagnosis. People find the topic fascinating."

"I'm in excellent health, Ms. Das. I guess I don't understand what brought you to my doorstep."

"One of the people I'm writing about is a roofer who suddenly contracted a strange illness that none of his doctors seem to be able to figure out. The individual recently worked here on your roof repairs."

"Why would a freelance writer be interested in such a humdrum story? I mean, the world's on fire. Surely there must be something more interesting and timely to write about."

"The topics writers select are something we could talk about all day," she explained, having no interest in responding in detail to his comment. "You just never know where a story might lead you."

"I see."

"I'm sorry, but I didn't get your name."

"I didn't provide it. I met a few of the workers. What's his name?"

Perhaps it was of no significance, but she hadn't mentioned the patient she was writing about was a man. Though mentioning he was a roofer made it reasonable for him to assume she was talking about a man.

"Abul Kahn."

"Doesn't ring a bell."

"The questions I'd like to ask you are more of a general nature. Whether you met him briefly or not probably isn't important." Kiara purposely looked past him, hoping to prompt him to invite her in.

"Even so, I don't see how I can possibly help you."

"I recently came across some interesting information that I suspect you'll be able to help me understand a little better," she told him, taking note of his long, hardened face with a birthmark at the corner of his mouth, and a commanding presence.

"Sorry, but as hard as I'm trying, I still can't imagine how."

"If you'll give me a few minutes of your time, I'll explain it to you."

She couldn't help but notice how his eyes moved across her face.

"Come in, Ms. Das." He opened the door and escorted her into a tastefully decorated living area with vaulted ceilings, a large wool area rug, and a baroque hardwood bookcase with a brass library ladder that covered the entire far wall.

"That's quite a collection of books."

"I'm very proud of it. If there's one thing that defines me, it's my books. You can learn a lot about somebody from the books they read. Please feel free to take a closer look."

"If you're sure you wouldn't mind—I also fancy myself a bibliophile," Kiara said, strolling over to the other side of the room. With what little she knew of her host, she wasn't surprised to see his books were arranged with precision. Glancing briefly at his collection, she was impressed with the breadth of their subject matter. She took particular notice of the vast number of works about various aspects of the animal kingdom.

"I'm quite jealous," she told him as she returned to the couch.. "I've always dreamed of having a house with a grand library." Despite his eccentricity, Kiara found herself impressed with the man. In a way, she was intrigued by him, and she suspected the more somebody got to know him, the more they'd realize he was an enigma wrapped in a riddle.

"Maybe this story you're working on will lead to a book. When it becomes a bestseller, you'll be able to fulfill your dream and build that library of yours."

He finally took a seat in a large high-backed chair, motioning for her to do the same in a loveseat.

"Before I ask you any questions about Abul Kahn, do you think you're now comfortable enough to share your name with me?"

"My name's Marcus."

"Is that a first or last name?"

"First."

"Thanks," she said, reaching into her purse and removing a pen and her orange spiral notebook. "That's a step in the right direction. As I mentioned, I'm looking into the work-related circumstances surrounding Mr. Kahn's illness."

"You mentioned he works for Quality Choice Roofers."

"That's correct. Obviously, all the physicians involved in caring for him are pulling their hair out trying to figure out how he became so ill."

"And you think he may have gotten sick while he was working here?" Marcus inquired.

"Not necessarily here, but I am suspicious his illness is work-related. I'm looking into all the locations Abul has worked for the past few months. Timing wise, I do have a particular interest in the possibility that he acquired the illness while he worked here."

"Interesting. And why is that, if you don't mind me asking?"

"His coworker mentioned to me that Abul's from Bangladesh, and as many Bangladeshis do, he very much enjoys drinking the fresh sap of date palm trees."

"As do thousands of the inhabitants of West Bengal," he said with a smile. "You'll have to excuse me, but I've always been fascinated by accents of the world, and yours is a dead giveaway."

"I'm impressed. The coworker mentioned to me that I might be interested in speaking with you."

"I see. It's funny how a frank conversation like the one we're having can reveal the truth. I now have a much better idea of why you came to see me. Why did Mr. Kahn's coworker suspect you'd benefit from talking with me?"

"While he insists he didn't personally participate, he told me that Abul couldn't resist sampling the sap that you're collecting from your small grove of date palms."

"Which gave you sufficient information to educate yourself on the possible health risks of drinking date palm sap." Grinning, he wagged a finger her way. "That answers one question I had."

"What question is that?" Kiara asked.

"I watched you when you got out of your car. I was wondering why you were so interested in my palm trees."

She forced a sugary smile to her face, hoping to keep the atmosphere light.

"I had to jump on the internet, but I do have an idea of the basics. It's amazing how such a sweet-tasting nectar can make somebody so sick."

"So you're wondering if my sap's the cause of his illness? Did any of the other workers also partake and get sick?"

"The information I have is that none of the workers besides Abul became seriously ill. I can't dismiss the possibility that the sap made him ill. Can you?"

"Actually, I think I can." He reached over, plucked a wrapped chocolate from a crystal dish, and popped it into his mouth. He extended the dish across the glass coffee table, offering Kiara one. She declined with a polite hand motion. "You're overlooking one rather important point," he said. "I drink the sap regularly, and it's never made me ill."

"I assume you're referring to the last few months," Kiara said. He nodded. "And the last time?"

"A few days ago."

"It's kind of far away, but I didn't notice any covers on the pots."

He chuckled. "I was just about to checkmate you with the same question. Do you happen to know how the palm sap becomes contaminated?"

"From the saliva and urine of fruit bats."

"That's correct. I'm impressed and suspect you know why I see no reason to cover the collecting pots."

Marcus was correct but she said nothing.

"I tend to believe that both of us are well aware there aren't any disease carrying fruit bats within nine thousand miles of here."

"I get the feeling you're pretty well read on the topic," Kiara said.

"As I'm sure you noticed from my book collection, I have quite an interest in all sorts of topics that involve animals, especially those that have the ability to fly, whatever their species."

"How did you develop a taste for date palm sap?"

"My work has taken me to Malaysia on several occasions—once for almost a year. I acquired my taste for palm juice there, along with a liking for various fruit wines. The wine made from certain Asian fruits has become very popular in North America over the last several years. I couldn't see a reason to give it up when I moved home. As you may or may not know, date palm nectar is not commercially available in the U.S."

"You must really enjoy it," she said. As her eyes drifted away briefly, they fell upon an antique mahogany bureau desk that was about ten feet away. She hadn't noticed it when she first came in, but toward the back of the desk was an ID badge. She couldn't be completely sure, but from where she was sitting, it very much resembled a Mothers and Infants ID.

"Do you find something of interest on my desk, Ms. Das?"

"No. Not at all. Just admiring the workmanship." She returned her attention to him. "What do you do for a living, Marcus?"

"I've dabbled in several different things since leaving university and venturing out on my own. But truth be told, I'm what the envious call a trust-fund baby, which has afforded me the opportunity to dip my big toe into several different pools." With a poker face, he added, "You mentioned you're working on a piece about patients with a hard-to-pin-down diagnosis."

"That's correct."

"Have you thought about including any of the IPS patients?"

"Excuse me?"

"IPS. It's the horrible illness those poor women at Mothers and Infants are suffering from. I assumed, with you being a reporter and all…well, you'd know all about it."

Stunned by his anything-but-random comment, Kiara found herself without words.

Marcus stood up and started toward where she was sitting. He stopped when he was an arm's length away. Towering over her, and with a menacing look on his face, he said, "With all due respect, Ms. Das, I don't believe you're being truthful with me."

"You're making me uncomfortable, Marcus. Would you mind taking a few steps back."

"The problem is this—I don't believe you're writing an article about elusive diagnoses. I'm also getting the feeling you're more interested in me than Abul Kahn."

"I thank you for your help, but this interview is over."

She closed her notepad, put it back in her purse, and stood up. She could read the rising anger in his eyes, making her only thought to get out of Marcus's home as quickly as possible. Having no clear idea of what his intentions were, the worst of possibilities crossed her mind. Choked with a mixture of fear and anxiety, she did her level best to hang on to her composure.

He took another step toward her, blocking her from moving in any direction. Her only option was to retake her seat, which she resisted with purpose.

"Are you deaf? This interview is over. Get out of my way."

"Actually, Ms. Das, we're just getting started." Suddenly overtaken with heart-shaking fear, she took a gulp of air.

"I know more cops than you can ever imagine. If you don't get out of my way now and let me leave, I promise you, I'll see you go to jail."

He scoffed at her threat. "I'll be happy to let you leave. All you have to do is tell me what your real reason is for coming here today. The way your eyes are dilated with fear and your hands are shaking,

I'd give my offer every consideration. Tell me the truth, and I'll escort you to the front door and we'll part amicably."

Not believing a word of what he said and at a complete loss for words, Kiara fell into a terrified silence.

Chapter 65

Kiara quickly decided the smartest thing she could do was keep Marcus talking. Every second she could bargain for increased her chances of being able to, by either word or action, escape her dire situation.

"I've got no reason to lie to you, Marcus. Let me go right now, and you have my word I was never here today."

"If I agreed to that fool's deal, how long would it be until a dozen or so police cruisers with sirens blaring screeched to a halt in front of my home?"

"I'm telling you the truth."

"The truth? You've been dancing with the truth since you set foot in my house. I'll know the reason why, or you're going to regret ever coming through my door. The choice is yours. What's it going to be?" He impatiently blew out a blast of air.

Kiara had no illusions she'd be able to persuade Marcus to see things her way. She also didn't see a path to the front door by trying to make a mad dash past him. While her mind was still spinning, looking for her best option, Marcus suddenly leaned in with a clenched hand and back-fisted her across her right cheekbone and eye. The extraordinary force of his blow lifted her off her feet and sent her crashing into a burl wood coffee table before she collapsed to the marble floor below. She remained conscious, but blood spattered in every direction from a jagged laceration under her eye.

Stone-faced, he walked over to his desk and opened the middle drawer. By the time he returned, Kiara had managed to pull herself up into a jackknife position over the edge of the loveseat. Gasping for each breath she took, she suddenly felt him grab her wrist. With one hard twist, he flipped her over and back into a seated position.

With no warning, he struck Kiara again, this time on the left side of her face, snapping her head violently to the side and opening an angular gash above her left eye that resulted in a steady spurt of arterial blood. Studying her impassively, Marcus watched as she struggled to raise a hand to stop the blood from streaming down her ashen face. Inclining his head forward, he grinned at her labored breathing and pained moans.

Convinced she wasn't on the verge of passing out, nor likely to be going anywhere under her own power, he left the room and made his way to a large pantry off the kitchen. A minute later, he returned with a roll of red duct tape and a handful of zip ties. Once he had her hands and feet secured with the ties, he layered three pieces of the duct tape across her mouth.

The moment he was finished, he grabbed a fistful of her hair and dragged her from the loveseat to her feet. With one deliberate move, he hoisted Kiara over his shoulder and carried her through the covered walkway into the barn. From there, he mounted the single flight of wooden stairs to the loft. When he reached the area between his office and the store room, he released his grip, gave a quick shrug of his shoulders and allowed her to slip to the floor. Tilting his head slightly to the side, he looked at her briefly. She was still conscious but clearly feeling the effects of the blows to her head. He took a large step over her body and strolled into the store room where he grabbed a folding chair.

Placing it in front of her, he straddled the seat and rested his arms on the backrest. He took out his cell phone, opened it to the latest book he was reading on the great migration of the Serengeti, and picked up where he'd left off earlier that day. Though engrossed in his reading, he still remembered to check Kiara's level of consciousness every couple of minutes.

After twenty minutes, she was still moaning but moving with more purpose. He decided she was alert enough to talk. He stood up and walked over to where she was lying on the floor. Grabbing her by the shoulders, he pushed her back against the wall and steadied her in a sitting position. He then reached down and yanked the strips of tape from across her mouth. Both facial lacerations were still oozing, leaving her face crusted with dried, darkened blood.

He leaned forward until his lips were within six inches of her right ear. "I hope you're starting to feel better," he said to her in just above a whisper.

"You sick son of a bitch."

"Please, no name calling. It's so uncivilized."

Consumed by panic and with every muscle and bone in her body aching, she said, "There are people who know I'm here. How stupid do you think I am?"

"You came to my home, didn't you? To my way of seeing things, that makes you pretty stupid. Anyway, even if you did tell somebody, you won't be missed for hours, which gives me plenty of time to erase any evidence that you were ever here." He squatted down in front of her. "Now I want you to tell me everything you know about the cause of IPS. By the way, if you're anything but totally forthcoming with me, I promise you'll suffer the consequences, only worse this time."

Kiara didn't doubt for a second he meant what he said. She was quickly becoming convinced that Marcus intended to kill her, no matter how much information she agreed to share with him. She doubted that any amount of begging and pleading would save her. She knew how to think on her feet, and it was obvious that the only way she was getting out of this situation alive was to somehow mastermind an escape. Marcus was right about one thing—nobody was going to come crashing through the door to rescue her.

"What's in it for me to tell you what I know?" she asked, trying to endure the pain of her injuries.

"I guess that depends on what you know. Try me."

"Not a chance. Not without some guarantee that I come out of this alive."

"You'll just have to trust me. You know, Ms. Das, I was pretty vague about what I do for a living, but you didn't even have the curiosity to push the point."

"That's because it has no bearing on the piece I'm writing."

"I don't believe that for a second. I don't think you wanted to let on that you suspected I work at Mothers and Infants."

"Do you?"

"We both know you saw my ID."

"Florida still has capital punishment. Maybe if you knew how close the authorities were to dropping a net on you, you'd call it quits right now and avoid the prison in Raiford and the big IV they'll be putting in your arm."

"Are you suggesting that I may have killed somebody or somehow arranged for an outbreak of an incurable illness? Thanks for the compliment, but that would be a pretty neat trick even for a man with my talents."

In a voice dripping with desperation, Kiara said, "I don't know for sure one way or the other, nor do I care. I'm saying if you let me walk out of here, I can easily forget about what's happened here. I'm willing to give you the time you need to escape."

"Anything else?

"I have the type of influence that can help you if you need it."

"And I'd believe that…why?"

"Because it would be the smart move on your part," she told him, tears beginning to form in her eyes.

"I might consider your offer if it weren't for the fact that I think you're bluffing and lying. I suspect, if the police were in desperate pursuit of me as you're implying, I'd know about it. Nobody from the authorities has even spoken to me."

"What the hell makes somebody like you tick?"

He fixed his eyes on Kiara. "Oh, I see. You think I should be counted among the homicidal psychopaths of the world—kind of like Ted Bundy and Son of Sam. Is that it? I'm not sure now is the time for feisty, Ms. Das. I would think somebody in your line of work would know that everything's not what it appears."

"What are you trying to say?"

"That different things motivate different people." With his fingertips pointed up, he tapped his hands together. "You've managed to connect some things that I believed nobody ever would have. I'm impressed, but I'm left wondering what to do now. Your visit here has created some interesting choices for me to consider."

He came out of his catcher's crouch and stood straight up. "Until I figure out exactly what I'm going to do with you, I'm going to keep you right here with me." He wrung his hands together and then clapped them a single time. "I guess that's enough talking for now." Without another word, he disappeared into his office.

While Kiara kept her gaze locked on the door to Marcus's office, she twisted and pulled at the bonds on her wrists with every ounce of strength she could muster, ignoring the pain as she tried to free her hands. A minute or so passed, and she had to stop to rest. She was still trying to catch her breath when she suddenly heard the office door open. Marcus emerged and started toward her with a grim look on his face. Intense fear swept over her when she saw his right hand tucked behind his back.

"Okay," he began with an infantile smirk as he raised his concealed hand and showed her a small syringe. He stared at it briefly as he tilted it from side to side. "There are two ways we can do this. You can either remain calm and allow me to give you this sedative, or, if you'd like to be difficult, I can knock you unconscious and do it. So what's it going to be, Ms. Das?"

Her mind was spinning, making it almost impossible for her to hold a straight thought in her head. She had no reason to believe the syringe contained a drug from which she'd ever awaken. Not believing for an instant he was bluffing, the only hope she saw of saving herself was to keep Marcus talking in the hopes it would delay any sinister intention he had as long as possible.

"Whatever you've got planned, you're only making things worse for yourself. Just let me go, and you have my word none of this ever happened."

"Will you back that up with a pinky swear?" he asked with a chuckle. "Did I forget to look in the mirror this morning? Do I have gullible tattooed on my forehead?"

"I have a family," she screamed, overtaken with terror.

"Oh, why didn't you say so? That changes everything."

"What do you gain by harming me?"

"My continued freedom." He held up the syringe again. "Now, what's it going to be?"

"I'll hold still."

"Wise choice."

"What are you giving me?"

"Ketamine. It's a short-acting sedative. It'll wear off in about twenty minutes." Leaning over, he pushed up her sleeve and thrust the needle into her upper arm. "I'm sorry about all this, Ms. Das, but for the life of me, I can't figure out how much of my work you've managed to piece together. You strike me as a smart lady, but I'm pretty smart myself, and if there's one thing I've learned, it's never to take any chances."

Marcus capped the syringe and sat back down to wait for the first signs that Kiara was feeling the effects of the ketamine. Five minutes later, her head was slumped forward with her chin flush against the top of her breastbone. Coming to his feet, he grabbed her by one ankle and dragged her inside the storeroom limp as a Raggedy Anne doll. Guessing he had about fifteen minutes before the ketamine would begin to wear off, he used the first five to return to the barn-house and locate Kiara's purse.

Making his way back to the loft, he put the finishing touches on his plan to permanently deal with his uninvited guest. For the moment, the most pressing matter was to conceal her vehicle from sight. After a few moments of thought, he decided the deserted horse barn at the north end of the farm would be the ideal location.

Addressing the bigger picture, he reminded himself that there were untold benefits of living so close to a watershed like the Everglades. For his purposes tonight, perhaps the biggest one was the hundreds of miles of isolated canals. The sheer number of bodies and automobiles that had found their permanent and undiscovered home in the swamp was legendary.

Marcus's plan was a simple one. A little before midnight, he'd load his ATV into the back of his pickup truck and find a suitable canal to dump both Ms. Das and her SUV. He'd then drop off the ATV, conceal it in a convenient location, and use it to return to the farm once he'd commended his uninvited guest and her vehicle to a swampy grave. If the accounts he'd read of such burials in the Everglades were accurate, it would be fifty years before somebody happened to stumble across the SUV.

With Kiara's purse in hand, Marcus entered the barn, climbed the stairs to the loft, and went into the storeroom From the way she was stirring, he surmised the drug was wearing off sooner than he'd expected. He walked over to her, kneeled down, and checked to make sure the zip ties were in place. He then replaced the tape across her mouth.

He decided to secure her bound hands to the floor-to-ceiling copper water pipe as a final layer of security. Satisfied she was tucked in and that he wouldn't be bothered by her again until it was time to make the trip into the Everglades, he patted her a couple of times on the head. Marcus paused to open her purse before returning to his office. Thinking it might make for interesting reading, he removed her spiral notebook, tossed her purse at her feet, and left her on the floor.

Once he was seated at his desk, he checked the weather app on his phone to get a forecast for the evening. The corners of his mouth creased into a smile when he read that, not only was the lunar cycle in its darkest phase, but the forecast called for a heavy cloud cover with a low ceiling. It would be a particularly dark night, even for the Everglades.

Marcus found himself wondering about the days that would follow Kiara's disappearance. Once she was considered a missing person, he assumed he'd be visited by the authorities as part of their routine investigation. He hadn't quite decided yet if he'd simply deny that she'd ever been to his farm or report to them that he'd spoken with her very briefly and she left. Marcus was in no way short on confidence. He'd always been comfortable thinking on his feet, and critical situations never made him nervous. He was certain his inevitable interview with the police would cast no suspicions on him, and he'd quickly become a faint memory in their investigation.

Chapter 66

As she had arranged with Kiara, Libby entered Alexandra's Bistro at exactly seven o'clock. Walking up to the hostess desk, she noticed the restaurant was considerably busier than it had been at lunchtime. The young lady who'd greeted her earlier was still working and smiled when they made eye contact.

"Welcome back, Ms. Rafferty," she said, checking her laptop. "The other guest in your party hasn't checked in as of yet. Your table's ready if you'd like to be seated. If you prefer, you can wait at the bar, and I'll come find you as soon as she arrives."

"I think I'd rather be seated now."

"Of course," she said as she waved to another hostess who came over, grabbed two menus, and showed Libby to the table.

Within a few minutes, a young man wearing a black vest over a gray shirt walked up to the table.

"Can I interest you in a drink while you're waiting?"

"Thank you, but I think I'll wait."

Libby had had a busy afternoon at work and hadn't given much further thought to her lunch meeting with Kiara. She was comfortable that she hadn't agreed to anything that was a violation of her code of conduct as a police officer—not yet at least. She checked the time. It was ten past seven. Looking toward the front of the restaurant, she didn't see Kiara. Waiting until she caught the server's eye, she signaled him, and he returned to the table.

"I think I will have something to drink. Can I trouble you for an unsweetened iced tea please."

"Of course."

By the time Libby finished her drink, it was almost seven thirty, and there was still no sign of Kiara. Reaching into her purse, she grabbed her phone and called her. The call went straight to voicemail. Thinking it was a little unusual that Kiara hadn't called to let her know she was running late, Libby assumed she was in the middle of an interview and couldn't excuse herself to take a call. But when another few minutes passed and there was still no sign of her, Libby called her home number.

Her husband picked up on the first ring.

"Hi. This is Libby Rafferty calling. I'm a friend of Kiara's. I think we've spoken on the phone a few times."

"Of course. Kiara told me you guys were meeting for dinner tonight."

"Actually, that's what I'm calling about. She's over half an hour late, and I can't seem to reach her."

"That doesn't sound like Kiara. She's a fanatic when it comes to punctuality."

"If you don't mind me asking, when was the last time you heard from her?"

"A few hours ago. She told me she'd spoken to some roofer who gave her a promising lead for the story she's currently working on and that she planned on interviewing somebody before meeting you for dinner. She seemed excited that she'd come across something important."

"I don't suppose she mentioned his name by any chance."

"No, but the lead came from Quality Choice Roofing. The only reason I remember that is because they did some work for us a few years ago. It's a small company owned by a couple of brothers. I'm pretty sure I have one of their cell phone numbers. Give me a sec," he told her. Libby drummed the table while she waited. "Here it is.

The guy's name is Bryan Kurtz. I'll share his contact information with you."

"Thank you," Libby said, grateful she wouldn't have to waste a lot of time trying to track down the number herself.

"Kiara will probably come through the door of the restaurant before you can call him."

"I hope so," she said, but for reasons she couldn't quite get her head around, she doubted he was right.

I'm trying to reach Mr. Bryan Kurtz."

"This is he. Is there a problem?"

"I'm trying to locate an individual, and I'm hoping you may be able to help me. Her name's Kiara Das, and I think she may have spoken to one of your employees earlier today."

"Actually, I took the call from Ms. Das and arranged for her to talk to my foreman. I spoke with him later, and he told me that she'd interviewed Pintu Nundan. She was interested in a recent job Abul Kahn was on and wanted to speak with the owner of the barnhouse we worked on."

"Is there any way you can provide me with that address, Mr. Kurtz?"

"I think so. Give me a sec while I bring it up on my computer." Libby held on, looking toward the entrance every minute or so, hoping to see Kiara come through the door. "The location is in the west part of the county. It's 240 Willis Run."

"Thank you, sir."

"My pleasure. If we can be of any further help, please call me back."

Libby motioned to the server. While she waited for him, she thought about what she'd just learned from Bryan. As hard as she tried to write it off as nothing other than Kiara getting held up and her phone being dead, she couldn't convince herself that's what happened. She was certain if her partner, Paul, were sitting across from her, he'd tell her she was overreacting. The thought crossed her mind to give him a call, but he and his wife had gone to Fort Myers for a couple of days, and she opted not to disturb him. She looked down at the piece of paper she'd written the address on. While she was still lost in thought, the server returned to the table.

"Is there anything I can get you?" he asked. From the sympathetic look that appeared on his face, Libby assumed he had come to the conclusion she'd been stood up.

"No thanks. In fact, I've kind of run out of time, so if you'll give me the check, I'd appreciate it."

"Happens all the time. Don't worry about it. The iced tea's on me. Have a nice evening."

"Thank you," she said, coming to her feet. She made sure to leave a five-dollar bill on the table and wasted no time leaving the restaurant and getting to her car.

Chapter 67

At a few minutes past nine, Marcus returned from moving Kiara's SUV to the abandoned horse stable. He had several hours before he'd head out to the Everglades to locate a suitable canal to dispose of her body. The details of how he'd accomplish the task were well set in his mind, leaving him with several hours to kill. He fancied himself an expert in solving puzzles based on logic. Remembering that he'd just received his latest book of high-complexity sudoku puzzles, his problem of how to fill his time was solved.

Making his first stop the library in the barn-house, he picked up the book and crossed the enclosed breezeway that led to the barn. Having no interest in his captive's condition, he skipped a stop in the tack room and went straight to his office. He'd been solving puzzles for a little over an hour when the barn-house's front door buzzer sounded.

"May I help you?" he asked through the two-way-talk device.

"This is Detective Rafferty with the Palm Beach Sheriff's Office. I'd like to speak with you."

"I'm in the barn. If you'll give me a few minutes, I'll finish up what I'm doing and walk up and meet you where you are."

"I'll save you the time. I'm already on my way to the barn."

He left his office, descended the stairs, and headed toward the entrance. He was almost to the front of the barn when he spotted a woman he guessed to be in her mid to late thirties enter through the partially open sliding wooden doors. Libby walked toward him and held up her credential wallet.

"I'm Marcus Parry. How can I help you?"

"Detective Rafferty. I'm investigating a missing person report. I'd like to ask you a few questions."

"Of course. I have an office up in the loft. I'm afraid it's the only place to sit down."

"That will be fine," she said, following him toward the stairs.

"Since you're here, am I to assume I know this missing person you're looking for?"

Marcus injected an appropriate amount of concern into his voice as he followed her up the stairs. He noticed her looking around at her surroundings. From the way she was gazing toward the rafters, he assumed she'd taken note of the dozens of bats that were roosting upside down.

Are you afraid of bats, Detective?" he asked, lighting a cigarette.

"I never gave it much thought. Are you?"

"I'd say I was at one time, but I've kind of gotten used to them. I've done quite a bit of reading about them. They're fascinating creatures. I never figured out why, but over time, they seem to have taken a liking to my barn. They may be uninvited guests, but they've never cared enough to bother me, and we seem to respect each other's space."

"My recollection is they carry rabies and all kinds of other terrible diseases. There must be a dozen companies you could hire to deal with them."

"I could never harm any living creature," he responded with a slow shake of his head. "No, Detective. They're here to stay, and I'm fine with it." They reached the top of the staircase and headed down the hall to his office.

"Don't they hibernate in the cold weather?"

"According to what I've read, most bats sleep during the day and spend their nights feasting on insects before returning the next morning. I assume the ones who live in my barn aren't the type that hibernate for months at a time."

Once they entered his office, Libby took a seat on a wooden chair that had seen better days. It faced his garage-sale desk that was piled high with all manner of papers, magazines, and stationery supplies.

"Do you own this farm, sir?"

"No, I'm a long-term renter. It's owned by a large real estate consortium. Don't bother asking me the name, because I'd have to look it up."

"How long have you lived here?"

"I've been in South Florida for quite some time, but I rented this place about three years ago."

"Does anybody else live here with you?"

"I have guests from time to time, but I prefer to live alone," Marcus answered. "Who is it that you're looking for, Detective? Perhaps, if I knew her name, it might spark my memory."

"I don't recall mentioning it was a woman."

"I guess I just assumed."

"You're correct. I'm looking for a young woman from the Miami area. Her name's Kiara Das. She's a reporter. Do you happen to know her?"

Marcus was instantly suspicious that Rafferty wasn't being honest with him. He wondered if she was just casting her line in the water and doing some trolling or if she had a reasonable suspicion that Kiara had been to his home. But one thing was plain as day. Even if somebody had filed a missing person report, it would have been only a few hours ago. Based on that time frame, unless there were extraordinary circumstances, it was highly unlikely the police would launch an immediate missing person investigation. Libby rephrased her question. "Has Ms. Das been here today, or has she tried to contact you in any way?"

Marcus was expecting the question—it was inevitable. The best way to answer it was a little more tricky.

"Ms. Das showed up at my door this afternoon completely

unannounced," he said in a nonchalant tone. "If you don't mind me asking, who reported her missing?"

"I'm not allowed to share that information with you, but I'm intrigued that you'd ask."

"Well, I guess I'm intrigued that you're pursuing a missing person investigation for somebody who was simply going on about her job a few hours ago."

"Tell me about your conversation with her."

"She was alone, quite calm, and came across as somebody who was serious about her job."

"What do you do for a living?"

"Many things, but my major area of interest is animal conservation. I have a master's degree in the area, which has opened a lot of academic and commercial employment opportunities for me."

"Can you give me some of the specifics of what you and she talked about?"

"She told me she was writing an article on a gentleman who had recently contracted a very unusual disease."

"Did she mention why she was interested in interviewing you specifically?"

"She told me the man she was writing about was a roofer and that he was part of a crew that did some work for me. I think she was interested in exploring the possibility that something in his work environment, either here or at another job site, made him ill."

"Did you meet the man she's writing about while he worked for you?"

"I didn't meet any of the roofers, Detective."

"Compared to a lot of areas within fifty miles of here, I'd say this looks like a pretty healthy area. I wonder why Ms. Das would think there was something about your farm's environment that could have made him sick."

"She asked me some pretty basic questions about the farm, which I answered. She seemed satisfied and left. It was a pretty short conversation. And as I mentioned, she told me she was investigating several of his recent job sites."

"Have you by any chance been following the story about the

group of women at Mothers and Infants who all became ill at the same time?" Libby asked.

"I'm aware of the illness."

"It's no secret that, in addition to those women, at least one other individual has been diagnosed with the disease."

"Are you saying you suspect that's the story Ms. Das is working on?"

"It's a possibility. Have you spent any time at Mothers and Infants in any capacity?" Libby asked him directly. She didn't raise her eyes. She simply continued jotting notes down.

"I'm a certified nursing assistant. I've worked staff relief at Mothers and Infants, but probably no more than a dozen shifts over the past year."

"I didn't notice any type of surveillance system on your property."

"That's because there isn't one. If I felt I needed that type of protection, I'd pack up and move to someplace more civilized. It also means I don't have any video of her being here, if that's what you're getting at."

As he spoke, Marcus watched Libby's eyes move across the top of his desk.

"How long did you speak to Ms. Das for?"

"I'd say twenty minutes or so."

"Did she mention she'd like to speak with you again?"

"No, and she revealed very little about the piece she was working on. As soon as she figured out that I wasn't a fount of information on anything she was researching for her story, she wrapped things up pretty quickly."

"I see."

"Do you have any other questions for me, Detective?"

"Just a couple. Did she say where she was headed after you two spoke?"

"No, she didn't."

"Did she seem nervous or upset?"

"Not at all."

"Did you actually see her car pull away?"

"I'm afraid I didn't."

"Is there anything else she said that you feel might help us?"

"Not that I can think of. As I said, she acted normally, our conversation was brief, and she left as quickly as she showed up."

Libby came to her feet. "Thank you. I may want to speak with you again."

He reached into the central drawer of his desk and handed her card. "Please call me anytime you wish. I'll show you the way out."

Even while he was getting up from his chair, Marcus was already thinking about the interview. He wasn't concerned about the way he'd responded to Detective Rafferty's questions, but what did concern him was her apparent mounting level of suspicion that had begun from the moment he'd greeted her at the barn door entrance.

Chapter 68

While Libby waited for Marcus to come out from behind his desk, she couldn't help but wonder at how composed he'd been during their talk. As a police officer, she'd come across other individuals like him—the type with ice water in their veins who were able to stand up to almost any nail-biting situation with a combination of facility and flair. Regardless of the reason, most people confronted with a police interview are visibly uneasy. In Marcus's case, it was as if he viewed their conversation as a game of cerebral chess that he was enjoying immensely. Libby had a lot to think about, but at the moment, the one thing that was clear in her mind was her belief that Marcus knew more about IPS and Kiara Das than he had admitted.

While she waited for him to stack a few file folders and set them on his writing pad, she casually scanned the top of his desk. Out of the corner of her eye she spotted a spiral notebook with an orange cover. When she realized it was identical to the one she'd seen Kiara remove from her purse at lunch, she was a little taken back. Well-practiced in not demonstrating emotion when she was on the job, Libby said nothing and followed Marcus out of his office. She cautioned herself to reel in her imagination, reasoning it was more likely that they'd both happened to purchase the same color notebook than that the one on his desk belonged to Kiara.

"I hope I've been of some help," he said to her as they started down the hall toward the staircase.

"I appreciate you taking the time to speak with me."

She hadn't taken more than a few steps when a faint, dimly familiar scent filled her nostrils. As they moved toward the end of the hall and were within a few feet of the storeroom, the sweet, woody aroma strengthened. She instantly recognized it, and her stomach clenched—the scent was undeniably that of a sandalwood perfume, indistinguishable from the one Kiara was wearing at lunch. All at once, the possibility that Marcus and Kiara both favored orange-colored office supplies seemed a lot less likely.

Libby intentionally allowed herself to fall another step behind him. She eased her hand toward her belt holster that held her Smith & Wesson M&P 2.0. Just before they reached the steps, she stopped and drew the weapon. Widening her stance, she leveled the handgun between his shoulder blades.

"Hold it right there," she called out to him. "You're under arrest. Put your hands where I can see them, and don't move." Marcus slowed his pace but didn't stop, nor did he put his hands up. For her own safety, Libby decided to make the arrest using a ground-control technique. "On the floor, spread eagle, right now." Marcus stopped but didn't move to the floor. Instead, he casually glanced over his shoulder, grinned menacingly, and slid his hand into his right pocket. "Get your hands where I can see them, and get on the floor. I won't tell you again."

"Certainly," he said, removing his hand from his pocket, revealing the small remote control he was holding between his thumb and index finger.

"Toss it on the floor and put your hands behind your back."

"As you say." He drew his hand back and held up the device. He then pushed its only button and tossed it her way. Before it hit the ground, an ear-piecing wail of a high-decibel, mixed-frequency siren filled the air. Instantly, the barn filled with a large swarm of terrified bats in frenzied flight. Before Libby could stop him, Marcus dashed the last few feet to the staircase, took the first few steps, and then vaulted over the banister to the floor below. Landing securely on his feet, he fled the barn through the covered breezeway.

The chaotic flightpaths of the bats with their shrill screeches and chitters joined with the blaring siren. It took every drop of discipline and training Libby could muster to prevent herself from covering her head and falling to the floor. But she knew that would make her supremely vulnerable if Marcus returned. Instead, she reset her service weapon, assumed a ready position, and kept it trained on the area at the top of the staircase. She could feel the air currents created by the bats as they continued their furious flight, passing within inches of her head and neck. Situational awareness was everything, and Libby focused on not losing sight of reality.

Beginning with one cautious step, she made her way down the hallway to the tack room. It was at this moment that she looked up again at the fleeing bats that had now formed a steady stream of flight and were escaping from the barn. Libby swung her gaze to the tack room door, reminding herself that adhering to everything she'd ever learned about critical situation procedures was the key to staying alive. Her eyes flashed in every direction, checking again to assure herself that Marcus was nowhere in sight.

The best she could do was take an educated guess as to whether he was still nearby or if he'd fled the area. An even mixture of experience and instinct convinced her he was still around and undoubtedly had harmful intent. Before dealing with the door, she reached for her cell phone to call for backup. She was unsurprised to discover there was no signal. When she tried her standard-issue two-way radio, she encountered the same problem.

She reached out and turned the door handle. As she expected, it was locked. Looking at the frame, she saw no hinges, which indicated the door probably opened into the room. She ran her hand along its middle. The construction didn't strike her as particularly sophisticated, leading her to believe the door was probably a hollow-core design and could be easily broken. She tapped the door's central portion. The characteristic sound confirmed her suspicion. Taking one step backward, Libby elevated her leg, flexed it fully at the knee, and front-kicked the door just below the handle. Being its weakest point, the area around the lock shattered, and the door flew open.

Libby wasted no time entering the room. Enough light filtered in from the hallway for her to spot the light switch and flip it on. She looked to the far wall and spotted Kiara sitting with her back pressed against the metal pipe. With her eyes remaining glued on the door, she backed up slowly until she reached Kiara, and she kneeled down beside her. From the condition of the door, she knew if Marcus returned he wouldn't be able to lock them in, but her position from a tactical standpoint was a precarious one. She needed to free Kiara from her restraints and get them both the hell out of the tack room as quickly as possible.

Kiara let out a low moan. "I have you," Libby told her as she started to evaluate the situation. Even though help had arrived, a look of terror remained frozen on Kiara's face.

The last batch of duct tape Marcus had applied to her face crisscrossed her mouth, extending all the way to the tops of her jawbones. Kiara's eyes flooded with tears. The expression on her face clearly betrayed her terror. The moment she lifted her head, Libby saw the two large gashes on her face and the blood stains on her clothes. She had no way of estimating how much blood Kiara had already lost or how much more she was likely to lose.

Libby cautiously removed the tape. "Hang on, Kiara. You're safe. He's gone. C'mon, we need to get out of here. Do you think you can walk?"

"I...I think so."

"Let's get this tape and the zip ties off you. Don't try to talk. Just concentrate on breathing normally."

Libby always carried a tactical folding knife. She quickly removed it from the same holster she used to carry her firearm. Shifting her eyes back and forth between Kiara and the entrance to the room, she used an appropriate mixture of speed and caution to cut the zip ties and remove the tape. Before assisting Kiara to her feet, Libby made sure she was in a good position to fire her weapon in the direction of the door if the need should arise.

Still partially under the effects of the drug, Kiara needed a moderate amount of assistance to make it to her feet.

"Are you ready?" Libby asked, placing her free hand under Kiara's arm to help support her weight.

"I think so."

"You're doing great. We're going to do this one step at a time. If anything happens, I want you to fall to the floor.

"That means you think he may come back."

"That would be a major error in judgment on his part."

They started to move toward the door. For Kiara's protection, Libby used her free arm to keep Kiara a half step behind her and tucked in along her side. Once they were out in the hall, they headed straight for the stairs. If Marcus was waiting for them, Libby realized that coming down the stairs put them in a particularly vulnerable position.

They reached the first step of the staircase with no problem. As they started down, Libby's attention was divided between keeping Kiara from falling and staying constantly vigilant to the possibility Marcus was lying in wait for them. With each step they took, Libby turned and looked toward the top steps, just in case Marcus knew of a different way to get to the loft. It took them longer than she was comfortable with, but they finally reached the bottom.

"How are you doing? Can you make it to the door?"

"I'm having some trouble breathing, but I'll make it."

"Catch your breath for a few seconds. Once we start heading for the door, we need to keep moving."

Realizing they were a long way from being out of harm's way, Libby urged Kiara on, and they started across the barn. The lighting wasn't nearly as bright as it was in the loft, and there was a distinct lack of cover along their path to the door. Libby worked under the assumption that Marcus had concealed himself close by and was waiting for just the right moment to make his move.

"How's the breathing?" Libby whispered, noting one of Kiara's lacerations had begun to ooze a steady stream of fresh blood.

"I'm okay. I can make it."

With her eyes and ears keenly attuned to her surroundings,

Libby continued to guide Kiara across the silent barn. When they were about halfway to the door, she caught sight of movement out of the corner of her eye. She immediately swung her gaze to the right and saw Marcus come out of one of the converted stalls with a shotgun in his hands. Instantly pushing Kiara to the floor, Libby set her preferred two-handed grip on her Smith & Wesson and rotated her shoulders toward him. She could see Marcus raising the single-barrel shotgun. Her mind flashed to her training, which dictated *simplify, focus, and execute*. By the time he'd tucked the butt of the Winchester into his shoulder and raised the barrel, Libby had already leveled her firearm at his upper torso. She prayed he wasn't wearing a vest.

She opened fire before he could get off his first shot. He staggered forward and fell, but was able to hold himself up on his knees in a seiza position. Libby fired another few rounds and watched him topple to the side. She kept her weapon leveled on him. To her surprise, he still had his hands on his shotgun. When she saw him begin to move it, trying to raise the gun, she opened fire again and didn't stop until the magazine was empty. The shotgun fell away as he tumbled back, coming to rest face-up on the cold clay floor.

Libby dropped that clip and replaced it with another. Marcus was motionless.

"Don't move," she told Kiara.

Libby moved cautiously to Marcus's fallen body. With her foot, she pushed the shotgun several feet away. There was a considerable amount of blood on the floor, and she could easily identify multiple wounds to his chest and flank. Checking again, she saw no signs of him breathing. Libby was as certain as she could be that she'd fatally wounded him, although she'd leave confirming his death to the paramedics.

At this point, she needed to secure the scene, get Kiara to safety, and call for medical assistance.

She returned to where Kiara was resting on the floor. "Are you okay?"

"A lot better than I was an hour ago."

"There's no cell phone or two-way radio signal in here. Let's get outside and call for help. We need to get you to the hospital."

"I should call my husband."

They left the barn and walked about twenty feet toward the barn-house. Libby tried her cell phone and was able to call for backup and medical assistance. They sat down right where they were standing.

"I'm guessing, when you suggested we collaborate, this wasn't exactly what you had in mind," Libby said.

"I don't want you to think I'm ungrateful about saving my life, so the next time we go to Alexandra's Bistro, my treat."

"Who do you think he was?" Libby asked.

"I didn't speak to him that long and he was very cautious about what he said, but I'd bet my life he's up to his eyeballs in the IPS outbreak."

"What makes you so sure?"

"I suspect if you get your CSI team out here and get a sample of the fresh sap he's harvesting from those date palm trees over there, you'll have proof positive of what's causing IPS."

"Any idea why he might have done that?"

"I don't have the first clue. Maybe he's just insane. You'll have to find out the answer to that question yourself."

They exchanged a look of relief when they heard the distant sirens. An ambulance and several Palm Beach County Sheriff's vehicles pulled up in front of the house.

"Help me up, please," Kiara said.

"Are you sure? The paramedics will be here in a few moments."

"I think I'd like to get up."

Libby stood up and helped Kiara get to her feet. As Libby gave her an enormous hug, the floodgates opened, and Kiara finally began crying profusely.

Chapter 69

INFUSION–DAY TWO

EIGHT AM

The first person Madison and Jack saw when they entered the progressive care unit was David Phillips. His scrubs were rumpled and his rusty red hair disheveled. He caught sight of them almost immediately and raised his container of coffee to signal them to join him. The pure exhaustion he was suffering from reflected in his eyes.

"How did everything go when you gave the second drug?" Jack asked, with a feeling in his gut that the experimental monoclonal antibody infusions hadn't gone nearly as well as the sintenimab.

"At first, everything was okay," David said. "But at about thirty minutes in, things started to get interesting. Four of the patients experienced a significant reaction."

"Manifested by what?" Jack asked.

"The first thing we noticed was blood pressure instability and a fast heart rate. That was followed by a significant number of hives. We'd just started treatment for what we assumed was an allergic reaction when all four patients developed fever, chills, and profuse sweating."

"Did the reactions reach the level of an emergency anaphylactic response?" Madison asked.

"No, but it got pretty close. One of them developed a moderate amount of respiratory distress. We thought she might need to be intubated and put on a ventilator, but we maxed out her meds, and although I can't be completely sure, it looks like she'll get through the crisis."

"Was Emma Collymore one of the patients affected?" Madison inquired.

"I'm afraid she was. Her parents are in her room now, chomping at the bit to see you two."

"How's she doing?" Madison inquired.

"Stable, but I'm not exactly ready to do a victory dance just yet."

She asked, "Did all the patients receive both monoclonal antibodies?"

"Yes."

"As I recall, up to forty percent of patients receiving a monoclonal antibody will manifest some reaction to the drug." Jack said.

"The early reactions tend to almost all be allergic in nature, but there are other side effects and complications that can appear months and even years later that can be very serious," David said. Just as he finished speaking, Teri walked up and joined them.

"What's the initial feeling among the nurses?" David asked.

Holding up crossed fingers, she answered, "I don't want to sound foolishly optimistic, but I saw each of the patients about an hour ago. The ones who didn't experience an allergic response are doing fine. I'd even go so far as to say that, compared to their pre-infusion condition, they're a little better. As far as the ones who suffered side effects, I'm not as convinced. I guess we'll just have to wait a few more hours to see how things play out."

"We need to keep things in perspective," Madison said. "Assuming all the patients tolerate the infusions, the big question's going to be whether the combined therapy will offer them a chance at recovery."

"Have you made a decision about using the experimental vaccine?" Teri inquired.

"All the arrangements are made," Madison told her. "If we decide to pull the trigger, we'll have the vaccine here in twenty-four hours."

"What's going to push us one way or the other?" Teri asked.

"I guess it'll be a rather subjective decision," Jack said. "I suspect it will be obvious if the monoclonal antibodies fail to eradicate the infection. If that's the case, we'll offer the vaccine to the families."

"I assume Dr. Phillips told you the Collymores are anxiously awaiting your arrival."

"We're headed there now," said Jack.

David tapped his watch. "I'd better get going. I'll touch base with you guys later."

Jack and Madison made their way to Emma's room and quietly stepped inside. The governor and Carmela were standing at the foot of her bed.

"Good morning," Madison said.

Carmela gave her a weak smile. "Good morning. Our girl had a rough night, but Dr. Phillips told us he thought she pulled through it okay." Her voice held an echo of hope.

"We just spoke with Dr. Phillips and Teri," Madison said. "We're obviously concerned about her allergic reaction, although we don't feel that ultimately it will interfere with her receiving the second round of monoclonal antibodies."

Jack moved to the head of the bed while Madison took the lead in responding to the Collymores' questions. To his surprise, Emma looked better than he expected. Her eyes were open, and for the first time in the last few days, she seemed to be able to focus. Her complexion still had an alabaster look to it, but it was improved. Checking her monitor, he noted her vital signs, oxygenation, and other physiological indicators were all normal. Jack took the next few minutes to do a physical examination. Both her rash and jaundice were showing signs of improvement.

"What do you think, Jack?" the governor asked.

"I'm cautiously encouraged."

"Dr. Phillips checked her about forty minutes ago, and he seemed to feel the same way."

"You'll recall from the first time we talked about monoclonal antibody therapy, we mentioned the possibility of seeing improvement within the first few days." Jack's voice gained positivity. "I think that may be the case with Emma."

The governor's voice was more assured. "Just to confirm, Emma will still receive another round of the two monoclonal antibodies beginning late this afternoon?"

"We have to monitor her condition carefully," Jack explained. "If she remains stable over the next several hours, we'll pre-treat her with medications to prevent another allergic reaction and begin the second round of treatment."

"So where do we go from here?" Carmela asked, coming to stand near Emma's head.

"We continue intensive support and close monitoring."

With a face radiating confidence, Carmela pushed a few stubborn strands of hair from Emma's brow. "She's still not speaking, but Sam and I are both getting the feeling she knows we're here and that she's trying to communicate with us."

"Give it a little time," Madison said. "Even if we see signs of improvement, the time she'll need to recover could be prolonged."

Carmela was quick to respond, "As long as she gets better, Dr. Shaw, we don't care how long it takes."

"Thank you again for everything," the governor said.

Jack and Madison left Emma's room and started down the hall to see their next patient.

"I generally don't find you so stingy on optimism," she said.

"My fear of the unknown has a way of bringing out my pessimistic side."

"There's got to be more to it than that."

"Everybody seems to be focused on if the patients are tolerating the monoclonal antibodies instead of whether they'll do them any good or not."

"The staff's desperate for some good news, Jack. It's only natural."

"I've thought about the cases we've consulted on over the years. In almost all of them, once we identified the cause of the illness and a treatment plan, I felt pretty optimistic about things. For some reason, that optimism is sorely lacking this time. I keep feeling as if we're in the eye of the hurricane, and that in a blink of an eye this honeymoon period's going to be over, and all hell is going to break loose."

Chapter 70

INFUSION–DAY THREE

TEN A.M.

When Jack and Madison finished making rounds on Emma Collymore, they briefed her nurse on the treatment plan for the next twenty-four hours and made their way to the core desk to speak with the medical unit secretary.

Janet Arenson, a longstanding employee of the hospital, looked up as they approached.

"Good morning, Doctors."

"Good morning," Madison said. "Would you happen to know if the Collymores arrived yet?"

"I think they got here a little while ago. They were here until pretty late last night."

Madison inquired, "Do you know if they've been in to see Emma yet?"

"I don't think so. They usually stop in the office we fixed up for the governor before they visit her."

"Thanks, Janet."

Jack and Madison headed down the unit's back corridor that ended in the area designated for administrative offices. The door to the governor's makeshift office was open. He was on the phone, but the moment he looked up and saw them, he waved them forward and quickly ended his call. Madison's eyes swung to Carmela, who was sitting on a loveseat with a blank look on her face.

She spotted them and stood up. "Good morning, Doctors."

"Good morning," Madison said. "Have you seen Emma yet?"

"No, but I spoke to her nurse around midnight, and she told me she was about the same. Have you and Dr. Wyatt already seen her?"

"We made rounds on her a little while ago."

"Last evening, right before Sam and I left, we noticed she seemed to be doing her best to focus on us. I even saw her lips move a little, as if she were trying to speak to us."

"If you're headed over to her room now, we'd be happy to walk with you," Madison offered, her gaze shifting to the governor. The uncertainty and trepidation on his face were ever-present.

"We'd appreciate that," Carmela said, and they left the office and made the short walk to Emma's room.

The Collymores had barely stepped into the room when they both froze in place at the sight of Emma sitting up in bed sipping water through a straw with her nurse's assistance. When she raised her eyes and saw them, the corners of her mouth curled into an adoring smile. Carmela covered her mouth and began to sob. The governor took Carmela's hand, and they hurried to the bedside.

"Thank God," he whispered.

Carmela's face flushed scarlet and her eyes danced with joy at the sight of Emma. "My God, sweetie, you… you look wonderful."

"I feel a lot better, Mom." She had obvious difficulty projecting her words, but they were intelligible.

Sam and Carmela leaned in from opposite sides of the bed and together gently hugged her. The brief silence that followed further enhanced the pure elation that filled the room.

For a man who was never at a loss for words, Sam couldn't remember a word of what he'd planned to say to his cherished daughter if this moment ever came. Consumed by the same brand of elation Carmela was feeling, he held Emma's hand in his.

He turned to Jack and Madison. "I think this is exactly the kind of Christmas miracle Carmela and I have been praying for," he told them in a voice rich with appreciation.

"You said you saw her this morning, but you purposely didn't tell us," Carmela said with a smile.

"We didn't want to ruin the surprise," Madison said.

Tears came to her eyes. "You two are modern-day miracle workers."

"Let's give present-day medicine some credit," Jack said. "It's possible that Emma's ability to heal herself and the monoclonal antibody therapy just happened to come together at the same time."

"We'll give you full credit for everything you did, Doctors, but I think Carmela and I will still always consider her recovery a miracle," Sam said, gesturing to them to join him at Emma's bedside.

"Honey, I'd like you to meet two individuals who have dedicated themselves heart and soul to getting you better."

"I met them a few minutes ago, Dad." She grinned before adding, "I guess I'm a pretty lucky lady."

"How much longer will she have to be in the hospital?" Carmela asked.

"Let's not get too far ahead of ourselves," Madison said. "We have a lot of evidence this morning that Emma's turned the corner. For the first time in days, her liver function tests have started to improve. We're not even thinking about a potential discharge date at this point. It's way too early."

"Within the bounds of what you can share with me, how are the other patients doing?" the governor asked.

"We're very encouraged."

Carmela hugged Sam, struggling to hold back a new deluge of tears. "I told you her time wasn't at hand." She lifted her gaze to Jack and Madison. "There's something I'd like to tell you. Fifteen years ago, my twin sister lost her only child to cancer. I remember what she went through like it happened yesterday. Sam and I will never forget that it was you, Dr. Shaw, and you, Dr. Wyatt, who saved us from the worst nightmare any parent could ever imagine."

Chapter 71

FIVE DAYS LATER

News of Marcus Parry's death and his alleged role in the IPS outbreak became front-page news, and the details of his involvement spread through the hospital like a brush fire in a stiff afternoon breeze.

Counting himself among those who were beyond gratified that the crisis was over, Dr. Josef Church felt as if the weight of the world had been lifted from his shoulders. It didn't take long for the powers that be at Mothers and Infants to completely vindicate him of all wrongdoing in the care of the IPS patients. Between re-familiarizing himself with his patients and interacting with an endless number of well-wishers, he felt well on his way to reestablishing his lost life.

Earlier in the day, he'd received a call from Detective Paul Allensworth requesting a meeting. Josef agreed without hesitation, and the interview was set for later that day in Josef's office. The call from the detective came as no great surprise to him, being an inevitability that he'd already given considerable thought to. His plan was simple. He'd maintain a cooperative nature and be completely forthcoming about everything he knew.

At exactly five o'clock, Josef's administrative assistant escorted Detectives Allensworth and Rafferty into his office. After introductions had been completed, he invited them to join him at his conference table, where they all settled in without delay.

Paul took the lead. "Thank you for taking the time to speak with us, Doctor."

"Of course. I hope you don't mind, but since my son was instrumental in dealing with the situation for both our practice and the hospital, I asked him to join us."

"That will be fine, Doctor."

"He's just getting out of surgery and will be here shortly."

"Since his death," Paul began, interlacing his fingers and setting his hands on the table, "we've been able to gather quite a bit of information about the man we believe was responsible for the IPS outbreak. He used the name Marcus Parry when he applied for a nursing assistant's position here at Mothers and Infants two years ago. We now know that was an alias. His real name was Adrian Voss. We've also learned he worked at Caring Hearts in Sarasota on the postpartum unit—also as a nursing assistant. What's of particular interest is that he was working the day you visited Caring Hearts and that he was involved in the care of the two women who contracted IPS and who were later transferred to this hospital."

Paul looked at his notes. "Voss was an educated man. He was a biology major as an undergraduate and went on to obtain a master's degree in animal conservation. From what we can decipher, he had an academic position for a few years before moving into the private sector. At first, he joined a company as a consultant dealing in bat surveying, research, and technology. He was eventually fired and it was from there that he lost his moral compass, becoming involved in unethical specimen trading. We have a pretty good idea that he was importing live bats from Malaysia with the Nipah virus. We have a lot more work to sift out the details, but our suspicion is that Voss had a confederate in Malaysia who worked at an unprincipled research center who was sending him live fruit bats infected with Nipah."

Before the detectives could pose their next question, Zach came through the door. They came to their feet and introduced themselves.

"It's nice to meet you both," he told them as he sat down next to his father. "I apologize for being a little late. I hope I haven't kept you waiting too long."

"Not at all," Paul said. We're just getting started."

"Do you have any idea why Voss selected my patients to commit these deplorable acts upon?"

"That's the same question Detective Rafferty and I have been asking ourselves since his death. What we've discovered about Voss leads us to believe he was a highly motivated individual who spent an enormous amount of time working out every detail of his plan."

"I'm interested in learning what motivated him to hurt my patients, Detective, not what special skills he acquired."

"You've hit on the main reason Detective Allensworth and I set up this meeting. Until we figure out why Voss was focused on you and your patients, I doubt we'll ever be able to fully understand what happened."

"Is there always a rational reason why dangerously psychotic individuals commit these kinds of acts?" Zach asked.

"Unfortunately, what you're alluding to is true. Crimes like this have been committed with no apparent motive," Libby answered.

"Were you aware that he worked in the birthing center?" Paul asked Josef.

"Only recently via the hospital scuttlebutt, but I have no recollection of him."

"I heard that he was using a phony name," Zach said.

"We were just sharing with your father that we discovered Parry was an alias. His real name was Adrian Voss," Libby said.

"Do you know why he used a fictitious name?" Zach asked.

"Our best guess is it was simply part of his scheme not to get caught," she said.

"Unbelievable," Josef muttered.

"Do either of you recall working with him?" Libby asked, sliding a picture of him from his employment file across the table.

Josef lowered his reading glasses and studied it. "I don't recognize him. Someone mentioned to me that he worked as staff relief and that his schedule was pretty sporadic. You have to remember, we're the busiest maternity hospital in the country. There are literally hundreds of employees working in different areas of the hospital. It's hard enough to remember the full-time ones." Shaking his head, he added, "I don't think either of us would recognize any of the staff-relief employees."

"Assuming for a moment that Voss did have a motive," Paul began, "wouldn't the most logical explanation be that he was a disgruntled family member of one of your patients?"

"No doctor makes every patient happy, Detective, and I've had my fair share of unhappy patients and family members," Josef said, handing the photo to Zach. "But I can't think of a single one mad enough to be driven to an act of insane revenge."

Paul noticed a pensive look suddenly appear on Zach's face. He continued to watch as he held his silence and absently massaged the bridge of his nose.

"Does he look familiar to you?" he asked Zach.

"Not really. I don't think so."

"Can you recall a disgruntled patient that you thought was capable of anything violent?" Paul asked.

"Actually, I was just thinking about that," Zach answered. "It's a slim possibility, but there was a family member I recall from a few years ago who was rather upset with my father."

"We'd like to hear about it," Libby was quick to say.

"I can't say the photo rings any bells, but I've been thinking about the name Adrian Voss since you mentioned it. When did you say he began working at Mothers and Infants?"

"About two years ago."

Zach inclined his head slightly to one side and asked his father, "Do you remember the patient we operated on about three years ago who came into the emergency room bleeding from an ectopic pregnancy?"

"Not really. We've probably operated on ten patients with that diagnosis in the last three years or so."

"The thing about this case that sticks out in my memory is that it was around the holidays. I remember because we were all having dinner together, and we had to leave urgently to get her up to surgery."

"What was it about this case that makes you think there was a disgruntled family member involved?" Paul asked.

"As I mentioned, it was an emergency operation. We managed to stop the bleeding and get her off the operating table. But the problems from her enormous blood loss and the number of transfusions she required led to severe complications. A couple of days after the operation, she was still in the ICU. I had just left the hospital and was on my way to the parking lot when I was approached by a man. He told me his name and that he was engaged to the patient. I remember him saying that he knew a lot about medical things. He was convinced we'd made a lot of mistakes in caring for his fiancée and that, if she died, it would be due directly to the inept care she'd received. Our conversation only lasted a couple of minutes, but he became increasingly more agitated and then just walked away."

Libby asked, "Did he threaten your father or anybody else in any way?"

"No, not in so many words. But he did say he was prepared to take action if she died. They weren't outright threats, but I would say they were implied."

"Did he mention what type of action he was prepared to take?" Paul asked.

"He didn't say...not that I recall. I must have assumed at the time he was referring to suing for malpractice or filing a complaint with the medical board."

"Do you remember if he mentioned his name?"

"He probably did, but I don't recall it."

"And the patient's name?" he asked.

"I don't remember that either, off the top of my head, but if you think it's worth pursuing, I should be able to find out."

"We'd appreciate her name. Is there anything else you recall about this guy that might help us?" Libby asked.

"Nothing, other than that the name Adrian Voss kind of rings a dim bell, but I can't be sure. It's a pretty distinctive name, and for reasons I can't explain, I've always remembered strange names."

"I don't remember a problem with a fiancé," Josef said.

"I probably didn't mention it to you, Dad."

Paul asked, "Were these implied threats against your father or the hospital?"

"As I recall, both. He went on about how incompetent the hospital and my father were and that they should both be held accountable for the inferior care they provided to his fiancée."

"Did you report him to security?" Libby asked.

"No. I probably didn't think it rose to that level of concern. It was only one time, and sometimes you just catch a family member when they're having a bad moment. I probably assumed I'd have another chance to speak with him and that I'd be able to work things out with him."

"It doesn't sound like you had that chance."

"No. I never saw or spoke to him again."

"Did the patient eventually recover?" Libby asked.

"Actually, she died a few days later of complications related to the surgery."

Libby turned to Josef. "Are you absolutely sure this man never attempted to get in touch with you?"

"If he did, I have no recollection of it. But I can tell you this," he said with a wrinkled brow. "If a patient's family member spoke to me in a manner such as my son just described, I doubt I'd forget it."

Libby couldn't help smiling inwardly, as his tone and manner reminded her very much of her father. "Did you happen to place a note in the patient's chart about any of this?" she asked Zach.

"I'm sure I didn't. That's something I would've only done if I'd decided to get security or the hospital administration involved."

Libby looked up from her notepad. "And you're quite sure you can't match this guy's face to Voss's photo?"

"No. I'm sorry, Detective. I can't."

The four of them continued to talk for another twenty minutes before the detectives deemed it time to bring the meeting to an end.

"As I mentioned, it might be helpful if you provide us with the name of the patient," Paul said.

"I'll have to do a little digging, but I'm sure I can find it. You'll have it by tomorrow."

Libby handed him a business card as they all came to their feet. "Thank you. And we appreciate you both taking the time to speak with us."

Josef walked the detectives to the door, and his assistant escorted them to the elevators.

As soon as they were alone, Paul said, "That wasn't too helpful." The elevator doors rolled open and they stepped inside.

"I don't know. It shouldn't be too difficult to track down the patient's family. Maybe chatting with them might open a door."

"I'm not sure," he said. "Since the guilty party in all this is now dead, I don't know how much rope the captain's going to give us on pursuing a bunch of details that won't matter much from a law enforcement point of view."

"What about Regina Leggett's murder?"

They stepped off the elevator and started across the lobby.

"What about it? We've identified the DNA samples we got from under her fingernails as Voss's. It's kind of a closed case. I guess the most important thing is the lesson we learned about taking people more seriously. Obviously, she did know something about the IPS cases, and it wound up getting her killed."

"The question is, how did Voss know she knew something and wanted to talk with us about it?"

"I suspect that's not a question we're likely to find the answer to," Paul said.

"Are you suggesting there was something going on between them?"

"That's one possibility. They were about the same age."

"Now there's a piece of indisputable evidence if I've ever heard one," Libby said with a laugh.

He grinned. "You know what they say. The only place where there's more fooling around going on than a police department is a hospital."

Chapter 72

As soon as Josef finished dinner, he retreated to his library. Now that he had been fully reinstated, including all clinical and administrative responsibilities, he had a lot of catching up to do. He took a seat at his ornate demilune style desk to begin reviewing a dozen or so operational and financial reports in preparation for the Mothers and Infants monthly Board of Trustees meeting. He'd been working his way through the documents for about an hour when the door opened and Zach entered.

"What's up, Dad?"

"Hi, Zach, good to see you," he said, raising his eyes from his laptop screen. "To what do I owe this unexpected visit?" Zach looked at him with affection but wagged a finger his way at the same time. Josef nodded apologetically. "It's the second Tuesday of the month, isn't it?"

"Which is also our inviolate brandy and cigar night."

Don't get old, son. It wreaks havoc on your memory."

"We can call it off for tonight and reschedule if you're too busy."

"Not on your life. There's nothing I'm doing that's more important than cigar night. I'll grab the Remy Martin and the snifters. Why don't you choose a couple of cigars out of the humidor. I just restocked it, so the choice is ample."

"Tonight we celebrate your total vindication from all matters related to the IPS cases."

"You won't get any pushback from me on that plan, son."

Josef walked over to the bar and reached for the bottle of brandy and two tulip snifters. Making his way over to the high-backed leather chairs that were positioned kitty-corner to each other with a table between them, he set the bottle and glasses down. Zach joined him and handed him one of his favorite Dominicans. He then poured them each the appropriate amount of brandy, angling each snifter on its side until the fine cognac reached the rim of the glass.

"How are things going?" Zach asked him, watching his father toast the foot of the cigar before lighting it.

"I'm slowly getting back to my normal schedule."

"It's been a rough few weeks. There's no rush. Take your time," he told him, placing a hand on his shoulder. "You'll excuse me for saying this, Dad, but you look like a man with something on his mind."

Josef's expression turned grim as a glance passed between them. "Actually, there is something I'd like to talk to you about."

"Okay, but I was hoping to keep things on a light note tonight. We're supposed to be celebrating, Dad."

"It won't take too long."

"I'm just teasing you a little. Go ahead."

"I've been thinking about our meeting with the detectives from the Palm Beach Sheriff's Office."

Zach lifted his snifter and took the first sip of his brandy. "I think it might be better to forget about it. Especially if you're trying to put this whole unfortunate IPS experience behind you."

"In a way, that's what I am trying to do."

"Sorry, go ahead."

"I think we both know that I haven't taken any emergency room calls for several years. And I can't remember the last time I operated on a woman with a ruptured ectopic. The other interesting thing is that you've always told me every little thing that happens when you're covering my patients."

"What are you trying to say?"

"It's very hard for me to believe you wouldn't inform me about a patient of mine with a disgruntled fiancé who threatened me."

Zach swirled the fine cognac as he listened. "That's because, when I told the detectives the story, I embellished it a little."

"I kind of suspected that. Would you mind telling me why?"

"Because I love you, Dad, and I can't even imagine the amount of stress you've already had to endure. And for what? I mean, you did nothing wrong. And now, all these people who've been lining up the last few days to wish you the best and tell you they never doubted you for a second…well, they're the same two-faced hypocrites who were screaming behind your back for you to retire last week."

"We're all capable of some hypocrisy from time to time. It's human nature."

"I don't get you sometimes. You have to be the most understanding and forgiving person on the face of the earth."

"Tell me why you misled the police, even if it was only a little bit."

"I was hoping that if I hinted at what they were looking for, they might take the bait and leave you alone. The sooner all of this is last week's news, the better it will be for everybody."

"I see."

"The detectives are looking for the last piece of the puzzle they need to close the file on this case. I provided them with that. That's all I did, and I was very careful how I worded things."

"Did this patient really exist?"

"Of course. I operated on her about five years ago. Everything about her ruptured ectopic, surgery, clinical course, and family is true. I'd say my account of the case was largely true, but I did take some creative liberties and embellish parts of it."

"Allow me to remind you that we were talking to the police. I don't think they take kindly to inventive half versions of the truth. You could be leaving yourself open to some real trouble."

"I'm not worried about it."

"I wouldn't be so cavalier about this. Supposing they figure it out? It could impact your career."

"I doubt very much they'll delve into the case. They want this thing to go away just as much as everybody else does."

"I hope you're right, because if you're not, you may wind up paying a pretty steep price."

"How? If worse comes to worst, I'll tell them I must have gotten Voss confused with another family member. Let them arrest me for first-degree bad memory. If I wind up in trouble…well, that's a chance I'm willing to take, because if it weren't for you, Dad, I wouldn't have a career. The way I see it, the guy's dead, and for all intents and purposes, we cured IPS. It's time to move on and make Adrian a faint memory."

"All of this still begs the question: Why do you think this guy came after me?" When Zach didn't answer, Josef looked up at his son. He could easily see the uneasy look that had landed on his face. Setting his brandy snifter down on the side table, he said, "What is it?"

Zach exhaled a deep breath. "Does the name Adrian Voss mean anything to you?"

Josef pondered the question briefly. "I'm not sure, but I must admit when the detectives mentioned his name, it did ring a distant bell."

"There's a reason for that. He was your stepson."

"Oh, my God. I'd completely forgotten about—"

"Hold on a sec, Dad. I know Adrian played no role in our family's life. You never talked about why, and I never asked. I'm not surprised you didn't recall his name at our meeting. Mom always used her maiden name, even when she got married the first time. It all happened a very long time ago, and it was a rare occasion when Adrian's last name even came up."

After a long moment, Josef put his finger to his lips and said, "I think I owe you an explanation."

"You don't owe me any explanations, Dad."

"I'd feel better if I could share this with you. Looking at things now, with two decades of hindsight, I feel like I should have explained certain things to you long before this. When Mom and I first spoke seriously about getting married, I explained to her that I very much wanted a family, but under no circumstances did I want any stepchildren. I also told her I had no interest in having any type of a significant relationship with her son. In fact, I think the last time I saw him, he couldn't have been more than about seven years old. He never spent one night in our house, and if I met him three times, I'd be surprised." Josef raised a halting hand. "Instead of me trying to explain why I felt so strongly about Adrian not being a part of my life, let's just leave it that it was a personal life's choice."

"As I said, Dad. You have no obligation to explain anything to me."

"Have you stayed in touch with Adrian over the years?"

"The last time I spoke to him, I was in my ob-gyn residency. Before that, we touched base from time to time, but around the time of Mom's death, we spoke frequently. When the police were conducting their investigation, they interviewed him. A day or two afterward, he called me."

"Seeing as I now know Adrian was responsible for what happened at the hospital, I have to assume he must have held me responsible for Mom's death, and that he despised me."

"Adrian absolutely adored Mom. He was devastated when he learned that she'd taken her own life. He never accepted the authorities' conclusion of your lack of involvement in Mom's suicide." Zach paused. Josef could easily see the discomfort that showed on his face. "There's no other way to say this other than to tell you that you're correct—Adrian blamed you for Mom's death. As I mentioned, I spoke with him about his feelings several times for the next few months. As hard as I tried, I didn't have any success in getting him to see Mom's suicide in a different light. In fact, I'd say his feelings intensified, and he became more obsessed with holding you accountable."

"Did he ever make any actual threats?"

"No, not that I recall. Eventually he stopped calling me, and I made no effort to reach out to him."

"But you said you spoke to him when you were a resident. Did he say anything at that time?"

"That was years later, and I think both of us chose to stay away from the topic. But what concerned me was that he mentioned he was having mental issues and that he'd been under the care of a psychiatrist. He even told me that he'd voluntarily committed himself for treatment."

"This is unbelievable," Josef said, dropping his chin and supporting his forehead against his fingertips. "You've shone a light on this entire thing for me. Apparently, Adrian figured out some way to create the IPS crisis to get even with me for Mom's death." Shaking his head with purpose, he added, "We have to call the detectives and share this information with them. It's the right thing to do."

"With all due respect, Dad, it's the absolute wrong thing to do."

"What are you saying?"

"I'm saying that going to the police is the absolute last thing we should consider doing."

"You're going to have to explain that to me."

"Informing the police about Adrian's relationship to our family would serve no useful purpose and would probably create a whole new set of problems. If it becomes public knowledge that we're related to Adrian, forget about the hospital problems it would cause, you could easily find yourself in the middle of a media circus. The other problem is that I won't be able to blame my bad memory to explain away the bedtime story I told the police about a disgruntled fiancé. They'll know I was lying, and that will create a serious problem for me."

"I hadn't thought of that."

"Dad, please listen to me. The cops shot the right guy. Adrian deserved what he got. For now, just promise me that you won't do anything rash. Take some time to think about all this logically and carefully. After you've done that, we'll sit down and talk again."

Josef set his half-smoked cigar down in the crystal ashtray. "Okay, I'll do it your way. For now," he finally said in a reluctant voice.

"I'm glad to hear that. Now, let's drink some brandy, talk about something else a little more pleasant, and enjoy the evening."

Chapter 73

By the second week after the monoclonal antibody infusions had been completed, all the women except Nell, who was slowly gaining strength after her emergency liver transplantation, were well on their way to a complete recovery. Dr. Phillips and his intensive care colleagues anticipated they would all be ready for discharge in two to three days. His team, in conjunction with Jack and Madison, reported to the administration and the other treating physicians that, although it was still too early to make a definitive judgment, they had no reason to suspect there was a likelihood of any significant long-term complications.

Jack and Madison were reaching the point in their out-of-town consultation when they were giving thought to returning to Ohio. At the governor's request, they had met with his healthcare team to thoroughly brief them on all aspects of the illness and offer their opinion whether they felt, from a public health standpoint, the matter of the IPS outbreak could be considered resolved.

They were now sitting in the library of Charlotte's house, organizing and packing the dozens of articles and monographs they'd accumulated since they first suspected IPS was a zoonotic infection. It had always been their custom to retain all the supportive material they acquired while investigating an elusive diagnosis. Once they returned to Columbus, they'd create an electronic file that covered every aspect of the illness from presentation to diagnosis and conclude with an account of the treatment and patient outcome.

The room was warmer than Madison would have liked, but the overhead fan she'd just turned on did wonders to rectify the situation. She never stopped wondering why Charlotte, regardless of the outside temperature, set the thermostat at seventy-seven degrees.

Charlotte walked into the room carrying a plate of the apple cinnamon oatmeal cookies she'd just pulled out of the oven. While Jack was still considering indulging, Madison had already taken the first bite of hers.

"You've really made a mess of this place," Charlotte said to Jack.

He threw his hands up in the air and shook his head several more times than was necessary. "We'll have it looking the way we found it in an hour," he promised.

"Did you ever notice how much Jack gestures when he speaks?" Madison asked.

"I've always believed my son was born to speak with his hands."

They chuckled while Jack ignored them.

"By the way," Charlotte said, "I want to thank you both for the beautiful butterfly garden teapot. I'll display it proudly with the rest of my collection."

"It's the least we could do for you allowing us to barge in on you on such short notice," Madison said.

"It wasn't necessary, but I thank you both again," she said. "I've got a meeting this afternoon I need to prepare for, so while I tackle that annoyance, I'll leave you two to work." Charlotte left the plate of cookies on the coffee table and strolled out of the room.

As they were well within range of a Moose attack, Madison immediately moved them to one of the wall unit's higher shelves.

Madison had already filled one box with an assortment of material when she started working on another large pile of resources she and Jack had reviewed. She'd worked her way down to a monograph that reviewed the history of bat research in the United States. Still nibbling away at her cookie to make it last longer, she picked up the monograph and made her way over to a matching recliner and ottoman.

The moment Madison looked at the cover, her breath caught. "You got a sec, Jack? You have to see this."

He put down the patient file he was looking at and joined her. "What's up?"

Madison held up the monograph and pointed to the author's name. "Does that name look remotely familiar to you?"

"Adrian Voss," he said. "That's some coincidence. At least, in his prior life, he made a positive contribution to society."

"I just can't believe this."

"I agree it's a fluke, but we know that Voss was a master bat biologist, and he had a credible academic job before his psychosis caught up with him and he turned to different means of making a living."

"I guess so."

With her interest piqued, she took a couple of minutes to thumb through the monograph. She wasn't interested in delving into any particular chapter. When she was finished, she leafed back to the beginning and was just about to close it when her eye caught the acknowledgment page, which listed all the research scientists who had assisted Voss in the writing of the monograph. In all, there were about a dozen names.

All at once, her eyes became laser focused on the page, and her breath caught. She slowly came to her feet, but her gaze remained frozen on the monograph.

"Oh my God," she uttered, feeling the type of disbelief that goes all the way to one's fingertips. "Jack."

"Yeah?"

"I think you'd better take a look at this."

"Again?"

Madison didn't respond, but when he looked over at her and read the shock in her eyes, he pulled his feet out from under Moose, got off the couch, and joined her on the other side of the room.

"This is Voss's acknowledgment page. She placed her finger on the page and ran it down the list. After a few moments, Jack looked up at her.

"I think we have a phone call to make," he told her as soon as he lifted his eyes from the page.

"I agree, but give me about half an hour. I have a hunch about something and want to check a couple of things."

Chapter 74

With a container of coffee in one hand and a cheese Danish in the other, Paul Allensworth strolled into Libby's office. She pointed at the chair in front of her desk and mouthed to him that she'd be off the phone shortly. While she was listening, she wrote the name Kiara on a legal pad and turned it around for Paul to see. He nodded, taking another bite of his pastry.

"I'm glad to hear you're feeling a little better," Libby told her. "How's the therapy going? Is it helping?"

"It's hard to tell," she answered. "It's funny, but I thought I was a lot tougher than this. I should be over it by now. Even with therapy, I'm still shaken by what happened."

"Anybody who went through what you did would feel the same way, and it hasn't been that long."

"I can't even close my eyes without seeing the way that monster looked at me when he came at me with that syringe in his hand."

"I hate to be so blunt, but just remember the monster's dead and can never hurt you again."

"That's very logical, but the reality only seems to help a little. The whole post-trauma thing has really gotten to me."

"You'll be fine. You just need more time. As soon as you're ready to meet for lunch, call me. No shop talk. I promise."

"Maybe next week, Libby. Thanks for caring."

"If you need anything, and I mean anything at all, don't hesitate for a second to call me."

"I won't and thanks, Libby. And thanks for spending so much time on the gun range."

"See, you're already starting to get your snarky sense of humor back. Bye."

Libby ended the call by turning off the speaker mode of her desk phone. For a few moments she sat there in silence, looking more downcast than Paul was used to seeing her.

"That didn't sound great," he said.

"I guess if somebody beat, drugged, and gagged me, and then zip-tied me to a pipe in a dark room, I wouldn't be doing so well either."

"Kiara's a tough lady. She'll be okay in time." He tilted his head to get a peek at the file in front of her. "Are you working on the Regina Leggett case?"

"Zach Church called. He found the patient's name. Unfortunately, she didn't have anybody listed on her medical chart as either next of kin or even a close family member. I'll do some more digging, but since she died several years ago, I doubt I'll come up with too much. As you keep telling me, it's beyond a long shot."

He extended his hand with the cheese Danish in it. "Bite?"

"Are you kidding?"

"I'll take that as a no. So the big question is just what are you looking for?"

"I'm just trying to make sure we have all of our loose ends tied up before we close the investigation," she told him.

"What loose ends are those?" After waiting for a few seconds without getting an answer he said, "Look, Libby, it was a horrible case, and there's no question Voss had one of the sickest minds I've ever encountered. But in the end, we've got a pretty good timeline of what happened and know why he targeted Dr. Church's patients.

It's also worth mentioning that Voss is dead, which in itself kind of wraps things up. I'm not sure what loose ends you're looking for."

They were still talking when Paul's cell phone rang.

"Detective, this is Ely Stanberry calling. Do you have a minute to speak?"

"Good morning, Doctor. Of course," he answered, extending his legs and then crossing them at the ankles.

He slowly straightened as he listened. "I appreciate you giving us a call. Of course, Doctor. We can be there in about forty minutes. Thank you for reaching out to us so promptly."

"What was that all about?" Libby asked.

"It seems Doctors Wyatt and Shaw would like to see us."

"The consulting doctors from Ohio?"

"That's them. Evidently, they came across some information they'd very much like to share with us," Paul said.

"What kind of information?"

"Doctor Church didn't say, but he did mention that he'd like to see us as soon as possible—and he said it very politely."

"Did you get the feeling his extreme courtesy was a bit of a jab because he felt we had a relaxed sense of urgency regarding Regina Leggett's request to meet with us?"

"Absolutely."

She shot him a grin. "This should be interesting. I can't wait to see what this vital piece of information is."

Chapter 75

"Thank you for coming to meet with us on such short notice," Ely said to Detectives Paul Allensworth and Libby Rafferty as he led them to his meeting table.

Madison and Jack were already seated and came to their feet as they approached. Madison had a sudden pang of anxiety, wondering how the police would react to what they were about to share with them. Ely completed the formal introductions, and they all found a seat at the table.

"May I offer anybody something to drink before we get started?" Ely began. After they all courteously declined, he went on, "As I suspect you're aware, Doctors Wyatt and Shaw are visiting us from Ohio and were key members of the physician team who investigated the IPS outbreak."

"I don't think there's anybody in Palm Beach County who owns a television or reads the newspaper who isn't familiar with the part the doctors played in curing the disease," Paul said.

"That's kind of you to say," Jack responded.

"Doctors Wyatt and Shaw came to see me earlier today to inform me of some information they'd discovered. After they shared it with me, I agreed with them that it should be brought to your attention." He turned to Madison. "I'll let Dr. Shaw take it from here."

As she gathered her thoughts, Madison removed Voss's monograph from her purse and set it on the table. She snuck a look at the detectives, who sat there plain-faced. All at once, she felt a slight chill travel down her spine.

"Earlier today, Dr. Wyatt and I were organizing the medical reference materials we used to help us in our investigation of IPS. One of those references was this monograph on bat behavior that was written with a particular focus on their ability to transmit viral diseases. We had consulted the monograph several times when we first suspected that IPS was a bat-borne disease." She paused, reached across the table, and handed the monograph to Libby. "As you can see, the monograph was authored by Adrian Voss."

Libby picked it up, thumbed through it briefly, and then handed it to Paul. "When was this work published?" she asked.

"About thirteen years ago," Madison answered, getting the feeling that the two detectives weren't very excited by the monograph Voss had authored.

"That would have been about the same time he had a full-time university appointment and was teaching and doing research," Paul stated.

Madison nodded. "That's correct."

"I can't say I have the faintest idea how big the bat scientist community is, but it can't be so large that Voss's monograph would necessarily raise any eyebrows. Do you think there's anything more to this other than it being a coincidence?" Paul asked.

"If the matter of authorship was the only thing of interest about the monograph, Dr. Wyatt and I might agree with you. But Voss included an acknowledgment page, which listed the name of Zachery M. Church as one of the contributing authors."

From the looks on their faces, Madison was certain she'd gotten their attention.

"And you think it may be the same Dr. Zach Church who's on staff here at Mothers and Infants?" Libby asked.

"We're certain of it, Detective," Madison said, watching with interest as the two detectives found the acknowledgment page and stared at it briefly. From the glance they exchanged, Madison was reasonably sure the idea that they were dealing with nothing more than a twist of fate was rapidly fading from their minds.

"Dr. Shaw, how can you be certain that the Dr. Church who's on staff here at Mothers and Infants and the one Voss acknowledged in his monograph are one and the same?" Paul asked.

"As is the case with most hospital websites, physician biographies are included for potential patients to read. According to the one that appears on the Mothers and Infants website, Dr. Church enrolled in a master's degree program in epidemiology in Philadelphia after he got his bachelor's."

Jack said, "If you look at Voss's acknowledgment of Dr. Church in his monograph, it mentions the same master's degree."

"Can we assume that, because of this collaboration, it's likely that Voss and Church knew each other?"

"That's a little hard to say," Ely jumped in. "As an ex-academician who has acknowledged a lot of contributors in my publications, I can say I knew many of them well, while for some of the others, our relationship consisted only of a couple of phone calls."

"So, just to go back to what we discussed before," Libby said. "Even as strange as these findings are, it's possible that Dr. Church and Voss barely knew each other."

Madison cleared her throat. "If you rely only on the information available in the monograph and on the hospital website, then yes, it's possible."

Paul and Libby both pushed back in their chairs at the same time. Tapping his fingertips together and looking at Madison through searching eyes, Paul asked. "Are you trying to tell us that there's something else linking Voss and Church together?"

"I was a little intrigued about what we learned from the monograph," Madison began after clearing her throat. "So I decided to see what else I might be able to find out." Madison paused, offering the detectives the opportunity to either comment on what she'd told them or ask a question.

"Don't stop now, Doctor," Libby told her.

"Voss is about three years older than Church. They were both born in South Florida. Voss's mother and father were divorced before his first birthday. His mother kept her maiden name of Clara Lynge while she was married. About a year after her divorce, she remarried. This time to Dr. Josef Church. Twelve months later, she gave birth to another boy who she and Josef named Zach. Their marriage came to an end about seventeen years later when Clara committed suicide."

Libby blinked with surprise. "I know a lot of the events you've mentioned are public record, but those kinds of details are not always so easy to come across. How sure are you that your information is accurate?"

Madison rolled her tongue across the inside of her right cheek. "I have a friend in Ohio who's a vice president of an IT company. She also has an avid interest in ancestry. She was kind enough to assist me."

Paul thumb stroked the two-day stubble on his chin. "Just to make sure there's no chance of a miscommunication here, are you saying that Voss and Zach Church had the same biological mother?"

Madison answered with no hesitation. "That's exactly what we're saying, Detective. Adrian Voss and Zach Church are half-brothers."

An immediate silence descended on the room.

"Does anybody else know about this?" Libby asked.

"Not that we're aware of," Ely assured her.

"What little we know about Dr. Church and his son is that they have a pretty good relationship. Would you say that's true?" Libby asked.

"I know the family well," Ely responded. "Absolutely. They're as close as any father and son I know."

"And as far as you know, Dr. Zach Church has never had any issues raised about his skill as a doctor or his character?"

"Never, and I'd say he's emblematic of the type of physician we strive to recruit to Mothers and Infants."

"Thank you," Libby said, swapping a glance with Paul.

"Is there anything else that you and Dr. Wyatt have come across that you think we should know about?" he asked.

"I believe we've briefed you on everything we discovered," Madison said.

"In that case, if you don't have any additional questions for Detective Allensworth and me, we'll be getting on our way."

Ely looked at Jack and Madison. They indicated no with a shake of their heads. "I think we're good," he told Libby.

"We thank you for taking the time to speak with us," Allensworth said. "If anything else comes to your attention please feel free to contact us."

"Of course," Ely said.

The detectives came to their feet, walked out into the hall, and started down the wide corridor toward the elevators.

"Without overthinking things, what's your gut feeling about Zach Church and Adrian being half-brothers?" Paul asked.

"I guess the spectrum stretches from an incredible coincidence to the possibility of some pretty serious criminal behavior."

"Which way are you leaning?"

"Coincidence. It's pretty obvious that Voss was mentally disturbed, and perhaps that accounts for what he did. As far as Dr. Zach's concerned, I don't see a motive. You heard what Dr. Stanberry said. He and his father have a great relationship."

"Which begs the question: Why would Zach lie right to our faces?"

"I assume that as soon as he heard Adrian Voss's name, he knew exactly who he was," Libby answered. "It's understandable that the last thing either of them would want would be for the police to know they were related to Voss."

"I'm not sure Church Senior recognized the name."

"If he did, he sure didn't act like it, " Libby said. "Regardless of who knew what, I still think Zach and Adrian being half-brothers is probably nothing more than an odd coincidence."

Based on his love of mentoring, she had a good idea what his next question would be.

"Got any ideas of what our next move should be?"

Holding off a knowing grin, she answered, "Despite Dr. Stanberry's impression of the Churches' father-son relationship we're obligated to learn as much as we can about what the dynamic was between all three of them," she answered with assurance. "And before you ask me, the first person I'd recommend we interview is Dr. Church Senior."

"Good thinking, Libby. Not bad at all."

The elevator doors opened, and they stepped aboard. Paul pushed the button for the twelfth floor.

Libby smiled. "Since we're going up instead of down, let me guess. Dr. Church's office is on twelve."

"You got it."

They stepped off the elevator and made their way around a curved hallway until they reached Josef Church's office. They continued through the open door into his reception area.

"May I help you?" Church's administrative coordinator asked.

"I'm Detective Allensworth. This is Detective Rafferty. If he's in, we'd like to speak with Dr. Church."

"Do you have an appointment?" Through dubious eyes, Paul regarded her briefly before pulling out his identification wallet and showing the young lady his gold badge. She said, "I think he's on a call at the moment, but if you'll have a seat, I'll let him know you're here." She waited until Paul and Libby found their way over to a pair of matching chairs before she picked up the phone.

A minute later Josef opened his door.

"Please come in, Detectives," he said in a level tone as he showed them into his office. "I'm a little surprised to see you. I thought my son and I answered all of your questions at our meeting. Is there something specific I can help you with?"

"Actually, we'd like to talk to you about your relationship with Adrian Voss."

The look on Josef's face suddenly changed, betraying his heart-shaking anxiety of what he feared was to come. Struggling to maintain his composure and not unmask his skyrocketing anguish, he quietly escorted the detectives to his conference table.

Chapter 76

ONE WEEK LATER

Josef Church prepared a cappuccino for himself, then walked over and sat down in the solid wooden rocking chair he'd put in the Florida room the day they'd moved into their Key Largo vacation house. thought about all the spectacular Florida daybreaks and sunsets he'd watched from his coveted chair, guessing the total number had to be well into the hundreds.

Over the past few days, he'd struggled to spend less time dwelling on his sobering conversation with Detectives Rafferty and Allensworth. To say the least, he'd found their interest in his and Zach's relationship with Voss intriguing. More out of instinct than anything else, he was as elusive as possible in answering their questions. It didn't surprise him that the detectives played their cards close to their vest, revealing little of what they intended to do with the limited information he shared with them. For reasons that he still didn't fully appreciate, he elected not to mention to Zach that the detectives had dropped in on him uninvited.

At a few minutes past nine, Zach strolled into the Florida room with his usual confident flair and gave his father's right shoulder an affectionate double-pat.

"Hey, Dad."

"Good morning. I know you're taking the float plane out today, but you didn't mention where you're heading."

"Actually, I moved up my vacation plans. I'm going to fly to Exuma and spend a few days there bone-fishing and diving. After that, it's anybody's guess."

"How long will you be gone?"

"I was hoping to take off about ten days," he answered as he crossed the room on his way to the table that held the cappuccino maker. "You'll forgive me for mentioning this, but you look like a man with something on his mind."

"I've been thinking a lot about Adrian and the conversation you and I had last week. As implausible and fantastic as it sounds, I'm certain Adrian conceived a plan to make a lot of women deathly ill as a twisted means to destroy my career."

"I agree with you."

"You said that quite nonchalantly."

"What Adrian did was vile, but it really doesn't matter. The important thing is whether you view what he did as simply an act that made for good theater or if you're going to do something about it."

"And that's exactly what I'd like to talk to you about, because I'm very interested in your input."

"I suspect you already know how I feel about all this, but I have no objection to discussing it again," Zach assured his father as he prepared a latte.

"I'm glad to hear that. You're one of the few people I'm comfortable talking to about this awful situation," Josef said. "I know you mentioned that you had stayed in touch with Adrian over the years, but how would you characterize your relationship?"

"I wouldn't call it a friendship. After we lost Mom, we communicated from time to time, rarely spoke about anything of importance, and we each went on with our lives."

"From what you told me, it sounds like you and Adrian had a similar reaction to Mom's passing."

"I'd say we were both deeply saddened by it, but I'd say I went through the grieving process better than he did."

"I would assume you agree with me that Adrian believed I was responsible for Mom's suicide?"

"He certainly did when it happened, and for some time after that. But I never imagined he'd eventually be driven to insane acts of vengeance."

"There's no doubt that revenge can be a powerful motive, especially when its flames are being stoked by hatred," Josef said. "I guess, as the years went by, his contempt for me festered until it reached a point that he found the courage to act."

"Maybe that was the way of things. I guess anything's possible."

"Oh, I think it's more than possible. I think it's damn probable."

"I'll echo what I said when we spoke last week. Even if you're right about Adrian, it doesn't matter," Zach said. "It doesn't make a particle of difference who his biological mother was or what atrocities he committed. Our only concern has to be what we should do about it."

"And your position is that we do nothing."

"Absolutely," he said, raising his index finger for emphasis. "Adrian's dead and gone. It's best if you and I just forget him. We should be happy and focused on the prospect of getting back to our normal lives." Zach raised the cup to his lips and took a final sip of his latte. "You have to find a way to get past this, Dad. Ultimately, you're going to have to do whatever you think is right. You asked me for my opinion, and I've given it to you. Now, if you don't mind, I'd like to put all this unpleasantness behind me and get started on my vacation."

"I'm sorry you view my concerns as unworthy of further conversation, but I'll agree to your request regarding your vacation if you'll agree to answer one final question."

"Sure, Dad. Go ahead. I didn't mean to upset you," he said, coming to his feet and walking toward the wet bar to place his cup in the sink. "You said you had a question for me. What is the question?"

Josef stood up and asked, "How much would a son have to despise his father to go to any length to destroy him?"

Zach's eyes instantly spun around. "Is there something compelling me to answer that bizarre question?"

"No, but as your father, there are things I need to know."

"With all due respect, it sounds to me like you think you already know the answer."

"Perhaps, but my question's still on the table."

"Instead of me answering it, why don't you simply tell me what's really on your mind?"

Josef approached his son and laid a hand on his shoulder. "Did you have a hand in any of Adrian Voss's criminal behavior?" Josef waited several seconds for an answer. When the silence remained unbroken, he said, "Your silence speaks volumes. I just want the truth, son. I think you owe me that."

"What truth is that?"

"I was never certain you were being honest when you swore to me that you didn't believe I would ever have done anything to intentionally harm Mom."

"You can choose to believe whatever you want," he said, folding his arms in front of his chest. "I'm sorry, Dad, but this conversation's over."

Josef turned and took a few steps toward the door before stopping. Looking into Zach's contemptuous eyes, his temper flared. Calling on every bit of restraint he could muster not to fly off the handle, Josef said evenly, "I'm not going to ask you again. Were you or were you not part of Adrian's plan to destroy me?"

"You're damn right I was."

Chapter 77

Ten minutes after Josef had walked out of his Florida room, he returned. He was surprised to see Zach had retaken his seat in the club chair. During his brief absence, Josef had done everything in his power to grasp how his son could have so inexplicably fallen from grace. Even though the truth was staring him in the face, Josef was incapable of believing how Zach had completely lost his moral compass and joined ranks with a man of Adrian's amorality. The reality staring him in the face was the harsh knowledge that his relationship with Zach was all but over.

"I thought you were in a hurry to get your vacation started," Josef said, strolling over to the large bay window and looking out at the choppy ocean.

"Figuring you'd be back sooner rather than later, I decided to hang around."

"Why? You said with such conviction that our conversation was over," Josef reminded him.

"I was curious how you arrived at your accusation that I was involved with Adrian in formulating and carrying out his plan."

Without turning around, Josef explained, "You may or may not recall this, but many years ago, you and I signed a general power of attorney granting each other mutual authority to access our personal and financial records."

"I remember."

"It made retracing your footsteps rather easy. For instance, I learned you're the principal owner of a limited liability corporation registered in Delaware that has a significant number of real estate holdings. The name of the company is Conyers Properties Limited. One of those holdings is the farm where Adrian Voss was living when he was killed by the police. Adrian was a renter with a five-year lease on the property that you owned. Additionally, you've personally made a significant number of deposits into the corporation over the past three years. Adrian was authorized by the bank tied to the LLC to make unlimited withdrawals, which he's been doing quite liberally, also for the past three years. In the records, there's also a letter of recommendation written by you to the director of human resources at Caring Hearts Medical Center in Sarasota, supporting Adrian Voss's application for employment as a nursing assistant."

"That was very industrious of you."

Without turning around to face Zach, Josef said, "Even loathing me as much as you do, how could you have become involved in something so depraved and vindictive?"

"I could share every detail with you, but at this point, what difference does it make?"

"Maybe none, but since I'm the person who raised you and have always thought of you as a kindhearted, compassionate human being and a person of integrity, it beggars my imagination how you could have decided to become involved in such a heinous crime."

Zach responded by lowering his chin and slowly shaking his head. His shoulders curled above his chest.

"Okay, Dad," he said, briefly closing his eyes. "Contrary to what I recently told you, Adrian and I have always maintained our relationship. The other thing I'm guilty of is understating how much he hated you and wanted to get even. Several years ago, he came to me with an idea of how to destroy your career as an obstetrician and render you thoroughly disgraced in the medical community."

Josef nodded. "For reasons that have now become obvious to me, it seems you were quite interested in listening to his proposal."

Zach's failure to comment on the accusation was more than sufficient to confirm its accuracy.

Zach said, "Adrian worked for several years at a large bat research facility in the Far East. What they possessed in size and contracts, they lacked in ethics. Adrian had worked on several strains of viruses that bats hosted. One in particular became the inspiration for his plan. What started as an amusing mental exercise for him eventually took on a life of its own and became the cornerstone of his plan to get even with you by ruining your life. That was when he decided to come see me in person."

"He'd never done that?"

"No. In all those years, we communicated frequently but never visited each other. He claimed this strain of virus would cause a very serious, but nonfatal, illness in humans. There were no diagnostic tests available for it, and your patients could be infected with the virus via an oral route. He believed if we carefully constructed the plan together, we could move it from the drawing board to the playing field in less than a year. On schedule, Adrian moved to South Florida, had the date palm trees planted, and arranged for the bats to be shipped to him by an unscrupulous confederate of his who still worked at the research lab."

"It sounds like Adrian had everything figured out. Why did he feel the need to recruit you and turn his plan into a conspiracy?"

"He wanted me to provide the necessary funds to bring the plan to fruition and use my connections at Mothers and Infants to make sure everything went off smoothly. I was also key to getting him the nursing positions he needed."

"So you're saying he was the mastermind, and you were the facilitator."

"I guess so, but I won't lie to you and tell you I was manipulated or threatened. The decision to go along with Adrian's plan was mine and mine alone."

"Adrian never would have come to you with this insane plan unless he was certain that, one, you wouldn't betray his trust if you weren't interested in conspiring with him, and two, that you wanted to see me destroyed every bit as much as he did."

"That's correct. Plus, I had no direct role in harming anybody."

"At the risk of bursting your bubble, I don't think that makes you any less guilty morally or in the eyes of the law."

"I understand that, Dad."

"According to the police, Adrian had managed to get himself involved with some pretty shady enterprises. I'm surprised he didn't suggest that you two simply kill me."

"He thought that was too good for you, and I have no appetite for murder, be it yours or anybody else's."

"Does that include Regina Legget?"

"Excuse me?"

"Despite your efforts to keep your romantic relationship with her under wraps, it wasn't the deep dark secret you thought or hoped it was."

"I'm a doctor. It's always been my policy to keep my window shades pulled down. Even so, I'm a single adult, and so was Regina. There's no crime in expecting a little privacy."

"But there is in murder. She knew there was something that didn't add up regarding IPS. I'm guessing she saw or overheard something she wasn't supposed to. Her fatal mistake was telling you about it. How else would Adrian have known she was in a position to ruin your plans?"

"Your assumption is wrong. I had nothing to do with her murder. You were right about one thing, though. She was suspicious. She'd seen him tampering with the unit doses of sodium citrate. Her mistake was confronting him about the possibility. She legitimately wanted to give him a chance to explain himself. He obviously denied it, but he was never certain she believed him. Concerned that Regina would go to the police and the powers that be at the hospital, he dealt with the problem. He didn't tell me about killing her until after the fact."

"Why didn't he discuss his plan with you before he ended Regina's life?"

"I told you. Adrian knew from the outset that I wouldn't become involved in anything that could possibly result in somebody losing their life."

"You're a doctor, for God's sake. How could you believe for a second that you could infect a group of women with a highly virulent virus that was unknown to modern medicine and be sure none of them would die from it?"

"I've asked myself that same question more times than I can remember."

"What happened after that?" Josef asked.

"We assumed that once we infected a large group of your patients, the brightest medical minds in the state would remain stumped as to how to treat it. As the level of frustration grew among the medical staff, and the public became increasingly aware of the untreatable illness that was ravaging Mothers and Infants' postpartum patients, the blame would eventually fall entirely on you. Once that happened, all we'd have to do is sit back and wait for the general public and medical community to come after you with pitchforks and lanterns."

"Obviously, you two weren't as clever as you thought." Josef stood up and walked over to the grandfather clock he'd given his father as a sixtieth birthday present. He reached up to a higher shelf of a wall unit, found the key, and began winding the clock. "You overlooked the possibility that, once the illness resolved on its own or we found a cure for it, IPS would soon become last week's news, and there would no longer be a spotlight on me."

"I'm not diminishing the impact of Doctors Shaw and Wyatt's unexpected presence at Mothers and Infants. But we did think about exactly what you're suggesting and concluded that curing the disease wouldn't change the ultimate outcome," Zach answered.

"You'll have to explain to me what you mean by that."

"A deadly viral outbreak is a pretty scary event. Just the mere possibility that you'd been the one who transmitted the virus would have been more than enough to dissuade patients from coming to you. No current or future mother would have asked for proof positive. Just the idea that you were responsible for the outbreak would have shuttered your office for good. The finger of blame would have been pointed squarely at your heart. No pregnant woman or self-respecting hospital would have touched you with a ten-foot pole."

By this point, Josef was convinced that, even though Zach was unlikely to agree, there was an overwhelming likelihood that his illicit and unlawful activities had sealed his fate. Since the die was cast, Josef saw no reason to conceal anything.

"The sad thing is that Adrian Voss's immoral behavior was most likely the result of his insanity. What's your justification? I thought you were a decent, law-abiding person. For God's sake, how could you have done such a despicable thing?"

Zach said in a defeated tone of voice, "You may not believe this, but it's almost as hard for me as it is for you to believe I could've allowed myself to become involved in such a senseless and stupid act. All I can do from this point forward is do everything in my power to regain my decency."

Josef looked at him through doubting eyes. "You're talking almost as if you don't believe you'll have to pay a price for what you've done."

"I'm hopeful that won't happen."

"I see," Josef began with his head bent forward in frustration. "You've convinced yourself that you'll get off scot-free because I'd never disclose anything that might bring the police to your front door. Is that it?"

"We've already discussed this, Dad, and we both know it's the truth. You are who you are, and you're not going to do anything that would ruin my life."

"You mean contrary to what you tried to do to me?"

"There's nothing to be gained by going over this ground again."

"Has it crossed your mind that it's remotely possible you've misjudged me?" Josef asked.

"Let's see. Have you already spoken to the authorities?" When Josef didn't respond, Zach shrugged and said, "That's what I thought. Let's face it, Dad, in the end, you're not going to send me to jail for the rest of my life… or worse."

"Maybe I was hoping you'd do the right thing whether I went to the police or not."

"Sorry. I've thought about it, but right now I don't have the courage or the character to ruin my life for one stupid mistake. So if you're about to try and convince me that the honorable thing for me to do is throw myself on the mercy of the court, you'd better pull up a chair, because you're going to be here for a long while."

"The irony here is shocking. If you had just found it in your heart to give me the benefit of the doubt about hurting your mother, I don't believe we'd be standing here now having this conversation. None of this ever would have happened if you'd simply believed me that I never did anything to intentionally harm your mother. Sometimes it takes the courage and character you just mentioned to do the right thing."

Poker-faced, Zach said flatly, "You're a fine one to be preaching about the virtues of character. And by the way, I did believe you, and I still do."

The skin bunched up on Josef's brow, and his eyes widened in disbelief. "What are you saying, Zach? Because if you're trying to change your story now to save yourself…well—"

"I'm not changing my story, as you put it. You've simply jumped to a wrong conclusion."

"I don't understand," Josef said.

"Well, I'll make it perfectly clear for you—I'm positive you weren't responsible for Mom's death."

"How could you possibly say that with such certainty?"

"Because the morning Mom took her own life, I'm the one who left the drawer unlocked, not you."

"My God, Zach. In all this time, you never said anything."

"I probably would have if the state had decided to charge you with negligent homicide. But once I found out you were in the clear, I didn't see any reason to sacrifice myself. I was a few days short of my high school graduation when Mom committed suicide, and I'd been fascinated by guns for years. I knew where you kept the key to your desk drawer hidden, and I took your gun out to handle it on more than one occasion."

"I don't know whether to believe any of this or not."

"After you left for the hospital that morning, I was sitting at your desk looking at your gun when I thought I heard the housekeeper coming down the hall. I knew she'd tell you if she saw me with your gun, so I quickly put it back in the drawer, returned the key to its hiding place, and got out of your den as fast as I could. It wasn't until after Mom shot herself that I remembered that I had forgotten to lock the drawer."

Josef was stunned into silence. Unable to hold a straight thought in his head, he battled to gather himself. Finally, he said, "Once I knew you were involved with Adrian, I naturally assumed your contempt for me was the result of Mom's death."

"I guess you made another assumption that wasn't true," Zach said glibly.

"If this isn't about your mother, what in God's name did I do to make you loathe me to the point of wanting to destroy my life?"

Displaying no outward emotion, Zach set his hands on the armrests and turned searching eyes to his father.

"What do you remember about the night Sarah died?"

Josef drew back in bewilderment. "Sarah? I'm not sure I recall exactly, but why would you ask me that now?"

"If you're having trouble remembering, I'll help you. The day we lost her, Sarah went off to school a healthy kid, came home with flu symptoms, and died sixteen hours later from meningococcemia"

"Aren't things bad enough for me at the moment without you causing me more pain?"

Zach glared at him. "This isn't about you. Everything isn't always about you. For just this once, you're going to have to understand that. So I ask you again, what were you doing the night Sarah died?"

Josef instantly noticed an extreme change in Zach's demeanor. He was no longer contrite or cooperative.

Zach continued, "It was Friday, and Mom was in Orlando with Adrian. Sarah was in eighth grade. She came from school at three with a headache, a sore throat, and a low-grade fever. She fell asleep on the couch for a couple of hours. I remember you taking a look at her when she woke up and then calling Mom. You told her Sarah wasn't feeling well and that she probably had the beginnings of the flu. You also told her you had no plans and that you'd be staying home to keep an eye on her. At about seven, you got a call from one of your partners who informed you he needed your help in the operating room. That's when you told me you had to go to the hospital and that I should keep an eye on Sarah."

"I remember the call. I also remember checking her again and feeling comfortable leaving, knowing that you'd be keeping a careful eye on her. You weren't a child, for goodness' sake. You were sixteen years old."

"What was Sarah's condition when you left?"

"I thought she was worse, but I still felt she had nothing more than the typical early onset flu symptoms."

"After you left, I kept a careful eye on Sarah. I called you an hour or so later in the operating room and told you her fever had gone up and that her headache was much worse. Do you recall what you told me?"

"Not exactly. I was preoccupied with a patient who was about to bleed to death on the operating table."

"You told me you'd be home in a couple of hours and just to keep an eye on things. I called you again about two hours later and told you she was vomiting and looked worse to me. You told me she had the flu and that it was expected that she'd get worse before she got better."

"Which is almost always the case."

"Not this time. I saw the rash less than an hour later. I hadn't been to medical school yet, so I didn't recognize it as the distinctive rash that accompanies severe bacterial meningitis. I phoned Mom, and she told me to call 9-1-1. After I did, I called you, and you said you were just getting out of the OR and that you'd meet me at the children's hospital as soon as you could. The paramedics arrived, realized how sick Sarah was, and transported her to the children's hospital. They were still in the ambulance when she had her first seizure."

"Okay, Zach. What happened to Sarah was tragic and just as traumatic to me as to you and Mom. I've lived with more guilt than you could ever imagine."

A disgusted look came to Zach's face. "We lost Sarah, Dad. If she'd gotten medical care sooner, there's a good chance she would have survived. That's not only my opinion. The review of her case by the children's hospital quality care committee concluded her death was likely avoidable if she'd had earlier intervention."

"With all due respect to the committee, they have no way of knowing that."

"I think we both know what this was about. When you got that call from your partner, you knew he was in over his head, and you wanted to be the one who saved the day. It's always been the same with you. All you've ever cared about is your medical practice and everybody thinking you were the most talented and smartest doctor in the room." Zach's face reddened. "Well, you weren't that night. You didn't call Mom to let her know you were leaving Sarah alone with me."

"I didn't think it was necessary."

"But you promised her that you wouldn't leave her side. You assured her you'd be at home for the entire evening."

"It was an emergency, Zach. Mom knew that I was a doctor and sometimes had to respond to emergency situations."

"Don't you dare try to take the moral high ground about Sarah's death. Fool yourself if you'd like, but you never fooled me or Mom. You had any number of partners who could have responded that night. It didn't have to be you."

"So now I know the real reason you hate me," Josef said. "I guess I could explain myself, but you wouldn't listen, and I'm afraid I'd be shouting at the rain."

"I doubt there's anything you could say to me that would cause me to forgive you. What I did to you was unforgivably deplorable, and I freely admit I'm a weak person with a faulty moral compass. I probably should have gotten help years ago to deal with my demons. I understand that, and maybe, in time, I'll gather the strength to do the right thing."

After a sustained silence, Zach came to his feet, made his way to the door, and left the room without so much as a backward glance.

Chapter 78

Zach made his way out of the house and across the backyard until he reached his custom-built floatplane dock. He removed his electric tablet from his bag and began pre-flighting the plane. He was working his way around to the engine when he spotted a Monroe County Sheriff's Department Marine Patrol boat about half a mile away moving slowly to the south. He ignored it and continued his pre-flight.

Josef returned to the far side of the room and watched Zach attending to the aircraft. After five minutes came and went, he reached for his phone and made a call.

"He's out back on the dock," he said.

"We'll be there in a couple of minutes."

Josef sat down for a very brief period of time before making his way over to the door. When he opened it, Detectives Allensworth and Rafferty were approaching from the living room.

"Good morning, Doctor," Libby said.

Slowly and carefully, Josef began to remove the recording/transmitting unit that the detectives had helped him place behind his belt earlier that morning.

"Please excuse my clumsiness," Josef said in a bothered way. "I'm not at all accustomed to wearing electronic spying devices."

"You did fine," Paul said, helping collect the wire, microphone, and transmitter from Josef's pants pocket and the underside of his belt.

"That was the hardest thing I've ever done in my life," he said in a near inconsolable monotone.

"I'm sure it was," Libby said.

"Did the device work okay?" he asked

"Yes, the audio was quite clear."

"You want to hear something funny, Detective? There's a part of me that's very unhappy to hear that. I'm not sure, knowing what I do now, I would have agreed to wear a wire."

Paul said, "I'm not diminishing the emotional strain of what you did this morning, but in time, I hope you'll come to believe you did the right thing. I don't think you ever would've known your personal safety was in jeopardy."

Libby stole a glance at Josef. "I'll stay here with Dr. Church," she said.

Paul left the house via the back door and joined two uniformed officers and a detective from the Monroe County Sheriff's Office.

Zach was just about finished with the preflight when he looked out toward the ocean. To his shock, he saw the police marine boat had moved into a position about a hundred yards away. His breath caught as his eyes immediately flashed to the Florida room's bay window. He saw his father and Libby staring directly at him. A moment later his attention shifted. Paul and the other police officers coming toward him. Folding his arms in front of himself, he turned and waited on the dock.

"Zach Church," the detective from the Monroe County Sheriff's Office said as the uniformed officers turned him and placed him in handcuffs. "You're under arrest for conspiracy to commit murder. You have the right to remain silent…"

Epilogue

FIVE DAYS LATER

It was a few minutes past eleven in the morning when Jack and Madison exited the hospital after visiting Nell Thacker. She was a couple of weeks post-op after undergoing an emergency liver transplantation. After cutting through enough red tape to stretch from one end of Dade County to the other, and with the help of the governor's healthcare team, arrangements had been made to have Nell undergo dual monoclonal antibody treatment as soon as she was stable following her transplant. Her rapid recovery from both the urgent transplant and IPS were the talk of the hospital.

"I can't believe how incredible Nell looks," Madison said as they entered the visitors parking lot and headed toward their rental.

"Of all the success stories we've seen over the years, if Nell's recovery isn't number one on the miracle list, it's right up there."

When they were a few feet from the car, Jack's phone rang. "Hi, Ely."

"What time today are you two heading back to Columbus?"

"We're scheduled to leave at four," Jack said.

"Great. Are you doing anything right now?"

"We just visited Nell Thacker. We were going to head back to the house and finish up some last-minute packing."

"Do you have time to stop at my office? I'd like to see you two before you leave."

"Sure," Jack said, looking over at Madison who responded with a thumbs up. "We can be there in about forty minutes. Does that work for you?"

"I'll be here waiting for you."

"We'll see you then." Ending the call, he asked, "I wonder if this is business or personal?"

"From what I've learned about Ely, probably a little of both. Before that mind of yours starts going off in ten different directions and you get all worked up, let's wait and see what's on his mind."

"Okay, but I have a feeling this isn't as innocent as it seems."

As Jack had anticipated, there was very little traffic, and they arrived at Mothers and Infants in forty-five minutes. They parked and wasted no time entering the hospital and going up to Ely's office.

The moment they walked through the door, they spotted Ely standing in the middle of his office, flanked by the governor, Carmela, and Emma.

Emma met them as they crossed the office and gave them both a grand hug.

"This is quite a pleasant surprise," Madison said.

"We couldn't let you leave our proud state without one last goodbye," the governor said, shaking Jack's hand.

"I can't think of a nicer final memory of all the wonderful people we've met than this," Madison said, turning to Emma. "How are you feeling?"

"Maybe a little more fatigued than usual, but I'm back to working half days and feeling great."

"That's great to hear," Jack told her.

Emma leaned in and said in a loud whisper, "Keep an eye on my Dad. He's probably going to try and recruit you both to his staff."

Governor Collymore laughed. "C'mon, Emma. That's ridiculous… although, I learned recently that my surgeon general's going to retire at the end of the year."

"Keep us in the loop," Jack said, tongue in cheek.

He looked at his daughter through adoring eyes. "As soon as Emma's a hundred percent, I'm going to start working on her again to come work for the state."

"Not once chance in a million, Pop. It's never going to happen."

"Nobody with sound judgment would want to work with you, Sam," Carmela said.

Just as the chuckling was dying down, the door opened, and Charlotte Duffy entered the office. Ely walked over and was the first to greet her. Jack noticed that everybody in the room except himself and Madison were doing their best to conceal a coy grin.

"Am I late?" she asked Ely.

"You're right on time, Charlotte."

The governor walked over. "How are you, Dr. Duffy?"

"I'm fine, but you look a little tired, Sam."

Jack closed his eyes and dropped his head slightly, wondering if his mother remembered she was talking to one of the most prominent governors in the entire country. Sometimes he tended to forget that Charlotte had first met the governor when he was barely out of law school and considering running for public office for the first time.

"You need to take this man on a vacation, Carmela," she said.

Carmela's smile didn't fade a bit as she gave Charlotte a kiss on each cheek. "Actually, I was thinking the same thing. So, I decided the three of us and my precious granddaughter will be taking a week off to go someplace warm over New Year's."

"That's wonderful to hear," Madison said.

Jack couldn't restrain himself any longer. "Okay, Mom. What's going on?"

"Be patient, dear, and let me say hello to everybody." When she was finished with her greetings, she moved center stage and said, "Imagine my surprise when our governor and Carmela called me last night, asking me if I had any ideas for a gift they could give you and Madison. That got me thinking about the big news you shared with me the night before last."

Jack responded, "I hope you're not—"

"I wasn't finished, dear."

Jack exhaled and held any further comments until his mother was finished.

"After giving it some thought, I took the liberty of sharing with them that you and Madison have decided to make things official and get married."

"Mom, you didn't," Jack said, voice just above a whisper, while Madison did everything in her power not to laugh at Jack's impending meltdown.

"I certainly did. I think, now that Madison has finally agreed to marry you… well, it's high time we started celebrating. So I want to let you and Madison know that I've invited the entire Collymore family to attend the wedding, and they've agreed."

"Congratulations from all of us," Emma said. "We're so very happy for you."

"Mom, we haven't even decided on a time or place yet."

"Whenever you do," Emma said, "just let us know, and we'll be on the next plane out."

Ely had a huge smile on his face. "I can't even begin to count the number of times a day a family or staff member tells me how grateful they are to Doctors Shaw and Wyatt for what you two accomplished here," he said. "Before you leave South Florida, I just wanted to make sure I offered you a huge collective thanks from all those individuals."

"Those are very kind words," Madison said.

"It was a great privilege for us to work with everybody associated with Mothers and Infants," Jack added.

The governor walked up to Madison and took both of her hands in his. "You're a brilliant doctor, Madison. My family and I became the luckiest people on the face of the earth when you stepped into our lives. We'll never forget your selfless dedication and devotion to Emma."

Madison's throat constricted with emotion. "Jack and I have never known a finer family than yours, governor."

Sam released her hands and walked up to Jack. "I don't know if you already have somebody in mind, Jack. But if you don't…well, in a small way of showing my gratitude for what you've done for my family, it would be my great honor if you'd allow me to serve as your best man."

Jack shifted his gaze to Madison before he answered. He could read the emotion in her eyes.

"I'd be equally honored, Governor," Jack said.

And with that, Governor Sam Collymore took another few steps forward while wiping a single tear from each cheek and gave Jack Wyatt a long hug.

HUNGRY FOR MORE OF Gary Birken, MD's chillingly authentic medical mysteries?

^^^ Scan the code above, or click here in your ebook to binge his hair-raising standalone novels.

Acknowledgments

To all those who tirelessly contributed to making this novel a reality. I thank you all.

Deborah Bealmear, Alison Birken, DVM, Susan Carew, Steven Dolchin, esq, Charles Jaffee, esq., Leslie Kellner Lemon, Robert Reid, md., and Cyndi Sandusky.

And a special thanks to Jen Lassalle, who continues to be my mentor and guiding light in the world of publishing.

For our grandchildren: Charlee, Heyden, Jacob, Jaxson, Leah, Leo, Libby, Luke, Madison, Mason, and Maya.

About Gary Birken, M.D.

When I first set pen to paper, I was a busy pediatric surgeon. I completed eight years of surgical training at Ohio State University and Nationwide Children's Hospital and remain to this day an ardent Buckeyes fan. Upon completing my training, I relocated to South Florida and joined the medical staff of Joe DiMaggio Children's Hospital, where I served as the Surgeon-in-Chief.

Now that my schedule is more relaxed, I'm able to devote greater time to writing and getting more involved with my readers. My approach to story-writing has always been to utilize fiction not only as a means to entertain, but also to offer some insight into an interesting or controversial topic in medicine. I'm often asked by aspiring authors for suggestions as to the best way to get started. The best advice I can offer any individual who seriously wants to write is to take the time to learn the craft of fiction writing, and then - read a lot and write a lot.

I am a member of the Mystery Writers of America and have had the opportunity of teaching writing at various conferences and other forums. I have also had the pleasure of serving as a panel member at the SleuthFest Conference. In addition to spending time with my family, including my ten grandchildren, I am a private pilot, and an avid tennis player. I also enjoy auditing university level courses and just hanging out with my English Setter, Eliza Doolittle. I hold a black belt in martial arts and frequently teach courses in women's self-defense.

Printed in Dunstable, United Kingdom